PENGUIN C

SERIES ADVISOR: PHILIP HORNE

WHAT MAISIE KNEW

HENRY JAMES was born in 1843 in Washington Place, New York, of Scottish and Irish ancestry. His father was a prominent theologian and philosopher and his elder brother, William, also became famous as a philosopher. James attended schools in New York and later in London, Paris and Geneva, before briefly entering the Law School at Harvard in 1862. In 1865 he began to contribute reviews and short stories to American journals. He visited Europe twice as an adult before moving to Paris in 1875, where he met Flaubert, Turgenev and other literary figures. However, after a year he moved to London, where he met with such success in society that he confessed to accepting 107 invitations in the winter of 1878–9 alone. In 1898 he left London and went to live at Lamb House, Rye, Sussex. Henry James became a naturalized British citizen in 1915, and was awarded the Order of Merit in 1916, shortly before his death in February of that year.

In addition to many short stories, plays, books of criticism, biography and autobiography, and much travel writing, he wrote some twenty novels, the first of which, *Watch and Ward*, appeared serially in the *Atlantic Monthly* in 1871. His novella 'Daisy Miller' (1878) established him as a literary figure on both sides of the Atlantic. Other novels include *Roderick Hudson* (1875), *The American* (1877), *The Europeans* (1878), *Washington Square* (1880), *The Portrait of a Lady* (1881), *The Bostonians* (1886), *The Princess Casamassima* (1886), *The Tragic Muse* (1890), *The Spoils of Poynton* (1897), *What Maisie Knew* (1897), *The Awkward Age* (1899), *The Wings of the Dove* (1902), *The Ambassadors* (1903) and *The Golden Bowl* (1904).

CHRISTOPHER RICKS is Warren Professor of the Humanities and Co-Director of the Editorial Institute at Boston University, having formerly been professor of English at Bristol and at Cambridge. He is a member of the Association of Literary Scholars and Critics, and He has

25p

CL 1228312 6

edited *The Poems of Tennyson* (3 vols., 1987), *The New Oxford Book of Victorian Verse* (1987), *Inventions of the March Hare: Poems 1909–1917 by T. S. Eliot* (1996), *The Oxford Book of English Verse* (1999), *Selected Poems of James Henry* (2002), Samuel Menashe's *New and Selected Poems* (2005), Samuel Beckett's *The Expelled / The Calmative / The End / First Love* (2009), and for Penguin Books *Alfred Lord Tennyson: Selected Poems* (2007). He is the author of *Milton's Grand Style* (1963), *Keats and Embarrassment* (1974), *The Force of Poetry* (1984), *T. S. Eliot and Prejudice* (1988), *Tennyson* (1989), *Beckett's Dying Words* (1993), *Essays in Appreciation* (1996), *Allusion to the Poets* (2002), *Reviewery* (2002), *Decisions and Revisions in T. S. Eliot* (2003), *Dylan's Visions of Sin* (2004), and *True Friendship: Geoffrey Hill, Anthony Hecht, and Robert Lowell under the Sign of Eliot and Pound* (2010). He was Professor of Poetry at Oxford, 2004–2009; in 2010, Waywiser Press published his anthology, *Joining Music with Reason: 34 Poets, British and American, Oxford 2004–2009*.

PHILIP HORNE is a Professor of English at University College London. He is the author of *Henry James and Revision: The New York Edition* (1990), editor of *Henry James: A Life in Letters* (1999) and co-editor of *Thorold Dickinson: A World of Film* (2008). He has also edited Henry James, *A London Life & The Reverberator*; and for Penguin, Henry James, *The Tragic Muse*, and Charles Dickens, *Oliver Twist*. He has written articles on Henry James, and on a wide range of other subjects, including telephones and literature, zombies and consumer culture, the films of Powell and Pressburger and of Martin Scorsese, the texts of Emily Dickinson and the criticism of F. R. Leavis.

HENRY JAMES

What Maisie Knew

Edited with an Introduction and Notes by
CHRISTOPHER RICKS

PENGUIN BOOKS

PENGUIN CLASSICS

Published by the Penguin Group
Penguin Books Ltd, 80 Strand, London WC2R 0RL, England
Penguin Group (USA) Inc., 375 Hudson Street, New York, New York 10014, USA
Penguin Group (Canada), 90 Eglinton Avenue East, Suite 700, Toronto, Ontario, Canada M4P 2Y3
(a division of Pearson Penguin Canada Inc.)
Penguin Ireland, 25 St Stephen's Green, Dublin 2, Ireland (a division of Penguin Books Ltd)
Penguin Group (Australia), 707 Collins Street, Melbourne, Victoria 3008, Australia
(a division of Pearson Australia Group Pty Ltd)
Penguin Books India Pvt Ltd, 11 Community Centre, Panchsheel Park, New Delhi – 110 017, India
Penguin Group (NZ), 67 Apollo Drive, Rosedale, Auckland 0632, New Zealand
(a division of Pearson New Zealand Ltd)
Penguin Books (South Africa) (Pty) Ltd, Block D, Rosebank Office Park,
181 Jan Smuts Avenue, Parktown North, Gauteng 2193, South Africa

Penguin Books Ltd, Registered Offices: 80 Strand, London WC2R 0RL, England

www.penguin.com

First published 1897
Published in Penguin Classics 2010
This edition published 2013
001

Introduction, A Note on the Text and Notes copyright © Christopher Ricks, 2010
Chronology and Further Reading copyright © Philip Horne, 2007

All rights reserved

Typeset in 10.25/12.25 pt PostScript Adobe Sabon
Typeset by MPS Limited, A Macmillan Company
www.macmillansolutions.com
Printed in Great Britain by Clays Ltd, St Ives plc

Except in the United States of America, this book is sold subject
to the condition that it shall not, by way of trade or otherwise, be lent,
re-sold, hired out, or otherwise circulated without the publisher's
prior consent in any form of binding or cover other than that in
which it is published and without a similar condition including this
condition being imposed on the subsequent purchaser

ISBN: 978-0-141-39403-9

www.greenpenguin.co.uk

MIX
Paper from
responsible sources
FSC
www.fsc.org   FSC™ C018179

Penguin Books is committed to a sustainable
future for our business, our readers and our planet.
This book is made from Forest Stewardship
Council™ certified paper.

Contents

Chronology

1843 *15 April*: HJ born at 21 Washington Place in New York City, second of five children of Henry James (1811–82), speculative theologian and social thinker, whose strict entrepreneur father had amassed wealth estimated at $3 million, one of the top ten American fortunes of his time, and his wife Mary (1810–82), daughter of James Walsh, a New York cotton merchant of Scottish origin.

1843–5 Accompanies parents to Paris and London.

1845–7 James family returns to USA and settles in Albany, New York.

1847–55 Family settles in New York City; HJ taught by tutors and in private schools.

1855–8 Family travels in Europe: Geneva, London, Paris, Boulogne-sur-Mer. Returns to USA and settles in Newport, Rhode Island.

1859–60 Family in Europe again: HJ attends scientific school, then the Academy (later the University) in Geneva. Learns German in Bonn.

   September 1860: Family returns to Newport. HJ makes friends with future critic T. S. Perry (who records that HJ 'was continually writing stories, mainly of a romantic kind') and artist John La Farge.

1861–3 Injures his back helping to extinguish a fire in Newport and is exempted from military service in American Civil War (1861–5).

   Autumn 1862: Enters Harvard Law School for a term. Begins to send stories to magazines.

1864 *February*: First short story, 'A Tragedy of Error', published anonymously in *Continental Monthly*.

May: Family moves to 13 Ashburton Place, Boston,
Massachusetts.

October: Unsigned review published in *North American
Review*.

1865 *March*: First signed tale, 'The Story of a Year', appears in
Atlantic Monthly. HJ's criticism published in first number of
the *Nation* (New York).

1866–8 Continues reviewing and writing stories.

Summer 1866: W. D. Howells, novelist, critic and influential
editor, becomes a friend.

November 1866: Family moves to 20 Quincy Street, beside
Harvard Yard, in Cambridge, Massachusetts.

1869 Travels for his health to England, where he meets John
Ruskin, William Morris, Charles Darwin and George Eliot;
also visits Switzerland and Italy.

1870 *March*: Death in USA of his much-loved cousin Minny
Temple.

May: HJ, still unwell, is reluctantly back in Cambridge.

1871 *August–December*: First short novel, *Watch and Ward*,
serialized in *Atlantic Monthly*.

1872–4 Accompanies invalid sister Alice and aunt Catherine
Walsh ('Aunt Kate') to Europe in May 1872. Writes travel
pieces for the *Nation*. Between October 1872 and September
1874 spends periods of time in Paris, Rome, Switzerland,
Homburg and Italy without his family.

Spring 1874: Begins first long novel, *Roderick Hudson*,
in Florence.

September 1874: Returns to USA.

1875 *January*: Publishes *A Passionate Pilgrim, and Other Tales*,
his first work to appear in book form. It is followed by *Trans-
atlantic Sketches* (travel pieces) and then by *Roderick Hudson*
in November. Spends six months in New York City (111 East
25th Street), then three in Cambridge.

11 November: Arrives at 29 rue de Luxembourg, Paris, as
correspondent for the *New York Tribune* on return to Europe.

December: Begins new novel, *The American*.

1876 Meets Gustave Flaubert, Ivan Turgenev, Edmond de Goncourt, Alphonse Daudet, Guy de Maupassant and Emile Zola.

December: Moves to London and settles at 3 Bolton Street, just off Piccadilly.

1877 Visits Paris, Florence and Rome.

May: *The American* is published.

1878 Meets William Gladstone, Alfred Tennyson and Robert Browning.

February: Collection of essays, *French Poets and Novelists*, is the first book HJ publishes in London.

July: Novella 'Daisy Miller' serialized in the *Cornhill Magazine*; in November *Harper's* publishes it in the USA, establishing HJ's reputation on both sides of the Atlantic.

September: Publishes novel *The Europeans*.

1879 *December*: Publishes novel *Confidence* and *Hawthorne* (critical study).

1880 *December*: Publishes novel *Washington Square*.

1881 *October*: Returns to USA; visits Cambridge.

November: Publishes novel *The Portrait of a Lady*.

1882 *January*: Death of mother. Visits New York and Washington DC.

May: Travels back to England but returns to USA on death of father in December.

1883 *Summer*: Returns to London.

November: Fourteen-volume collected edition of fiction published by Macmillan.

December: Publishes *Portraits of Places* (travel writings).

1884 Sister Alice moves to London and settles near HJ.

September: Publishes *A Little Tour in France* (travel writings) and *Tales of Three Cities*; his important artistic statement 'The Art of Fiction' appears in *Longman's Magazine*.

Becomes a friend of R. L. Stevenson and Edmund Gosse. Writes to his American friend Grace Norton: 'I shall never marry ... I am both happy enough and miserable enough, as it is.'

1885–6 Publishes two serial novels, *The Bostonians* and *The Princess Casamassima*.

6 March 1886: Moves into flat at 34 De Vere Gardens.

1887 *Spring and summer*: Visits Florence and Venice. Continues friendship (begun in 1880) with American novelist Constance Fenimore Woolson.

1888 Publishes novel *The Reverberator*, a story collection *The Aspern Papers* and *Partial Portraits* (criticism).

1889 Collection of tales *A London Life* published.

1890 Novel *The Tragic Muse* published.

1891 Play version of *The American* has a short run in the provinces and London.

1892 *February*: Publishes *The Lesson of the Master* (story collection).

   March: Death of Alice James in London.

1893 Three volumes of tales published: *The Real Thing* (March), *The Private Life* (June), *The Wheel of Time* (September).

1894 Deaths of Constance Fenimore Woolson and R. L. Stevenson.

1895 *5 January*: Play *Guy Domville* is greeted by boos and applause on its premiere at St James's Theatre; HJ abandons playwriting for many years.

   Visits Ireland. Takes up cycling. Publishes two volumes of tales, *Terminations* (May) and *Embarrassments* (June).

1896 Publishes novel *The Other House*.

1897 Two novels, *The Spoils of Poynton* and *What Maisie Knew*, published.

   February: Starts dictating, due to wrist problems.

   September: Takes lease on Lamb House, Rye, Sussex.

1898 *June*: Moves into Lamb House. Sussex neighbours include the writers Joseph Conrad, H. G. Wells and Ford Madox Hueffer (Ford).

   August: Publishes *In the Cage* (short novel).

   October: 'The Turn of the Screw', ghost story included in *The Two Magics*, proves his most popular work since 'Daisy Miller'.

1899 *April*: Novel *The Awkward Age* published.

   August: Buys the freehold of Lamb House.

1900 Shaves off his beard.

   August: Publishes collection of tales *The Soft Side*.

   Friendship with American novelist Edith Wharton develops.

1901 *February*: Publishes novel *The Sacred Fount*.

1902 *August*: Publishes novel *The Wings of the Dove*.

1903 *February*: Publishes collection of tales *The Better Sort*.

September: Publishes novel *The Ambassadors*.

October: Publishes memoir *William Wetmore Story and his Friends*.

1904 *August*: Sails to USA, his first visit for twenty-one years. Will travel to New England, New York, Philadelphia, Washington, the South, St Louis, Chicago, Los Angeles and San Francisco.

November: Publishes novel *The Golden Bowl*.

1905 *January*: Is President Theodore Roosevelt's guest at a White House dinner. Elected to the American Academy of Arts and Letters.

July: Back in Lamb House, begins revising works for the New York Edition of *The Novels and Tales of Henry James*.

October: Publishes *English Hours* (travel essays).

1906–8 Selects, arranges, writes prefaces and has illustrations made for New York Edition (published 1907–9, twenty-four volumes).

1907 *January*: Publishes *The American Scene* (travel book).

1908 *March*: Play *The High Bid* produced at Edinburgh.

1909 *October*: Publishes *Italian Hours* (travel essays). Health problems.

1910 *August*: Travels to USA with brother William, who dies a week after their return.

October: Publishes *The Finer Grain* (tales).

1911 *August*: Returns to England.

October: Publishes *The Outcry* (novel adapted from play). Begins work on autobiography.

1912 *June*: Receives honorary doctorate from Oxford University.

October: Takes flat at 21 Carlyle Mansions, Cheyne Walk, Chelsea; suffers from shingles.

1913 *March*: Publishes *A Small Boy and Others* (first volume of autobiography). Portrait painted by John Singer Sargent for seventieth birthday.

1914 *March*: Publishes *Notes of a Son and Brother* (second volume of autobiography).

August: Outbreak of World War One; HJ becomes passionately engaged with the British cause and helps Belgian refugees and wounded soldiers.

October: Publishes *Notes on Novelists*.

1915 Is made honorary president of the American Volunteer Motor Ambulance Corps.

July: Becomes a British citizen.

Writes essays about the war (collected in *Within the Rim* (1919)) and the Preface to *Letters from America* (1916) by the poet Rupert Brooke, who had died the previous year.

2 December: Suffers a stroke.

1916 Awarded the Order of Merit in New Year Honours.

28 February: Dies. After his funeral in Chelsea Old Church, his ashes are smuggled back to USA by sister-in-law and buried in the family plot in Cambridge.

Philip Horne

Introduction

[*Publisher's Note: First-time readers should be aware that details of the plot are revealed in this Introduction.*]

Of all Henry James's novels, *What Maisie Knew* may well be the one that 'strikes its root deepest into the human heart'. The thrilled phrase is William Hazlitt's in *Characters of Shakespear's Plays* (1817), and he shaped it for *King Lear*, the dramatic tragedy that, like James's tragi-comedy of a novel, unwincingly contemplates the selfishness, self-delusion and self-destruction infecting a family that yet is graced by the goodness of a daughter.

'Marriage has many pains, but celibacy has no pleasures': this was the proposition of Dr Johnson, or rather of the princess in his fable of a novel *Rasselas* (1759). Divorce has many pains, but it has one pleasure, the pleasure vengeful. Custody? We are told of Maisie's parents that 'They had wanted her not for any good they could do her, but for the harm they could, with her unconscious aid, do each other' (5). The ill parenthood and ill step-parenthood would come to change the line of attack but not the lust for revenge. 'It would still be essentially a struggle, but its object would now be *not* to receive her' (37).

The *Chicago Tribune* (22 November 1897) praised this novel that had just appeared from a Chicago and New York publisher, and concluded: 'Mr. James has achieved a success; and his book, which is published by Herbert S. Stone & Co., is rightly described as "important". So long as parents are to be divorced, so long will it remain a problem what it is that the Maisies are to know.' True. Less true, more tendentious, was the heading that the *Tribune* gave to its review: 'Henry James' Study of the Moral Effects of Divorce.'

What Maisie Knew is a family romance of a kind, a family necromance, much of the book being communications of the

living dead. But what saves the book, and saves it from being a
tragedy only – not merely – is that Maisie is saved. Or, to put it
more prudently (since the book ends with her adult life in prospect only), with a good chance of being saved, of being good
still. It is she, in large part, who saves herself. Yet it is thanks to
something incorruptible in the two far-from-perfect people
who do respect her: her stepfather Sir Claude and her elderly
governess Mrs. Wix. In Maisie's escaping the worst of what
threatens to corrupt her, of what might have seemed all but
certain to damage her for life, it is her feeling for life that sees
her right. She looks likely (but who can be confident what is in
store for her or for any of us?) to survive what it was to have
two rancorous parents, Beale and Ida, and two dismaying step-
parents, one of whom, Sir Claude, is amiably weak, and the
other, Mrs. Beale, emptily strong.

Ezra Pound, remarking that 'Artists are the antennae of the
race', had arrived at this thought in praise of Henry James, who
had foreseen and had foreknown Armageddon, thirty years
before the Great War.[1] *What Maisie Knew* anticipates the col-
lateral damage in the great war between the sexes, the expanding fracture of the nuclear family and the dissolution of the
extended one. No longer would the destructive agent be death
in childbirth, it would be death in divorce. On the first page of
this novel, we hear of the court's judgement on Mr Farange,
'that he should refund to his late wife the twenty-six hundred
pounds put down by her, as it was called, some three years
before, in the interest of the child's maintenance'. *His late wife*
is still very much alive in her unremittingly frictive way. The
marriage lasted till a form of death did them part. *His ex-wife*?
This ungentlemanly term was let fall by the *Gentleman's Magazine* in 1876, the first instance of its use in the *Oxford English
Dictionary*. As for James, the narrative moves within two pages
from 'his late wife' to 'her ex-husband'.

Like some other children, Maisie was doomed to have four
parents, and it would prove to be as dire as having no parents
at all. The single-parent family may have its exhaustions, but so
does the quadruple-parent family. Maisie is an only child, but
one of her fictive sisters is Jane Eyre, indeflectible, a girl whose

progress into womanhood nothing can dent or daunt. Chapter
23 of Ecclesiasticus opens: 'He that toucheth pitch shall be
defiled therewith.' And *she*, likewise? Maisie has no choice but
to touch pitch. She remains, and she remains a child undefiled.
So far, so good, she is. At the book's conclusion, she may have
a chance to put her old young life behind her. The world is all
before her, where to choose her place of rest, and providence
(in the unlikely guise of Mrs Wix, who is not her divine gover-
nor but her all-too-human governess), her guide.

Composition and Publication

On 12 November 1892, Henry James set down in his Notebooks a social conversation that roused, yet once more, the
writer in him.

> – Two days ago, at dinner at James Bryce's Mrs. Ashton, Mrs.
> Bryce's sister, mentioned to me a situation that she had known of,
> of which it immediately struck me that something might be made
> in a tale. A child (boy or girl would do, but I see a girl, which
> would make it different from *The Pupil*) was *divided* by its parents
> in consequence of their being divorced. The court, for some rea-
> son, didn't, as it might have done, give the child exclusively to
> either parent, but decreed that it was to spend its time equally with
> each – that is alternately. Each parent married again, and the child
> went to them a month, or three months, about – finding with the
> one a new mother and with the other a new father.

The entry, which runs to twenty lines, proceeded to elaborate
an ensuing situation or likelihood.[2]

Nine months later (26 August 1893), James set down a further dozen lines about 'the idea of the little story on the subject
of the *partagé* [divided] child – of the divorced parents – as to
which I have already made a note here'. Four months later
(22 December 1893), the artistic promise moved him to half a
dozen summary pages of plot and character and mystery;
he was moved to a commercial promise, too, for the entry
began by naming an editor: 'Promising H. Harland a 10,000

(a *real* 10,000) for the April *Yellow Book*.' This, in '8 or 10 little chapters'. It was almost three years later, on 22 September 1896, that he had a few lines in the Notebook ('I've brought my little history of "Maisie" to the point at which I ought to be able to go on very straight with it'), and next month, 26 October, he told himself with stern exhilaration that 'a really detailed scenario of the rest is indispensable for a straight and sure advance to the end'. Sure enough, such a scenario followed at once: six or eight pages long, it is an extraordinary document and a fascinating demonstration of James's powers of creation. Two months later, 21 December 1896, he seized a truth: 'I realize – none too soon – that the *scenic* method is my absolute, my imperative, my *only* salvation.' It alone could 'see me out of the wood, at all, of this interminable little *Maisie; 10,000 more words* of which I have still to do'.

It had come to seem interminable. James had been indefatigable. The estimated ten thousand words had become ninety thousand. But then his estimates as to the number of words that he would precipitate, or that would precipitate him, are notorious for falling preposterously short.[3]

What Maisie Knew was first published in 1897 in America and in England, serialized at first and then appearing in volume form from William Heinemann (London) and from Herbert Stone & Co. (Chicago and New York) in September and October respectively.[4]

Children in Novels

It was a conversation at dinner that prompted *What Maisie Knew*, but James had long recognized that he had a duty and a responsibility. As a reviewer, he had returned repeatedly to what was urgently wrong with the novels of his day when they came to set children within the world of their factitious convictions. James's great novel on degradation is a creative critique of all those novels that, in their delusive sanctimony, constituted for him a powerful immorality. In this sense, he (like us) owes them a very great deal, immensely more than they deserve.

In the *North American Review*, October 1865, James had passed judgement on Adeline Dutton Whitney's *The Gayworthys*:

> Its radical defect is the degradation of sentiment by making children responsible for it. This practice is becoming the bane of our novels. It signifies little where it began, or what authority it claims: it is, in our opinion, as fatal to the dignity of serious feeling and to the grandeur of strong passions as the most flagrant immoralities of French fiction. Heaven defend us from the puerile![5]

The terms of censure are the very ones that were to figure in the hostile reviews of *What Maisie Knew* in 1897, reviews that James, a decade later, set himself to answer in his Preface of 1908.[6]

James's loathing of puerility animates others of his early review-essays.[7] The one devoted to Elizabeth Rundle Charles's *Winifred Bertram and the World She Lived In* finds the child-heroine 'far too good to be true'.[8] 'This very competency to the various cares and difficulties of her position, on which the author dwells so lovingly, is to us a thoroughly unpleasant spectacle' and 'We can conceive of nothing more pernicious for a child than a premature sense of the seriousness of life.' It was in the impassioned creation of *What Maisie Knew*, thirty years later, that James turned to advantage, and to a different apprehension, his insistence in this sharp review that 'children grow positively good only as they grow wise, and they grow wise only as they grow old and leave childhood behind them'. The end of *What Maisie Knew*, James was to say in a letter, was 'the stroke of the hour of the end of that childhood'. And what had been for him the 'thoroughly unpleasant spectacle' of too wise a child was to be for *his* reviewer the 'unedifying spectacle' of *What Maisie Knew*. It is James's sense of *waste* that moves him in 1884 to regret Edmond de Goncourt's novel *Chérie*, 'which strikes me as having failed deplorably in what it attempts – that is in tracing the development of the moral consciousness of a child'.[9]

James in 1865, then, had lamented a moral degradation that he judged to be as fatal as the most flagrant immoralities of French fiction. Heaven defend us! Those who were to deplore *What Maisie Knew* deployed the same terms: 'In what it says, still more in what it suggests, it ranks, except for a terrible underlying dullness, with the worst schools of French fiction.'[10] It presents an 'unedifying spectacle', 'the portraiture of half a dozen as unlovely and squalid souls . . . as it has been our misfortune to encounter in the range of modern fiction'.[11] The verdict and the sentence deny that there are any extenuating circumstances. 'Its author exhibits not one ray of pity or dismay at this spectacle of a child with the pure current of its life thus poisoned at its source', and 'the readers of the story – may they be few – will probably never understand exactly what any one concerned said or did or meant. This is just as well, for what little one is able to understand is alike repellent to taste and feeling, to law and gospel.'[12] But then, in a manner that would have to acknowledge that the hostile reviews have got hold of the right thing by the wrong end, a favourable review proclaims that the squalid and the repellent are active and alive in the book, while insisting that *What Maisie Knew* is a triumph over these horrors, and that the pure current of Maisie's life is *not* poisoned. Against all-but-all odds.

> I have read this book with amazement and delight: with amazement at its supreme delicacy; with delight that its author, in spite of such discouragement as may come from lack of popular acclaim, retains an unswerving allegiance, to a literary conscience that forbids him to leave a slipshod phrase, or a single word out of its appointed place.

Acknowledging as the very enterprise of *What Maisie Knew* (not admitting, as a concession about it) 'the whole sordid drama of petty jealousy, rancour, wantonness, and vacillation', the reviewer agrees as to the battlefield but insists that the victory is James's: 'Certainly there is no living writer who has achieved the feat which Mr. James has here achieved, in analysing and purifying the baser passions of our nature by passing them through the pure mind of a little child.'[13]

What James finds base is the pious claptrap that passes for purity and then bestsells it short. *What Maisie Knew* is the thinking man's *What Katy Did*. In 1872 Susan M. Coolidge gave the world her very memorable title; she ended the introductory exposition of the first two pages with 'Here it is – the story of What Katy Did'; and the book's final words were 'that Katy did'. The paragraph was of thirteen words:

But although she said she didn't deserve it, I think that Katy did.

The opening page of James's much-more-than-retort to *What Katy Did* displays his title, followed at once with some words that constitute a witty way to *begin* an enterprise:

WHAT MAISIE KNEW

The litigation had seemed interminable, and had in fact been complicated;

And how does this book itself terminate? With a sixteen-word paragraph:

Mrs. Wix gave a sidelong look. She still had room for wonder at what Maisie knew.

We may return to the last of James's Notebook entries and 'this interminable little *Maisie*'.

What Katy Did owed everything to its sanctimonious sentimentalities. Katy is a girl who *owns up*, enabling the novelist to reassure any parent (any child, less amenable) that 'There is a saving grace in truth which helps truth-tellers through the worst of their troubles, and Katy found this out now' (Chapter 3). But Maisie finds out no such things; she knows that it is not as simple as that, given the world. The truth will not necessarily save you, especially if the truth were so imprudent as to choose to go about naked.

Katy is punished by the hand of God, which does not push her on the swing.

As she passed the shed the new swing caught her eye.

'How exactly like Aunt Izzie,' she thought, 'ordering the children not to swing till she gives them leave. I suppose she thinks it's too hot, or something. *I* shan't mind her, anyhow.' (Chapter 8)

The swing crashes, Katy badly injures her spine, and all the second half of the book is about her pain – capitalized upon as The School of Pain – and her slow effort to walk.

'My legs feel so queer,' she said, one morning; 'they are just like the Prince's legs which were turned to black marble in the *Arabian Nights*. What do you suppose is the reason, Papa? Won't they feel natural soon?'

'Not soon,' answered Dr. Carr. Then he said to himself: 'Poor child! she had better know the truth.' So he went on, aloud: 'I am afraid, my darling, that you must make up your mind to stay in bed a long time.' . . .

'Oh, Papa!' gasped Katy, between her sobs, 'doesn't it seem dreadful that just getting into the swing for few minutes should do so much harm? Such a little thing as that!'

'Yes, such a little thing!' repeated Dr. Carr, sadly. 'And it was only a little thing too, forgetting Aunt Izzie's order about the swing. Just for the want of the small "horseshoe nail" of obedience, Katy.' (Chapter 9)[14]

Such moralizing, and the immorality of it, would be enough to make any self-respecting child into a psychopath. It made Susan M. Coolidge a great success. It confirmed James's understanding of a great novel still to be written.

The Art of the Novel

Mrs Wix found safety in novels of a certain sort:

She took refuge on the firm ground of fiction, through which indeed there flowed the blue river of truth. She knew swarms of stories, mostly those of the novels she had read; relating them

with a memory that never faltered and a wealth of detail that
was Maisie's delight. They were all about love and beauty and
countesses and wickedness. (22)

But then *What Maisie Knew* is all about love and beauty and
countesses and wickedness. Its art is that these are realized in
words that do not pretend. Not so much 'complex words' in
general, to take up William Empson's term in *The Structure of
Complex Words* (1951), but a clutch of particular complexities
that especially relate to vulnerability. For truth is not necessarily
or not solely a blue river. It can be a sewer. 'Lot of water under
the bridge, lot of other stuff too', as Bob Dylan sings.

There is the vulnerability of *innocence*, a word the repetition
of which throughout the novel would be maddening if it were
not that James assists us to stay sane – and to see how Maisie
manages to stay sane – with the word's help. The book's second
paragraph acknowledges that 'neither parent figured in the
least as a happy example to youth and innocence' (4); the entire
book attends to those four nouns. There is not only the setting
of innocence against experience (a commonplace and indispensable antithesis), there is James's understanding that innocence
is the altogether positive word in the English language that has
a negative prefix. 'Not nocent yet', Milton wrote of the snake
that had not yet been possessed by Satan. Not doing harm.

There are the paradoxes by which innocence becomes something that has to be striven for, palpable in the mild word *tried*
when Maisie understands what Maisie is asking of herself:

'What do you know about Lord Eric?'
    She tried innocently to be odd in return. 'Oh, I know more
than you think! Is it Lord Eric?' she repeated. (105)

Hers is a complex fate, 'an innocence so saturated with knowledge
and so directed to diplomacy' (135), with this child's innocence
astonishingly unharmed by the knowledge and the diplomacy.
T. S. Eliot famously said of Maisie's creator that 'He had a mind so
fine that no idea could violate it.'[15] Of Maisie, it could be said that
she had a disposition so fine that no knowledge could violate it.

There is the vulnerability of a child in the face of time. '"She loves him – she adores him. A woman knows." Mrs. Wix spoke not only as if Maisie were not a woman, but as if she would never be one' (230). Or the vulnerability of Maisie's armour itself, disguise, 'the effect she studied, the effect of harmless vacancy' (54), as Maisie self-protectively (she has a self worth protecting) makes out that she is stupid, while being neither ingenuous nor disingenuous. Georg Christoph Lichtenberg noted that 'Many people reveal a gift for pretending to be stupid before they are wise; girls very often possess this gift.'[16]

There is the vulnerability of *little*, so easy to condescend to or with, or to descend to (sentimentally), or to bid with. James needs the word countless times, but he exercises his vigilance, and is magnificently resourceful in establishing different kinds of *cordon sanitaire* around the word that is in danger of being too appealing.

There is the vulnerability of what it is to be a *gentleman*. Sir Claude is called, again and again, both 'a perfect gentleman' and 'the perfect gentleman'. 'A fellow must behave like a gentleman, damn it, dear good Mrs. Wix' (189). But it is a hardship, although it may not seem to be one, to be in a position to do without *work*. Mrs Wix and her subordinates are the only people in the book who have to work (Miss Overmore escaped her work as the pretty governess by marrying her master and becoming Mrs Beale), and Sir Claude's amiable life is one of which the butterfly flutter is the direct result of his having nothing to *do*. There are the wages of sin and there is the pin money of indolence. Added to which, not only is it the case that to have 'independent means' is not really to be in every respect independent (rather as someone who has money *in his own right* usually has it from someone else), but Sir Claude insufficiently has independent means. True, he doesn't sell himself as Beale Farange and as Ida and Mrs Beale variously do, at the beck of the higher prostitution, but he is always at a loss, fiscally and physically. Carlyle, he of the work-ethic, was convincingly stern: 'The folly of that impossible precept, "Know thyself"; till it be translated into this partially possible one, "Know what thou canst work at."'[17] Maisie is not yet of an age to work, and anyway she has her work cut out as it is, trying to stay unimpaired. Everyone else (except Mrs Wix?) is debarred from knowing himself or herself by not knowing what they could work at.

Instead of working, they trade upon – trade in – *charm*. 'Certainly mamma had a charm which, when turned on, became a large explanation' (156). And yet Henry James is gentleman enough to be delighted by one of Ida's great moments, when she suddenly warms again to Sir Claude: '"Don't be an old goose," she said charmingly. "Let us alone"' (158).

Then there is the vulnerability of the cognate concept, *decency*, sometimes weakly inviting indecency to wound it, sometimes settling for what James identifies as Sir Claude's 'plea of mere "decency"' (96), as against heroism and aspiration.[18] There is the vulnerability of *fear*, felt in Maisie's apprehension of Sir Claude:

Why was such a man so often afraid? It must have begun to come to her now that there was one thing just such a man above all could be afraid of. He could be afraid of himself. His fear at all events was there; his fear was sweet to her, beautiful and tender to her, was having coffee and buttered rolls and talk and laughter that were no talk and laughter at all with her; his fear was in his jesting, postponing, perverting voice ...

and the severely loving sentence rolls immitigably on for a further half-dozen lines, to end with 'Mrs. Beale rose suddenly before her' (238–9). 'When at last they lounged off it was as if his fear, his fear of his weakness, leaned upon her heavily as they followed the harbour' (253). Perfect fear casteth out love. For there is the vulnerability of love, *passim*.

Every reader knows that what it is to *know* is endlessly matter for responsible speculation in *What Maisie Knew*. Pretty well all the word's senses in the *Oxford English Dictionary* will have a claim to consideration, and teasing them out is a game worth many a candle. Less manifest is an unobtrusive little word like *charge*. James starts from the reiterated fondling of the foundling Maisie as 'her little charge', 'his little charge', 'his little accepted charge' (ah), 'his intelligent little charge' (ah, again), 'a little charge'. This is the theme, of which the variations exploit a dozen capacities of the word. From that of a material load; that which can be borne, taken or received; through the explosive possibilities of powder and shot (many of the book's explosions involve her little charge); the accumulation of electricity; the load of trouble, expense, responsibility, blame etc.; the pecuniary burden, expense, cost; rising to the responsibilities, a task or duty laid on one; commission, trust, an office entrusted to one; and the duty or responsibility of taking care of (a person or thing); care, custody, superintendence. And bearing down on all these, there are the reproofs to them all: their neglecting the injunction, mandate or order, so that in various ways they all become open to a charge, an accusation, an indictment upon which each of them is brought up for trial.

What we don't know in this book is no less intriguing than what we do know. This may be a matter of a wide and crucial context. Of the precise legal position (custody, and so on), the reader is as vague, baffled and helpless as are those in the book who regularly say things like 'We take our stand on the law' (263) without really having an inkling of what the law actually and exactly is. 'For all she knew, a legal rule' (222)? Or there are those keywords that constitute a different kind of word: a name. The first sentence of the book ends 'as to the assignment of the child' and the last sentence of this prologue begins 'The child was provided for ...' The particular child is granted her name only in the second paragraph of the book, where it arrives within the chilling sequence, 'that of sending Maisie to a Home'. There is a great deal of teasing play not only with her name, and with what people elect to call her, but with other names that are never granted. We never learn the name that follows 'Sir Claude':

'She sends you her particular love and announces to you that she's engaged to be married to Sir Claude.'

'Sir Claude?' Maisie wonderingly echoed. (36–7)

Maisie is wondering who he is; we are left forever wondering what his other name is. So that Ida when she marries him becomes simply *her ladyship*, lest we be in a know. (It is as though Sir Claude were nothing but his knighthood.) And complementing this suspect game, there is the fact that we never know what Mrs Beale's first name is. Unlike Mrs Wix, Mrs Beale carries about the Christian name of her husband (even when the marriage is in ruins). When she was Miss Overmore, we knew her only by that form of address. 'And the difference began of course in her being addressed, even by Maisie, from that day and by her particular request, as Mrs. Beale' (42). That we don't know Moddle's first name is a consequence of our being upstairs, not downstairs. That we don't know the Captain's name, or the Countess's, will have quite other implications. All this within a book that makes such play with names, calls upon them and calls them out so often. The supreme name is Maisie.

Susan M. Coolidge did well by proceeding immediately from *What Katy Did* (1872) to *What Katy Did at School* (1873). For her part, Maisie never did proceed to school, although we sometimes enter the bleached dour schoolroom at her home. (*Her home?* The second paragraph of the book had considered 'sending Maisie to a Home'.) What Coolidge did next was *What Katy Did Next* (1885). However, the author of *What Maisie Knew* (1897) knew better than to suppose that he knew – that he was in any position to tell us – *What Maisie Knew Next*. The year after publication, he wrote to an inquirer. It was a typed letter, and for this he somewhat apologized:

Dear Mrs. Bancroft,
Forgive this brutal way of acknowledging a sympathy expressed by yourself in a manner so much more personal. But it is my inexorable fate to have, now, to dictate almost altogether; for whenever I intermit it and return to the use of my hand, which I moreover hate, I pay for it, collapse again and have to fall back on Remington. The sight of *your* hand hooks on to the remembrance of the autumn afternoons and the snug little corner on the edge of Piccadilly. If you were still in that snug little corner and I on the other side of the fire, perhaps I should

be able to make you believe a little how very much I don't know of what Maisie 'became'. I'm afraid I told all I *can* tell – for the money! Send me another five dollars. Seriously, the case seems to me to illustrate the marked difference between that which is in old-fashioned parlance a 'story' and that which has the distinctive characteristics of what *I* call a Subject. The story, in the old-fashioned sense, isn't, I dare say, told – told to the end that is, – in the book. But what the end – *where* the end, in that sort of thing, ever is, I feel that I can never say: the place, the point, the limit seem to me so arbitrary. Whereas, as regards the Subject of the poor little wretch, somehow – isn't it so? – *that* is treated. There would doubtless be another Subject later – but my mind, as yet, refuses to tackle it; for the reason, after all, I think, that it can only be essentially less interesting. The situation certainly didn't stay where I left it – the edifying stepparents didn't probably, for very long, make a very good thing of it together. Sir Claude and the lone infant bumped again against each other – and heaven only knows what *may* have occurred. Only, whatever it was, the best of it, for Art – forgive the vulgar expression – was over. The best of it was in other words all the *worst* of it – it must have been, though still doubtless curious and queer, less interesting afterwards. The subject was girl's childhood – it was the fact of that that was the whole note of the situation; and my climax, arrived at, was marked *by*, and consisted *of*, the stroke of the hour of the end of that childhood. Voilà. I'm afraid I haven't told you much – but all thanks for the interest expressed in your inquiry.[19]

In being so imaginatively circumspect as to what Maisie's future held for her, and what she held for her future, Henry James the novelist is at one with a great exemplar, from France to boot. ('The most flagrant immoralities of French fiction', James; 'the worst schools of French fiction', one of his reviewers.) Voilà. The reviewer of *What Maisie Knew* in the *Pall Mall Gazette* (11 October 1897) saw that James 'had selected a strange medley of sordid intrigue, in which some vivid and curious characters perform the antics of that human comedy on which Mr. James loves to dwell as much as his great contemporary'. Of Honoré de Balzac, author of *La Comédie Humaine*, James was to write in 1905 that 'We do not, at any rate, get away from him; he is behind us, at the worst, when he is not before; and I feel that any course about the country we explore is ever best held by keeping him, through the trees of the forest, in sight.'[20] For Balzac, it might be not only the future of his characters that would be withheld from him, but their past. James Fitzjames Stephen (a contemporary of James's, one who, as it happens, wrote for the *Pall Mall Gazette*) liked this about Balzac. 'One of the characters in *Ursule Mirouet*, a certain Captain de Jordy, excited the curiosity of Balzac's friends. M. de Jordy is represented as living at Nemours, weighed down by some secret grief, and Madame Surville was anxious to know the cause of it. "I did not know M. de Jordy before he came to Nemours", was her brother's answer.'[21] Henry James did not know Maisie Farange after she came from Boulogne.

Christopher Ricks

NOTES

1. 'Henry James' (1918); *Literary Essays of Ezra Pound*, ed. T. S. Eliot (London: Faber and Faber, 1954), p. 297.

2. See *The Complete Notebooks*, ed. Leon Edel and Lyall H. Powers (New York and Oxford: Oxford University Press, 1987). For the Notebook entries as they relate to Maisie, see 'Henry James on *What Maisie Knew*' (pp. 275–86 below).

3. See Philip Horne, 'Henry James and the Economy of the Short Story', *Modernist Writers and the Marketplace*, ed. Ian Willison, Warwick Gould and Warren Chernaik (London: Macmillan, 1996).

4. See A Note on the Text, p. xxxi.

5. *Literary Criticism*, vol.1, *Essays on Literature, American Writers & English Writers*, ed. Leon Edel and Mark Wilson (New York: Library of America, 1984), p. 637.

6. See 'Five Reviews of *What Maisie Knew*' and, 'Henry James on *What Maisie Knew*' (pp. 267–74 and 286–94 below).

7. James wrote of Lousia M. Alcott's *Eight Cousins*: 'The smart satirical tone is the last one in the world to be used in describing to children their elders and betters and the social mysteries that surround them. Miss Alcott seems to have a private understanding with the youngsters she depicts, at the expense of

their pastors and masters.' (*Nation*, 14 October 1875; *Literary Criticism: Essays on Literature, American Writers & English Writers*, pp. 195–6.) But one of the tones in *What Maisie Knew* (a novel that engages with the social mysteries that surround children) *is* the smart satirical one. James's double chimings chimed for me: *elders and betters, pastors and masters*? One genius at satirical tone, akin to James rather than to Alcott, is the author of *Elders and Betters* (1944) and *Pastors and Masters* (1925), I. Compton-Burnett.

8. *Nation* (1 February 1866); *Literary Criticism: Essays on Literature, American Writers & English Writers*, pp. 831–2.

9. 'The Art of Fiction', *Longman's Magazine* (September 1884); *Literary Criticism: Essays on Literature, American Writers & English Writers*, p. 61.

10. *Literary World* (11 December 1897).

11. *The Spectator* (30 October 1897).

12. *Literary World* (11 December 1897).

13. *The Academy* (16 October 1897).

14. For James's very different ways with the *Arabian Nights*, see the Notes, p. 298. And for this very different ways with a swing, see Chapter XXX, where the swing breaks 'under the weight and the extravagant patronage of the cook' (241; see also A Note on the Text, p. xxxiii). At least it wasn't under the weight and the extravagant patronage of God.

15. 'In Memory of Henry James', *The Egoist* (January 1918), reprinted in *Little Review* V (August 1918), p. 46.

16. *Aphorisms*, tr. R. J. Hollingdale (London: Penguin, 1990), p. 113.

17. Thomas Carlyle, *Sartor Resartus* (1833–4), Book 2, Chapter 7.

18. James has an ear for sound effects, audible in 'Beale's was a house in which no decent woman would consent to be seen' (17), in 'the dingy decencies, of Maisie's simple instructress' (56) and in 'Have I lost all delicacy, all decency' (207). Stylized dismay is to be heard, too, in the chime of '"They're a pretty pair of parents!" Mrs. Beale exclaimed' (46).

19. Letter to Mrs John Chandler Bancroft, 21 March 1898; see *Henry James: A Life in Letters*, ed. Philip Horne (London: Penguin, 1999), pp. 299–300.

20. 'The Lesson of Balzac', *Atlantic Monthly* (August 1905); *Literary Criticism*, vol. 2, *French Writers, Other European Writers, the Prefaces to the New York Edition*, p. 139.

21. *Saturday Review* (19 December 1857).

Further Reading

BY HENRY JAMES

Autobiography, ed. Frederick W. Dupee (Princeton: Princeton University Press, 1983).

Collected Travel Writings, ed. Richard Howard, 2 vols. (New York: Library of America, 1993).

The Complete Letters of Henry James, ed. Pierre A. Walker and Greg W. Zacharias (Lincoln, Nebr.: University of Nebraska Press, 2006–).

The Complete Notebooks, ed. Leon Edel and Lyall H. Powers (New York and Oxford: Oxford University Press, 1987).

The Complete Plays of Henry James, ed. Leon Edel (London: Rupert Hart-Davis, 1949).

Complete Stories, 5 vols. (New York: Library of America, 1996–9).

Henry James: A Life in Letters, ed. Philip Horne (London: Penguin, 1999).

Henry James: Letters, ed. Leon Edel, 4 vols. (Cambridge, Mass.: Belknap Press, 1974–84).

The Letters of Henry James, ed. Percy Lubbock, 2 vols. (London: Macmillan, 1920).

Literary Criticism, ed. Leon Edel and Mark Wilson, 2 vols. (New York: Library of America, 1984).

BIOGRAPHY, CRITICISM AND REFERENCE

Edel, Leon, *Henry James: A Life* (New York: Harper & Row, 1985).

— and Laurence, Dan H. *A Bibliography of Henry James*, 3rd edn., revised with the assistance of James Rambeau (Oxford: Oxford University Press, 1982).

Gard, Roger, ed., *Henry James: The Critical Heritage* (London: Routledge & Kegan Paul, 1968). Contains a very full selection of contemporary reviews and comments.

Graham, Kenneth, *Henry James: A Literary Life* (Basingstoke: Macmillan, 1995).

Kaplan, Fred, *Henry James: The Imagination of Genius* (London: Hodder & Stoughton, 1992).

Nowell-Smith, Simon (compiler), *The Legend of the Master* (London: Constable, 1947).

CRITICAL WORKS RELATING TO
WHAT MAISIE KNEW

Bewley, Marius, with an Introduction and two Interpolations by F. R. Leavis, *The Complex Fate: Hawthorne, Henry James and Some Other American Writers* (New York: Grove Press, 1954), pp. 96–144.

Poole, Adrian, Introduction to *What Maisie Knew*, Oxford World's Classics (New York and Oxford: Oxford University Press, 1996).

Supino, David J., *Henry James: A Bibliographical Catalogue of a collection of Editions to 1921* (Liverpool University Press, 2006).

Wood, Michael, 'What Henry Knew', *Literature and the Taste of Knowledge* (Cambridge: Cambridge University Press, 2005), pp. 13–36 (discussion not confined to *What Maisie Knew*).

A Note on the Text

What Maisie Knew appeared in 1897. Serialized both in America (*The Chap Book*, 15 January to 1 August) and in England (the *New Review*, February to September, abridged), the novel was promptly issued by the journals' publishers: William Heinemann (London) in September, and Herbert Stone & Co. (Chicago and New York) in October. There were four versions, then, in the year of publication. Yet the textual variants within 1897 were on a smaller scale than the revisions that Henry James started upon in 1907 for the New York Edition of the Novels and Tales of Henry James, published in twenty-four volumes by Charles Scribner's Sons between 1907 and 1909. Volume XI (1908) consisted of *What Maisie Knew*, *In the Cage* and 'The Pupil'.

Of the 1897 editions, Heinemann's is preferred here (for a detailed discussion of its dating, see below). This, not least for its English spelling: 'many-coloured and many-odoured' has a different colour and odour from 'many-colored and many-odored'. For this is a novel with an English setting (presented again now by an English publisher). The practice for a long time has been to adopt the text of the New York Edition (1908). This was the course taken by the previous Penguin Classics edition introduced by Paul Theroux with additional notes by Patricia Crick (1985), and the Oxford World's Classics volume edited by Adrian Poole (1996). An exception in choosing 1897 has been the Library of America: *Novels 1896–1899: The Other House, The Spoils of Poynton, What Maisie Knew, The Awkward Age*, with notes by Myra Jehlen (2003), where the brief Note on the Texts has two paragraphs comparing the texts of the American and English periodical publications but not offering any comparison with 1908 other than the observation, 'revised to reflect the further evolution of his style'.

The decision here, to make the early version more available, derives from 1897's less idiosyncratic wordings, its relaxed ease, and its effecting (more often than 1908 chose to do) a touching simplicity. James's revisions in 1908 assuredly made the book more Jamesian, but while this brought subtleties and nuances, it does suggest a caveat. For just as Keats is not at his very best when Keatsian, or Tennyson when Tennysonian, so James, too, surrenders some valuable qualities when he becomes so very much himself, his late self, so involuted and convoluted, so voluted, even. The New York Edition, with its re-creative energies bent upon almost all of James's fiction, precipitated changes that were ubiquitous. Sometimes, in their way, iniquitous.

Even such an unremitting admirer of Henry James as Simon Nowell-Smith, the compiler of *The Legend of the Master* (1947), an unfailing illumination of the many-sided Master, came to choose for his 1949 re-issue of *The Reverberator* its earliest volume publication (1888), as against the New York Edition. He acknowledged that 'Often the expansion of a phrase, or even the interpolation of a whole sentence, is felicitous', but of James's stylistic change over the course of a decade or two, he remarked: 'Whether it was a change for the better or the worse is a matter of opinion.' Whereupon he made good his own opinion, with instances and analyses. He asked whether 'the gain in the subtle use of imagery, which is great, outweighs the loss, also great, of immediacy', and proceeded to particularize just what such a loss amounts to, in human terms: in the later version, 'we are told nothing either of Delia's complexion or of her smile.' I should repeat of *What Maisie Knew* an admonition by Nowell-Smith:

> It is matter of fact, not of opinion, that these and other remodelled phrases were the work of an older man than the author, in 1888, of *The Reverberator*, a man whose tortuosity of expression, alike in writing and in speech, had in the interval become legendary. That James's 'third manner' may be an essential part

of the brilliance of later novels more brilliant perhaps in their way than *The Reverberator* is beside the point: the manner remains, for *The Reverberator*, an anachronism.

It was perhaps in order to elude any such anachronism that James in 1908 found himself concluding his Preface to *What Maisie Knew* with a sturdy unreliable terseness: '"Maisie" is of 1907.' Adrian Poole, in his Oxford World's Classics edition, emends to 1897: 'The New York Edition reads "1907", but this seems to be a slip. It is true that James revised the novel in 1907, but when he assigns dates elsewhere in the Prefaces it is always the year of initial publication of which he thinks, describing the tale "Europe", for example, as "of 1899".'

There is one correction to the 1897 text. 'James had nodded' (Poole gives us the nod) when in Chapter XXX the wrong person is blamed for the swing's breaking: 'under the weight and the extravagant patronage of Susan Ash'. For Susan Ash was at The Other House. So I adopt the 1908 reading that corrects 1897: 'of the cook'.

I need to give at least some instances to justify my sense of the impulse that mostly animates the 1908 changes, with their gains and losses. Let me note with gratitude that Poole provides nine pages that valuably display a selection of the revisions, observing especially James's newly added similes, his adverbs, and his words placed within inverted commas ('branded as "low" in character').

Bear in mind that Maisie is a child, and that much of the narration observes her reflections or her effect upon others. Grant, perhaps, that even though the expansive version is often deliciously sly or intricately *outré*, it may lack a relative simplicity that is germane to the child's eye view.

1897 text	1908 text
Chapter IV	
She was passively comical	She was as droll as a charade or an animal toward the end of the 'natural history'

this sense of a tenderness that would never give way

this sense of a support, like a breast-high banister in a place of 'drops', that would never give way

Chapter VI

a very different class of person from

lower in the scale of 'form' than

Chapter VII

something still more bewildering

something portentous

She raised to Miss Overmore's face all the timidity of her eyes

She looked at Miss Overmore much as she had a way of looking at persons who treated her to 'grown up' jokes

Chapter XI

he was distinctly fat

he was 'too fat for the pace'

Chapter XV

With her great hard eyes on him for a moment she smiled

She directed to him the face that was like an illuminated garden, turnstile and all, for the frequentation of which he had his season-ticket

Chapter XVI

being ugly

having a face so informally put together that the only kindness could be to call it funny

Chapter XVIII

her tears

the friendly suffusion of her eyes

Chapter XXVI

I so despair of tracing	I so despair of courting her
her steps that I must	noiseless mental footsteps here
crudely give you	that I must crudely give you
my word	my word

Sometimes when faced by the elaborations of the New York Edition, you do so despair of courting James's noiseless mental footsteps as to make you wish that he might crudely give you his words.

It was the earlier wording of the novel that moved a reviewer in the *Indianapolis News* (3 November 1897) to an insistence: 'It is true, indeed, that Mr. James uses many words, sometimes pages of words, just to portray one little thought of a little child, but he uses his words – he is not used by them. This is not a book to be read hastily, with skipping of passages, with a cloudy mind; it is a story that demands keen intelligence, alert brain, perceptions, fresh and eager.'

There is clearly a case for respecting James's final decisions, and Philip Horne's *Henry James and Revision: The New York Edition* (Clarendon Press, 1990) is a Masterly account of the intricacies of appreciation, and is fascinatingly alive to the delights of the revisions and of the revising. But there is a counter-case for a particular edition's making a different editorial decision, the better to realize James's varying art. The work of an older man than he had once been, mused Nowell-Smith. William Empson explained his decision scarcely to revise *Seven Types of Ambiguity* for its second edition (1947) by invoking a sympathetic figure who happens to have parodied Henry James with the utmost respect: 'Sir Max Beerbohm has a fine reflection on revising one of his early works; he said he tried to remember how angry he would have been when he wrote it if an elderly pedant had made corrections, and how certain he would have felt that the man was wrong.'

But this is not a matter of a simple right or wrong. When a genius revises his or her work, it is never the case that the gain or loss is pure. Pope's re-imagining of *The Rape of the Lock* as well as of *The Dunciad*, Wordsworth's lifelong attentions to *The Prelude*, Whitman's determination that *Leaves of Grass* enjoy some such freedom as attends upon a performing art, Robert Graves's yearning never really to have done with a poem, Wyndham Lewis's resourceful vexation at the exuberance of *Tarr* as he had first published it: all of these should act as reminders that there will always be countless particular judgements to be made, as well as pleasures (not simultaneously to be experienced, unfortunately) to be chosen from. To choose the *What Maisie Knew* of 1897 is not to refuse the one 'of 1907', which is in any case not far to seek.

A NOTE ON THE HEINEMANN EDITION

Thanks to the good offices of Philip Horne, I have learnt of the paramount authority possessed by David J. Supino and his *Henry James: A Bibliographical Catalogue of a Collection of Editions to 1921* (Liverpool University Press, 2006).

Mr Supino, to whom I am most grateful, kindly allows me to quote here the account that he sent me of the Heinemann edition (London, 1897):

The first English edition of *What Maisie Knew* has the date 1898, or more correctly MDCCCXCVIII, on the title page of all three impressions. However, it is clear that all three were printed and published in 1897 not 1898. The three impressions of this first edition were printed from the same set of plates.

The first impression can be identified by the fact that the title-page verso is blank except for the words *All rights reserved* in the lower left, it being printed on laid paper. The second impression title-page verso has the additional wording: *First Edition* [i.e. impression], *September 1897* | *Reprinted, October 1897*. The third Edition [i.e. impression] has the further wording: *First Edition, September 1897* | *Reprinted, October 1897* | *Reprinted, December 1897*. All three were priced at 6s. They are all printed on laid paper, and bound in blue diagonal fine-ribbed cloth, with the title in gold serifed caps on the front cover, below which are four irises in blind [tooled impression without addition of colour].

The only English printing that has an 1897 date on the title page is the colonial impression of the first English edition, although it was not published until March 1898. It was issued in bright red cloth (price 3s. 6d.), and also in paper wrappers (price 2s. 6d.). It is possible (although this is a conjecture) that it was printed before the impressions for domestic publication, and it is clearly printed from the same set of plates as the three domestic impressions. However, while the domestic impressions are printed on laid paper, and the title pages are printed in black and red, the colonial impression has a title page printed only in black, and the text is printed on wove paper.

To complicate matters Heinemann must have run short of sheets of the first English edition (he did this frequently with James titles), and instead of printing it again, he bound some of the sheets of the colonial impression (printed on wove paper) in the same blue cloth (but with nine tulips in blind on the front cover rather than four irises) as the domestic impressions and sold them on the English market. The title page of these copies is printed in black and there is the date 1897 at the foot. The title-page verso has only *All rights reserved* in the lower left.

The first impression of the American edition (dated 1897, or rather M DCCC XCVII, spaced so) was published after the English first impression.

In the Library of America *Henry James: Novels 1896–1899* (2003, p. 1029), Myra Jehlen corrected six typos of 1897, of which one was dangerous: for *drove me*, read *drove to me* (p. 117 below). I am grateful likewise to Susan Kennedy who spotted two further typos of 1897. I have corrected, with the aid of the American edition of 1897, *which she* to *to which she* (p. 94), and on a few occasions when James has been inconsistent in such a matter as hyphenation (having both *shopfront* and *shop-front*), I have standardized with the help of the American edition of 1897.

Publisher's Note

Some minor adjustments of punctuation have been made for this edition. They include the substitution of n-rule dashes for long ones, single quotation marks for double and the standardization of '-ize' spellings throughout, in accordance with Penguin Classics house style.

What Maisie Knew

The litigation had seemed interminable and had in fact been complicated; but by the decision on the appeal the judgment of the divorce-court was confirmed as to the assignment of the child. The father, who, though bespattered from head to foot, had made good his case, was, in pursuance of this triumph, appointed to keep her: it was not so much that the mother's character had been more absolutely damaged as that the brilliancy of a lady's complexion (and this lady's, in court, was immensely remarked) might be more regarded as showing the spots. Attached, however, to the second pronouncement was a condition that detracted, for Beale Farange, from its sweetness – an order that he should refund to his late wife the twenty-six hundred pounds put down by her, as it was called, some three years before, in the interest of the child's maintenance and precisely on a proved understanding that he would take no proceedings: a sum of which he had had the administration and of which he could render not the least account. The obligation thus attributed to her adversary was no small balm to Ida's resentment; it drew a part of the sting from her defeat and compelled Mr. Farange perceptibly to lower his crest. He was unable to produce the money or to raise it in any way; so that after a squabble scarcely less public and scarcely more decent than the original shock of battle his only issue from his predicament was a compromise proposed by his legal advisers and finally accepted by hers.

His debt was by this arrangement remitted to him and the little girl disposed of in a manner worthy of the judgment-seat of Solomon. She was divided in two and the portions tossed impartially to the disputants. They would take her, in rotation, for six months at a time; she would spend half the year with each. This was odd justice in the eyes of those who still blinked in the fierce light projected from the tribunal – a light in which neither parent figured in the least as a happy example to youth and innocence. What was to have been expected on the evidence was the nomination, *in loco parentis*, of some proper third person, some respectable or at least some presentable friend. Apparently, however, the circle of the Faranges had been scanned in vain for any such ornament; so that the only solution finally meeting all the difficulties was, save that of sending Maisie to a Home, the partition of the tutelary office in the manner I have mentioned. There were more reasons for her parents to agree to it than there had ever been for them to agree to anything; and they now prepared with her help to enjoy the distinction that waits upon vulgarity sufficiently attested. Their rupture had resounded, and after being perfectly insignificant together they would be decidedly striking apart. Had they not produced an impression that warranted people in looking for appeals in the newspapers for the rescue of the little one – reverberation, amid a vociferous public, of the idea that some movement should be started or some benevolent person should come forward? A good lady came indeed a step or two: she was distantly related to Mrs. Farange, to whom she proposed that, having children and nurseries wound up and going, she should be allowed to take home the bone of contention and, by working it into her system, relieve at least one of the parents. This would make every time, for Maisie, after her inevitable six months with Beale, much more of a change.

'More of a change?' Ida cried. 'Won't it be enough of a change for her to come from that low brute to the person in the world who detests him most?'

'No, because you detest him so much that you'll always talk to her about him. You'll keep him before her by perpetually abusing him.'

Mrs. Farange stared. 'Pray, then, am I to do nothing to counteract his villainous abuse of *me*?'

The good lady, for a moment, made no reply: her silence was a grim judgment of the whole point of view. 'Poor little monkey!'

she at last exclaimed; and the words were an epitaph for the tomb of Maisie's childhood. She was abandoned to her fate. What was clear to any spectator was that the only link binding her to either parent was this lamentable fact of her being a ready vessel for bitterness, a deep little porcelain cup in which biting acids could be mixed. They had wanted her not for any good they could do her, but for the harm they could, with her unconscious aid, do each other. She should serve their anger and seal their revenge, for husband and wife had been alike crippled by the heavy hand of justice, which, in the last resort, met on neither side their indignant claim to get, as they called it, everything. If each was only to get half, this seemed to concede that neither was so base as the other pretended, or, to put it differently, offered them as both bad indeed, since they were only as good as each other. The mother had wished to prevent the father from, as she said, 'so much as looking' at the child; the father's plea was that the mother's lightest touch was 'simply contamination'. These were the opposed principles in which Maisie was to be educated – she was to fit them together as she might. Nothing could have been more touching at first than her failure to suspect the ordeal that awaited her little unspotted soul. There were persons horrified to think what those who had charge of it would combine to try to make of it: no one could conceive in advance that they would be able to make nothing ill.

This was a society in which, for the most part, people were occupied only with chatter, but the disunited couple had at last grounds for expecting a period of high activity. They girded their loins; they felt as if the quarrel had only begun. They felt indeed more married than ever, inasmuch as what marriage had mainly suggested to them was the high opportunity to quarrel. There had been 'sides' before, and there were sides as much as ever; for the sider too the prospect opened out, taking the pleasant form of a superabundance of matter for desultory conversation. The many friends of the Faranges drew together to differ about them; contradiction grew young again over tea-cups and cigars. Everybody was always assuring everybody of something very shocking, and nobody would have been jolly if nobody had been outrageous. The pair appeared to have a social attraction which failed merely as regards each other: it was indeed a great deal to be able to say for Ida that no one but Beale desired her blood, and for Beale that if he should ever have his eyes scratched out it would be only by his wife. It was generally felt, to begin with, that they were awfully good-looking – they had really not been analysed to a deeper residuum. They made up together, for instance, some twelve feet of stature, and nothing was more discussed than the apportionment of this quantity. The sole flaw in Ida's beauty was a length and reach of arm conducive perhaps to her having so often beaten her ex-husband at billiards, a game in which she showed a superiority largely accountable, as she maintained, for the resentment finding expression in his physical violence. Billiards were her great accomplishment and the distinction her name always first produced the mention of. Notwithstanding some very long lines everything about her that might have been large and that in many women profited by the licence was, with a single exception, admired and cited for its smallness. The exception was her eyes, which might have been of mere regulation size, but which overstepped the modesty of nature; her mouth, on the other hand, was barely perceptible, and odds were freely taken as to the measurement of her waist. She was a person who, when she was out – and she was always out – produced everywhere a sense of having been seen often, the sense indeed of a kind of abuse of visibility, so that it would have been, in the usual places, rather vulgar to wonder at her. Strangers only did that; but they, to the amusement of the familiar, did it very much: it was an inevitable way of betraying an alien habit. Like her husband, she carried clothes, carried them as a train carries passengers: people had been known to compare their taste and dispute about the accommodation they gave these articles, though inclining on the whole to the commendation of Ida as less overcrowded, especially with jewellery and flowers. Beale Farange had natural decorations, a kind of costume in his vast fair beard, burnished like a gold breastplate, and in the eternal glitter of the teeth that his long moustache had been trained not to hide and that gave him, in every possible situation, the look of the joy of life. He had been destined in his youth for diplomacy and momentarily attached, without a salary, to a legation which enabled him often to say 'In *my* time, in the East': but contemporary history had somehow had no use for him, had hurried past him and left him in perpetual Piccadilly. Every one knew what he had – only twenty-five hundred. Poor Ida, who had run through everything, had now nothing but her carriage and her paralysed uncle. This old brute, as he was called, was supposed to have a lot put away. The child was provided for, thanks to a crafty godmother, a defunct aunt of Beale's, who had left her something in such a manner that the parents could appropriate only the income.

I

The child was provided for, but the new arrangement was inevitably confounding to a young intelligence, intensely aware that something had happened which must matter a good deal and looking anxiously out for the effects of so great a cause. It was to be the fate of this patient little girl to see much more than, at first, she understood, but also, even at first, to understand much more than any little girl, however patient, had perhaps ever understood before. Only a drummer-boy in a ballad or a story could have been so in the thick of the fight. She was taken into the confidence of passions on which she fixed just the stare she might have had for images bounding across the wall in the slide of a magic-lantern. Her little world was phantasmagoric – strange shadows dancing on a sheet. It was as if the whole performance had been given for her – a mite of a half-scared infant in a great dim theatre. She was in short introduced to life with a liberality in which the selfishness of others found its account, and there was nothing to avert the sacrifice but the modesty of her youth.

Her first term was with her father, who spared her only in not letting her have the wild letters addressed to her by her mother: he confined himself to holding them up at her and shaking them, while he showed his teeth, and then amusing her by the way he chucked them, across the room, bang into the fire. Even at that moment, however, she had a scared anticipation of fatigue, a guilty sense of not rising to the occasion, feeling the charm of the violence with which the stiff unopened envelopes, whose big monograms – Ida bristled with monograms – she would have liked to see, were made to whizz, like dangerous missiles, through the air. The greatest effect of the great cause was her own greater importance, chiefly revealed to her in the larger freedom with which she was handled, pulled hither and thither and kissed, and the proportionately greater niceness she was obliged to show. Her features had somehow become prominent; they were so perpetually nipped by the gentlemen who came to see her father and the smoke of whose cigarettes went into her face. Some of these gentlemen made her strike matches and light their cigarettes; others, holding her on knees violently jolted, pinched the calves of her legs until she shrieked – her shriek was much admired – and reproached them with being toothpicks. The word stuck in her mind and contributed to her feeling from this time that she was deficient in something that would meet the general desire. She found out what it was: it was a congenital tendency to the production of a substance to which Moddle, her nurse, gave a short, ugly name, a name painfully associated with the part of the joint, at dinner, that she didn't like. She had left behind her the time when she had no desires to meet, none at least save Moddle's, who, in Kensington Gardens, was always on the bench when she came back to see if she had been playing too far. Moddle's desire was merely that she shouldn't do that, and she met it so easily that the only spots in that long brightness were the moments of her wondering what would become of her if, on her rushing back, there should be no Moddle on the bench. They still went to the Gardens, but there was a difference even there; she was impelled perpetually to look at the legs of other children and ask her nurse if *they* were toothpicks. Moddle was terribly truthful; she always said: 'Oh, my dear, you'll not find such another pair as your own.' It seemed to have to do with something else that Moddle often said: 'You feel the strain – that's where it is; and you'll feel it still worse, you know.'

Thus, from the first, Maisie not only felt it, but knew that she felt it. A part of it was the consequence of her father's telling her that he felt it too, and telling Moddle, in her presence, that she must make a point of driving that home. She was familiar, at the age of six, with the fact that everything had been changed on her account, everything ordered to enable him to give himself up to her. She was to remember always the words in which Moddle impressed upon her that he did so give himself: 'Your papa wishes you never to forget, you know, that he has been dreadfully put about.' If the skin on Moddle's face had to Maisie the air of being unduly, almost painfully, stretched, it never presented that appearance so much as when she uttered, as she often had occasion to utter, such words. The child wondered if they didn't make it hurt more than usual; but it was only after some time that she was able to attach to the picture of her father's sufferings, and more particularly to her nurse's manner about them, the meaning for which these things had waited. By the time she had grown sharper, as the gentlemen who had criticized her calves used to say, she found in her mind a collection of images and echoes to which meanings were attachable – images and echoes kept for her in the childish dusk, the dim closet, the high drawers, like games she wasn't yet big enough to play. The great strain meanwhile was that of carrying by the right end the things her father said about her mother – things mostly indeed that Moddle, on a glimpse of them, as if they had been complicated toys or difficult books, took out of her hands and put away in the closet. It was a wonderful assortment of objects of this kind that she discovered there later, all tumbled up too with the things, shuffled into the same receptacle, that her mother had said about her father.

She had the knowledge that, on a certain occasion which every day brought nearer, her mother would be at the door to take her away, and this would have darkened all the days if the ingenious Moddle had not written on a paper, in very big, easy words, ever so many pleasures that she would enjoy at the other house. These promises ranged from 'a mother's fond love' to 'a nice poached egg to your tea,' and took by the way the prospect of sitting up ever so late to see the lady in question dressed, in silks and velvets and diamonds and pearls, to go out: so that it was a real support to Maisie, at the supreme hour, to feel that, by Moddle's direction, the paper was thrust away in her pocket and there clenched in her fist. The supreme hour was to furnish her with a vivid reminiscence, that of a strange outbreak in the drawing-room on the part of Moddle, who, in reply to something her father had just said, cried aloud: 'You ought to be perfectly ashamed of yourself – you ought to blush, sir, for the way you go on!' The carriage, with her mother in it, was at the door; a gentleman who was there, who was always there, laughed out very loud; her father, who had her in his arms, said to Moddle: 'My dear woman, I'll settle *you* presently!' – after which he repeated, showing his teeth more than ever at Maisie while he hugged her, the words for which her nurse had taken him up. Maisie was not at the moment so fully conscious of them as of the wonder of Moddle's sudden disrespect and crimson face; but she was able to produce them in the course of five minutes when, in the carriage, her mother, all kisses, ribbons, eyes, arms, strange sounds and sweet smells, said to her: 'And did your beastly papa, my precious angel, send any message to your own loving mamma?' Then it was that she found the words spoken by her beastly papa to be, after all, in her little bewildered ears, from which, at her mother's appeal, they passed, in her clear, shrill voice, straight to her little innocent lips. 'He said I was to tell you, from him,' she faithfully reported, 'that you're a nasty, horrid pig!'

II

In that lively sense of the immediate which is the very air of a child's mind the past, on each occasion, became for her as indistinct as the future: she surrendered herself to the actual with a good faith that might have been touching to either parent. Crudely as they had calculated, they were at first justified by the event: she was the little feathered shuttlecock that they fiercely kept flying between them. The evil they had the gift of thinking, or pretending to think, of each other, they poured into her little gravely gazing soul as into a boundless receptacle; and each of them had, doubtless, the best conscience in the world as to the duty of teaching her the stern truth that should be her safeguard against the other. She was at the age for which all stories are true and all conceptions are stories. The actual was the absolute; the present alone was vivid. The objurgation, for instance, launched in the carriage by her mother after she had, at her father's bidding, punctually performed, was a missive that dropped into her memory with the dry rattle of a letter falling into a pillar-box. Like the letter it was, as part of the contents of a well-stuffed post-bag, delivered in due course at the right address. In the presence of these overflowings, after they had continued for a couple of years, the associates of either party sometimes felt that something should be done for what they called 'the real good, don't you know?' of the child. The only thing done, however, in general, took place when it was sighingly remarked that she fortunately wasn't all the year round where she happened to be at the awkward moment, and that, furthermore, either from extreme cunning or from extreme stupidity, she appeared not to take things in.

The theory of her stupidity, eventually embraced by her parents, corresponded with a great date in her small, still life: the complete vision, private but final, of the strange office she filled. It was literally a moral revolution, and it was accomplished in the depths of her nature. The stiff dolls on the dusky shelves began to move their arms and legs: old forms and phrases began to have a sense that frightened her. She had a new feeling, the feeling of danger; on which a new remedy rose to meet it, the idea of an inner self, or, in other words, of concealment. She puzzled out with imperfect signs, but with a prodigious spirit, that she had been a centre of hatred and a messenger of insult, and that everything was bad because she had been employed to make it so. Her parted lips locked themselves with the determination to be employed no longer. She would forget everything, she would repeat nothing, and when, as a tribute to the successful application of her system, she began to be called a little idiot, she tasted a pleasure altogether new. When therefore, as she grew older, her parents in turn, in her presence, announced that she had grown shockingly dull, it was not from any real contraction of her little stream of life. She spoiled their fun, but she practically added to her own. She saw more and more; she saw too much. It was Miss Overmore, her first governess, who, on a momentous occasion, had sown the seeds of secrecy; sown them not by anything she said, but by a mere roll of those fine eyes which Maisie already admired. Moddle had become at this time, after alternations of residence of which the child had no clear record, an image faintly embalmed in the remembrance of hungry disappearances from the nursery and distressful lapses in the alphabet, sad embarrassments, in particular, when invited to recognize something that her nurse called 'the important letter haitch'. Miss Overmore, however hungry, never disappeared: this marked her somehow as a being more exalted, and the character was confirmed by a prettiness that Maisie supposed to be extraordinary. Mrs. Farange had said that she was almost too pretty, and some one had asked what that mattered so long as Beale wasn't there. 'Beale or no Beale,' Maisie had heard her mother reply, 'I take her because she's a lady and yet awfully poor. Rather nice people, but there are seven sisters at home. What do people mean?'

Maisie didn't know what people meant, but she knew very soon all the names of all the sisters; she could say them off better than she could say the multiplication-table. She privately wondered moreover, though she never asked, about the awful poverty, of which her companion also never spoke. Food, at any rate, came up by mysterious laws; Miss Overmore never, like Moddle, had on an apron, and when she ate she held her fork with her little finger curled out. The child, who watched her at many moments, watched her particularly at that one. 'I think you're lovely,' she often said to her; even mamma, who was lovely too, had not such a pretty way with the fork. Maisie associated this showier presence with her now being 'big', knowing of course that nursery-governesses were only for little girls who were not, as she said, 'really' little. She vaguely knew, further, somehow, that the future was still bigger than she, and that a part of what made it so was the number of governesses lurking in it and ready to dart out. Everything that had happened when she was really little was dormant, everything but the positive certitude, bequeathed from afar by Moddle, that the natural way for a child to have her parents was separate and successive, like her mutton and her pudding or her bath and her nap.

'*Does* he know that he lies?' – that was what she had vivaciously asked Miss Overmore on the occasion which was so suddenly to lead to a change in her life.

'Does he know—?' Miss Overmore stared; she had a stocking pulled over her hand and was pricking at it with a needle which she poised in the act. Her task was homely, but her movement, like all her movements, graceful.

'Why, papa.'

'That he "lies"?'

'That's what mamma says I'm to tell him – "that he lies and he knows he lies".' Miss Overmore turned very red, though she laughed out till her head fell back; then she pricked again at her muffled hand so hard that Maisie wondered how she could bear it. '*Am* I to tell him?' the child went on. It was then that her companion addressed her in the unmistakable language of a pair of eyes of deep dark-grey. 'I can't say No,' they replied as distinctly as possible; 'I can't say No, because I'm afraid of your mamma, don't you see? Yet how can I say Yes after your papa has been so kind to me, talking to me so long the other day, smiling and flashing his beautiful teeth at me the time we met him in the Park, the time when, rejoicing at the sight of us, he left the gentleman he was with and turned and walked with us, stayed with us for half an hour?' Somehow, in the light of Miss Overmore's lovely eyes, that incident came back to Maisie with a charm it hadn't had at the time, and this in spite of the fact that after it was over her governess had never but once alluded to it. On their way home, when papa had quitted them, she had expressed the hope that the child wouldn't mention it to mamma. Maisie liked her so, and had so the charmed sense of being liked by her, that she accepted this remark as settling the matter and wonderingly conformed to it. The wonder now lived again, lived in the recollection of what papa had said to Miss Overmore: 'I've only to look at you to see that you're a person to whom I can appeal to help me to save my daughter.' Maisie's ignorance of what she was to be saved from didn't diminish the pleasure of the thought that Miss Overmore was saving her. It seemed to make them cling together.

III

She was therefore all the more startled when her mother said to her in connection with something to be done before her next migration: 'You understand, of course, that she's not going with you.'

Maisie turned quite faint. 'Oh, I thought she was.'

'It doesn't in the least matter, you know, what you think,' Mrs. Farange loudly replied; 'and you had better indeed for the future, miss, learn to keep your thoughts to yourself.' This was exactly what Maisie had already learned, and the accomplishment was just the source of her mother's irritation. It was of a horrid little critical system, a tendency, in her silence, to judge her elders, that this lady suspected her, liking as she did, for her own part, a child to be simple and confiding. She liked also to hear the report of the whacks she administered to Mr. Farange's character, to his pretensions to peace of mind: the satisfaction of dealing them diminished when nothing came back. The day was at hand, and she felt it, when she should feel more delight in hurling Maisie at him than in snatching her away; so much so that her conscience winced under the acuteness of a candid friend who had remarked that the real end of all their tugging would be that each parent would try to make the little girl a burden to the other – a sort of game in which a fond mother clearly wouldn't show to advantage. The prospect of not showing to advantage, a distinction in which she held that she had never failed, begot in Ida Farange an ill-humour of which several persons felt the effect. She determined that Beale, at any rate, should feel it; she reflected afresh that in the study of how to be odious to him she must never give way. Nothing could incommode him more than not to get the good, for the child, of a nice female appendage who had clearly taken a fancy to her. One of the things Ida said to the appendage was that Beale's was a house in which no decent woman could consent to be seen. It was Miss Overmore herself who explained to Maisie that she had had a hope of being allowed to accompany her to her father's, and that this hope had been dashed by the way her mother took it. 'She says that if I ever do such a thing as enter his service, I must never, in this house, expect to show my face again. So I've promised not to attempt to go with you. If I wait patiently till you come back here we shall certainly be together once more.'

Waiting patiently, and above all waiting till she should come back there, seemed to Maisie a long way round – it reminded her of all the things she had been told, first and last, that she should have if she would be good, and that, in spite of her goodness, she had never had at all. 'Then who will take care of me at papa's?'

'Heaven only knows, my own precious!' Miss Overmore replied, tenderly embracing her. There was indeed no doubt that she was dear to this beautiful friend. What could have proved it better than the fact that before a week was out, in spite of their distressing separation, and her mother's prohibition, and Miss Overmore's scruples and Miss Overmore's promise, the beautiful friend had turned up at her father's? The little lady already engaged there to come by the hour, a fat, dark little lady, with a foreign name and dirty fingers, who wore, throughout, a bonnet that had at first given her a deceptive air of not staying long, besides asking her pupil questions that had nothing to do with lessons, questions that Beale Farange himself, when two or three were repeated to him, admitted to be awfully vulgar – this strange apparition faded before the bright creature who had braved everything for Maisie's sake. The bright creature told her little charge frankly what had happened – that she had really been unable to hold out. She had broken her vow to Mrs. Farange; she had struggled for three days, then she had come straight to Maisie's papa and told him the simple truth. She adored his daughter; she couldn't

give her up; she would make any sacrifice for her. On this basis
it had been arranged that she should stay; her courage had been
rewarded; she left Maisie in no doubt as to the amount of courage she had required. Some of the things she said made a particular impression on the child – her declaration, for instance,
that when her pupil should get older she would understand
better just how 'dreadfully bold' a young lady, to do exactly
what she had done, had to be.

'Fortunately your papa appreciates it; he appreciates it
immensely' – that was one of the things Miss Overmore also
said, with a striking insistence on the adverb. Maisie herself
was no less impressed with what her friend had gone through,
especially after hearing of the terrible letter that had come
from Mrs. Farange. Mamma had been so angry that, in Miss
Overmore's own words, she had loaded her with insult – proof
enough indeed that they must never look forward to being
together again under mamma's roof. Mamma's roof, however,
had its turn, this time, for the child, of appearing but remotely
contingent, so that, to reassure her, there was scarce a need of
her companion's secret, solemnly confided – the idea that there
should be no going back to mamma at all. It was Miss
Overmore's private conviction, and a part of the same communication, that if Mr. Farange's daughter would only show a
really marked preference she would be backed up by 'public
opinion' in holding on to him. Poor Maisie could scarcely grasp
that incentive, but she could surrender herself to the day. She
had conceived her first passion, and the object of it was her
governess. It had not been put to her, and she couldn't, or at
any rate she didn't, put it to herself, that she liked Miss
Overmore better than she liked papa; but it would have
sustained her under such an imputation to feel herself able
to reply that papa too liked Miss Overmore exactly as much.
He had particularly told her so. Besides, she could easily see it.

IV

All this led her on, but it brought on her fate as well, the day when her mother would be at the door in the carriage in which Maisie now rode on no occasions but these. There was no question, at present, of Miss Overmore's going back with her: it was universally recognized that her quarrel with Mrs. Farange was much too acute. The child felt it from the first; there was no hugging nor exclaiming as that lady drove her away – there was only a frightening silence, unenlivened even by the invidious inquiries of former years, which culminated, according to its stern nature, in a still more frightening old woman, a figure awaiting her on the very doorstep. 'You're to be under this lady's care,' said her mother. 'Take her, Mrs. Wix,' she added, addressing the figure impatiently and giving the child a push in which Maisie felt that she wished to set Mrs. Wix an example of energy. Mrs. Wix took her, and Maisie felt, the next day, that she would never let her go. She had struck her at first, just after Miss Overmore, as terrible; but something in her voice at the end of an hour touched the little girl in a spot that had never even yet been reached. Maisie knew later what it was, though doubtless she couldn't have made a statement of it: these were things that a few days' conversation with Mrs. Wix lighted up. The principal one was a matter that Mrs. Wix herself always immediately mentioned: she had had a little girl quite of her own, and the little girl had been killed on the spot. She had had absolutely nothing else in all the world, and her affliction had broken her heart. It was comfortably established between them that Mrs. Wix's heart was broken. What Maisie felt was that she had been, with passion and anguish, a mother, and that this was something Miss Overmore was not, something, strangely, confusingly, that mamma was even less.

So it was that in the course of an extraordinarily short time she found herself as deeply absorbed in the image of the little dead Clara Matilda, who, on a crossing in the Harrow Road, had been knocked down and crushed by the cruellest of hansoms, than she had ever found herself in the family group made vivid by one of seven. 'She's your little dead sister,' Mrs. Wix ended by saying, and Maisie, all in a tremor of curiosity and compassion, addressed from that moment a particular piety to the small infectious sentiment. Somehow she wasn't a real sister, but that only made her the more romantic. It contributed to this view of her that she was never to be spoken of in that character to any one else – least of all to Mrs. Farange, who wouldn't care for her nor recognize the relationship: it was to be just an unutterable and inexhaustible little secret with Mrs. Wix. Maisie knew everything about her that could be known, everything she had said or done in her little mutilated life, exactly how lovely she was, exactly how her hair was curled and her frocks were trimmed. Her hair came down far below her waist – it was of the most wonderful golden brightness, just as Mrs. Wix's own had been a long time before. Mrs. Wix's own was indeed very remarkable still, and Maisie had felt at first that she should never get on with it. It played a large part in the sad and strange appearance, the appearance as of a kind of greasy greyness, which Mrs. Wix had presented on the child's arrival. It had originally been yellow, but time had turned its glow to ashes, to a turbid, sallow, unvenerable white. Still excessively abundant, it was dressed in a manner of which the poor lady appeared not yet to have recognized the supersession, with a glossy braid, like a large diadem, on the top of the head, and behind, at the nape of the neck, a dingy rosette like a large button. She wore glasses which, in humble reference to a divergent obliquity of vision, she called her straighteners, and a little ugly snuff-coloured dress trimmed with satin bands in the form of scallops and glazed with antiquity. The straighteners, she explained to Maisie, were put on for the sake of others, whom, as she believed, they helped to recognize the direction, otherwise misleading, of her glance; the rest of the melancholy attire could only have been put on for herself. With the added suggestion of her goggles it reminded her pupil of the polished shell or corslet of a horrid beetle. At first she had looked cross and almost cruel; but this impression passed away with the child's increased perception of her being in the eyes of the world a figure mainly for laughter. She was passively comical – a person whom people, to make talk lively, described to each other and imitated. Every one knew the straighteners; every one knew the diadem and the button, the scallops and satin bands; every one, though Maisie had never betrayed her, knew even Clara Matilda.

It was on account of these things that mamma got her for so little money, really for nothing: so much, one day when Mrs. Wix had accompanied her into the drawing-room and left her, the child heard one of the ladies she found there – a lady with eyebrows arched like skipping-ropes and thick black stitching, like ruled 'lines', on beautiful white gloves – announce to another. She knew governesses were poor; Miss Overmore was unmentionably and Mrs. Wix familiarly so. Neither this, however, nor the old brown frock, nor the diadem, nor the button, made a difference for Maisie in the charm put forth through everything, the charm of Mrs. Wix's conveying that, somehow, in her ugliness and her poverty, she was peculiarly and soothingly safe; safer than any one in the world, than papa, than mamma, than the lady with the arched eyebrows; safer even, though so much less beautiful, than Miss Overmore, on whose loveliness, as she supposed it, the little girl was faintly conscious that one couldn't rest with quite the same tucked-in and kissed-for-good-night feeling. Mrs. Wix was as safe as Clara Matilda, who was in heaven and yet, embarrassingly, also in Kensal Green, where they had been together to see her little huddled grave. It was from something in Mrs. Wix's tone, which, in spite of caricature, remained indescribable and inimitable, that Maisie, before her term with her mother was over, drew this sense of a tenderness that would never give way. If she knew her instructress was poor and queer she also knew that she was not nearly so 'qualified' as Miss Overmore, who could say lots of dates straight off (letting you hold the book yourself), state the position of Malabar, play six pieces without notes, and, in a sketch, put in beautifully the trees and houses and difficult parts. Maisie herself could play more pieces than Mrs. Wix, who was moreover visibly ashamed of her houses and trees and could only, with the help of a smutty forefinger, of doubtful legitimacy in the field of art, do the smoke coming out of the chimneys.

They dealt, the governess and her pupil, in 'subjects', but there were many the governess put off from week to week and that they never got to at all: she only used to say 'We'll take that in its proper order.' Her order was a circle as vast as the untravelled globe. She had not the spirit of adventure, and the child could perfectly see how many subjects she was afraid of. She took refuge on the firm ground of fiction, through which indeed there flowed the blue river of truth. She knew swarms of stories, mostly those of the novels she had read; relating them with a memory that never faltered and a wealth of detail that was Maisie's delight. They were all about love and beauty and countesses and wickedness. Her conversation was practically an endless narrative, a great garden of romance, with sudden vistas into her own life and gushing fountains of fact. These were the parts where they most lingered; she made the child take with her again every step of her long, lame course and think it a journey in an enchanted land. Her pupil acquired a vivid vision of every one who had ever, in her phrase, knocked against her – some of them, oh, so hard! – every one literally but Mr. Wix, her husband, as to whom nothing was mentioned save that he had been dead for ages. He had been rather remarkably absent from his wife's existence, and Maisie was never taken to see his grave.

V

The second parting from Miss Overmore had been bad enough, but this first parting from Mrs. Wix was much worse. The child had lately been to the dentist's and had a term of comparison for the screwed-up intensity of the scene. It was dreadfully silent, as it had been when her tooth was taken out; Mrs. Wix had on that occasion grabbed her hand and they had clung to each other with the frenzy of their determination not to scream. Maisie, at the dentist's, had been heroically still, but just when she felt most anguish had become aware, on the part of her companion, of an audible shriek, a spasm of stifled sympathy. This was reproduced by the only sound that broke their supreme embrace when, a month later, the 'arrangement', as her periodical uprootings were called, played the part of the horrible forceps. Embedded in Mrs. Wix's nature as her tooth had been socketed in her gum, the operation of extracting her would really have been a case for chloroform. It was a hug that fortunately left nothing to say, for the poor woman's want of words at such an hour seemed to fall in with her want of everything. Maisie's alternate parent, in the outermost vestibule – he liked the impertinence of crossing as much as that of his late wife's threshold – stood over them with his open watch and his still more open grin, while from the only corner of an eye on which something of Mrs. Wix's didn't impinge the child saw at the door a brougham in which Miss Overmore also waited. She remembered the difference when, six months before, she had been torn from the breast of that more spirited protectress. Miss Overmore, then also in the vestibule, but of course in the other one, had been thoroughly audible and voluble; her protest had rung out bravely and she had declared that something – her pupil didn't know exactly what – was a regular wicked shame. That had at the time dimly recalled to Maisie the far-away moment of Moddle's great outbreak: there seemed always to be 'shames' connected in one way or another with her migrations. At present, while Mrs. Wix's arms tightened and the smell of her hair was strong, she further remembered how, in pacifying Miss Overmore, papa had made use of the words 'you dear old duck!' – an expression which, by its oddity, had stuck fast in her young mind, having moreover a place well prepared for it there by what she knew of the governess whom she now always mentally characterized as the pretty one. She wondered whether this affection would be as great as before: that would at all events be the case with the prettiness Maisie could see in the face which showed brightly at the window of the brougham.

The brougham was a token of harmony, of the fine conditions papa, this time, would offer: he had usually come for her in a hansom with a four-wheeler behind for the boxes. The four-wheeler with the boxes on it was actually there; but mamma was the only lady with whom she had ever been in a conveyance of the kind always of old spoken of by Moddle as a private carriage. Papa's carriage was, now that he had one, still more private, somehow, than mamma's; and when at last she found herself quite on top, as she felt, of its inmates and gloriously rolling away she put to Miss Overmore, after another immense and talkative squeeze, a question of which the motive was a desire for information as to the continuity of a certain sentiment. 'Did papa like you just the same while I was gone?' she inquired – full of the sense of how markedly his favour had been established in her presence. She had bethought herself that this favour might, like her presence, and as if depending on it, be only intermittent and for the season. Papa, on whose knee she sat, burst into one of those loud laughs of his that, however prepared she was, seemed always, like some trick in a frightening game, to leap forth to make her jump; and before Miss Overmore could speak he replied: 'Why, you little donkey, when you're away what have I left to do but just to love her?' Miss Overmore hereupon immediately took her from him, and they had, over her, an hilarious little scrimmage of which Maisie caught the surprised observation in the white stare of an old lady who passed in a victoria. Then her beautiful friend remarked to her very gravely: 'I shall make him understand that if he ever again says anything as horrid as that to you I shall carry you straight off and we'll go and live somewhere together and be good, quiet little girls.' The child couldn't quite make out why her father's speech had been horrid, since it only expressed that appreciation which their companion herself, of old, described as 'immense'. To enter more into the truth of the matter she appealed to him again directly, asked if in all those months Miss Overmore hadn't been with him just as she had been before and just as she would be now. 'Of course she has, old girl – where else could the poor dear be?' cried Beale Farange, to the still greater scandal of their companion, who protested that unless he straightway 'took back' his nasty wicked fib it would be, this time, not only him she would leave, but his child too and his house and his tiresome troubles – all the impossible things he had succeeded in putting on her. Beale, under this frolic menace, took nothing back at all: he was indeed apparently on the point of repeating his assertion, but Miss Overmore instructed her little charge that she was not to listen to his bad jokes: she was to understand that a lady couldn't stay with a gentleman that way without some awfully proper reason.

Maisie looked from one of her companions to the other; this was the freshest, merriest start she had yet enjoyed, but she had a shy fear of not exactly believing them. 'Well, what reason *is* proper?' she thoughtfully demanded.

'Oh, a long-legged stick of a tomboy: there's none so good as that.' Her father enjoyed both her drollery and his own and tried again to get possession of her – an effort deprecated by their comrade and leading again to something of a public scuffle. Miss Overmore declared to the child that she had been all the while with good friends; on which Beale Farange went on: 'She means good friends of mine, you know – tremendous friends of mine. There has been no end of *them* about – that I *will* say for her!' The child felt bewildered and was afterwards for some time

conscious of a vagueness, just slightly embarrassing, as to the
subject of so much amusement and as to where her governess
had really been. She didn't feel at all as if she had been seriously
told, and no such feeling was supplied by anything that occurred
later. Her embarrassment, of a precocious, instinctive order,
attached itself to the idea that this was another of the matters
that it was not for her, as her mother used to say, to go into.
Therefore, under her father's roof, during the time that followed,
she made no attempt to clear up her ambiguity by a sociable
interrogation of housemaids; and it was an odd truth that the
ambiguity itself took nothing from the fresh pleasure promised
her by renewed contact with Miss Overmore. The confidence
looked for by that young lady was of the fine sort that explanation cannot improve, and she herself at any rate was a person
superior to any confusion. For Maisie moreover concealment
had never necessarily seemed deception, and she had grown up
among things as to which her foremost knowledge was that she
was not to ask about them. It was far from new to her that the
questions of the small are the peculiar diversion of the great:
except the affairs of her doll Lisette there had scarcely ever been
anything at her mother's that was explicable with a grave face.
Nothing was so easy to her as to send the ladies who gathered
there off into shrieks, and she might have practised upon them
largely if she had been of a more calculating turn. Everything
had something behind it: life was like a long, long corridor with
rows of closed doors. She had learned that at these doors it was
wise not to knock – this seemed to produce, from within, such
sounds of derision. Little by little, however, she understood
more, for it befell that she was enlightened by Lisette's questions,
which reproduced the effect of her own upon those for whom
she sat in the very darkness of Lisette. Was she not herself convulsed by such innocence? In the presence of it she often imitated the shrieking ladies. There were at any rate things she
really couldn't tell even a French doll. She could only pass on her
lessons and study to produce on Lisette the impression of having
mysteries in her life, wondering the while whether she succeeded
in the air of shading off, like her mother, into the unknowable.
When the reign of Miss Overmore followed that of Mrs. Wix

she took a fresh cue, emulating her governess and bridging over the interval with the simple expectation of trust. Yes, there were matters one couldn't 'go into' with a pupil. There were for instance days when, after prolonged absence, Lisette, while she took off her things, tried hard to discover where she had been. Well, she discovered a little, but she never discovered all. There was an occasion when, on her being particularly indiscreet, Maisie replied to her – and precisely about the motive of a disappearance – as she, Maisie, had once been replied to by Mrs. Farange: 'Find out for yourself!' She mimicked her mother's sharpness, but she was rather ashamed afterwards, though as to whether of the sharpness or the mimicry was not quite clear.

VI

She became aware in time that this would be a period not remarkable for lessons, the care of her education being now only one of the many duties devolving on Miss Overmore; a circumstance as to which she was present at various passages between that lady and her father – passages significant, on either side, of dissent and even of displeasure. It was gathered by the child on these occasions that there was something in the situation for which her mother might 'come down' on them all, though indeed the suggestion, always thrown out by her father, was greeted on his companion's part with particular derision. Such scenes were usually brought to a climax by Miss Overmore's demanding, in a harsher manner than she applied to any other subject, in what position under the sun such a person as Mrs. Farange would find herself for coming down. As the months went on the little girl's interpretations thickened, and the more effectually that this period was the longest she had yet known without a break. She became familiar with the idea that her mother, for some reason, was in no hurry to reinstate her: that idea was forcibly expressed by her father whenever Miss Overmore, differing and decided, took him up on the question, which he was always putting forward, of the urgency of sending her to school. For a governess Miss Overmore differed surprisingly; far more, for instance, than would ever have entered into the head of poor Mrs. Wix. She remarked to Maisie many times that she was quite conscious of not doing her justice, and that Mr. Farange equally measured and equally lamented this deficiency. The reason of it was that she had mysterious responsibilities that interfered – responsibilities, Miss Overmore intimated, to Mr. Farange himself and to the friendly, noisy little house and those who came there. Mr. Farange's remedy for every inconvenience was that the child should be put at school – there were such lots of splendid schools, as everybody knew, at Brighton and all over the place. That, however, Maisie learned, was just what would bring her mother down: from the moment he should delegate to others the housing of his little charge he hadn't a leg to stand on before the law. Didn't he keep her away from her mother precisely because Mrs. Farange was one of these others?

There was also the solution of a second governess, a young person to come in by the day and really do the work; but to this Miss Overmore wouldn't for a moment listen, arguing against it with great public relish and wanting to know from all comers (she put it even to Maisie herself) if they didn't see how frightfully it would give her away. 'What am I supposed to be at all, don't you see, if I'm not here to look after her?' She was in a false position and so freely and loudly called attention to it that it seemed to become almost a source of glory. The way out of it of course was just to do her plain duty; but that was unfortunately what, with his excessive, his exorbitant demands on her, which every one indeed appeared quite to understand, he practically, he selfishly prevented. Beale Farange, for Miss Overmore, was now never anything but 'he', and the house was as full as ever of lively gentlemen with whom, under that designation, she chaffingly talked about him. Maisie meanwhile, as a subject of familiar gossip on what was to be done with her, was left so much to herself that she had hours of wistful thought of the large loose discipline of Mrs. Wix: yet she none the less held it under her father's roof a point of superiority that none of his visitors were ladies. It added to this odd security that she had once heard a gentleman say to him as if it were a great joke and in obvious reference to Miss Overmore: 'Hanged if she'll let another woman come near you – hanged if she ever will. She'd let fly a stick at her as they do at a strange cat!' Maisie greatly preferred gentlemen as inmates in spite of their also having their way – louder but sooner over – of laughing out at her. They pulled and pinched, they teased and tickled her; some of them even, as they termed it, shied things at her, and all of them thought it funny to call her by names having no resemblance to her own. The ladies, on the other hand, addressed her as 'You poor pet' and scarcely touched her even to kiss her. But it was of the ladies she was most afraid.

She was old enough now to understand how disproportionate a stay she had already made with her father; and also old enough to enter a little into the ambiguity that surrounded this circumstance and that oppressed her particularly whenever the question had been touched upon in talk with her governess. 'Oh, you needn't worry: she doesn't care!' Miss Overmore had often said to her in reference to any fear that her mother might resent her prolonged detention. 'She has other people than poor little *you* to think about, and she has gone abroad with them, and you needn't be in the least afraid that she'll stickle this time for her rights.' Maisie knew Mrs. Farange had gone abroad, for she had had, weeks and weeks before, a letter from her, beginning 'My precious pet' and taking leave of her for an indeterminate time; but she had not seen in it a renunciation of hatred or of the writer's policy of asserting herself, for the sharpest of all her impressions had been that there was nothing her mother would ever care so much about as to torment Mr. Farange. What at last, however, in this connection was bewildering and a little frightening was the dawn of a suspicion that a better way had been found to torment Mr. Farange than to deprive him of his periodical burden. This was the question that worried our young lady and that Miss Overmore's confidences and the frequent observations of her employer only rendered more mystifying. It was a contradiction that if Ida had now a fancy for shirking the devotion she had originally been so hot about, her late husband shouldn't jump at the monopoly for which he had also in the first instance so fiercely fought; but when Maisie, with a subtlety beyond her years, sounded this new ground her main success was in hearing her mother more freshly abused. Miss Overmore, up to now, had rarely deviated from a decent reserve, but the day came when she expressed herself with a vividness not inferior to Beale's own on the subject of the lady who had fled to the Continent to wriggle out of her job.

It would serve this lady right, Maisie gathered, if that contract, in the shape of an overgrown and underdressed daughter, should be shipped straight out to her and landed at her feet in the midst of scandalous pastimes.

The picture of these pursuits was what Miss Overmore took refuge in when the child tried timidly to ascertain if her father were in danger of feeling that he had too much of her. She evaded the point and only kicked up all round it the dust of Ida's heartlessness and folly, of which the supreme proof, it appeared, was the fact that she was accompanied on her journey by a gentleman whom, to be painfully plain about it, she had – well, 'picked up'. The only terms on which, unless they were married, ladies and gentlemen might, as Miss Overmore expressed it, knock about together, were the terms on which she and Mr. Farange had exposed themselves to possible misconception. She had indeed, as I have intimated, often explained this before, often said to Maisie: 'I don't know what in the world, darling, your father and I should do without you, for you just make the difference, as I've told you, of keeping us perfectly proper.' The child took in the office it was so endearingly presented to her that she performed a comfort that helped her to a sense of security even in the event of being abandoned by her mother. Familiar as she had become with the idea of the great alternative to the proper, she felt that her governess and her father would have a substantial reason for not emulating that detachment. At the same time she had heard somehow of little girls – of exalted rank, it was true – whose education was carried on by instructors of the other sex, and she knew that if she were at school at Brighton it would be thought an advantage to her to be more or less in the hands of masters. She meditated on these mysteries and she at last remarked to Miss Overmore that if she should go to her mother perhaps the gentleman might become her tutor.

'The gentleman?' The proposition was complicated enough to make Miss Overmore stare.

'The one who's with mamma. Mightn't that make it right – as right as your being my governess makes it for you to be with papa?'

Miss Overmore considered; she coloured a little; then she embraced her ingenious disciple. 'You're too sweet! I'm a *real* governess.'

'And couldn't he be a real tutor?'

'Of course not. He's ignorant and bad.'

'Bad—?' Maisie echoed, with wonder.

Her companion gave a queer little laugh at her tone. 'He's ever so much younger—' The speaker paused.

'Younger than you?'

Miss Overmore laughed again; it was the first time Maisie had seen her approach so nearly to a giggle. 'Younger than – no matter whom. I don't know anything about him, and I don't want to,' she rather inconsequently added. 'He's not my sort, and I'm sure, my own darling, he's not yours.' And she repeated the embrace with which her colloquies with Maisie almost always terminated and which made the child feel that *her* affection, at least, was a gage of safety. Parents had come to seem precarious, but governesses were evidently to be trusted. Maisie's faith in Mrs. Wix, for instance, had suffered no lapse from the fact that all communication with her was temporarily at an end. During the first weeks of their separation Clara Matilda's mamma had repeatedly and dolefully written to her, and Maisie had answered with an excitement qualified only by orthographical delays; but the correspondence had been duly submitted to Miss Overmore, with the final consequence of incurring a lively disapproval. It was this lady's view that Mr. Farange wouldn't care for it at all; and she ended by confessing – since her pupil pushed her – that she didn't care for it herself. She was furiously jealous, she said; and that circumstance was only a new proof of her disinterested affection. She pronounced Mrs. Wix's effusions moreover illiterate and unprofitable and made no scruple of declaring it extraordinary that a woman in her senses should have placed the formation of her daughter's mind in such ridiculous hands. Maisie was well aware that the proprietress of the old brown dress and the old, odd headgear was a very different class of person from Miss Overmore; but it was now brought home to her with pain that she was educationally quite out of the question. She was

buried for the time beneath a conclusive remark of Miss Overmore's: 'She's really beyond a joke!' This remark was made as
that charming woman held in her hand the last letter that
Maisie was to receive from Mrs. Wix; it was fortified by a
decree abolishing the preposterous tie. 'Must I then write and
tell her?' the child bewilderingly inquired: she grew pale at the
image of the dreadful things it appeared to be prescribed for
her to say. 'Don't dream of it, my dear – *I'll* write: you may
trust me!' cried Miss Overmore; who indeed wrote to such purpose that a hush in which you could have heard a pin drop
descended upon poor Mrs. Wix. She gave for weeks and weeks
no sign whatever of life: it was as if she had been as effectually
disposed of by Miss Overmore's communication as her little
girl, in the Harrow Road, had been disposed of by the terrible
hansom. Her very silence became, after this, one of the largest
elements of Maisie's consciousness; it proved a warm and
habitable air, into which the child penetrated further than
she dared ever to mention to her companions. Somewhere in the
depths of it the dim straighteners were fixed upon her; somewhere out of the troubled little current Mrs. Wix intensely waited.

VII

It quite fell in with this intensity that one day, on returning from a walk with the housemaid, Maisie should have found her in the hall, seated on the stool usually occupied by the telegraph-boys who haunted Beale Farange's door and kicked their heels while, in his room, answers were concocted with the aid of smoke-puffs and growls. It had seemed to her on their parting that Mrs. Wix had reached the last limits of the squeeze, but she now felt those limits to be transcended and that the duration of her visitor's hug was a direct reply to Miss Overmore's act of abolition. She understood in a flash how the visit had come to be possible – that Mrs. Wix, watching her chance, must have slipped in under protection of the fact that papa, always tormented in spite of arguments with the idea of a school, had, for a three days' excursion to Brighton, absolutely insisted on the attendance of her adversary. It was true that when Maisie explained their absence and their important motive Mrs. Wix wore an expression so peculiar that it could only have had its origin in surprise. This contradiction, however, peeped out only to vanish, for at the very moment that, in the spirit of it, she threw herself afresh upon her young friend a hansom crested with neat luggage rattled up to the door and Miss Overmore bounded out. The shock of her encounter with Mrs. Wix was less violent than Maisie had feared on seeing her and didn't at all interfere with the sociable tone in which, in the presence of her rival, she explained to her little charge that she had returned, for a particular reason, a day sooner than she first intended. She had left papa – in such nice lodgings – at Brighton; but he would come back to his dear little home on the morrow. As for

Mrs. Wix, papa's companion supplied Maisie in later converse with the right word for the attitude of this personage: Mrs. Wix 'stood up' to her in a manner that the child herself felt at the time to be astonishing. This occurred indeed after Miss Overmore had so far waived her interdict as to make a move to the dining-room, where, in the absence of any suggestion of sitting down, it was scarcely more than natural that even poor Mrs. Wix should stand up. Maisie immediately inquired if at Brighton, this time, anything had come of the possibility of a school; to which, much to her surprise, Miss Overmore, who had always grandly repudiated it, replied, after an instant, but quite as if Mrs. Wix were not there:

'It may be, darling, that something *will* come. The objection, I must tell you, has been quite removed.'

At this it was still more startling to hear Mrs. Wix speak out with great firmness. 'I don't think, if you'll allow me to say so, that there's any arrangement by which the objection *can* be "removed". What has brought me here to-day is that I've a message for Maisie from dear Mrs. Farange.'

The child's heart gave a great thump. 'Oh, mamma's come back?'

'Not yet, sweet love, but she's coming,' said Mrs. Wix, 'and she has – most thoughtfully, you know – sent me on to prepare you.'

'To prepare her for what, pray?' asked Miss Overmore, whose original serenity began, with this news, to turn to sharpness.

Mrs. Wix quietly applied her straighteners to Miss Overmore's florid loveliness. 'Well, miss, for a very important communication.'

'Can't dear Mrs. Farange, as you so oddly call her, make her communications directly? Can't she take the trouble to write to her only daughter?' the younger lady demanded. 'Maisie herself will tell you that it's months and months since she has had so much as a word from her.'

'Oh, but I've written to mamma!' cried the child as if this would do quite as well.

'That makes her treatment of you all the greater scandal,' the governess in possession promptly declared.

'Mrs. Farange is too well aware,' said Mrs. Wix with sustained spirit, 'of what becomes of her letters in this house.'

Maisie's sense of fairness hereupon interposed for her visitor. 'You know, Miss Overmore, that papa doesn't like everything of mamma's.'

'No one likes, my dear, to be made the subject of such language as your mother's letters contain. They were not fit for the innocent child to see,' Miss Overmore observed to Mrs. Wix.

'Then I don't know what you complain of, and she's better without them. It serves every purpose that I'm in Mrs. Farange's confidence.'

Miss Overmore gave a scornful laugh. 'Then you must be mixed up with some extraordinary proceedings!'

'None so extraordinary,' cried Mrs. Wix, turning very pale, 'as to say horrible things about the mother to the face of the helpless daughter!'

'Things not a bit more horrible, I think,' Miss Overmore rejoined, 'than those you, madam, appear to have come here to say about the father!'

Mrs. Wix looked for a moment hard at Maisie; then turning again to her other interlocutress she spoke with a trembling voice. 'I came to say nothing about him, and you must excuse Mrs. Farange and me if we are not so irreproachable as the companion of his travels.'

The young woman thus described stared an instant at the audacity of the description – she apparently needed time to take it in. Maisie, however, gazing solemnly from one of the disputants to the other, observed that her answer, when it came, perched upon smiling lips. 'It will do quite as well, no doubt, if you come up to the requirements of the companion of Mrs. Farange's!'

Mrs. Wix broke into a queer laugh: it sounded to Maisie like an unsuccessful imitation of a neigh. 'That's just what I'm here to make known – how perfectly the poor lady comes up to them herself.' She straightened herself before the child. 'You must take your mamma's message, Maisie, and you must feel that her wishing me to come to you with it this way is a great proof of interest and affection. She sends you her particular love and announces to you that she's engaged to be married to Sir Claude.'

'Sir Claude?' Maisie wonderingly echoed. But while Mrs. Wix explained that this gentleman was a dear friend of Mrs. Farange's, who had been of great assistance to her in getting to Florence and in making herself comfortable there for the winter, she was not too violently shaken to perceive her old friend's enjoyment of the effect of this news on Miss Overmore. That young lady opened her eyes and flushed; she immediately remarked that Mrs. Farange's marriage would of course put an end to any further pretension to take her daughter back. Mrs. Wix inquired with astonishment why it should do anything of the sort, and Miss Overmore promptly gave as a reason that it was clearly but another dodge in a system of dodging. She wanted to get out of the bargain: why else had she now left Maisie on her father's hands weeks and weeks beyond the time about which she had originally made such a fuss? It was vain for Mrs. Wix to represent – as she speciously proceeded to do – that all this time would be made up as soon as Mrs. Farange returned: she, Miss Overmore, knew nothing, thank heaven, about her confederate, but she was very sure that any person capable of forming that sort of relation with the lady in Florence was a person who could easily be put forward as objecting to the presence in his house of the fruit of a union that his dignity must ignore. It was a game like another, and Mrs. Wix's visit was clearly the first move in it. Maisie found in this exchange of asperities a fresh incitement to the unformulated fatalism in which her observation of her own career had long since taken refuge; and it was the beginning for her of a deeper prevision that, in spite of Miss Overmore's brilliancy and Mrs. Wix's passion, she should live to see a change in the nature of the struggle she appeared to have come into the world to produce. It would still be essentially a struggle, but its object would now be *not* to receive her.

Mrs. Wix, after Miss Overmore's last demonstration, addressed herself wholly to the little girl, and, drawing from the pocket of her dingy old pelisse a small flat parcel, removed its envelope and wished to know if *that* looked like a gentleman

who wouldn't be nice to everybody – let alone to a person he
would be so sure to find so nice. Mrs. Farange, in the geniality
of new-found happiness, had enclosed a 'cabinet' photograph
of Sir Claude, and Maisie lost herself in admiration of the fair,
smooth face, the regular features, the kind eyes, the amiable
air, the general glossiness and smartness of her prospective
stepfather – only vaguely puzzled to think that she should now
have two fathers at once. Her researches had hitherto indicated
that to incur a second parent of the same sex you had usually
to lose the first. '*Isn't* he sympathetic?' asked Mrs. Wix, who
had clearly, on the strength of his charming portrait, made up
her mind that Sir Claude promised her a future. 'You can see,
I hope,' she added, with much expression, 'that *he's* a perfect
gentleman!' Maisie had never before heard the word
'sympathetic' applied to anybody's face; it struck her very much
and from that moment it agreeably remained with her. She testified moreover to the force of her own perception in a long, soft
little sigh of response to the pleasant eyes that seemed to seek her
acquaintance, to speak to her directly. 'He's quite lovely!' she
declared to Mrs. Wix. Then eagerly, irrepressibly, as she still held
the photograph and Sir Claude continued to fraternize, 'Oh, can't
I keep it?' she broke out. No sooner had she done so than she
looked up from it at Miss Overmore: this was with the sudden
instinct of appealing to the authority that had long ago impressed
on her that she mustn't ask for things. Miss Overmore, to
her surprise, looked distant and rather odd, hesitating and giving
her time to turn again to Mrs. Wix. Then Maisie saw that lady's
long face lengthen; it was stricken and almost scared, as if her
young friend really expected more of her than she had to give. The
photograph was a possession that, direly denuded, she clung to,
and there was a momentary struggle between her fond clutch of it
and her capability of every sacrifice for her precarious pupil. With
the acuteness of her years, however, Maisie saw that her own avidity would triumph, and she held out the picture to Miss Overmore
as if she were quite proud of her mother. 'Isn't he just lovely?' she
demanded while poor Mrs. Wix hungrily wavered, her straighteners
largely covering it and her pelisse gathered about her with an
intensity that strained its ancient seams.

'It was to *me*, darling,' the visitor said, 'that your mamma so generously sent it; but of course if it would give you particular pleasure—' She faltered, only gasping her surrender.

Miss Overmore continued extremely remote. 'If the photograph's your property, my dear, I shall be happy to oblige you by looking at it on some future occasion. But you must excuse me if I decline to touch an object belonging to Mrs. Wix.'

Mrs. Wix by this time had grown very red. 'You might as well see him this way, miss,' she retorted, 'as you certainly never will, I believe, in any other! Keep the pretty picture, by all means, my precious,' she went on: 'Sir Claude will be happy himself, I daresay, to give me one with a kind inscription.' The pathetic quaver of this brave little boast was not lost upon Maisie, who threw herself so gratefully upon Mrs. Wix's neck that on the termination of their embrace, the public tenderness of which, she felt, made up for the sacrifice she imposed, their companion had had time to lay a quick hand on Sir Claude and, with a glance at him or not, whisk him effectually out of sight. Released from the child's arms Mrs. Wix looked about for the picture; then she fixed Miss Overmore with a hard, dumb stare; and finally, with her eyes on the little girl again, achieved the grimmest of smiles. 'Well, nothing matters, Maisie, because there's another thing your mamma wrote about. She has made sure of me.' Even after her loyal hug Maisie felt a bit of a sneak as she glanced at Miss Overmore for permission to understand this. But Mrs. Wix left them in no doubt of what it meant. 'She has definitely engaged me – for her return and for yours. Then you'll see for yourself.' Maisie, on the spot, quite believed she should; but the prospect was suddenly thrown into confusion by an extraordinary demonstration from Miss Overmore.

'Mrs. Wix,' said that young lady, 'has some undiscoverable reason for regarding your mother's hold on you as strengthened by the fact that she's about to marry. I wonder then – on that system – what Mrs. Wix will say to your father's.'

Miss Overmore's words were directed to her pupil, but her face, lighted with an irony that made it prettier even than ever before, was presented to the dingy figure that had stiffened itself for departure. The child's discipline had been bewildering – it had ranged freely between the prescription that she was to answer when spoken to and the experience of lively penalties on obeying that prescription. This time, nevertheless, she felt emboldened for risks; above all as something still more bewildering seemed to have leaped into her sense of the relations of things. She raised to Miss Overmore's face all the timidity of her eyes. 'Do you mean papa's hold on me – do you mean *he's* about to marry?'

'Papa is not about to marry – papa *is* married, my dear. Papa was married the day before yesterday at Brighton.' Miss Overmore glittered more gaily; meanwhile it came over Maisie, and quite dazzlingly, that her pretty governess was a bride. 'He's my husband, if you please, and I'm his little wife. So *now* we'll see who's your little mother!' She caught her pupil to her bosom in a manner that was not to be outdone by the emissary of her predecessor, and a few moments later, when things had lurched back into their places, that poor lady, quite defeated of the last word, had soundlessly taken flight.

VIII

After Mrs. Wix's retreat Miss Overmore appeared to recognize that she was not exactly in a position to denounce Ida Farange's second union; but she drew from a table-drawer the photograph of Sir Claude and, standing there before Maisie, bent her eyes on it for some moments.

'Isn't he beautiful?' the child ingenuously asked.

Her companion hesitated. 'No – he's horrid,' she, to Maisie's surprise, sharply returned. But she considered another minute; after which she handed back the picture. It appeared to Maisie herself to exhibit a fresh attraction, and she was embarrassed, for she had never before had occasion to differ from her lovely friend. So she only could ask what, such being the case, she should do with it: should she put it quite away – where it wouldn't be there to offend? On this Miss Overmore again deliberated; then she said unexpectedly: 'Put it on the schoolroom mantelpiece.'

Maisie had apprehensions. 'Won't papa dislike to see it there?'

'Very much indeed; but that won't matter *now*.' Miss Overmore spoke with peculiar significance and to her pupil's mystification.

'On account of the marriage?' Maisie inquired.

Miss Overmore laughed, and Maisie could see that in spite of the irritation produced by Mrs. Wix she was in high spirits. 'Which marriage do you mean?'

With the question put to her it suddenly seemed to the child that she didn't know, and she felt that she looked foolish. So she took refuge in saying: 'Shall *you* be different——?' This was a full implication that the bride of Sir Claude would be.

'As your father's wedded wife? Utterly!' Miss Overmore replied. And the difference began of course in her being addressed, even by Maisie, from that day and by her particular request, as Mrs. Beale. It was there indeed principally that it ended, for except that the child could reflect that she should presently have four parents in all, and also that at the end of three months the staircase, for a little girl hanging over banisters, sent up the deepening rustle of more delicate advances, everything made the same impression as before. Mrs. Beale had very pretty frocks, but Miss Overmore's had been quite as good, and if papa was much fonder of his second wife than he had been of his first Maisie had foreseen that fondness and followed its development almost as closely as the victim of it. There was little indeed in the relations of her companions that her precocious experience couldn't explain, for if they struck her as after all rather deficient in that air of the honeymoon of which she had so often heard – in much detail, for instance, from Mrs. Wix – it was natural to judge this circumstance in the light of papa's proved disposition to contest the empire of the matrimonial tie. His honeymoon, when he came back from Brighton – not on the morrow of Mrs. Wix's visit, and not, oddly, till several days later – his honeymoon was perhaps perceptibly tinged with the dawn of a later stage of wedlock. There were things as to which, for Mrs. Beale, as the child had learnt, his dislike wouldn't matter now, and their number increased so that such a trifle as his hostility to the photograph of Sir Claude quite dropped out of view. This pleasing object found a conspicuous place in the schoolroom, which, in truth, Mr. Farange seldom entered and in which silent admiration formed, during the time I speak of, almost the sole scholastic exercise of Mrs. Beale's pupil.

Maisie was not long in seeing just what her stepmother had meant by the difference she should show as Mrs. Beale. If she was her father's wife she was not her own governess, and if her presence had had formerly to be made regular by the theory of a humble function she was now on a footing that dispensed with all theories and was inconsistent with all servitude. That was what she had meant by the removal of the obstacle to a school; her small companion was no longer required at home as – it was Mrs. Beale's own amusing word – a little duenna. The objection to a successor to Miss Overmore remained: it was composed frankly of the fact, of which Mrs. Beale granted the full absurdity, that she was too awfully fond of her step-daughter to bring herself to see her in vulgar and mercenary hands. The note of this particular danger emboldened Maisie to put in a word for Mrs. Wix, the modest measure of whose avidity she had taken from the first; but Mrs. Beale disposed afresh and effectually of a candidate who would be sure to act in some horrible and insidious way for Ida's interest and who moreover was personally loathsome and as ignorant as a fish. She made also no less of a secret of the awkward fact that a good school would be hideously expensive, and of the further circumstance, which seemed to put an end to everything, that when it came to the point papa, in spite of his previous clamour, was really most nasty about paying. 'Would you believe,' Mrs. Beale confidentially asked of her little charge, 'that he says I'm a worse expense than ever, and that a daughter and a wife together are really more than he can afford?' It was thus that the splendid school at Brighton lost itself in the haze of larger questions, though the fear that it would provoke Ida to leap into the breach subsided with her prolonged, her quite shame-less non-appearance. Her daughter and her successor were therefore left to gaze in united but helpless blankness at all that Maisie was not learning.

This quantity was so great as to fill the child's days with a sense of intermission to which even French Lisette gave no accent – with finished games and unanswered questions and dreaded tests; with the habit, above all, in her watch for a change, of hanging over banisters when the door-bell sounded. This was the great refuge of her impatience, but what she heard at such times was a clatter of gaiety downstairs; the impression of which, from her earliest childhood, had built up in her the belief that the grown-up time was the time of real amusement and above all of real intimacy. Even Lisette, even Mrs. Wix had never, she felt, in spite of hugs and tears, been so intimate with her as so many persons at present were with Mrs. Beale and as so many others of old had been with Mrs. Farange. The note of

hilarity brought people together still more than the note of
melancholy, which was the one exclusively sounded, for instance,
by poor Mrs. Wix. Maisie, in these days, preferred none the less
that domestic revels should be wafted to her from a distance:
she felt sadly unsupported for facing the interrogatory of the
drawing-room. That was a reason the more for making the most
of Susan Ash, who in her quality of under-housemaid moved at
a very different level and who, none the less, was much depended
upon out of doors. She was a guide to peregrinations that had
little in common with those intensely definite airings that had
left with the child a vivid memory of the regulated mind of
Moddle. There were under Moddle's system no dawdles at
shop-windows and no nudges, in Oxford Street, of 'I *say*, look
at '*er*!' There was an inexorable treatment of crossings and a
serene exemption from the fear that – especially at corners, of
which she was yet weakly fond – haunted the housemaid, the
fear of being, as she ominously said, 'spoken to'. The dangers of
the town equally with its diversions added to Maisie's sense of
being untutored and unclaimed.

The situation, however, had taken a twist when, on another
of her returns, at Susan's side, extremely tired, from the pursuit
of exercise qualified by much hovering, she encountered another
emotion. She on this occasion learnt at the door that her instant
attendance was requested in the drawing-room. Crossing the
threshold in a cloud of shame she discerned through the blur
Mrs. Beale seated there with a gentleman who immediately
drew the pain from her predicament by rising before her as the
original of the photograph of Sir Claude. She felt the moment
she looked at him that he was by far the most radiant person
with whom she had yet been concerned, and her pleasure in
seeing him, in knowing that he took hold of her and kissed her,
as quickly throbbed into a strange, shy pride in him, a perception of his making up for her fallen state, for Susan's public
nudges, which quite bruised her, and for all the lessons that, in
the dead schoolroom, where at times she was almost afraid to
stay alone, she was bored with not having. It was as if he had
told her on the spot that he belonged to her, so that she could
already show him off and see the effect he produced. No, nothing

else that was most beautiful that had ever belonged to her could kindle that particular joy – not Mrs. Beale at that very moment, not papa when he was gay, nor mamma when she was dressed, nor Lisette when she was new. The joy almost overflowed in tears when he laid his hand on her and drew her to him, telling her, with a smile of which the promise was as bright as that of a Christmas-tree, that he knew her ever so well by her mother, but had come to see her now so that he might know her really. She could see that his view of the way 'really' to know her was to make her come away with him, and, further, that this was what he was there for and had already been some time: arranging it with Mrs. Beale and getting on with that lady in a manner evidently not at all affected by her having, on the arrival of his portrait, thought of him so ill. They had grown almost intimate – or had the air of it – over their discussion; and it was still further conveyed to Maisie that Mrs. Beale had made no secret, and would make yet less of one, of all that it cost to let her go. 'You seem so tremendously eager,' she said to the child, 'that I hope you're at least clear about Sir Claude's relation to you. It doesn't appear to occur to him to give you the necessary reassurance.'

Maisie, a trifle mystified, turned quickly to her new friend. 'Why, it's of course that you're *married* to her, isn't it?'

Her anxious emphasis started them off, as she had learned to call it; this was the echo she infallibly and now quite resignedly produced; moreover, Sir Claude's laughter was an indistinguishable part of the sweetness of his being there. 'We've been married, my dear child, three months, and my interest in you is a consequence, don't you know? of my great affection for your mother. In coming here it's of course for your mother I'm acting.'

'Oh, I know,' Maisie said with all the candour of her competence. 'She can't come herself – except just to the door.' Then as she thought afresh: 'Can't she come even to the door now?'

'There you are!' Mrs. Beale exclaimed to Sir Claude. She spoke as if his dilemma were ludicrous.

His kind face, in an hesitation, seemed to recognize it; but he answered the child with a frank smile. 'No – not very well.'

'Because she has married you?'

He promptly accepted this reason. 'Well, that has a good deal to do with it.'

He was so delightful to talk to that Maisie pursued the subject. 'But, papa – *he* has married Miss Overmore.'

'Yes, and you'll see that he won't come for you at your mother's,' that lady interposed.

'Yes, but that won't be for a long time,' Maisie hastened to respond.

'We won't talk about it now – you've months and months to put in first.' And Sir Claude drew her closer.

'Ah, that's what makes it so hard to give her up!' Mrs. Beale sighed, holding out her arms to her stepdaughter. Maisie, quitting Sir Claude, went over to them and, clasped in a still tenderer embrace, felt entrancingly the expansion of the field of happiness. '*I'll* come for you,' said her stepmother, 'if Sir Claude keeps you too long: we must make him quite understand that! Don't talk to me about her ladyship!' she went on, to their visitor, so familiarly that it was almost as if they must have met before. 'I know her ladyship as if I had made her. They're a pretty pair of parents!' Mrs. Beale exclaimed.

Maisie had so often heard them called so that the remark diverted her but an instant from the agreeable wonder of this grand new form of allusion to her mother; and that, in its turn, presently left her free to catch at the pleasant possibility, in connection with herself, of a relation much happier as between Mrs. Beale and Sir Claude than as between mamma and papa. Still the next thing that happened was that her interest in such a relation brought to her lips a fresh question. 'Have you seen papa?' she asked of Sir Claude.

It was the signal for their going off again, as her small stoicism had perfectly taken for granted that it would be. All that Mrs. Beale had nevertheless to add was the vague apparent sarcasm: 'Oh, papa!'

'I'm assured he's not at home,' Sir Claude replied to the child; 'but if he had been I should have hoped for the pleasure of seeing him.'

'Won't he mind your coming?' Maisie went on.

'Oh, you bad little girl!' Mrs. Beale humorously protested.

The child could see that at this Sir Claude, though still moved to mirth, coloured a little; but he spoke to her very kindly. 'That's just what I came to see, you know – whether your father *would* mind. But Mrs. Beale appears strongly of the opinion that he won't.'

This lady promptly justified her opinion to her stepdaughter. 'It will be very interesting, my dear, you know, to find out what it is, to-day, that your father does mind. I'm sure *I* don't know!' – and she repeated, though with perceptible resignation, her sigh of a moment before. 'Your father, darling, is a very odd person indeed.' She turned with this, smiling, to Sir Claude. 'But, perhaps, it's hardly civil for me to say that of his not objecting to have *you* in the house. If you knew some of the people he does have!'

Maisie knew them all, and none indeed were to be compared to Sir Claude. He laughed back at Mrs. Beale; he looked at such moments quite as Mrs. Wix, in the long stories she told her pupil, always described the lovers of her distressed beauties – 'the perfect gentleman and strikingly handsome'. He got up, to the child's regret, as if he were going. 'Oh, I daresay we should be all right!'

Mrs. Beale once more gathered in her little charge, holding her close and looking thoughtfully over her head at their visitor. 'It's so charming – for a man of your type – to have wanted her so much!'

'What do you know about my type?' Sir Claude inquired. 'Whatever it may be, I daresay it deceives you. The truth about me is simply that I'm the most unappreciated of – what do you call the fellows? – "family-men". Yes, I'm a family-man; upon my honour I am!'

'Then why on earth,' cried Mrs. Beale, 'didn't you marry a family-woman?'

Sir Claude looked at her hard. '*You* know who one marries, I think. Besides, there *are* no family-women – hanged if there are! None of them want any children – hanged if they do!'

His account of the matter was most interesting, and Maisie, as if it were of bad omen for her, stared at the picture in some dismay. At the same time she felt, through encircling arms, her protectress hesitate. 'You do come out with things! But you mean her ladyship doesn't want any – really?'

'Won't hear of them – simply. But she can't help the one she *has* got.' And with this Sir Claude's eyes rested on the little girl in a way that seemed to her to mask her mother's attitude with the conscientiousness of his own. 'She must make the best of her, don't you see? If only for the look of the thing, don't you know? one wants one's wife to take the proper line about her child.'

'Oh, I know what one wants!' Mrs. Beale asserted with a competence that evidently impressed her interlocutor.

'Well, if you keep *him* up – and I daresay you've had worry enough – why shouldn't I keep Ida? What's sauce for the goose is sauce for the gander – or the other way round, don't you know? I mean to see the thing through.'

Mrs. Beale, for a minute, still with her eyes on him as he leaned upon the chimneypiece, appeared to turn this over. 'You're just a wonder of kindness – that's what you are!' she said at last. 'A lady's expected to have natural feelings. But *your* horrible sex——! Isn't it a horrible sex, little love?' she demanded with her cheek upon her stepdaughter's.

'Oh, I like gentlemen best,' Maisie lucidly replied.

The words were taken up merrily. 'That's a good one for *you*!' Sir Claude exclaimed to Mrs. Beale.

'No,' said that lady: 'I've only to remember the women she sees at her mother's.'

'Ah, they're very nice now,' Sir Claude returned.

'What do you call "nice"?'

'Well, they're all right.'

'That doesn't answer me,' said Mrs. Beale; 'but I daresay you do take care of them. That makes you more of an angel to want this job too.' She playfully whacked her smaller companion.

'I'm not an angel – I'm an old grandmother,' Sir Claude declared. 'I like babies – I always did. If we go to smash I shall look for a place as responsible nurse.'

Maisie, in her charmed mood, drank in an imputation on her years which at another moment might have been bitter; but the charm was sensibly interrupted by Mrs. Beale's screwing her round and gazing fondly into her eyes. 'You're willing to leave me, you wretch?'

The little girl deliberated; even her attachment to this bright presence had become as a cord she must suddenly snap. But she snapped it very gently. 'Isn't it my turn for mamma?'

'You're a horrible little hypocrite! The less, I think, now said about "turns" the better,' Mrs. Beale made answer. '*I* know whose turn it is. You've not such a passion for your mother!'

'I say, I say: *do* look out!' Sir Claude quite amiably protested.

'There's nothing she hasn't heard. But it doesn't matter – it hasn't spoiled her. If you knew what it costs me to part with you!' she pursued to Maisie.

Sir Claude watched her as she charmingly clung to the child. 'I'm so glad you really care for her. That's so much to the good.'

Mrs. Beale slowly got up, still with her hands on Maisie, but emitting a little soft exhalation. 'Well, if you're glad, that may help us; for I assure you that I shall never give up any rights in her that I may consider that, by my own sacrifices, I've acquired. I shall hold very fast to my interest in her. What seems to have happened is that she has brought you and me together.'

'She has brought you and me together,' said Sir Claude.

The cheerfulness of his assent to this proposition was contagious, and Maisie broke out almost with enthusiasm: 'I've brought you and her together!'

Her companions of course laughed anew and Mrs. Beale gave her an affectionate shake. 'You little monster – take care what you do! But that's what she does do,' she continued to Sir Claude. 'She did it to me and Beale.'

'Well, then,' he said to Maisie, 'you must try the trick at *our* place.' He held out his hand to her again. 'Will you come now?'

'Now – just as I am?' She turned with an immense appeal to her stepmother, taking a leap over the mountain of 'mending', the abyss of packing that had loomed and yawned before her. 'Oh, *may* I?'

Mrs. Beale addressed her assent to Sir Claude. 'As well so as any other way. I'll send on her things to-morrow.' Then she gave a tug to the child's coat, glancing at her up and down with some ruefulness. 'She's not turned out as I should like – her mother will pull her to pieces. But what's one to do – with nothing to do it on? And she's better than when she came – you can tell her mother that. I'm sorry to have to say it to you – but the poor child was a sight!'

'Oh, I'll turn her out myself!' the visitor cordially announced.

'I shall like to see how!'——Mrs. Beale appeared much amused. 'You must bring her to show me – we can manage that. Good-bye, little fright!' And her last word to Sir Claude was that she would keep him up to the mark.

IX

The idea of what she was to make up and the prodigious total it came to were kept well before Maisie at her mother's. These things were the constant occupation of Mrs. Wix, who arrived there by the back-stairs, but in tears of joy, the day after her own arrival. The process of making up, as to which the good lady had an immense deal to say, took, through its successive phases, so long that it promised to be a period at least equal to the child's last period with her father. But this was a fuller and richer time: it bounded along to the tune of Mrs. Wix's constant insistence on the energy they must both put forth. There was a fine intensity in the way the child agreed with her that under Mrs. Beale and Susan Ash she had learned nothing whatever; the wildness of the rescued castaway was one of the forces that would henceforth make for a career of conquest. The year therefore rounded itself as a receptacle of retarded knowledge – a cup brimming over with the sense that now at least she was learning. Mrs. Wix fed this sense from the stores of her conversation and with the immense bustle of her reminder that they must cull the fleeting hour. They were surrounded with subjects they must take at a rush and perpetually getting into the attitude of triumphant attack. They had certainly no idle hours, and the child went to bed each night as tired as from a long day's play. This had begun from the moment of their reunion, begun with all Mrs. Wix had to tell her young friend of the reasons of her ladyship's extraordinary behaviour at the very first.

It took the form of her ladyship's refusal for three days to see her child – three days during which Sir Claude made hasty, merry dashes into the schoolroom to smooth down the odd situation, to say 'She'll come round, you know; I assure you she'll come round,' and a little even to compensate Maisie for the indignity he had caused her to suffer. There had never in the child's life been, in all ways, such a delightful amount of reparation. It came out by his sociable admission that her ladyship had not known of his visit to her late husband's house and of his having made that person's daughter a pretext for striking up an acquaintance with the dreadful creature installed there. Heaven knew she wanted her child back and had made every plan of her own for removing her; what she couldn't for the present at least forgive any one concerned was the meddling, underhand way in which Sir Claude had brought about the transfer. Maisie carried more of the weight of this resentment than even Mrs. Wix's confidential ingenuity could lighten for her, especially as Sir Claude himself was not at all ingenuous, though indeed on the other hand he was not at all crushed. He was amused and intermittent and at moments most startling; he brought out to his young companion, with a frankness that agitated her much more than he seemed to guess, that he depended on her not letting her mother, when she should see her, get anything out of her about anything Mrs. Beale might have said to him. He came in and out; he professed, in joke, to take tremendous precautions; he showed a positive disposition to romp. He chaffed Mrs. Wix till she was purple with the pleasure of it, and reminded Maisie of the reticence he expected of her till she set her teeth like an Indian captive. Her lessons these first days and indeed for long after seemed to be all about Sir Claude, and yet she never really mentioned to Mrs. Wix that she was prepared, under his inspiring injunction, to be vainly tortured. This lady, however, had formulated the position of things with an acuteness that showed how little she needed to be coached. Her explanation of everything that seemed not quite pleasant – and if her own footing was perilous it met that danger as well – was that her ladyship was passionately in love. Maisie accepted this hint with infinite awe and pressed upon it much when she was at last summoned into the presence of her mother.

There she encountered matters in which it seemed really to help to give her a clue – an almost terrifying strangeness, full, none the less, after a little, of reverberations of Ida's old fierce, demonstrative recoveries of possession. They had been some time in the house together, and this demonstration came late. Preoccupied, however, as Maisie was with the idea of the sentiment Sir Claude had inspired, and familiar, in addition, by Mrs. Wix's anecdotes, with the ravages that in general such a sentiment could produce, she was able to make allowances for her ladyship's remarkable appearance, her violent splendour, the wonderful colour of her lips and even the hard stare, like that of some gorgeous idol described in a story-book, that had come into her eyes in consequence of a curious thickening of their already rich circumference. Her professions and explanations were mixed with eager challenges and sudden drops, in the midst of which Maisie recognized as a memory of other years the rattle of her trinkets and the scratch of her endearments, the odour of her clothes and the jumps of her conversation. She had all her old clever way – Mrs. Wix said it was 'aristocratic' – of changing the subject as she might have slammed the door in your face. The principal thing that was different was the tint of her golden hair, which had changed to a coppery red and, with the head it profusely covered, struck the child as now lifted still further aloft. This picturesque parent showed literally a grander stature and a nobler presence, things which, with some others that might have been bewildering, were handsomely accounted for by the romantic state of her affections. It was her affections, Maisie could easily see, that led Ida to break out into questions as to what had passed at the other house between that horrible woman and Sir Claude; but it was also just here that the little girl was able to recall the effect with which in earlier days she had practised the pacific art of stupidity. This art again came to her aid: her mother, in getting rid of her after an interview in which she had achieved a hollowness beyond her years, allowed her fully to understand that she had not grown a bit more amusing.

She could bear that; she could bear anything that helped her to feel she had done something for Sir Claude. If she hadn't told Mrs. Wix how Mrs. Beale seemed to like him she certainly couldn't tell her ladyship. In the way the past revived for her there was a queer confusion. It was because mamma hated papa that she used to want to know bad things of him; but if at present she wanted to know the same of Sir Claude it was quite from the opposite motive. She was awe-struck at the manner in which a lady might be affected through the passion mentioned by Mrs. Wix; she held her breath with the sense of picking her steps among the tremendous things of life. What she did, however, now, after the interview with her mother, impart to Mrs. Wix was that, in spite of her having had her 'good' effect, as she called it – the effect she studied, the effect of harmless vacancy – her ladyship's last words had been that her ladyship's duty by her would be thoroughly done. Over this announcement governess and pupil looked at each other in silent profundity; but as the weeks went by it had no consequences that interfered gravely with the breezy gallop of making up. Her ladyship's duty took at times the form of not seeing her child for days together, and Maisie led her life in great prosperity between Mrs. Wix and kind Sir Claude. Mrs. Wix had a new dress and, as she was the first to proclaim, a better position; so it all struck Maisie as a crowded, brilliant life, with, for the time, Mrs. Beale and Susan Ash simply 'left out' like children not invited to a Christmas party. Mrs. Wix had a secret terror which, like most of her secret feelings, she discussed with her little companion, in great solemnity, by the hour: the possibility of her ladyship's coming down on them, in her sudden high-bred way, with a school. But she had also a balm to this fear in a conviction of the strength of Sir Claude's grasp of the situation. He was too pleased – didn't he constantly say as much? – with the good impression made, in a wide circle, by Ida's sacrifices; and he came into the schoolroom repeatedly to let them know how beautifully he felt everything had gone off and everything would go on.

He disappeared at times for days, when his patient friends understood that her ladyship would naturally absorb him; but he always came back with the drollest stories of where he had been, a wonderful picture of society, and even with pretty presents that showed how in absence he thought of his home. Besides giving Mrs. Wix by his conversation a sense that they almost themselves 'went out', he gave her a five-pound note and the history of France and an umbrella with a malachite knob, and to Maisie both chocolate-creams and story-books, and a lovely great-coat (which he took her out all alone to buy), besides ever so many games in boxes, with printed directions, and a bright red frame for the protection of his famous photograph. The games were, as he said, to while away the evening hour; and the evening hour indeed often passed in futile attempts on Mrs. Wix's part to master what 'it said' on the papers. When he asked the pair how they liked the games they always replied 'Oh, immensely!' but they had earnest discussions as to whether they hadn't better appeal to him frankly for aid to understand them. This was a course their delicacy shrank from; they couldn't have told exactly why, but it was a part of their tenderness for him not to let him think they had trouble. What dazzled most was his kindness to Mrs. Wix, not only the five-pound note and the 'not forgetting' her, but the perfect consideration, as she called it with an air to which her sounding of the words gave the only grandeur Maisie was to have seen her wear save on a certain occasion hereafter to be described, an occasion when the poor lady was grander than all of them put together. He shook hands with her, he recognized her, as she said, and above all, more than once, he took her, with his stepdaughter, to the pantomime and, in the crowd, coming out, publicly gave her his arm. When he met them in sunny Piccadilly he made merry and turned and walked with them, heroically suppressing his consciousness of the stamp of his company, a heroism that – needless for Mrs. Wix to sound *those* words – her ladyship, though a blood-relation, was little enough the woman to be capable of. Even to the hard heart of childhood there was something tragic in such elation at such humanities: it brought home to Maisie the way her humble companion had sidled and ducked through life. But it settled the question of the degree to which Sir Claude was a gentleman: he was more of one than anybody else in the world – 'I don't care,' Mrs. Wix repeatedly remarked, 'whom you may meet in grand society, nor even to whom you may be contracted in marriage.' There were questions that Maisie never asked; so her governess was spared the embarrassment of telling her if he were more of a gentleman than papa. This was not moreover from the want of opportunity, for there were no moments between them at which the topic could be irrelevant, no subject they were going into, not even the principal dates or the auxiliary verbs, in which it was further off than the turn of the page. The answer on the winter nights to the puzzle of cards and counters and little bewildering pamphlets was just to draw up to the fire and talk about him; and if the truth must be told this edifying interchange constituted for the time the little girl's chief education.

It must also be admitted that he took them far, farther perhaps than was always warranted by the old-fashioned conscience, the dingy decencies, of Maisie's simple instructress. There were hours when Mrs. Wix sighingly testified to the scruples she surmounted, seemed to ask what other line one *could* take with a young person whose experience had been, as it were, so peculiar. 'It isn't as if you didn't already know everything, is it, love?' and 'I can't make you any worse than you *are*, can I, darling?' – these were the terms in which the good lady justified to herself and her pupil her pleasant conversational ease. What the pupil already knew was indeed rather taken for granted than expressed, but it performed the useful function of transcending all text-books and supplanting all studies. If the child couldn't be worse it was a comfort even to herself that she was bad – a comfort offering a broad, firm support to the fundamental fact of the present crisis: the fact that mamma was fearfully jealous. This was another side of the circumstance of mamma's passion, and the deep couple in the schoolroom were not long in working round to it. It brought them face to face with the idea of the inconvenience suffered by any lady who marries a gentleman producing on other ladies the charming effect of Sir Claude. That such ladies would freely fall in love with him was a reflection naturally irritating to his wife. One day when some accident, some crash of a banged door or some scurry of a scared maid, had rendered this truth particularly vivid, Maisie, receptive and profound, suddenly said to her companion: 'And you, my dear, are you in love with him too?'

Even her profundity had left a margin for a laugh; so she was a trifle startled by the solemn promptitude with which

Mrs. Wix plumped out: 'Over head and ears. I've *never*, since you ask me, been so far gone.'

This boldness had none the less no effect of deterrence for her when, a few days later – it was because several had elapsed without a visit from Sir Claude – her governess turned the tables. 'May I ask you, miss, if *you* are?' Mrs. Wix brought it out, she could see, with hesitation, but clearly intending a joke. 'Why, *yes*!' the child made answer, as if in surprise at not having long ago seemed sufficiently to commit herself; on which her friend gave a sigh of apparent satisfaction. It might in fact have expressed positive relief. Everything was as it should be.

Yet it was not with them, they were very sure, that her ladyship was furious, nor because she had forbidden it that there befell at last a period – six months brought it round – when for days together he scarcely came near them. He was 'off', and Ida was 'off', and they were sometimes off together and sometimes apart; there were seasons when the simple students had the house to themselves, when the very servants seemed also to be 'off' and dinner became a reckless forage in pantries and sideboards. Mrs. Wix reminded her disciple on such occasions – hungry moments often, when all the support of the reminder was required – that the 'real life' of their companions, the brilliant society in which it was inevitable they should move and the complicated pleasures in which it was almost presumptuous of the mind to follow them, must offer features literally not to be imagined without being seen. At one of these times Maisie found her opening it out that, though the difficulties were many, it was Mrs. Beale who had now become the chief. Then somehow it was brought fully to the child's knowledge that her stepmother had been making attempts to see her, that her mother had deeply resented it, that her stepfather had backed her stepmother up, that the latter had pretended to be acting as the representative of her father, and that her mother took the whole thing, in plain terms, very hard. The situation was, as Mrs. Wix declared, an extraordinary muddle to be sure. Her account of it brought back to Maisie the happy vision of the way Sir Claude and Mrs. Beale had made acquaintance – an incident to which, with her stepfather, though she had had little to say about it to

Mrs. Wix, she had during the first weeks of her stay at her
mother's found more than one opportunity to revert. As to
what had taken place the day Sir Claude came for her, she had
been vaguely grateful to Mrs. Wix for not attempting, as her
mother had attempted, to put her through. That was what
Sir Claude had called the process when he warned her of it,
and again afterwards when he told her she was an awfully
good 'chap' for having foiled it. Then it was that, well aware
Mrs. Beale hadn't in the least really given her up, she had asked
him if he remained in communication with her and if for the
time everything must really be held to be at an end between her
stepmother and herself. This conversation had occurred in consequence of his one day popping into the schoolroom and
finding Maisie alone.

X

He was smoking a cigarette and he stood before the fire and looked at the meagre appointments of the room in a way that made her rather ashamed of them. Then before, on the subject of Mrs. Beale, he let her 'draw' him – that was another of his words; it was astonishing how many she gathered in – he remarked that really mamma kept them rather low on the question of decorations. Mrs. Wix had put up a Japanese fan and two rather grim texts; she had wished they were gayer, but they were all she happened to have. Without Sir Claude's photograph, however, the place would have been, as he said, as dull as a cold dinner. He had said as well that there were all sorts of things they ought to have; yet governess and pupil, it had to be admitted, were still divided between discussing the places where any sort of thing would look best if any sort of thing should ever come and acknowledging that mutability in the little girl's career which was naturally unfavourable to accumulation. She stayed long enough only to miss things, not half long enough to deserve them. The way Sir Claude looked about the schoolroom had made her feel with humility as if it were not very different from the shabby attic in which she had visited Susan Ash. Then he had said, in abrupt reference to Mrs. Beale: 'Do you think she really cares for you?'

'Oh, awfully!' Maisie had replied.

'But, I mean, does she love you for yourself, as they call it, don't you know? Is she as fond of you, now, as Mrs. Wix?'

The child turned it over. 'Oh, I'm not every bit Mrs. Beale has!'

Sir Claude seemed much amused at this. 'No; you're not every bit she has!'

He laughed for some moments; but that was an old story to Maisie, and she was not too much disconcerted to go on: 'But she'll never give me up.'

'Well, I won't either, old boy: so that's not so wonderful, and she's not the only one. But if she's so fond of you, why doesn't she write to you?'

'Oh, on account of mamma.' This was rudimentary, and she was almost surprised at the simplicity of Sir Claude's question.

'I see – that's quite right,' he answered. 'She might get at you – there are all sorts of ways. But of course there's Mrs. Wix.'

'There's Mrs. Wix,' Maisie lucidly concurred. 'Mrs. Wix can't endure her.'

Sir Claude seemed interested. 'Oh, she can't endure her? Then what does she say about her?'

'Nothing at all – because she knows I shouldn't like it. Isn't it sweet of her?' the child asked.

'Certainly; rather nice. Mrs. Beale wouldn't hold her tongue for any such thing as that, would she?'

Maisie remembered how little she had done so; but she desired to protect Mrs. Beale too. The only protection she could think of, however, was the plea: 'Oh, at papa's, you know, they don't mind!'

At this Sir Claude only smiled. 'No, I dare say not. But here we mind, don't we? – we take care what we say. I don't suppose it's the sort of thing I ought to say,' he went on; 'but I think we must on the whole be rather nicer here than at your father's. However, I don't press that; for it's a sort of question on which it's awfully awkward for you to speak. Don't worry, at any rate: I assure you I'll back you up.' Then, after a moment, while he smoked, he reverted to Mrs. Beale and the child's first inquiry. 'I'm afraid we can't do much for her just now. I haven't seen her since that day – upon my word I haven't seen her.' The next instant, with a laugh the least bit foolish, the young man slightly coloured: he felt this profession of innocence to be excessive as addressed to Maisie. It was inevitable to say to her, however, that of course her mother loathed the lady of the other house. He couldn't go there again with his wife's consent, and he wasn't the man – he begged her to believe, falling once more, in spite of himself, into the scruple of showing the child he didn't trip – to go there without it. He was liable in talking with her to take the tone of her being also a man of the world. He had gone to Mrs. Beale's to fetch away Maisie; but that was altogether different. Now that she was in her mother's house what pretext had he to give her mother for paying calls on her father's wife? And of course Mrs. Beale couldn't come to Ida's – Ida would tear her limb from limb. Maisie, with this talk of pretexts, remembered how much Mrs. Beale had made of her being a good one, and how, for such a function, it was her fate to be either much depended on or much missed. Sir Claude moreover recognized on this occasion that perhaps things would take a turn later on; and he wound up by saying: 'I'm sure she does sincerely care for you – how can she possibly help it? She's very young and very pretty and very clever: I think she's charming. But we must walk very straight. If you'll help me, you know, I'll help *you*,' he concluded in the pleasant fraternizing, equalizing, not a bit patronizing way which made the child ready to go through anything for him and the beauty of which, as she dimly felt, was that it was not a deceitful descent to her years, but a real indifference to them.

It gave her moments of secret rapture – moments of believing she might help him indeed. The only mystification in this was the imposing time of life that her elders spoke of as youth. For Sir Claude then Mrs. Beale was 'young', just as for Mrs. Wix Sir Claude was: that was one of the merits for which Mrs. Wix most commended him. What therefore was Maisie herself, and, in another relation to the matter, what therefore was mamma? It took her some time to puzzle out with the aid of an experiment or two that it wouldn't do to talk about mamma's youth. She even went so far one day, in the presence of that lady's thick colour and marked lines, as to wonder if it would occur to any one but herself to do so. Yet if she wasn't young then she was old; and this threw an odd light on her having a husband of a different generation. Mr. Farange was still older – that Maisie perfectly knew; and it brought her in due course to the perception of how much more, since Mrs. Beale was younger than Sir Claude,

papa must be older than Mrs. Beale. Such discoveries were
disconcerting and even a trifle confounding: these persons, it
appeared, were not of the age they ought to be. This was
somehow particularly the case with mamma, and the fact
made her reflect with some relief on her not having gone with
Mrs. Wix into the question of Sir Claude's attachment to his
wife. She was conscious that in confining their attention to
the state of her ladyship's own affections they had been con-
trolled – Mrs. Wix perhaps in especial – by delicacy and even
by embarrassment. The end of her colloquy with her stepfather in the schoolroom was her saying: 'Then if we're not to
see Mrs. Beale at all it isn't what she seemed to think when
you came for me.'

He looked rather blank. 'What did she seem to think?'

'Why, that I've brought you together.'

'She thought that?' Sir Claude inquired.

Maisie was surprised at his already forgetting it. 'Just as I had
brought papa and her. Don't you remember she said so?'

It came back to Sir Claude in a peal of laughter. 'Oh yes – she
said so!'

'And *you* said so,' Maisie lucidly pursued.

He recovered, with increasing mirth, the whole occasion.
'And *you* said so!' he retorted as if they were playing a game.

'Then were we all mistaken?' the child asked.

He considered a little. 'No; on the whole not. I dare say it's
just what you *have* done. We *are* together – in an extraordinary
sort of way. She's thinking of us – of you and me – though we
don't meet. And I've no doubt you'll find it will be all right
when you go back to her.'

'Am I going back to her?' Maisie brought out with a little
gasp which was like a sudden clutch of the happy present.

It appeared to make Sir Claude grave a moment; it might
have made him feel the weight of the pledge his action had
given. 'Oh, some day, I suppose! We've lots of time.'

'I've such a tremendous lot to make up,' Maisie said with a
sense of great boldness.

'Certainly; and you must make up every hour of it. Oh, I'll
see that you do!'

This was encouraging; and to show, cheerfully, that she was reassured she replied: 'That's what Mrs. Wix sees too.'

'Oh yes,' said Sir Claude; 'Mrs. Wix and I are shoulder to shoulder.'

Maisie took in a little this strong image; after which she exclaimed: 'Then I've done it also to you and her – I've brought *you* together!'

'Blest if you haven't!' Sir Claude laughed. 'And more, upon my word, than any of the lot. Oh, you've done for *us*! Now, if you could – as I suggested, you know, that day – only manage me and your mother!'

The child wondered. 'Bring you and *her* together?'

'You see we're not together – not a bit. But I oughtn't to tell you such things; all the more that you won't really do it – not you. No, old chap,' the young man continued; 'there you'll break down. But it won't matter – we'll rub along. The great thing is that you and I are all right.'

'*We're* all right!' Maisie echoed devoutly. But the next moment, in the light of what he had just said, she asked: 'How shall I ever leave you?' It was as if she must somehow take care of him.

His smile did justice to her anxiety. 'Oh, well, you needn't! It won't come to that.'

'Do you mean that when I do go you'll go with me?'

Sir Claude hesitated. 'Not exactly "with" you perhaps; but I shall never be far off.'

'But how do you know where mamma may take you?'

He laughed again. 'I don't, I confess!' Then he had an idea, but it seemed a little too jocose. 'That will be for you to see – that she sha'n't take me too far.'

'How can I help it?' Maisie inquired in surprise. 'Mamma doesn't care for me,' she said very simply. 'Not really.' Child as she was, her little long history was in the words; and it was as impossible to contradict her as if she had been venerable.

Sir Claude's silence was an admission of this, and still more the tone in which he presently replied: 'That won't prevent her from – some time or other – leaving me with you.'

'Then we'll live together?' she eagerly demanded.

'I'm afraid,' said Sir Claude, smiling, 'that that will be Mrs. Beale's real chance.'

Her eagerness just slightly dropped at this; she remembered Mrs. Wix's pronouncement that it was all an extraordinary muddle. 'To take me again? Well, can't you come to see me there?'

'Oh, I dare say!'

Though there were parts of childhood Maisie had lost she had all childhood's preference for the particular promise. 'Then you *will* come – you'll come often, won't you?' she insisted, while at the moment she spoke the door opened for the return of Mrs. Wix. Sir Claude hereupon, instead of replying, gave her a look which left her silent and embarrassed.

When he again found privacy convenient, however – which happened to be long in coming – he took up their conversation very much where it had dropped. 'You see, my dear, if I shall be able to go to you at your father's it isn't at all the same thing for Mrs. Beale to come to you here.' Maisie gave a thoughtful assent to this proposition, though conscious that she could scarcely herself say just where the difference would lie. She felt how much her stepfather saved her, as he said with his habitual amusement, the trouble of that. 'I shall probably be able to go to Mrs. Beale's without your mother's knowing it.'

Maisie stared with a certain thrill at the dramatic element in this. 'And she couldn't come here without mamma's——?' She was unable to articulate the word for what mamma would do.

'My dear child, Mrs. Wix would tell of it.'

'But I thought,' Maisie objected, 'that Mrs. Wix and you——'

'Are such brothers-in-arms?' – Sir Claude caught her up. 'Oh yes, about everything but Mrs. Beale. And if you should suggest,' he went on, 'that we might somehow or other hide her peeping in from Mrs. Wix——'

'Oh, I don't suggest *that*!' Maisie in turn cut him short.

Sir Claude looked as if he could indeed quite see why. 'No; it would really be impossible.' There came to her from this glance at what they might hide the first small glimpse of something in him that she wouldn't have expected. There had been times when she had had to make the best of the impression that she was herself deceitful; yet she had never concealed anything bigger than a thought. Of course she now concealed this thought of how strange it would be to see *him* hide; and while she was so actively engaged he continued: 'Besides, you know, I'm not afraid of your father.'

'And you are of my mother?'

'Rather, old man!' Sir Claude replied.

XI

It must not be supposed that her ladyship's intermissions were not qualified by demonstrations of another order – triumphal entries and breathless pauses during which she seemed to take of everything in the room, from the state of the ceiling to that of her daughter's boot-toes, a survey that was rich in intentions. Sometimes she sat down and sometimes she surged about, but her attitude wore equally in either case the grand air of the practical. She found so much to deplore that she left a great deal to expect, and bristled so with calculations that she seemed to scatter remedies and pledges. Her visits were as good as an outfit; her manner, as Mrs. Wix once said, as good as a pair of curtains; but she was a person addicted to extremes – sometimes barely speaking to her child and sometimes pressing this tender shoot to a bosom cut, as Mrs. Wix had also observed, remarkably low. She was always in a fearful hurry, and the lower the bosom was cut the more it was to be gathered she was wanted elsewhere. She usually broke in alone, but sometimes Sir Claude was with her, and during all the earlier period there was nothing on which these appearances had had so delightful a bearing as on the way her ladyship was, as Mrs. Wix expressed it, under the spell. 'But *isn't* she under it!' Maisie used in thoughtful but familiar reference to exclaim after Sir Claude had swept mamma away in peals of natural laughter. Not even in the old days of the convulsed ladies had she heard mamma laugh so freely as in these moments of conjugal surrender, to the gaiety of which even a little girl could see she had at last a right – a little girl whose thoughtfulness was now all happy selfish meditation on good omens and future fun.

Unaccompanied, in subsequent hours, and with an effect of changing to meet a change, Ida took a tone superficially disconcerting and abrupt – the tone of having, at an immense cost, made over everything to Sir Claude and wishing others to know that if everything wasn't right it was because Sir Claude was so dreadfully vague. 'He has made from the first such a row about you,' she said on one occasion to Maisie, 'that I've told him to do for you himself and try how he likes it – see? I've washed my hands of you; I've made you over to him; and if you're discontented it's on him, please, you'll come down. So don't haul poor *me* up – I assure you I've worries enough.' One of these, visibly, was that the spell rejoiced in by the schoolroom fire was already in danger of breaking; another was that she was finally forced to make no secret of her husband's unfitness for real responsibilities. The day came indeed when her breathless auditors learnt from her in bewilderment that what ailed him was that he was, alas, simply not serious. Maisie wept on Mrs. Wix's bosom after hearing that Sir Claude was a butterfly; considering moreover that her governess patched it up but ill in coming out at various moments the next few days with the opinion that it was proper to his 'station' to be light and gay. That had been proper to every one's station that she had yet encountered save poor Mrs. Wix's own, and the particular merit of Sir Claude had seemed precisely that he was different from every one. She talked with him, however, as time went on, very freely about her mother; being with him, in this relation, wholly without the fear that had kept her silent before her father – the fear of bearing tales and making bad things worse. He appeared to accept the idea that he had taken her over and made her, as he said, his particular lark; he quite agreed also that he was an awful humbug and an idle beast and a sorry dunce. And he never said a word to her against her mother – he only remained dumb and discouraged in the face of her ladyship's own overtopping earnestness. There were occasions when he even spoke as if he had wrenched his little charge from the arms of a parent who had fought for her tooth and nail.

This was the very moral of a scene that flashed into vividness one day when the four happened to meet without company in the drawing-room and Maisie found herself clutched to her mother's breast and passionately sobbed and shrieked over, made the subject of a demonstration that evidently formed the sequel to a sharp passage enacted just before. The connection required that while she almost cradled the child in her arms Ida should speak of her as hideously, as fatally estranged, and should rail at Sir Claude as the cruel author of the outrage. 'He has taken you *from* me,' she cried; 'he has set you *against* me, and you've been won away and your horrid little mind has been poisoned! You've gone over to him, you've given yourself up to side against me and hate me. You never open your mouth to me – you know you don't; and you chatter to him like a dozen magpies. Don't lie about it – I hear you all over the place. You hang about him in a way that's barely decent, and he can do what he likes with you. Well then, let him, to his heart's content: he has been in such a hurry to take you that we'll see if it suits him to keep you. I'm very good to break my heart about it when you've no more feeling for me than a clammy little fish!' She suddenly thrust the child away and, as a disgusted admission of failure, sent her flying across the room into the arms of Mrs. Wix, whom at this moment and even in the whirl of her transit Maisie saw, very red, exchange a quick, queer look with Sir Claude.

The impression of the look remained with her, confronting her with such a critical little view of her mother's explosion that she felt the less ashamed of herself for incurring the reproach with which she had been cast off. Her father had once called her a heartless little beast, and now, though decidedly scared, she was as stiff and cold as if the description had been just. She was not even frightened enough to cry, which would have been a tribute to her mother's wrongs: she was only, more than anything else, curious about the opinion mutely expressed by their companions. Taking the earliest opportunity to question Mrs. Wix on this subject she elicited the remarkable reply: 'Well, my dear, it's her ladyship's game, and we must just hold on like grim death.' Maisie could interpret at her leisure these ominous words. Her reflections indeed at this moment thickened apace, and one of them made her sure that her governess had conversations, private, earnest and not infrequent, with her frivolous step-father. She perceived in the light of a second episode that something beyond her knowledge had taken place in the house. The things beyond her knowledge – numerous enough in truth – had not hitherto, she believed, been the things that had been nearest to her: she had even had in the past a small smug conviction that in the domestic labyrinth she always kept the clue. This time too, however, she at last found out, with the discreet aid, it had to be confessed, of Mrs. Wix. Sir Claude's own assistance was abruptly taken from her, for his comment on her ladyship's game was to start on the spot, quite alone, for Paris, evidently because he wished to show a spirit when accused of positive wickedness. He might be fond of his stepdaughter, Maisie felt, without wishing her to be after all thrust on him in such a way; his absence therefore, it was clear, was a protest against the thrusting. It was while this absence lasted that our young lady finally discovered what had happened in the house to be that her mother was no longer in love.

The limit of a passion for Sir Claude had certainly been reached, she judged, some time before the day on which her ladyship burst suddenly into the schoolroom to introduce Mr. Perriam, who, as she announced from the doorway to Maisie, wouldn't believe his ears that one had a great hoyden of a daughter. Mr. Perriam was short and massive – Mrs. Wix remarked afterwards that he was distinctly fat; and it would have been difficult to say of him whether his head were more bald or his black moustache more bushy. He seemed also to have moustaches over his eyes, which, however, by no means prevented these polished little globes from rolling round the room as if they had been billiard-balls impelled by Ida's cele-brated stroke. Mr. Perriam wore on the hand that pulled his moustache a diamond of dazzling lustre, in consequence of which and of his general weight and mystery our young lady observed on his departure that if he had only had a turban he would have been quite her idea of a heathen Turk.

'He's quite my idea,' Mrs. Wix replied, 'of a heathen Jew.'

'Well, I mean,' said Maisie, 'of a person who comes from the East.'

'That's where he *must* come from,' her governess opined – 'he comes from the City.' In a moment she added as if she knew all about him: 'He's one of those people who have lately broken out. He'll be immensely rich.'

'On the death of his papa?' the child interestedly inquired.

'Dear no – nothing hereditary. I mean he has made a lot of money.'

'How much, do you think?' Maisie demanded.

Mrs. Wix reflected and sketched it. 'Oh, many millions.'

'A hundred?' said her questioner.

Mrs. Wix was not sure of the number, but there were enough of them to have seemed to warm up for the time the penury of the schoolroom – to linger there as an afterglow of the hot, heavy light Mr. Perriam sensibly shed. This was also, no doubt, on his part, an effect of that enjoyment of life with which, among her elders, Maisie had been in contact from her earliest years – the sign of happy maturity, the old familiar note of overflowing cheer. 'How d'ye do, ma'am? How d'ye do, little miss?' – he laughed and nodded at the gaping figures. 'She has brought me up for a peep – it's true I wouldn't take you on trust. She's always talking about you, but she would never produce you; so to-day I challenged her on the spot. Well, you ain't a myth, my dear – I back down on that,' the visitor went on to Maisie; 'nor you either, miss, though you might be, to be sure!'

'I bored him with you, darling – I bore every one,' Ida said, 'and to prove that you *are* a sweet thing, as well as a fearfully old one, I told him he could judge for himself. So now he sees that you're a dreadful bouncing business and that your poor old Mummy's at least sixty!' – and her ladyship smiled at Mr. Perriam with the charm that her daughter had heard imputed to her at papa's by the merry gentlemen who had so often wished to get from him what they called a 'rise'. Her manner at that instant gave the child a glimpse more vivid than any yet enjoyed of the attraction that papa, in remarkable language, always denied she could put forth.

Mr. Perriam, however, clearly recognized it in the grace with which he met her. 'I never said you ain't wonderful – did I ever say it, hey?' and he appealed with pleasant confidence to the testimony of the schoolroom, about which itself also he evidently felt that he ought to have something to say. 'So this is their little place, hey? Charming, charming, charming!' he repeated as he vaguely looked round. The interrupted students clung together as if they had been personally exposed; but Ida relieved their embarrassment by a hunch of her high shoulders. This time the smile she addressed to Mr. Perriam had a beauty of sudden sadness. 'What on earth is a poor woman to do?'

The visitor's grimace grew more marked as he continued to look, and the conscious little schoolroom felt still more like a cage at a menagerie. 'Charming, charming, charming!' Mr. Perriam insisted; but the parenthesis closed with a prompt click. 'There you are!' said her ladyship. 'By-bye!' she sharply added. The next minute they were on the stairs, and Mrs. Wix and her companion, at the open door and looking mutely at each other, were reached by the sound of the ample current that carried them back to their life.

It was singular perhaps after this that Maisie never put a question about Mr. Perriam, and it was still more singular that by the end of a week she knew all she didn't ask. What she most particularly knew – and the information came to her, unsought, straight from Mrs. Wix – was that Sir Claude wouldn't at all care for the visits of a millionaire who was in and out of the upper rooms. How little he would care was proved by the fact that under the sense of them Mrs. Wix's discretion broke down altogether: she was capable of a transfer of allegiance, capable, at the altar of propriety, of a desperate sacrifice of her ladyship. As against Mrs. Beale, she more than once intimated, she had been willing to do the best for her, but as against Sir Claude she could do nothing for her at all. It was extraordinary the number of things that, still without a question, Maisie knew by the time her stepfather came back from Paris – came bringing her a splendid apparatus for painting in water-colours and bringing Mrs. Wix, by a lapse of memory that would have been droll if it had not been a trifle disconcerting, a second and even a more elegant umbrella. He had forgotten all about the first, with which, buried in as many wrappers as a mummy of the Pharaohs, she wouldn't for the world have done anything so profane as use it.

Maisie knew above all that though she was now, by what she
called an informal understanding, on Sir Claude's 'side', she had
yet not uttered a word to him about Mr. Perriam. That gentleman became therefore a kind of flourishing public secret, out of
the depths of which governess and pupil looked at each other
portentously from the time their friend was restored to them. He
was restored in great abundance, and it was marked that, though
he appeared to have felt the need to take a stand against the risk
of being too roughly saddled with the offspring of others, he at
this period exposed himself more than ever before to the presumption of having created expectations.

If it had become now, for that matter, a question of sides,
there was at least a certain amount of evidence as to where
they all were. Maisie, of course, in such a delicate position,
was on nobody's; but Sir Claude had all the air of being on
hers. If therefore Mrs. Wix was on Sir Claude's, her ladyship
on Mr. Perriam's, and Mr. Perriam presumably on her ladyship's, this left only Mrs. Beale and Mr. Farange to account for.
Mrs. Beale clearly was, like Sir Claude, on Maisie's, and papa,
it was to be supposed, on Mrs. Beale's. Here indeed was a slight
ambiguity, as papa's being on Mrs. Beale's didn't somehow
seem to place him quite on his daughter's. It sounded, as this
young lady thought it over, very much like puss-in-the-corner,
and she could only wonder if the distribution of parties would
lead to a rushing to and fro and changing of places. She was in
the presence, she felt, of restless change: wasn't it restless
enough that her mother and her stepfather should already be
on different sides? That was the great thing that had domesti-
cally happened. Mrs. Wix besides had turned another face: she
had never been exactly gay, but her gravity was now an attitude
as conspicuous as a poster. She seemed to sit in her new dress
and brood over her lost delicacy, which had become almost as
doleful a memory as that of poor Clara Matilda. 'It *is* hard for
him,' she often said to her companion; and it was surprising
how competent on this point Maisie was conscious of being to
agree with her. Hard as it was, however, Sir Claude had never
shown to greater advantage than in the gallant, generous, sociable
way he carried it off: a way that drew from Mrs. Wix a hundred

expressions of relief at his not having suffered it to embitter him. It threw him more and more at last into the schoolroom, where he had plainly begun to recognize that if he was to have the credit of perverting the innocent child he might also at least have the amusement. He never came into the place without telling its occupants that they were the nicest people in the house – a remark which always led them to say to each other 'Mr. Perriam!' as loud as ever compressed lips and enlarged eyes could make them articulate. He caused Maisie to remember what she had said to Mrs. Beale about his having the nature of a good nurse and, rather more than she intended before Mrs. Wix, to bring the whole thing out by once remarking to him that none of her good nurses had smoked quite so much in the nursery. This had no more effect than it was meant to on his cigarettes: he was always smoking, but always declaring that it was death to him not to lead a domestic life.

He led one after all in the schoolroom, and there were hours of late evening, when she had gone to bed, that Maisie knew he sat there talking with Mrs. Wix of how to meet his difficulties. His consideration for this unfortunate woman even in the midst of them continued to show him as the perfect gentleman and lifted the object of his courtesy into an upper air of beatitude in which her very pride had the hush of anxiety. 'He leans on me – he leans on me!' she only announced from time to time; and she was more surprised than amused when, later on, she accidentally found she had given her pupil the impression of a support literally supplied by her person. This glimpse of a misconception led her to be explicit – to put before the child, with an air of mourning indeed for such a stoop to the common, that what they talked about in the small hours, as they said, was the question of his taking right hold of life. The life she wanted him to take right hold of was the public: 'she', I hasten to add, was, in this connection, not the mistress of his fate, but only Mrs. Wix herself. She had phrases about him that were full of tenderness, yet full of morality. 'He's a wonderful nature, but he can't live like the lilies. He's all right, you know, but he must have a high interest.' She had more than once remarked that his affairs were sadly involved, but that they must get

him – Maisie and she together apparently – into Parliament.
The child took it from her with a flutter of importance that
Parliament was his natural sphere, and she was the less prepared to recognize a hindrance as she had never heard of any
affairs whatever that were not involved. She had in the old
days once been told by Mrs. Beale that her very own were, and
with the refreshment of knowing that she *had* affairs the information hadn't in the least overwhelmed her. It was true and
perhaps a little alarming that she had never heard of any such
matters since then. Full of charm at any rate was the prospect
of some day getting Sir Claude in; especially after Mrs. Wix, as
the fruit of more midnight colloquies, once went so far as
to observe that she really believed it was all that was wanted to
save him. Mrs. Wix, with these words, struck her pupil as crop-
ping up, after the manner of mamma when mamma talked,
quite in a new place. The child stared as at the jump of a
kangaroo.

'Save him from what?'

Mrs. Wix hesitated; then she covered a still greater distance.
'Why, just from awful misery.'

XII

She had not at the moment explained her ominous speech, but the light of remarkable events soon enabled her companion to read it. It may indeed be said that these days brought on a high quickening of Maisie's direct perceptions, of her gratified sense of arriving by herself at conclusions. This was helped by an emotion intrinsically far from sweet – the increase of the alarm that had most haunted her meditations. She had no need to be told, as on the morrow of the revelation of Sir Claude's danger she was told by Mrs. Wix, that her mother wanted more and more to know why the devil her father didn't send for her: she had too long expected that mamma's curiosity on this point would break out with violence. Maisie could meet such pressure so far as meeting it was to be in a position to reply, in words directly inspired, that papa would be hanged before he'd again be saddled with her. She therefore recognized the hour that in troubled glimpses she had long foreseen, the hour when – the phrase for it came back to her from Mrs. Beale – with two fathers, two mothers and two homes, six protections in all, she shouldn't know 'wherever' to go. Such apprehension as she felt on this score was not diminished by the fact that Mrs. Wix herself was suddenly white with terror: a circumstance leading Maisie to the further knowledge that this lady was still more scared on her own behalf than on that of her pupil. A governess who had only one frock was not likely to have either two fathers or two mothers: accordingly if even with these resources Maisie was to be in the streets, where in the name of all that was dreadful was poor Mrs. Wix to be? She had had, it appeared, a tremendous brush with Ida, which had begun and ended with the request that she would be pleased on the spot to 'bundle'. It had come suddenly but completely, this signal of which she had gone in fear. The companions confessed to each other their long foreboding, but Mrs. Wix was better off than Maisie in having a plan of defence. She declined indeed to communicate it till it was quite mature; but meanwhile, she hastened to declare, her feet were firm in the schoolroom. They could only be loosened by force: she would 'leave' for the police perhaps, but she wouldn't leave for mere outrage. That would be to play her ladyship's game, and it would take another turn of the screw to make her desert her darling. Her ladyship had come down with extraordinary ferocity: it had been one of many symptoms of a situation strained – 'between them all,' as Mrs. Wix said, 'but especially between the two' – to the point of God only knew what.

Her description of the crisis made the child reflect. 'Between which two? – papa and mamma?'

'Dear, no. I mean between your mother and *him*.'

Maisie, in this, recognized an opportunity to be really deep. '"Him"? – Mr. Perriam?'

She fairly brought a blush to the scared face. 'Well, my dear, I must say what you *don't* know ain't worth mentioning. That it won't go on for ever with Mr. Perriam – since I *must* meet you – who can suppose? But I meant dear Sir Claude.'

Maisie stood corrected rather than abashed. 'I see. But it's about Mr. Perriam he's angry?'

Mrs. Wix hesitated. 'He says he's not.'

'Not angry? He has told you so?'

Mrs. Wix looked at her hard. 'Not about *him*.'

'Then about some one else?'

Mrs. Wix looked at her harder. 'About some one else.'

'Lord Eric?' the child promptly brought forth.

At this, of a sudden, her governess was more agitated. 'Oh, why, little unfortunate, should we discuss their dreadful names?' – and she threw herself for the millionth time on Maisie's neck. It took her pupil but a moment to feel that she quivered with insecurity, and, the contact of her terror aiding, the pair in another instant were sobbing in each other's arms. Then it was that, completely relaxed, demoralized as she had never been, Mrs. Wix suffered her wound to bleed and her resentment to gush. Her great bitterness was that Ida had called her false, denounced her hypocrisy and duplicity, reviled her spying and tattling, her lying and grovelling to Sir Claude. 'Me, *me*,' the poor woman wailed, 'who've seen what I've seen and gone through everything only to cover her up and ease her off and smooth her down? If I've been an 'ipocrite it's the other way round: I've pretended, to him and to her, to myself and to you and to every one, *not* to see! It serves me right to have held my tongue before such horrors!' What horrors they were her companion forbore too closely to inquire, showing even signs not a few of an ability to take them for granted. That put the couple more than ever, in this troubled sea, in the same boat, so that with the consciousness of ideas on the part of her fellow-mariner Maisie could sit close and wait. Sir Claude on the morrow came in to tea, and then the ideas were produced. It was extraordinary how the child's presence drew out their full richness. The principal one was startling, but Maisie appreciated the courage with which her governess handled it. It simply consisted of the proposal that whenever and wherever they should take refuge Sir Claude should consent to share their asylum. On his protesting with all the warmth in nature against this note of secession she asked what else in the world was left to them if her ladyship should stop supplies.

'Supplies be hanged, my dear woman!' said their delightful friend. 'Leave supplies to me – I'll take care of supplies.'

Mrs. Wix hesitated. 'Well, it's exactly because I knew you'd be so glad to do so that I put the question before you. There's a way to look after us better than any other. That way is just to come *with* us.'

It hung before Maisie, Mrs. Wix's way, like a glittering picture, and she clasped her hands in ecstasy. 'Come with us, come with us!' she echoed.

Sir Claude looked from his stepdaughter back to her governess. 'Do you mean leave this house and take up my abode with you?'

'It will be the right thing – if you feel as you've told me you feel.' Mrs. Wix, sustained and uplifted, was now as clear as a bell.

Sir Claude had the air of trying to recall what he had told her; then the light broke that was always breaking to make his face more pleasant. 'It's your suggestion that I shall take a house for you?'

'For the wretched homeless child. Any roof – over *our* heads – will do for us; but of course for you it will have to be something really nice.'

Sir Claude's eyes reverted to Maisie, rather hard, as she thought; and there was a shade in his very smile that seemed to show her – though she also felt it didn't show Mrs. Wix – that the accommodation prescribed must loom to him pretty large. The next moment, however, he laughed gaily enough. 'My dear lady, you exaggerate tremendously *my* poor little needs.' Mrs. Wix had once mentioned to her young friend that when Sir Claude called her his dear lady he could do anything with her; and Maisie felt a certain anxiety to see what he would do now. Well, he only addressed her a remark of which the child herself was aware of feeling the force. 'Your plan appeals to me immensely; but of course – don't you see? – I shall have to consider the position I put myself in by leaving my wife.'

'You'll also have to remember,' Mrs. Wix replied, 'that if you don't look out your wife won't give you time to consider. Her ladyship will leave *you*.'

'Ah, my good friend, I do look out!' the young man returned while Maisie helped herself afresh to bread and butter. 'Of course if that happens I shall have somehow to turn round; but I hope with all my heart it won't. I beg your pardon,' he continued to his stepdaughter, 'for appearing to discuss that sort of possibility under your sharp little nose. But the fact is that I forget half the time that Ida is your sainted mother.'

'So do I!' said Maisie, to put him the more in the right.

Her protectress, at this, was upon her again. 'The little desolate, precious pet!' For the rest of the conversation she was enclosed in Mrs. Wix's arms, and as they sat there interlocked Sir Claude, before them with his tea-cup, looked down at them in deepening thought. Shrink together as they might they couldn't help, Maisie felt, being a very massive image, a large loose, ponderous presentment, of what Mrs. Wix required of him. She knew moreover that this lady didn't make it better by adding in a moment: 'Of course *we* shouldn't dream of a whole house. Any sort of little lodging, however humble, would be only too blessed.'

'But it would have to be something that would hold us all,' said Sir Claude.

'Oh yes,' Mrs. Wix concurred; 'the whole point is our being together. While you're waiting, before you act, for her ladyship to take some step, our position here will come to an impossible pass. You don't know what I went through with her for you yesterday – and for our poor darling; but it's not a thing I can promise you often to face again. She has dismissed me in horrible language – she has instructed the servants not to wait on me.'

'Oh, the poor servants are all right!' Sir Claude eagerly cried.

'They're certainly better than their mistress. It's too dreadful that I should sit here and say of your wife, Sir Claude, and of Maisie's own mother, that she's lower than a domestic; but my being betrayed into such remarks is just a reason the more for our getting away. I shall stay till I'm taken by the shoulders, but that may happen any day. What also may perfectly happen, you must permit me to repeat, is that she'll go off to get rid of us.'

'Oh, if she'll only do that!' Sir Claude laughed. 'That would be the very making of us!'

'Don't say it – don't say it!' Mrs. Wix pleaded. 'Don't speak of anything so fatal. You know what I mean. We must all cling to the right. You mustn't be bad.'

Sir Claude set down his tea-cup; he had become more grave and he pensively wiped his moustache. 'Won't all the world say I'm awful if I leave the house before – before she has bolted? They'll say it was my doing it that made her bolt.'

Maisie could grasp the force of this reasoning, but it offered no check to Mrs. Wix. 'Why need you mind that – if you've done it for so high a motive? Think of the beauty of it,' the good lady pressed.

'Of bolting with *you*?' Sir Claude ejaculated.

She faintly smiled – she even faintly coloured. 'So far from doing you harm, it will do you the highest good. Sir Claude, if you'll listen to me, it will save you.'

'Save me from what?'

Maisie, at this question, waited with renewed suspense for an answer that would bring the thing to a finer point than their companion had brought it to before. But there was on the contrary only more mystification in Mrs. Wix's reply. 'Ah, from you know what!'

'Do you mean from some other woman?'

'Yes – from a real bad one.'

Sir Claude at least, the child could see, was not mystified; so little indeed that a smile of intelligence broke afresh in his eyes. He turned them in vague discomfort to Maisie, and then something in the way she met them caused him to chuck her playfully under the chin. It was not till after this that he good-naturedly met Mrs. Wix. 'You think me much worse than I am.'

'If that were true,' she returned, 'I wouldn't appeal to you. I do, Sir Claude, in the name of all that's good in you – and, oh, so earnestly! We can help each other. What you'll do for our young friend here I needn't say. That isn't even what I want to speak of now. What I want to speak of is what you'll *get* – don't you see? – from such an opportunity to take hold. Take hold of *us* – take hold of *her*. Make her your duty – make her your life: she'll repay you a thousand-fold!'

It was to Mrs. Wix, during this appeal, that Maisie's contemplation transferred itself: partly because, though her heart was in her throat for trepidation, she felt a certain delicacy about appearing herself to press the question; partly from the coercion of seeing Mrs. Wix come out as Mrs. Wix had never come before – not even on the day of her call at Mrs. Beale's with the news of mamma's marriage. On that day Mrs. Beale had surpassed her in dignity; but nobody could have surpassed her now. There was in fact at this moment a fascination for her pupil in the hint she seemed to give that she had still more of that surprise behind. So the sharpened sense of spectatorship was the child's main support, the long habit, from the first, of seeing herself in discussion and finding in the fury of it – she had had a glimpse of the game of football – a sort of compensation for the doom of a peculiar passivity. It gave her often an odd air of being present at her history in as separate a manner as if she could only get at experience by flattening her nose against a pane of glass. Such she felt to be the application of her nose while she waited for the effect of Mrs. Wix's eloquence. Sir Claude, however, didn't keep her long in a position so ungraceful: he sat down and opened his arms to her as he had done the day he came for her at her father's, and while he held her there, looking at her kindly, but as if their companion had brought the blood a good deal to his face, he said:

'Dear Mrs. Wix is magnificent, but she's rather too grand about it. I mean the situation isn't after all quite so desperate or quite so simple. But I give you my word before her, and I give it to her before you, that I'll never, never, forsake you. Do you hear that, old fellow, and do you take it in? I'll stick to you through everything.'

Maisie did take it in – took it with a long tremor of all her little being; and then as, to emphasize it, he drew her closer she buried her head on his shoulder and cried without sound and without pain. While she was so engaged she became aware that his own breast was agitated, and gathered from it with rapture that his tears were as silently flowing. Presently she heard a loud sob from Mrs. Wix – Mrs. Wix was the only one who made a noise.

She was to have made, for some time, none other but this, though within a few days, in conversation with her pupil, she described her relations with Ida as positively excruciating. There was as yet nevertheless no attempt to eject her by force, and she recognized that Sir Claude, taking such a stand as never before, had intervened with passion and with success. As Maisie remembered – and remembered wholly without disdain – that he had told her he was afraid of her ladyship, the little girl took this act of resolution as a proof of what, in the spirit of the engagement sealed by all their tears, he was really prepared to do. Mrs. Wix spoke to her of the pecuniary sacrifice by which she herself purchased the scant security she enjoyed and which,

if it was a defence against the hand of violence, was far from
making her safe from private aggression. Didn't her ladyship
find every hour of the day some insidious means to humiliate and
trample upon her? There was a quarter's salary owing her – a
great name, even Maisie could suspect, for a small matter; she
should never see it as long as she lived, but keeping quiet about
it put her ladyship, thank heaven, a little in one's power. Now
that he was doing so much else she could never have the gross-
ness to apply for it to Sir Claude. He had sent home for schoolroom consumption a huge frosted cake, a wonderful delectable
mountain with geological strata of jam, which might, with
economy, see them through many days of their siege; but it was
none the less known to Mrs. Wix that his affairs were more
and more involved, and her fellow-partaker looked back tenderly, in the light of these involutions, at the expression of face
with which he had greeted the proposal that he should set up
another establishment. Maisie felt that if their maintenance
should hang but by a thread they must still demean themselves
with the highest delicacy. What he was doing was simply acting without delay, so far as his embarrassments permitted,
on the inspiration of his elder friend. There was at this season
a wonderful month of May – as soft as a drop of the wind in a
gale that had kept one awake – when he took out his stepdaughter with a fresh alacrity and they rambled the great town
in search, as Mrs. Wix called it, of combined amusement and
instruction.

They rode on the top of 'buses; they visited outlying parks;
they went to cricket-matches where Maisie fell asleep; they tried
a hundred places for the best one to have tea. This was his direct
way of rising to Mrs. Wix's admirable lesson – of making his little accepted charge his duty and his life. They dropped, under
incontrollable impulses, into shops that they agreed were too
big, to look at things that they agreed were too small, and it was
during these hours that Mrs. Wix, alone at home, but a subject
of regretful reference as they pulled off their gloves for refreshment, subsequently described herself as most exposed to the
blows that her ladyship had achieved such ingenuity in dealing. She again and again repeated that she would not so much

have minded having her 'attainments' held up to scorn and her knowledge of every subject denied if she were not habitually denounced to her face as the basest of her sex. There was by this time no pretence on the part of any one of denying it to be fortunate that her ladyship habitually left London every Saturday and was more and more disposed to a return late in the week. It was almost equally public that she regarded as a preposterous 'pose', and indeed as a direct insult to herself, her husband's attitude of staying behind to look after a child for whom the most elaborate provision had been made. If there was a type Ida despised, Sir Claude communicated to Maisie, it was the man who pottered about town of a Sunday; and he also mentioned how often she had declared to him that if he had a grain of spirit he would be ashamed to accept a menial position about Mr. Farange's daughter. It was her ladyship's contention that he was in craven fear of his predecessor – otherwise he would recognize it as an obligation of plain decency to protect his wife against the outrage of that person's barefaced attempt to swindle her. The swindle was that Mr. Farange put upon her the whole intolerable burden; 'and even when I pay for you myself,' Sir Claude averred to his young friend, 'she accuses me the more of truckling and grovelling.' It was Mrs. Wix's conviction, they both knew, arrived at on independent grounds, that Ida's weekly excursions were feelers for a more considerable absence. If she came back later each week the week would be sure to arrive when she wouldn't come back at all. This appearance had of course much to do with Mrs. Wix's actual valour. Could they but hold out long enough the snug little home with Sir Claude would find itself informally constituted.

XIII

This might moreover have been taken to be the sense of a remark made by her stepfather as – one rainy day when the streets were all splash and two umbrellas unsociable and the wanderers had sought shelter in the National Gallery – Maisie sat beside him staring rather sightlessly at a roomful of pictures which he had mystified her much by speaking of with a bored sigh as a 'silly superstition'. They represented, with patches of gold and cataracts of purple, with stiff saints and angular angels, with ugly Madonnas and uglier babies, strange prayers and prostrations; so that she at first took his words for a protest against devotional idolatry – all the more that he had of late often come with her and with Mrs. Wix to morning church, a place of worship of Mrs. Wix's own choosing, where there was nothing of that sort; no haloes on heads, but only, during long sermons, beguiling backs of bonnets, and where, as her governess always afterwards observed, he gave the most earnest attention. It presently appeared, however, that his reference was merely to the affectation of admiring such ridiculous works – an admonition that she received from him as submissively as she received everything. What turn it gave to their talk need not here be recorded: the transition to the colourless schoolroom and lonely Mrs. Wix was doubtless an effect of relaxed interest in what was before them. Maisie expressed in her own way the truth that she never went home nowadays without expecting to find the temple of her studies empty and the poor priestess cast out. This conveyed a full appreciation of her peril, and it was in rejoinder that Sir Claude uttered, acknowledging the source of that peril, the reassurance at which I have glanced. 'Don't be afraid, my dear: I've squared her.' It required indeed a supplement when he saw that it left the child momentarily blank. 'I mean that your mother lets me do what I want so long as I let her do what she wants.'

'So you *are* doing what you want?' Maisie asked.

'Rather, Miss Farange!'

Miss Farange turned it over. 'And she's doing the same?'

'Up to the hilt!'

Again she considered. 'Then, please, what may it be?'

'I wouldn't tell you for the whole world.'

She gazed at a gaunt Madonna; after which she broke into a slow smile. 'Well, I don't care, so long as you do let her.'

'Oh, you monster!' laughed Sir Claude, getting up.

Another day, in another place – a place in Baker Street where at a hungry hour she had sat down with him to tea and buns – he brought out a question disconnected from previous talk. 'I say, you know, what do you suppose your father *would* do?'

Maisie had not long to cast about nor to question his pleasant eyes. 'If you were really to go with us? He would make a great complaint.'

He seemed amused at the term she employed. 'Oh, I shouldn't mind a "complaint"!'

'He would talk to every one about it,' said Maisie.

'Well, I shouldn't mind that either.'

'Of course not,' the child hastened to respond. 'You've told me you're not afraid of him.'

'The question is are you?' said Sir Claude.

Maisie candidly considered; then she spoke resolutely. 'No, not of papa.'

'But of somebody else?'

'Certainly, of lots of people.'

'Of your mother first and foremost of course.'

'Dear, yes; more of mamma than of——than of——'

'Than of what?' Sir Claude asked as she hesitated for a comparison.

She thought over all objects of dread. 'Than of a wild elephant!' she at last declared. 'And you are too,' she reminded him as he laughed.

'Oh yes, I am too.'

Again she meditated. 'Why then did you marry her?'

'Just because I *was* afraid.'

'Even when she loved you?'

'That made her the more alarming.'

For Maisie herself, though her companion seemed to find it droll, this opened up depths of gravity. 'More alarming than she is now?'

'Well, in a different way. Fear, unfortunately, is a very big thing, and there's a great variety of kinds.'

She took this in with complete intelligence. 'Then I think I've got them all.'

'You?' her friend cried. 'Nonsense! You're thoroughly "game".'

'I'm awfully afraid of Mrs. Beale,' Maisie announced.

He raised his smooth brows. 'That charming woman?'

'Well,' she answered, 'you can't understand it because you're not in the same state.'

She had been going on with a luminous 'But' when, across the table, he laid his hand on her arm. 'I *can* understand it,' he confessed. 'I *am* in the same state.'

'Oh, but she likes you so!' Maisie eagerly suggested.

Sir Claude literally coloured. 'That has something to do with it.'

Maisie wondered again. 'Being liked with being afraid?'

'Yes, when it amounts to adoration.'

'Then why aren't you afraid of *me*?'

'Because with you it amounts to that.' He had kept his hand on her arm. 'Well, what prevents is simply that you're the gentlest spirit on earth. Besides——' he pursued; but he came to a pause.

'Besides——?'

'I should be in fear if you were older – there! See – you already make me talk nonsense,' the young man added. 'The question's about your father. Is he likewise afraid of Mrs. Beale?'

'I think not. And yet he loves her,' Maisie mused.

'Oh no – he doesn't; not a bit!' After which, as his companion stared, Sir Claude apparently felt that he must make his announcement fit with her recollections. 'There's nothing of that sort *now*.'

But Maisie only stared the more. 'They've changed?'

'Like your mother and me.'

She wondered how he knew. 'Then you've seen Mrs. Beale again?'

He demurred. 'Oh no. She has written to me,' he presently subjoined. '*She's* not afraid of your father either. No one at all is – really.' Then he went on while Maisie's little mind, with its filial spring too relaxed, from of old, for a pang at this want of parental majesty, speculated on the vague relation between Mrs. Beale's courage and the question, for Mrs. Wix and herself, of a neat lodging with their friend. 'She wouldn't care a bit if Mr. Farange should make a row.'

'Do you mean about you and me and Mrs. Wix? Why should she care? It wouldn't hurt *her*.'

Sir Claude, with his legs out and his hand diving into his trousers-pocket, threw back his head with a laugh just perceptibly tempered, as she thought, by a sigh. 'My dear step-child, you're delightful! Look here, we must pay. You've had five buns?'

'How *can* you?' Maisie demanded, crimson under the eye of the young woman who had stepped to their board. 'I've had three.'

Shortly after this Mrs. Wix looked so ill that it was to be feared her ladyship had treated her to some unexampled passage. Maisie asked if anything worse than usual had occurred; whereupon the poor woman brought out with infinite gloom: 'He has been seeing Mrs. Beale.'

'Sir Claude?' The child remembered what he had said: 'Oh no – not *seeing* her!'

'I beg your pardon. I absolutely know it.' Mrs. Wix was as positive as she was dismal.

Maisie nevertheless ventured to challenge her. 'And how, please, do you know it?'

She faltered a moment. 'From herself. I've been to see her.' Then on Maisie's visible surprise: 'I went yesterday while you were out with him. He has seen her repeatedly.'

It was not wholly clear to Maisie why Mrs. Wix should be
prostrate at this discovery; but her general consciousness of the
way things could be both perpetrated and resented always
eased off for her the strain of the particular mystery. 'There
may be some mistake. He says he hasn't.'

Mrs. Wix turned paler, as if this were a still deeper ground
for alarm. 'He says so? – he denies that he has seen her?'

'He told me so three days ago. Perhaps she's mistaken,'
Maisie suggested.

'Do you mean perhaps she lies? She lies whenever it suits her,
I'm very sure. But I know when people lie – and that's what
I've loved in you, that you never do. Mrs. Beale didn't yesterday
at any rate. He *has* seen her.'

Maisie was silent a little. 'He says not,' she then repeated.
'Perhaps – perhaps——' Once more she paused.

'Do you mean perhaps *he* lies?'

'Gracious goodness, no!' Maisie shouted.

Mrs. Wix's bitterness, however, again overflowed. 'He does,
he does,' she cried, 'and it's that that's just the worst of it!
They'll take you, they'll take you, and what in the world will
then become of me?' She threw herself afresh upon her pupil
and wept over her with the inevitable effect of causing the
child's own tears to flow. But Maisie could not have told you if
she had been crying at the image of their separation or at that
of Sir Claude's untruth. As regards this deviation it was agreed
between them that they were not in a position to bring it home
to him. Mrs. Wix was in dread of doing anything to make him,
as she said, 'worse'; and Maisie was sufficiently initiated to be
able to reflect that in speaking to her as he had done he had
only wished to be tender of Mrs. Beale. It fell in with all her
inclinations to think of him as tender, and she forbore to let
him know that the two ladies had, as *she* would never do,
betrayed him.

She had not long to keep her secret, for the next day, when
she went out with him, he suddenly said in reference to some
errand he had first proposed: 'No, we won't do that – we'll do
something else.' On this, a few steps from the door, he stopped
a hansom and helped her in; then following her he gave the

driver over the top an address that she lost. When he was seated beside her she asked him where they were going; to which he replied: 'My dear child, you'll see.' She saw while she watched and wondered that they took the direction of the Regent's Park; but she didn't know why he should make a mystery of that, and it was not till they passed under a pretty arch and drew up at a white house in a terrace from which the view, she thought, must be lovely that, mystified, she clutched him and broke out: 'I shall see papa?'

He looked down at her with a kind smile. 'No, probably not. I haven't brought you for that.'

'Then whose house is it?'

'It's your father's. They've moved here.'

She looked about: she had known Mr. Farange in four or five houses, and there was nothing astonishing in this except that it was the nicest place yet. 'But I shall see Mrs. Beale?'

'It's to see her that I brought you.'

She stared, very white, and, with her hand on his arm, though they had stopped, kept him sitting in the cab. 'To leave me, do you mean?'

He hesitated. 'It's not for me to say if you *can* stay. We must look into it.'

'But if I do I shall see papa?'

'Oh, some time or other, no doubt.' Then Sir Claude went on: 'Have you really so very great a dread of that?'

Maisie glanced away over the apron of the cab – gazed a minute at the green expanse of the Regent's Park and, at this moment colouring to the roots of her hair, felt the full, hot rush of an emotion more mature than any she had yet known. It consisted of an odd, unexpected shame at placing in an inferior light, to so perfect a gentleman and so charming a person as Sir Claude, so very near a relative as Mr. Farange. She remembered, however, her friend's telling her that no one was seriously afraid of her father, and she turned round with a small toss of her head. 'Oh, I daresay I can manage him!'

Sir Claude smiled, but she noticed that the violence with which she had just changed colour had brought into his own face a slight compunctious and embarrassed flush. It was as if he had caught his first glimpse of her sense of responsibility. Neither of them made a movement to get out, and after an instant he said to her: 'Look here, if you say so we won't after all go in.'

'Ah, but I want to see Mrs. Beale!' the child murmured.

'But what if she does decide to take you? Then, you know, you'll have to remain.'

Maisie turned it over. 'Straight on – and give you up?'

'Well – I don't quite know about giving me up.'

'I mean as I gave up Mrs. Beale when I last went to mamma's. I couldn't do without you here for anything like so long a time as that.' It struck her as a hundred years since she had seen Mrs. Beale, who was on the other side of the door they were so near and whom she yet had not taken the jump to clasp in her arms.

'Oh, I daresay you'll see more of me than you've seen of Mrs. Beale. It isn't in *me* to be so beautifully discreet,' Sir Claude said. 'But all the same,' he continued, 'I leave the thing, now that we're here, absolutely with you. You must settle it. We'll only go in if you say so. If you don't say so we'll turn right round and drive away.'

'So in that case Mrs. Beale won't take me?'

'Well – not by any act of ours.'

'And I shall be able to go on with mamma?' Maisie asked.

'Oh, I don't say that!'

She considered. 'But I thought you said you had squared her?'

Sir Claude poked his stick at the splashboard of the cab. 'Not, my dear child, to the point she now requires.'

'Then if she turns me out and I don't come here——?'

Sir Claude promptly took her up. 'What do I offer you, you naturally inquire? My poor chick, that's just what I ask myself. I don't see it, I confess, quite as straight as Mrs. Wix.'

His companion gazed a moment at what Mrs. Wix saw. 'You mean *we* can't make a little family?'

'It's very base of me, no doubt, but I can't wholly chuck your mother.'

Maisie, at this, emitted a low but lengthened sigh, a slight sound of reluctant assent which would certainly have been amusing to an auditor. 'Then there isn't anything else?'

'I vow I don't quite see what there is.'

Maisie waited a moment; her silence seemed to signify that she too had no alternative to suggest. But she made another appeal. 'If I come here you'll come to see me?.'

'I won't lose sight of you.'

'But how often will you come?' As he hung fire she pressed him. 'Often and often?'

Still he faltered. 'My dear old woman——' he began. Then he paused again, going on at the next moment with a change of tone: 'You're too funny! Yes, then,' he said; 'often and often.'

'All right!' Maisie jumped out. Mrs. Beale was at home, but not in the drawing-room, and when the butler had gone for her the child suddenly broke out: 'But when I'm here what will Mrs. Wix do?'

'Ah, you should have thought of that sooner!' said her companion with the first faint note of asperity she had ever heard him sound.

Mrs. Beale fairly swooped upon her, and the effect of the whole hour was to show the child how much, how quite formidably indeed, after all, she was loved. This was the more the case as her stepmother, so changed – in the very manner of her mother – that she really struck her as a new acquaintance, somehow recalled more familiarity than Maisie could feel. A rich, strong, expressive affection in short pounced upon her in the shape of a handsomer, ampler, older Mrs. Beale. It was like making a fine friend, and they hadn't been a minute together before she felt elated at the way she had met the choice imposed upon her in the cab. There was a whole future in the combination of Mrs. Beale's beauty and Mrs. Beale's hug. She seemed to Maisie charming to behold, and also to have no connection at all with anybody who had once mended underclothing and had meals in the nursery. The child knew one of her father's wives was a woman of fashion, but she had always dimly made a distinction, not applying that epithet without reserve to the other. Mrs. Beale since their separation had acquired a conspicuous right to it, and Maisie's first flush of response to her present delight coloured all her splendour with meanings that, this time, were sweet. She had told Sir Claude that she was afraid of the lady in the Regent's Park; but she was not too much afraid to rejoice, aloud, on the very spot. 'Why, aren't you beautiful? Isn't she beautiful, Sir Claude, *isn't* she?'

'The handsomest woman in London, simply,' Sir Claude gallantly replied. 'Just as sure as you're the best little girl!'

Well, the handsomest woman in London gave herself up, with tender, lustrous looks and every demonstration of fondness, to a happiness at last recovered. There was almost as vivid a bloom in her maturity as in mamma's, and it took her but a short time to give her little friend an impression of positive power – an impression that opened up there like a new source of confidence. This was a perception, on Maisie's part, that neither mamma, nor Sir Claude, nor Mrs. Wix, with their immense and so varied respective attractions, had exactly kindled, and that made an immediate difference when the talk, as it promptly did, began to turn to her father. Oh yes, Mr. Farange was a complication, but she saw now that he would not be one for his daughter. For Mrs. Beale certainly he was an immense one; she speedily made known as much: but Mrs. Beale from this moment presented herself to Maisie as a person to whom a great gift had come. The great gift was just for handling complications. Maisie observed how little she made of them when, after she had dropped to Sir Claude some reference to a previous meeting, he exclaimed with an air of consternation and yet with something of a laugh that he had denied to their companion their having, since the day he came for her, seen each other till that moment.

Mrs. Beale diffused surprise. 'Why did you do anything so silly?'

'To protect your reputation.'

'From Maisie?' Mrs. Beale was much amused. 'My reputation with Maisie is too good to suffer.'

'But you believed me, you rascal, didn't you?' Sir Claude asked of the child.

She looked at him; she smiled. 'Her reputation did suffer. I discovered you had been here.'

He was not too chagrined to laugh. 'The way, my dear, you talk of that sort of thing!'

'How should she talk,' Mrs. Beale inquired, 'after all this wretched time with her mother?'

'It was not mamma who told me,' Maisie exclaimed. 'It was only Mrs. Wix.' She was hesitating whether to bring out before Sir Claude the source of Mrs. Wix's information; but Mrs. Beale, addressing the young man, showed her the vanity of her scruples.

'Do you know that preposterous person came to see me a day or two ago? – when I told her I had seen you repeatedly.'

Sir Claude, for once in a way, was disconcerted. 'The old cat! She never told me. Then you thought I had lied?' he demanded of Maisie.

She was flurried by the term with which he had qualified her gentle friend, but she felt the occasion to be one to which she must in every manner lend herself. 'Oh, I didn't mind! But Mrs. Wix did,' she added with an intention benevolent to her governess.

Her intention was not very effective as regards Mrs. Beale. 'Mrs. Wix is too idiotic!' that lady declared.

'But to you, of all people,' Sir Claude asked, 'what had she to say?'

'Why, that, like Mrs. Micawber – whom she must, I think, rather resemble – she will never, never, never desert Miss Farange.'

'Oh, I'll make that all right!' Sir Claude cheerfully returned.

'I'm sure I hope so, my dear man,' said Mrs. Beale, while Maisie wondered just how he would proceed. Before she had time to ask Mrs. Beale continued: 'That's not all she came to do, if you please. But you'll never guess the rest.'

'Shall *I* guess it?' Maisie demanded.

Mrs. Beale was again amused. 'Why, you're just the person! It must be quite the sort of thing you've heard at your awful mother's. Have you never seen women there crying to her to "spare" the men they love?'

Maisie, wondering, tried to remember; but Sir Claude was freshly diverted. 'Oh, they don't trouble about Ida! Mrs. Wix cried to you to spare *me*?'

'She regularly went down on her knees to me.'

'The darling old dear!' the young man exclaimed.

These words were a joy to Maisie – they made up for his previous description of Mrs. Wix. 'And *will* you spare him?' she asked of Mrs. Beale.

Her stepmother, seizing her and kissing her again, seemed charmed with the tone of her question. 'Not an inch of him! I'll pick him to the bone!'

'You mean that he'll really come often?' Maisie pressed.

Mrs. Beale turned lovely eyes to Sir Claude. 'That's not for me to say – it's for him.'

He said nothing for the time, however; with his hands in his pockets and vaguely humming a tune – even Maisie could see he was a little nervous – he only walked to the window and looked out at the Regent's Park. 'Well, he has promised,' Maisie said. 'But how will papa like it?'

'His being in and out? Ah, that's a question that, to be frank with you, my dear, hardly matters. In point of fact, however, Beale greatly enjoys the idea that Sir Claude too, poor man, has been forced to quarrel with your mother.'

Sir Claude turned round and spoke gravely and kindly. 'Don't be afraid, Maisie; you won't lose sight of me.'

'Thank you so much!' Maisie was radiant. 'But what I meant – don't you know? – was what papa would say to *me*.'

'Oh, I've been having that out with him,' said Mrs. Beale. 'He'll behave well enough. You see the great difficulty is that, though he changes every three days about everything else in the world, he has never changed about your mother. It's a caution, the way he hates her.'

Sir Claude gave a short laugh. 'It certainly can't beat the way she still hates *him*!'

'Well,' Mrs. Beale went on obligingly, 'nothing can take the place of that feeling with either of them, and the best way they can think of to show it is for each to leave you as long as possible on the hands of the other. There's nothing, as you've seen for yourself, that makes either so furious. It isn't, asking so little as you do, that you're much of an expense or a trouble; it's only that you make each feel so well how nasty the other wants to be. Therefore Beale goes on loathing your mother too much to have any great fury left for any one else. Besides, you know, I've squared him.'

'Oh Lord!' Sir Claude cried with a louder laugh and turning again to the window.

'*I* know how!' Maisie was prompt to proclaim. 'By letting him do what he wants on condition that he lets you also do it.'

'You're too delicious, my own pet!' – she was involved in another hug. 'How in the world have I got on so long without

you? I've not been happy, love,' said Mrs. Beale with her cheek
to the child's.

'Be happy now!' – Maisie throbbed with shy tenderness.

'I think I shall be. You'll save me.'

'As I'm saving Sir Claude?' the little girl asked eagerly.

Mrs. Beale, a trifle at a loss, appealed to her visitor. 'Is she really?'

He showed high amusement at Maisie's question. 'It's dear
Mrs. Wix's idea. There may be something in it.'

'He makes me his duty – he makes me his life,' Maisie set
forth to her stepmother.

'Why, that's what *I* want to do!' – Mrs. Beale, so anticipated,
turned pink with astonishment.

'Well, you can do it together. Then he'll *have* to come!'

Mrs. Beale by this time had her young friend fairly in her lap
and she smiled up at Sir Claude. 'Shall we do it together?'

His laughter had dropped, and for a moment he turned his
handsome, serious face not to his hostess, but to his stepdaughter. 'Well, it's rather more decent than some things. Upon my
soul, the way things are going, it seems to me the only decency!'
He had the air of arguing it out to Maisie, of presenting it,
through an impulse of conscience, as a connection in which
they could honourably see her participate; though his plea of
mere 'decency' might well have appeared to fall below her rosy
little vision. 'If we're not good for you,' he exclaimed, 'I'll be
hanged if I know who we shall be good for!'

Mrs. Beale showed the child an intenser light. 'I daresay you
will save us – from one thing and another.'

'Oh, I know what she'll save *me* from!' Sir Claude roundly
asserted. 'There'll be rows, of course,' he went on.

Mrs. Beale quickly took him up. 'Yes, but they'll be nothing –
for you at least – to the rows your wife makes as it is. I can bear
what *I* suffer – I can't bear what you do.'

'We're doing a good deal for you, you know, young woman,'
Sir Claude went on to Maisie with the same gravity.

His little charge coloured with a sense of obligation and the
eagerness of her desire it should be remarked how little was
lost on her. 'Oh, I know!'

'Then you must keep us all right!' This time he laughed.

CHAPTER XIV

'How you talk to her!' cried Mrs. Beale.

'No worse than you!' he gaily rejoined.

'Handsome is that handsome does!' she exclaimed in the same spirit. 'You can take off your things,' she went on, releasing Maisie.

The child, on her feet, was all emotion. 'Then I'm just to stop – this way?'

'It will do as well as any other. Sir Claude, to-morrow, will have your things brought.'

'I'll bring them myself. Upon my word I'll see them packed!' Sir Claude promised. 'Come here and unbutton.'

He had beckoned his young companion to where he sat, and he helped to disengage her from her coverings while Mrs. Beale, from a little distance, smiled at the hand he displayed. 'There's a stepfather for you! I'm bound to say, you know, that he makes up for the want of other people.'

'He makes up for the want of a nurse!' Sir Claude laughed. 'Don't you remember I told you so the very first time?'

'Remember? It was exactly what made me think so well of you!'

'Nothing would induce me,' the young man said to Maisie, 'to tell you what made me think so well of *her*.' Having divested the child he kissed her gently and gave her a little pat to make her stand off. The pat was accompanied with a vague sigh in which his gravity of a moment before came back. 'All the same, if you hadn't had the fatal gift of beauty——'

'Well, what?' Maisie asked, wondering why he paused. It was the first time she had heard of her beauty.

'Why, we shouldn't all be thinking so well of each other!'

'He isn't speaking of personal loveliness – you're not lovely in person, my dear, at all,' Mrs. Beale explained. 'He's just talking of plain, dull charm of character.'

'Her character's the most extraordinary thing in all the world,' Sir Claude communicated to Mrs. Beale.

'Oh, I know all about that sort of thing!' – she fairly bridled with the knowledge.

It gave Maisie somehow a sudden sense of responsibility from which she sought refuge. 'Well, you've got it too, "that sort of thing" – you've got the fatal gift; you both really have!' she broke out.

'Beauty of character? My dear boy, we haven't a pennyworth!' Sir Claude protested.

'Speak for yourself, sir!' leaped lightly from Mrs. Beale. 'I'm good and I'm clever. What more do you want? For you, I'll spare your blushes and not be personal – I'll simply say that you're as handsome as you can stick together.'

'You're both very lovely; you can't get out of it!' – Maisie felt the need of carrying her point. 'And it's beautiful to see you together.'

Sir Claude had taken his hat and stick; he stood looking at her a moment. 'You're a comfort in trouble! But I must go home and pack you.'

'And when will you come back? – to-morrow, to-morrow?'

'You see what we're in for!' he said to Mrs. Beale.

'Well, I can bear it,' she replied, 'if you can.'

Their companion gazed from one of them to the other, thinking that though she had been happy indeed between Sir Claude and Mrs. Wix she should evidently be happier still between Sir Claude and Mrs. Beale. But it was like being perched on a prancing horse, and she made a movement to hold on to something. 'Then, you know, sha'n't I bid good-bye to Mrs. Wix?'

'Oh, I'll make it all right with her,' said Sir Claude.

Maisie considered. 'And with mamma?'

'Ah, mamma!' he sadly laughed.

Even for the child this was scarcely ambiguous; but Mrs. Beale endeavoured to contribute to its clearness. 'Your mother will crow, she'll crow——'

'Like the early bird!' said Sir Claude as she looked about for a comparison.

'She'll need no consolation,' Mrs. Beale went on, 'for having made your father grandly blaspheme.'

Maisie stared. 'Will he grandly blaspheme?' It sounded picturesque, almost scriptural, and her question produced a fresh play of caresses, in which Sir Claude also engaged. She wondered meanwhile who, if Mrs. Wix was disposed of, would represent in her life the element of geography and anecdote; and she presently surmounted the delicacy she felt about asking. 'Won't there be any one to give me lessons?'

Mrs. Beale was prepared with a reply that struck her as absolutely magnificent. 'You shall have such lessons as you've never had in all your life. You shall go to courses.'

'Courses?' Maisie had never heard of such things.

'At institutions – on subjects.'

Maisie continued to stare. 'Subjects?'

Mrs. Beale was really splendid. 'All the most important ones. French literature – and sacred history. You'll take part in classes – with awfully smart children.'

'I'm going to look thoroughly into the whole thing, you know.' And Sir Claude, with characteristic kindness, gave her a nod of assurance accompanied by a friendly wink.

But Mrs. Beale went much further. 'My dear child, you shall attend lectures.'

The horizon was suddenly vast and Maisie felt herself the smaller for it. 'All alone?'

'Oh no; I'll attend them with you,' said Sir Claude. 'They'll teach me a lot I don't know.'

'So they will me,' Mrs. Beale gravely admitted. 'We'll go with her together – it will be charming. It's ages,' she confessed to Maisie, 'since I've had any time for study. That's another sweet way in which you'll be a motive to us. Oh, won't the good she'll do us be immense?' she broke out uncontrollably to Sir Claude.

He weighed it; then he replied: 'That's certainly our idea.' Of this idea Maisie naturally had less of a grasp, but it inspired her with almost equal enthusiasm. If in so bright a prospect there would be nothing to long for it followed that she wouldn't long for Mrs. Wix; but her consciousness of her assent to the absence of that fond figure caused a pair of words that had often sounded in her ears to ring in them again. It showed her in short what her father had always meant by calling her mother a 'low sneak' and her mother by calling her father one. She wondered if she herself shouldn't be a low sneak in learning to be so happy without Mrs. Wix. What would Mrs. Wix do?

Where would Mrs. Wix go? Before Maisie knew it, and at the door, as Sir Claude was off, these anxieties, on her lips, grew articulate and her stepfather had stopped long enough to answer them. 'Oh, I'll square her!' he cried; and with this he departed.

Face to face with Mrs. Beale Maisie, giving a sigh of relief, looked round at what seemed to her the dawn of a higher order. 'Then *every one* will be squared!' she peacefully said. On which her stepmother affectionately bent over her again.

XV

It was Susan Ash who came to her with the news: 'He's downstairs, miss, and he do look beautiful.'

In the schoolroom at her father's, which had pretty blue curtains, she had been making out at the piano a lovely little thing, as Mrs. Beale called it, a 'Moonlight Berceuse' sent her through the post by Sir Claude, who considered that her musical education had been deplorably neglected and who, the last months at her mother's, had been on the point of making arrangements for regular lessons. She knew from him familiarly that the real thing, as he said, was shockingly dear and that anything else was a waste of money, and she therefore rejoiced the more at the sacrifice represented by this composition, of which the price, five shillings, was marked on the cover and which was evidently the real thing. She was already on her feet. 'Mrs. Beale has sent up for me?'

'Oh no – it's not that,' said Susan Ash. 'Mrs. Beale has been out this hour.'

'Then papa!'

'Dear no – not papa. You'll do, miss, all but them wandering 'airs,' Susan went on. 'Your papa never came 'ome at all,' she added.

'From where?' Maisie responded a little absently and very excitedly. She gave a wild manual brush of her locks.

'Oh, that, miss, I should be very sorry to tell you! I'd rather tuck away that white thing behind – though I'm blessed if it's my work.'

'Do then, please. I know where papa was,' Maisie impatiently continued.

'Well, in your place I wouldn't tell.'

'He was at the club – the Chrysanthemum. So!'

'All night long? Why, the flowers shut up at night, you know!' cried Susan Ash.

'Well, I don't care' – the child was at the door. 'Sir Claude asked for me *alone*?'

'The same as if you was a duchess.'

Maisie was aware on her way downstairs that she was now quite as happy as one, and also, a moment later, as she hung round his neck, that even such a personage would scarce commit herself more grandly. There was moreover a hint of the duchess in the infinite point with which, as she felt, she exclaimed: 'And this is what you call coming *often*?'

Sir Claude met her, delightfully, in the same fine spirit. 'My dear old man, don't make me a scene – I assure you it's what every woman does that I look at. Let us have some fun – it's a lovely day: clap on something smart and come out with me; then we'll talk it over quietly.' They were on their way five minutes later to Hyde Park, and nothing that even in the good days at her mother's they had ever talked over had more of the sweetness of tranquillity than his present prompt explanations. He was at his best in such an office and with the exception of Mrs. Wix the only person she had met in her life who ever explained. With him, however, the act had an authority transcending the wisdom of woman. It all came back, all the plans that always failed, all the rewards and bribes that she was perpetually paying for in advance and perpetually out of pocket by afterwards – the whole great stress to be dealt with introduced her on each occasion afresh to the question of money. Even she herself almost knew how it would have expressed the strength of his empire to say that to shuffle away her sense of being duped he had only, from under his lovely moustache, to breathe upon it. It was somehow in the nature of plans to be expensive and in the nature of the expensive to be impossible. To be 'involved' was of the essence of everybody's affairs, and also at every particular moment to be more involved than usual. This had been the case with Sir Claude's, with papa's, with mamma's, with Mrs. Beale's and with Maisie's own at the particular moment, a moment of several weeks, that had elapsed since our young lady had been re-established at her father's. There wasn't 'two-and-tuppence' for anything or for any one, and that was why there had been no sequel to the classes in French literature with all the smart little girls. It was devilish awkward, didn't she see? to try, without even the modest sum mentioned, to mix her up with a remote array that glittered before her after this as the children of the rich. She was to feel henceforth as if she were flattening her nose upon the hard window-pane of the sweet-shop of knowledge. If the classes, however, that were select, and accordingly the only ones, were impossibly dear, the lectures at the institutions – at least at some of them – were directly addressed to the intelligent poor, and it therefore had to be easier still to produce on the spot the reason why she had been taken to none. This reason, Sir Claude said, was that she happened to be just going to be, though they had nothing to do with that in now directing their steps to the banks of the Serpentine. Maisie's own park, in the north, had been nearer at hand, but they rolled westward in a hansom because at the end of the sweet June days that was the direction taken by every one that any one looked at. They cultivated for an hour, on the Row and by the Drive, this opportunity for each observer to amuse and for one of them indeed, not a little hilari-ously, to mystify the other, and before the hour was over Maisie had elicited, in reply to her sharpest challenge, a further account of her friend's long absence.

'Why I've broken my word to you so dreadfully – promising so solemnly and then never coming? Well, my dear, that's a question that, not seeing me day after day, you must very often have put to Mrs. Beale.'

'Oh yes,' the child replied; 'again and again.'

'And what has she told you?'

'That you're as bad as you're beautiful.'

'Is that what she says?'

'Those very words.'

'Ah, the dear old soul!' Sir Claude was much diverted, and his loud, clear laugh was all his explanation. Those were just the words Maisie had last heard him use about Mrs. Wix. She clung to his hand, which was encased in a pearl-grey glove ornamented with the thick black lines that, at her mother's, always used to strike her as connected with the way the be-stitched fists of the long ladies carried, with the elbows well out, their umbrellas upside down. The mere sense of it in her own covered the ground of loss just as much as the ground of gain. His presence was like an object brought so close to her face that she couldn't see round its edges. He himself, however, remained showman of the spectacle even after they had passed out of the Park and begun, under the charm of the spot and the season, to stroll in Kensington Gardens. What they had left behind them was, as he said, only a pretty bad circus, and, through engaging gates and over a bridge, they had come in a quarter of an hour, as he also remarked, a hundred miles from London. A great green glade was before them, and high old trees, and under the shade of these, in the fresh turf, the crooked course of a rural footpath. 'It's the Forest of Arden,' Sir Claude had just delightfully observed, 'and I'm the banished duke, and you're – what was the young woman called? – the artless country wench. And there,' he went on, 'is the other girl – what's her name, Rosalind? – and (don't you know?) the fellow who was making up to her. Upon my word he *is* making up to her!'

His allusion was to a couple who, side by side, at the end of the glade, were moving in the same direction as themselves. These distant figures, in their slow stroll (which kept them so close together that their heads, drooping a little forward, almost touched), presented the back of a lady who looked tall, who was evidently a very fine woman, and that of a gentleman whose left hand appeared to be passed well into her arm, while his right, behind him, made jerky motions with the stick that it grasped. Maisie's fancy responded for an instant to her friend's idea that the sight was idyllic; then, stopping short, she brought out with all her clearness: 'Why, mercy – if it isn't mamma!'

Sir Claude paused with a stare. 'Mamma? Why, mamma's at Brussels.'

Maisie, with her eyes on the lady, wondered. 'At Brussels?'

'She's gone to play a match.'

'At billiards? You didn't tell me.'

'Of course I didn't!' Sir Claude ejaculated. 'There's plenty I don't tell you. She went on Wednesday.'

The couple had added to their distance, but Maisie's eyes more than kept pace with them. 'Then she has come back.'

Sir Claude watched the lady. 'It's much more likely she never went!'

'It's mamma!' the child said with decision.

They had stood still, but Sir Claude had made the most of his opportunity, and it happened that just at this moment, at the end of the vista, the others halted and, still showing only their backs, seemed to stay talking. 'Right you are, my duck!' he exclaimed at last. 'It's my own sweet wife!'

He had spoken with a laugh, but he had changed colour, and Maisie quickly looked away from him. 'Then who is it with her?'

'Blest if I know!' said Sir Claude.

'Is it Mr. Perriam?'

'Oh dear no – Perriam's smashed.'

'Smashed?'

'Exposed, in the City. But there are quantities of others!' Sir Claude smiled.

Maisie appeared to count them; she studied the gentleman's back. 'Then is this Lord Eric?'

For a moment her companion made no answer, and when she turned her eyes again to him he was looking at her, she thought, rather queerly. 'What do you know about Lord Eric?'

She tried innocently to be odd in return. 'Oh, I know more than you think! Is it Lord Eric?' she repeated.

'It may be. Blest if I care!'

Their friends had slightly separated and now, as Sir Claude spoke, suddenly faced round, showing all the splendour of her ladyship and all the mystery of her comrade. Maisie held her breath. 'They're coming!'

'Let them come.' And Sir Claude, pulling out his cigarettes, began to strike a light.

'We shall meet them!'

'No; they'll meet *us*.'

Maisie stood her ground. 'They see us. Just look.'

Sir Claude threw away his match. 'Come straight on.' The others, in the return, evidently startled, had half paused again, keeping well apart. 'She's horribly surprised and she wants to slope,' he continued. 'But it's too late.'

Maisie advanced beside him, making out even across the interval that her ladyship was ill at ease. 'Then what will she do?'

Sir Claude puffed his cigarette. 'She's quickly thinking.' He appeared to enjoy it.

Ida had faltered but an instant; her companion clearly gave her moral support. Maisie thought he somehow looked brave, and he had no likeness whatever to Mr. Perriam. His face, thin and rather sharp, was smooth, and it was not till they came nearer that she saw he had a remarkably fair little moustache. She could already see that his eyes were of the lightest blue. He was far nicer than Mr. Perriam. Mamma looked terrible from afar, but even under her guns the child's curiosity flickered and she appealed again to Sir Claude. 'Is it – *is* it Lord Eric?'

Sir Claude smoked composedly enough. 'I think it's the Count.'

This was a happy solution – it fitted her idea of a count. But what idea, as she now came grandly on, did mamma fit? – unless that of an actress, in some tremendous situation, sweeping down to the footlights as if she would jump them. Maisie felt really frightened and before she knew it had passed her hand into Sir Claude's arm. Her pressure caused him to stop, and at the sight of this the other couple came equally to a stand and, beyond the diminished space, remained a moment more in talk. This, however, was the matter of an instant; leaving the Count apparently to come round more circuitously – an out-flanking movement, if Maisie had but known – her ladyship resumed the onset. 'What *will* she do now?' her daughter asked.

Sir Claude was at present in a position to say: 'Try to pretend it's me.'

'You?'

'Why, that I'm up to something.'

In another minute poor Ida had justified this prediction, erect there before them like a figure of justice in full dress. There were parts of her face that grew whiter while Maisie looked, and other parts in which this change seemed to make other colours reign with more intensity. 'What are you doing with my daughter?' she demanded of her husband; in spite of the indignant tone of which Maisie had a greater sense than ever in her life before of not being personally noticed. It seemed to her that Sir Claude also grew pale as an effect of the loud defiance with which Ida twice repeated this question. He put her, instead of answering it, an inquiry of his own: 'Who the devil have you got hold of *now*?' and at this her ladyship turned tremendously to the child, glaring at her as if she were an equal plotter of sin. Maisie received in petrifaction the full force of her mother's huge painted eyes – they were like Japanese lanterns swung under festive arches. But life came back to her from a tone suddenly and strangely softened. 'Go straight to that gentleman, my dear; I have asked him to take you a few minutes. He's charming – go. I've something to say to *this* creature.'

Maisie felt Sir Claude immediately clutch her. 'No, no – thank you; that won't do. She's mine.'

'Yours?' It was confounding to Maisie to hear her speak quite as if she had never heard of Sir Claude before.

'Mine. You've given her up. You've not another word to say about her. I have her from her father,' said Sir Claude – a statement that astonished his companion, who could also measure its lively action on her mother.

There was visibly, however, an influence that made Ida consider; she glanced at the gentleman she had left, who, having strolled with his hands in his pockets to some distance, stood there with unembarrassed vagueness. With her great hard eyes on him for a moment she smiled; then she looked again at Sir Claude. 'I've given her up to her father to *keep* – not to get rid of by sending about the town either with you or any one else. If she's not to mind me, let *him* come and tell me so. I decline to take it from another person, and you're a fool to pretend that with your hypocritical meddling you've a leg to stand on. I know your game, and I've something now to say to you about it.'

Sir Claude gave a squeeze of the child's arm. 'Didn't I tell you she would have, Miss Farange?'

'You're uncommonly afraid to hear it,' Ida went on; 'but if you think she'll protect you from it you're mightily mistaken.' She gave him a moment. 'I'll give her the benefit as soon as look at you. Should you like her to know, my dear?' Maisie had a sense of her launching this inquiry at him with effect; yet our young lady was also conscious of hoping that Sir Claude would reply in the affirmative. We have already learned that she had come to like people's liking her to 'know'. Before he could reply at all, none the less, her mother opened a pair of arms of extraordinary elegance, and then she felt the loosening of his grasp. 'My own child,' Ida murmured in a voice – a voice of sudden confused tenderness – that it seemed to her she heard for the first time. She wavered but an instant, thrilled with the first direct appeal, as distinguished from the mere maternal pull, she had ever had from lips that, even in the old vociferous years, had always been sharp. The next moment she was on her mother's breast, where, amid a wilderness of trinkets, she felt as if she had suddenly been thrust into a jeweller's shop-front, but only to be as suddenly ejected with a push and the brisk injunction: 'Now go to the Captain!'

Maisie glanced at the gentleman submissively, but felt the want of more introduction. 'The Captain?'

Sir Claude broke into a laugh. 'I told her he was the Count.'

Ida stared; she rose so superior that she was colossal. 'You're too utterly loathsome,' she then declared. 'Be off!' she repeated to her daughter.

Maisie started, moved backward and, looking at Sir Claude, 'Only for a moment,' pleaded to him in her bewilderment.

But he was too angry to heed her – too angry with his wife; as she turned away she heard his anger break out. 'You damned old b——!' – she couldn't quite hear all. It was enough, it was too much: she fled before it, rushing even to a stranger in the terror of such a change of tone.

XVI

As she met the Captain's light blue eyes the greatest marvel occurred; she felt a sudden relief at finding them reply with anxiety to the horror in her face. 'What in the world has he done?' He put it all on Sir Claude.

'He has called her a damned old brute.' She couldn't help bringing that out.

The Captain, at the same elevation as her ladyship, gaped wide; then of course, like every one else, he was convulsed. But he instantly caught himself up, echoing her bad words. 'A damned old brute – your mother?'

Maisie had already her second movement. 'I think she tried to make him angry.'

The Captain's stupefaction was fine. 'Angry – *she*? Why, she's an angel!'

On the spot, as he said this, his face won her over; it was so bright and kind, and his blue eyes had such a reflection of some mysterious grace that, for him at least, her mother had put forth. Her fund of observation enabled her as she gazed up at him to place him: he was a candid, simple soldier; very brave – she came back to that – but at the same time very soft. At any rate he struck a note that was new to her and that after a moment made her say: 'Do you like her very much?'

He smiled down at her, hesitating, looking pleasanter and pleasanter. 'Let me tell you about your mother.'

He put out a big military hand which she immediately took, and they turned off together to where a couple of chairs had been placed under one of the trees. 'She told me to come to you,' Maisie explained as they went; and presently she was close to him in one of the chairs, with the prettiest of pictures – the sheen of the lake through other trees – before them, and the sound of birds, the plash of boats, the play of children in the air. The Captain, inclining his military person, sat sideways to be closer and kinder, and as her hand was on the arm of her seat he put his own down on it again to emphasize something he had to say that would be good for her to hear. He had already told her how her mother, from the moment of seeing her so unexpectedly with a person who was – well, not at all the right person, had promptly asked him to take charge of her while she herself tackled, as she said, the real culprit. He gave the child the sense of doing for the time what he liked with her; ten minutes before she had never seen him, but she could now sit there touching him, impressed by him and thinking it nice when a gentleman was thin and brown – brown with a kind of clear depth that made his straw-coloured moustache almost white and his eyes resemble little pale flowers. The most extraordinary thing was the way she didn't appear just then to mind Sir Claude's being 'tackled'. The Captain wasn't a bit like him, for it was an odd part of the pleasantness of mamma's friend that it resided in a manner in this friend's being ugly. An odder part still was that it finally made our young lady, to classify him further, say to herself that, of all people in the world, he reminded her most insidiously of Mrs. Wix. He had neither straighteners nor a diadem, nor, at least in the same place as the other, a button; he was sun-burnt and deep-voiced and smelt of cigars, yet he marvellously had more in common with her old governess than with her young stepfather. What he had to say to her that was good for her to hear was that her poor mother (didn't she know?) was the best friend he had ever had in his life. And he added: 'She has told me ever so much about you. I'm awfully glad to know you.'

She had never, she thought, been so addressed as a young lady, not even by Sir Claude the day, so long ago, that she found him with Mrs. Beale. It struck her as the way that at balls, by delightful partners, young ladies must be spoken to in the intervals of dances; and she tried to think of something that would meet it at the same high point. But this effort flurried her, and all she could produce was: 'At first, you know, I thought you were Lord Eric.'

The Captain looked vague. 'Lord Eric?'

'And then Sir Claude thought you were the Count.'

At this he laughed out. 'Why he's only five foot high and as red as a lobster!' Maisie laughed in return – the young lady at the ball certainly would – and was on the point, as conscientiously, of pursuing the subject with an agreeable question. But before she could speak her companion challenged her. 'Who in the world is Lord Eric?'

'Don't you know him?' She judged her young lady would say that with light surprise.

'Do you mean a fat man with his mouth always open?' She had to confess that their acquaintance was so limited that she could only describe the bearer of the name as a friend of mamma's; but a light suddenly came to the Captain, who quickly declared that he knew her man. 'What-do-you-call-him's brother, the fellow that owned Bobolink?' Then, with all his kindness, he contradicted her flat. 'Oh dear no; your mother never knew *him*.'

'But Mrs. Wix said so,' the child risked.

'Mrs. Wix?'

'My old governess.'

This again seemed amusing to the Captain. 'She mixed him up, your old governess. He's an awful beast. Your mother never looked at him.'

He was as positive as he was friendly, but he dropped for a minute after this into a silence that gave Maisie, confused but ingenious, a chance to redeem the mistake of pretending to know too much by the humility of inviting further correction. 'And doesn't she know the Count?'

'Oh, I daresay! But he's another ass.' After which abruptly, with a different look, he put down again on the back of her own the hand he had momentarily removed. Maisie even thought he coloured a little. 'I want tremendously to speak to you. You must never believe any harm of your mother.'

'Oh, I assure you I *don't*!' cried the child, blushing, herself, up to her eyes in a sudden surge of deprecation of such a thought.

The Captain, bending his head, raised her hand to his lips with a benevolence that made her wish her glove had been nicer. 'Of course you don't when you know how fond she is of *you*.'

'She's fond of me?' Maisie panted.

'Tremendously. But she thinks you don't like her. You *must* like her. She has had too much to bear.'

'Oh yes – I know!' She rejoiced that she had never denied it.

'Of course I've no right to speak of her except as a particular friend,' the Captain went on. 'But she's a splendid woman. She has never had any sort of justice.'

'Hasn't she?' – his companion, to hear the words, felt a thrill altogether new.

'Perhaps I oughtn't to say it to you; but she has had everything to suffer.'

'Oh yes – you can *say* it to me!' Maisie hastened to profess.

The Captain rejoiced. 'Well, you needn't tell. It's all for *you* – do you see?'

Serious and smiling, she only wanted to take it from him. 'It's between you and me! Oh, there are lots of things I've never told!'

'Well, keep this with the rest. I assure you she has had the most infernal time, no matter what any one says to the contrary. She's the cleverest woman I ever saw in all my life. She's too charming.' She had been touched already by his tone, and now she leaned back in her chair and felt something tremble within her. 'She's tremendous fun – she can do all sorts of things better than I've ever seen any one. She has the pluck of fifty – and I know; I assure you I do. She has the nerve for a tiger-shoot – by Jove I'd *take* her! And she's awfully open and generous, don't you know? there are women that are such horrid sneaks. She'll go through anything for any one she likes.' He appeared to watch for a moment the effect on his companion of this emphasis; then he gave a small sigh that mourned the limits of the speakable. But it was almost with the note of a fresh challenge that he wound up: 'Look here, she's *true*!'

Maisie had so little desire to assert the contrary that she found herself, in the intensity of her response, throbbing with a joy still less utterable than the essence of the Captain's admiration. She was fairly hushed with the sense that he spoke of her mother as she had never heard any one speak. It came over her as she sat silent that, after all, this admiration and this respect were quite new words, which took a distinction from the fact that nothing in the least resembling them in quality had on any occasion dropped from the lips of her father, of Mrs. Beale, of Sir Claude, or even of Mrs. Wix. What it appeared to her to come to was that, on the subject of her ladyship, it was the first real kindness she had heard, so that, at the touch of it, something strange and deep and pitying surged up within her – a revelation that, practically and so far as she knew, her mother, apart from this, had only been disliked. Mrs. Wix's original account of Sir Claude's affection seemed as empty now as the chorus in a children's game, and the husband and wife, but a little way off at that moment, were face to face in hatred and with the dreadful name he had called her still in the air. What was it the Captain, on the other hand, had called her? Maisie wanted to hear that again. The tears filled her eyes and rolled down her cheeks, which burned, under them, with the rush of a consciousness that for her too, five minutes before, the vivid, towering beauty whose assault she awaited had been for the moment an object of pure dread. She became on the spot indifferent to her usual fear of showing what in children was notoriously most offensive – presented to her companion, soundlessly but hideously, her wet, distorted face. She cried, with a pang, straight *at* him, cried as she had never cried at any one in all her life. 'Oh, do you love her?' she brought out with a gulp that was the effect of her trying not to make a noise.

It was, doubtless, another consequence of the thick mist through which she saw him that in reply to her question the Captain gave her such a queer blurred look. He stammered; yet in his voice there was also the ring of a great awkward insistence. 'Of course I'm tremendously fond of her – I like her better than any woman I ever saw. I don't mind in the least telling you that,' he went on, 'and I should think myself a great beast if I did.' Then to show that his position was superlatively clear he made her, with a kindness that even Sir Claude had never surpassed, tremble

again as she had trembled at his first outbreak. He called her by
her name, and her name drove it home. 'My dear Maisie, your
mother's an angel!'

It was an almost incredible balm – it soothed so her impression of danger and pain. She sank back in her chair; she covered
her face with her hands. 'Oh, mother, mother, mother!' she
sobbed. She had an impression that the Captain, beside her, if
more and more friendly, was by no means unembarrassed; in a
minute, however, when her eyes were clearer, he was erect in
front of her, very red and nervously looking about him and
whacking his leg with his stick. 'Say you love her, Mr. Captain;
say it, say it!' she implored.

Mr. Captain's blue eyes fixed themselves very hard. 'Of
course I love her, damn it, you know!'

At this she also jumped up; she had fished out somehow her
pocket-handkerchief. 'So do *I* then. I do, I do, I do!' she passionately asseverated.

'Then will you come back to her?'

Maisie, staring, stopped the tight little plug of her hand-
kerchief on the way to her eyes. 'She won't have me.'

'Yes, she will. She wants you.'

'Back at the house – with Sir Claude?'

Again he hung fire. 'No, not with him. In another place.'

They stood looking at each other with an intensity unusual
as between a Captain and a little girl. 'She won't have me in any
place.'

'Oh, yes she will, if *I* ask her!'

Maisie's intensity continued. 'Shall you be there?'

The Captain's, on the whole, did the same. 'Oh yes – some
day.'

'Then you don't mean now?'

He broke into a quick smile. 'Will you come now? – go with
us for an hour?'

Maisie considered. 'She wouldn't have me even now.' She
could see that he had his idea, but that her tone impressed him.
That disappointed her a little, though in an instant he rang out
again.

'She will if I ask her,' he repeated. 'I'll ask her this minute.'

Maisie, turning at this, looked away to where her mother and her stepfather had stopped. At first, among the trees, nobody was visible; but the next moment she exclaimed with expression: 'It's over – here he comes!'

The Captain watched the approach of her ladyship's husband, who lounged composedly over the grass, making to Maisie with his closed fingers a little movement in the air. 'I've no desire to avoid him.'

'Well, you mustn't see him,' said Maisie.

'Oh, he's in no hurry himself!' Sir Claude had stopped to light another cigarette.

She was vague as to the way it was proper he should feel; but she had a sense that the Captain's remark was rather a free reflection on it. 'Oh, he doesn't care!' she replied.

'Doesn't care for what?'

'Doesn't care who you are. He told me so. Go and ask mamma,' she added.

'If you can come with us? Very good. You really want me not to wait for him?'

'*Please* don't.' But Sir Claude was not yet near, and the Captain had with his left hand taken hold of her right, which he familiarly, sociably swung a little. 'Only first,' she continued, 'tell me this. Are you going to *live* with mamma?'

The immemorial note of mirth broke out at her seriousness. 'One of these days.'

She wondered, wholly unperturbed by his laughter. 'Then where will Sir Claude be?'

'He'll have left her of course.'

'Does he really intend to do that?'

'You have every opportunity to ask him.'

Maisie shook her head with decision. 'He won't do it. Not first.'

Her 'first' made the Captain laugh out again. 'Oh, he'll be sure to be nasty! But I've said too much to you.'

'Well, you know, I'll never tell,' said Maisie.

'No, it's all for yourself. Good-bye.'

'Good-bye.' Maisie kept his hand long enough to add: 'I like you too.' And then supremely: 'You *do* love her?'

'My dear child——!' The Captain wanted words.

'Then don't do it only for just a little.'

'A little?'

'Like all the others.'

'All the others?' – he stood staring.

She pulled away her hand. 'Do it always!' She bounded to meet Sir Claude, and as she left the Captain she heard him ring out with apparent gaiety:

'Oh, I'll keep it up!'

As she joined Sir Claude she perceived her mother, in the distance, move slowly off; and, glancing again at the Captain, saw him, swinging his stick, retreat in the same direction.

She had never seen Sir Claude look as he looked just then; flushed yet not excited – settled rather in an immovable disgust and at once very sick and very hard. His conversation with her mother had clearly drawn blood, and the child's old horror came back to her, begetting the instant moral contraction of the days when her parents had looked to her to feed their love of battle. Her greatest fear for the moment, however, was that her friend would see she had been crying. The next she became aware that he glanced at her, and it presently occurred to her that he didn't even wish to be looked at. At this she quickly removed her gaze, while he said rather curtly: 'Well, who in the world *is* the fellow?'

She felt herself flooded with prudence. 'Oh, *I* haven't found out!' This sounded as if she meant he ought to have done so himself; but she could only face doggedly the ugliness of seeming disagreeable, as she used to face it in the hours when her father, for her blankness, called her a dirty little donkey, and her mother, for her falsity, pushed her out of the room.

'Then what have you been doing all this time?'

'Oh, I don't know!' It was of the essence of her method not to be silly by halves.

'Then didn't the beast say anything?' They had got down by the lake and were walking fast.

'Well, not very much.'

'He didn't speak of your mother?'

'Oh yes, a little!'

'Then, what I ask you, please, is *how*?' She was silent a minute – so long that he presently went on: 'I say, you know – don't you hear me?'

At this she produced: 'Well, I'm afraid I didn't attend to him very much.'

Sir Claude, smoking rather hard, made no immediate rejoinder; but finally he exclaimed: 'Then, my dear, you were the perfection of an idiot!' He was so irritated – or she took him to be – that for the rest of the time they were in the Gardens he spoke no other word; and she meanwhile subtly abstained from any attempt to pacify him. That would only lead to more questions. At the gate of the Gardens he hailed a four-wheeled cab and, in silence, without meeting her eyes, put her into it, only saying 'Give him *that*' as he tossed half a crown upon the seat. Even when from outside he had closed the door and told the man where to go he never took her departing look. Nothing of this kind had ever yet happened to them, but it had no power to make her love him less, and she could not only bear it, she felt as she drove away that she could rejoice in it. It brought again the sweet sense of success that, ages before, she had had on an occasion when, on the stairs, returning from her father's, she had met a fierce question of her mother's with an imbecility as deep and had in consequence been dashed by Mrs. Farange almost to the bottom.

XVII

If for reasons of her own she could bear the sense of Sir Claude's displeasure her young endurance might have been put to a serious test. The days went by without his knocking at her father's door, and the time would have turned to dreariness if something had not conspicuously happened to give it a new difference. What took place was a marked change in the attitude of Mrs. Beale – a change that somehow, even in his absence, seemed to bring Sir Claude again into the house. It began practically with a conversation that occurred between them the day Maisie came home alone in the cab. Mrs. Beale had by that time returned, and she was more successful than their friend in extracting from our young lady an account of the extraordinary passage with the Captain. She came back to it repeatedly, and on the very next day it grew distinct to Maisie that she was already in full possession of what at the same moment had been enacted between her ladyship and Sir Claude. This was the real origin of her final perception that though he didn't come to the house her stepmother had some rare secret for not being deprived of him. That produced eventually a strange, a deeper communion with Mrs. Beale, the first sign of which had been – not on Maisie's part – a wonderful outbreak of tears. Mrs. Beale was not, as she herself said, a crying creature: she had not cried, to Maisie's knowledge, since the lowly governess days, the grey dawn of their connection. But she wept now with passion, professing loudly that it did her good and saying remarkable things to the child, for whom the occasion was an equal benefit, an addition to all the fine reasons stored up for not making anything worse. It hadn't somehow made anything worse, Maisie felt, for her to have told Mrs. Beale what she had not told Sir Claude, inasmuch as the greatest strain, to her sense, was between Sir Claude and Sir Claude's wife, and his wife was just what Mrs. Beale was unfortunately not. He sent his stepdaughter three days after the incident in Kensington Gardens a message as frank as it was tender, and that was how Mrs. Beale had had to bring out in a manner that seemed half an appeal, half a defiance: 'Well, yes, hang it – I *do* see him!'

How and when and where, however, were just what Maisie was not to know – an exclusion moreover that she never questioned in the light of a participation large enough to make him, in hours of solitude with Mrs. Beale, present like a picture on the wall. As far as her father was concerned such hours had no interruption; and then it was clear between them that they were each thinking of the absent and each thinking that the other thought, so that he was an object of conscious reference in everything they said or did. The wretched truth, Mrs. Beale had to confess, was that she had hoped against hope and that in the Regent's Park it was impossible Sir Claude should really be in and out. Hadn't they at last to look the fact in the face? – it was too disgustingly evident that no one after all had been squared. Well, if no one had been squared it was because every one had been vile. No one and every one were of course Beale and Ida, the extent of whose power to be nasty was a thing that, to a little girl, Mrs. Beale simply couldn't communicate. Therefore it was that to keep going at all, as she said, that lady had to make, as she also said, another arrangement – the arrangement in which Maisie was included only to the point of knowing that it existed and wondering wistfully what it was. Conspicuously at any rate it had a side that was responsible for Mrs. Beale's sudden emotion and sudden confidence – a demonstration, however, of which the tearfulness was far from deterrent to our heroine's thought of how happy she should be if she could only make an arrangement for herself. Mrs. Beale's own operated, it appeared, with regularity and frequency; for it was almost every day or two that she was able to bring Maisie a message and to take one back. It had been over the vision of what, as she called it, he did for her that she broke down; and this vision was kept in a manner before Maisie by a subsequent increase not only of the gaiety, but literally – it seemed not presumptuous to perceive – of the actual virtue of her friend. The friend was herself the first to proclaim it: he had pulled her up immensely – he had quite pulled her round. She had charming, tormenting words about him: he was her good fairy, her hidden spring – above all he was just her conscience. That was what had particularly come out with her startling tears: he had made her, dear man, think ever so much better of herself. It had been thus rather surprisingly revealed that she had been in a way to think ill, and Maisie was glad to hear of the corrective at the same time that she heard of the ailment.

She presently found herself supposing and in spite of her envy even hoping that whenever Mrs. Beale was out of the house Sir Claude had in some manner the satisfaction of it. This was now of more frequent occurrence than ever before – so much so that she would have thought of her stepmother as almost extravagantly absent had it not been that, in the first place, her father was a superior specimen of that habit: it was the frequent remark of his present wife, as it had been, before the tribunals of their country, a prominent plea of her predecessor, that he scarce came home even to sleep. In the second place Mrs. Beale, when she *was* on the spot, had now a beautiful air of longing to make up for everything. The only shadow in such bright intervals was that, as Maisie put it to herself, she could get nothing by questions. It was in the nature of things to be none of a small child's business, even when a small child had from the first been deluded into a fear that she might be only too much initiated. Things then were in Maisie's experience so true to their nature that questions were almost always improper; but she learned on the other hand soon to recognize that patient little silences and intelligent little looks could be rewarded from time to time by delightful little glimpses. There had been years at Beale Farange's when the monosyllable 'he' meant always, meant almost violently the master; but all that was changed at a period at which Sir Claude's merits were of themselves so much in the air that it scarce took even two letters to name him. 'He keeps me up splendidly – he does, my own precious,' Mrs. Beale would observe to her comrade; or else she would say that the situation at the other establishment had reached a point that could scarcely be believed – the point, monstrous as it sounded, of his not having laid eyes upon her for twelve days. 'She' of course at Beale Farange's had never meant any one but Ida, and there was the difference in this case that it now meant Ida with renewed intensity. Mrs. Beale was in a position strikingly to animadvert more and more upon her dreadfulness, the moral of all which appeared to be how abominably yet blessedly little she had to do with her husband. This flow of information came home to our two friends because, truly, Mrs. Beale had not much more to do with her own; but that was one of the reflections that Maisie could make without allowing it to break the spell of her present sympathy. How could such a spell be anything but deep when Sir Claude's influence, though operating from afar, at last really determined the resumption of his stepdaughter's studies? Mrs. Beale again took fire about them and was quite vivid, for Maisie, as to their being the great matter to which the dear absent one kept her up.

This was the second source – I have just alluded to the first – of the child's consciousness of something that, very hopefully, she described to herself as a new phase; and it also presented in the brightest light the fresh enthusiasm with which Mrs. Beale always reappeared and which really gave Maisie a happier sense than she had yet had of being very dear at least to two persons. That she had small remembrance at present of a third illustrates, I am afraid, a temporary oblivion of Mrs. Wix, an accident to be explained only by a state of unnatural excitement. For what was the form taken by Mrs. Beale's enthusiasm and acquiring relief in the domestic conditions still left to her but the delightful form of 'reading' with her little charge on lines directly prescribed and in works profusely supplied by Sir Claude? He had got hold of an awfully good list – 'mostly essays, don't you know?' Mrs. Beale had said; a word always august to Maisie, but henceforth to be softened by hazy, in fact by quite languorous edges. There was at any rate a week in which no less than nine volumes arrived, and the impression was to be gathered from Mrs. Beale that the obscure intercourse she enjoyed with Sir Claude not only involved an account and a criticism of studies, but was organized almost for the very purpose of report and consultation. It was for Maisie's education in short that, as she often repeated, she closed her door – closed it to the gentlemen who used to flock there in such numbers and whom her husband's practical desertion of her would have made it a course of the highest indelicacy to receive. Maisie was familiar from of old with the principle at least of the care that a woman, as Mrs. Beale phrased it, attractive and exposed must take of her 'character', and was duly impressed with the rigour of her stepmother's scruples. There was literally no one of the other sex whom she seemed to feel at liberty to see at home, and when the child risked an inquiry about the ladies who, one by one, during her own previous period, had been made quite loudly welcome, Mrs. Beale hastened to inform her that, one by one, they had, the fiends, been found out, after all, to be awful. If she wished to know more about them she was recommended to approach her father.

Maisie had, however, at the very moment of this injunction much livelier curiosities, for the dream of lectures at an institution had at last become a reality, thanks to Sir Claude's now unbounded energy in discovering what could be done. It stood out in this connection that when you came to look into things in a spirit of earnestness an immense deal could be done for very little more than your fare in the Underground. The institution – there was a splendid one in a part of the town but little known to the child – became, in the glow of such a spirit, a thrilling place, and the walk to it from the station through Glower Street – a pronunciation for which Mrs. Beale once laughed at her little friend – a pathway literally strewn with 'subjects'. Maisie seemed to herself to pluck them as she passed, though they thickened in the great grey rooms where the fountain of knowledge, in the form usually of a high voice that she took at first to be angry, plashed in the stillness of rows of faces thrust out like empty jugs. 'It *must* do us good – it's all so hideous,' Mrs. Beale had immediately declared, manifesting a purity of resolution that made these occasions quite the most harmonious of all the many on which the pair had pulled together.

Maisie certainly had never, in such an association, felt so uplifted and never above all been so carried off her feet as at the moments of Mrs. Beale's breathlessly re-entering the house and fairly shrieking upstairs to know if they would still be in time for a lecture. Her stepdaughter, all ready from the earliest hours, almost leaped over the banister to respond, and they dashed out together in quest of learning as hard as they often dashed back to release Mrs. Beale for other preoccupations. There had been in short no bustle like it since that last brief flurry when Mrs. Wix, blowing as if she were grooming her, 'made up' for everything previously lost at her father's.

These weeks as well were too few, but they were flooded with a new emotion, a part of which indeed came from the possibility that, through the long telescope of Glower Street, or perhaps between the pillars of the institution – which were what Maisie thought most made it one – they should some day spy Sir Claude. That was what Mrs. Beale, under pressure, had said – doubtless a little impatiently: 'Oh yes, oh yes – some day!' His joining them was clearly far less of a matter of course than was to have been gathered from his original profession of desire to improve, in their company, his own mind; and this sharpened our young lady's guess that since that occasion either something destructive had happened or something desirable hadn't. Mrs. Beale had thrown but a partial light in telling her how it had turned out that nobody had been squared. Maisie wished at any rate that somebody *would* be squared. However, though in every approach to the temple of knowledge she watched in vain for Sir Claude, there was no doubt about the action of his loved image as an incentive and a recompense. When the institution was most on pillars – or, as Mrs. Beale put it, on stilts – when the subject was deepest and the lecture longest and the listeners ugliest, then it was they both felt their patron in the background would be most pleased with them.

One day, abruptly, with a glance at this background, Mrs. Beale said to her companion: 'We'll go to-night to the thingumbob at Earl's Court;' an announcement putting forth its full lustre when she had made known that she referred to the great Exhibition just opened in that quarter, a collection of extraordinary foreign things, in tremendous gardens, with illuminations, bands, elephants, switchbacks and side-shows, as well as crowds of people among whom they might possibly see some one they knew. Maisie flew in the same bound at the neck of her friend and at the name of Sir Claude, on which Mrs. Beale confessed that – well, yes, there was just a chance that he would be able to meet them. He never of course, in his terrible position, knew what might happen from hour to hour; but he hoped to be free and he had given Mrs. Beale the tip. 'Bring her there on the quiet and I'll try to turn up' – this was clear enough on what so many weeks of privation had made of his desire to see the child: it even appeared to represent on his part a yearning as constant as her own. That in turn was just puzzling enough to make Maisie express a bewilderment. She couldn't see, if they were so intensely of the same mind, why the theory on which she had come back to Mrs. Beale – the general reunion, the delightful trio, should have broken down so in fact. Mrs. Beale, furthermore, only gave her more to think about in saying that their disappointment was the result of his having got into his head a kind of idea.

'What kind of idea?'

'Oh, goodness knows!' She spoke with an approach to asperity. 'He's so awfully delicate.'

'Delicate?' – that was ambiguous.

'About what he does, don't you know?' said Mrs. Beale. She fumbled. 'Well, about what *we* do.'

Maisie wondered. 'You and me?'

'Me and *him*, silly!' cried Mrs. Beale with, this time, a real giggle.

'But you don't do any harm – *you* don't,' said Maisie, wondering afresh and intending her emphasis as a decorous allusion to her parents.

'Of course we don't, you angel – that's just the ground *I* take!' her companion exultantly responded. 'He says he doesn't want you mixed up.'

'Mixed up with what?'

'That's exactly what *I* want to know: mixed up with what, and how you are any more mixed——?' But Mrs. Beale paused

without ending her question. She ended after an instant in a
different way. 'All you can say is that it's his fancy.'

The tone of this, in spite of its expressing a resignation, the
fruit of weariness, that dismissed the subject, conveyed so vividly how much such a fancy was not Mrs. Beale's own that our
young lady was led by the mere fact of contact to arrive at a
dim apprehension of the unuttered and the unknown. The relation between her step-parents had then a kind of mysterious
residuum: this was the first time she really had reflected that
except as regards herself it was not a relationship. To each other
it was only what they might have happened to make it, and she
gathered that this, in the event, had been something that led Sir
Claude to keep away from her. Didn't he fear she would be
compromised? The perception of such a scruple endeared him
the more, and it flashed over her that she might simplify everything by showing him how little she made of such a danger.
Hadn't she lived with her eyes on it from her third year? It was
the condition most frequently discussed at the Faranges', where
the word was always in the air and where at the age of five,
amid rounds of applause, she could gabble it off. She knew as
well in short that a person could be compromised as that a
person could be slapped with a hair-brush or left alone in the
dark, and it was equally familiar to her that each of these
ordeals was in general held to have too little effect. But the first
thing was to make absolutely sure of Mrs. Beale. This was done
by saying to her thoughtfully: 'Well, if you don't mind – and
you really don't, do you?'

Mrs. Beale, with a dawn of amusement, considered. 'Mixing
you up? Not a bit. For what does it mean?'

'Whatever it means I don't in the least mind *being* mixed.
Therefore if you don't and I don't,' Maisie concluded, 'don't
you think that when I see him this evening I had better just tell
him we don't and ask him why in the world *he* should?'

XVIII

The child, however, was not destined to enjoy much of Sir Claude at the 'thingumbob', which took for them a very different turn indeed. On the spot Mrs. Beale, with hilarity, had urged her to the course proposed; but later, at the Exhibition, she withdrew this allowance, mentioning as a result of second thoughts that when a man was so sensitive such a communication might only make him worse. It would have been hard indeed for Sir Claude to be 'worse', Maisie felt as, in the gardens and the crowd, when the first dazzle had dropped, she looked for him in vain up and down. They had all their time, the couple, for frugal, wistful wandering: they had partaken together at home of the light, vague meal – Maisie's name for it was a 'jam-supper' – to which they were reduced when Mr. Farange sought his pleasure abroad. It was abroad now entirely that Mr. Farange cultivated this philosophy, and it was the actual impression of his daughter, derived from his wife, that he had three days before joined a friend's yacht at Cowes.

The place was full of side-shows, to which Mrs. Beale could introduce the little girl only, alas, by revealing to her so attractive, so enthralling a name: the side-shows, each time, were sixpence apiece, and the fond allegiance enjoyed by the elder of our pair had been established from the earliest time in spite of a paucity of sixpences. Small coin dropped from her as half-heartedly as answers from bad children to lessons that had not been looked at. Maisie passed more slowly the great painted posters, pressing with a linked arm closer to her friend's pocket, where she hoped for the audible chink of a shilling. But the upshot of this was but to deepen her yearning: if Sir Claude would only at last come the shillings would begin to ring. The companions paused, for want of one, before the Flowers of the Forest, a large presentment of bright brown ladies – they were brown all over – in a medium suggestive of tropical luxuriance, and there Maisie dolorously expressed her belief that he would never come at all. Mrs. Beale hereupon, though discernibly disappointed, reminded her that he had not been promised as a certainty – a remark that caused the child to gaze at the Flowers of the Forest through a blur in which they became more magnificent, yet oddly more confused, and by which moreover confusion was imparted to the aspect of a gentleman who at that moment, in the company of a lady, came out of the brilliant booth. The lady was so brown that Maisie at first took her for one of the Flowers; but during the few seconds that this required – a few seconds in which she had also desolately given up Sir Claude – she heard Mrs. Beale's voice, behind her, gather both wonder and pain into a single sharp little cry.

'Of all the wickedness – *Beale*!'

He had already, without distinguishing them in the mass of strollers, turned another way – it seemed at the brown lady's suggestion. Her course was marked, over heads and shoulders, by an upright scarlet plume, as to the ownership of which Maisie was instantly eager. 'Who is she? – who is she?'

But Mrs. Beale for a moment only looked after them. 'The liar – the liar!'

Maisie considered. 'Because he's not – where one thought?' That was also, a month ago in Kensington Gardens, where her mother had not been. 'Perhaps he has come back,' she insinuated.

'He never went – the hound!'

That, according to Sir Claude, had been also what her mother had not done, and Maisie could only have a sense of something that in a maturer mind would be called the way history repeats itself. 'Who *is* she?' she asked again.

Mrs. Beale, fixed to the spot, seemed lost in the vision of an opportunity missed. 'If he had only seen me!' – it came from between her teeth. 'She's a brand-new one. But he must have been with her since Tuesday.'

Maisie took it in. 'She's almost black,' she then observed.

'They're always hideous,' said Mrs. Beale.

This was a remark on which the child had again to reflect. 'Oh, not his *wives*!' she remonstrantly exclaimed. The words at another moment would probably have set her friend off, but Mrs. Beale was now too intent in seeing what became of the others. 'Did you ever in your life see such a feather?' Maisie presently continued.

This decoration appeared to have paused at some distance, and in spite of intervening groups they could both look at it. 'Oh, that's the way they dress – the vulgarest of the vulgar!'

'They're coming back – they'll see us!' Maisie the next moment asserted; and while her companion answered that this was exactly what she wanted and the child returned 'Here they are – here they are!' the unconscious objects of so much attention, with a change of mind about their direction, quickly retraced their steps and precipitated themselves upon their critics. Their unconsciousness gave Mrs. Beale time to leap, under her breath, to a recognition which Maisie caught.

'It must be Mrs. Cuddon!'

Maisie looked at Mrs. Cuddon hard – her lips even echoed the name. What followed was extraordinarily rapid – a minute of livelier battle than had ever yet, in so short a span at least, been waged round our heroine. The muffled shock – lest people should notice – was so violent that it was only for her later thought the steps fell into their order, the steps through which, in a bewilderment not so much of sound as of silence, she had come to find herself, too soon for comprehension and too strangely for fear, at the door of the Exhibition with her father. He thrust her into a hansom and got in after her, and then it was – as she drove along with him – that she recovered a little what had happened. Face to face with them in the gardens he had seen them, and there had been a moment of checked concussion during which, in a glare of black eyes and a toss of red plumage, Mrs. Cuddon had recognized them, ejaculated and vanished. There had been another moment at which she became aware of Sir Claude, also poised there in surprise, but out of her father's view, as if he had been warned off at the very

moment of reaching them. It fell into its place with all the rest
that she had heard Mrs. Beale say to her father, but whether
low or loud was now lost to her, something about his having
this time a new one; on which he had growled something indistinct, but apparently in the tone and of the sort that the child,
from her earliest years, had associated with hearing somebody
retort to somebody that somebody was 'another'. 'Oh, I stick to
the old!' Mrs. Beale had exclaimed at this; and her accent, even
as the cab got away, was still in the air, for Maisie's companion
had spoken no other word from the moment of whisking her
off – none at least save the indistinguishable address which,
over the top of the hansom and poised on the step, he had given
the driver. Reconstructing these things later, Maisie believed
that she at this point would have put a question to him had not
the silence into which he charmed her or scared her – she could
scarcely tell which – come from his suddenly making her feel
his arm about her, feel, as he drew her close, that he was agitated in a way he had never yet shown her. It seemed to her that
he trembled, trembled too much to speak, and this had the
effect of making her, with an emotion which, though it had
begun to throb in an instant, was by no means all dread, con-
form to his portentous hush. The act of possession that his
pressure in a manner advertised came back to her after the
longest of the long intermissions that had ever let anything
come back. They drove and drove, and he kept her close; she
stared straight before her, holding her breath, watching one
dark street succeed another and strangely conscious that what
it all meant was somehow that papa was less to be left out of
everything than she had supposed. It took her but a minute to
surrender to this discovery, which, in the form of his present
embrace, suggested a fresh kind of importance in him and with
that a confused confidence. She neither knew exactly what he
had done nor what he was doing; she could only be rather
impressed and a little proud, vibrate with the sense that he had
jumped up to do something and that she had as quickly become
a part of it. It was a part of it too that here they were at a house
that seemed not large, but in the fresh white front of which the
street-lamp showed a smartness of flower-boxes. The child had

been in thousands of stories – all Mrs. Wix's and her own, to say nothing of the richest romances of French Elise – but she had never been in such a story as this. By the time he had helped her out of the cab, which drove away, and she heard in the door of the house the prompt little click of his key, the Arabian Nights had quite closed round her.

From this minute they were in everything, particularly in such an instant 'Open Sesame' and in the departure of the cab, a rattling void filled with relinquished step-parents; they were, with the vividness, the almost blinding whiteness of the light that sprang responsive to papa's quick touch of a little brass knob on the wall, in a place that, at the top of a short, soft staircase, struck her as the most beautiful she had ever seen in her life. The next thing she perceived it to be was the drawing-room of a lady – oh, of a lady, she could see in a moment, and not of a gentleman, not even of one like papa himself or even like Sir Claude – whose things were as much prettier than mamma's as it had always had to be confessed that mamma's were prettier than Mrs. Beale's. In the middle of the small bright room and the presence of more curtains and cushions, more pictures and mirrors, more palm-trees drooping over brocaded and gilded nooks, more little silver boxes scattered over little crooked tables and little oval miniatures hooked upon velvet screens than Mrs. Beale and her ladyship together could, in an unnatural alliance, have dreamed of mustering, the child became aware, with a swift possibility of compassion, of something that was strangely like a relegation to obscurity of each of those women of taste. It was a stranger operation still that her father should on the spot be presented to her as quite advantageously and even grandly at home in the dazzling scene and himself by so much the more separated from scenes inferior to it. She spent with him in it, while explanations continued to hang back, twenty minutes that, in their sudden drop of danger, affected her, though there were neither buns nor ginger-beer, like an extemporized expensive treat.

'Is she very rich?' He had begun to strike her as almost embarrassed, so shy that he might have found himself with a young lady with whom he had little in common. She was literally moved by this apprehension to offer him some tactful relief.

Beale Farange stood and smiled at his young lady, his back to the fanciful fireplace, his light overcoat – the very lightest in London – wide open, and his wonderful lustrous beard completely concealing the expanse of his shirt-front. It pleased her more than ever to think that papa was handsome and, though as high aloft as mamma and almost, in his specially florid evening-dress, as splendid, of a beauty somehow less belligerent, less terrible. 'The Countess? Why do you ask me that?'

Maisie's eyes opened wider. 'Is she a Countess?'

There was an unaccustomed geniality in his enjoyment of her wonder. 'Oh yes, my dear, but it isn't an English title.'

Maisie's manner appreciated this. 'Is it a French one?'

'No, nor French either. It's American.'

Maisie conversed agreeably. 'Ah then of course she must be rich.' She took in such a combination of nationality and rank. 'I never saw anything so lovely.'

'Did you have a sight of her?' Beale asked.

'At the Exhibition?' Maisie smiled. 'She was gone too quick.'

Her father laughed. 'She did slope!' She was for a moment afraid he would say something about Mrs. Beale and Sir Claude: his unexpected gentleness was too mystifying. All he risked was, the next minute: 'She has a horror of vulgar scenes.'

This was something Maisie needn't take up; she could still continue bland. 'But where do you suppose she went?'

'Oh, I thought she'd have taken a cab and have been here by this time. But she'll turn up all right.'

'I'm sure I *hope* she will,' Maisie said; she spoke with an earnestness begotten of the impression of all the beauty around her, to which, in person, the Countess might make further contribution. 'We came awfully fast,' she added.

Her father again laughed loud. 'Yes, my dear, I made you step out!' Beale hesitated; then he pursued: 'I want her to see you.'

Maisie, at this, rejoiced in the attention that, for their evening out, Mrs. Beale, even to the extent of personally 'doing up' her old hat, had given her appearance. Meanwhile her father went on. 'You'll like her awfully.'

'Oh, I'm sure I shall!' After which, either from the effect of having said so much or from that of a sudden glimpse of the impossibility of saying more, she felt an embarrassment and sought refuge in a minor branch of the subject. 'I thought she was Mrs. Cuddon.'

Beale's gaiety rather increased than diminished. 'You mean my wife did? My dear child, my wife's a damned fool!' He had the oddest air of speaking of his wife as of a person whom she might scarcely have known, so that the refuge of her scruple didn't prove particularly happy. Beale on the other hand appeared after an instant himself to feel a scruple. 'What I mean is, to speak seriously, that she doesn't really know anything about anything.' He paused, following the child's charmed eyes and tentative step or two as they brought her nearer to the pretty things on one of the tables. 'She thinks she has good things, don't you know!' He quite jeered at Mrs. Beale's delusion.

Maisie felt she must confess that it was one; everything she had missed at the side-shows was made up to her by the Countess's luxuries. 'Yes,' she considered; 'she does think that.'

There was again a dryness in the way Beale replied that it didn't matter what she thought; but there was an increasing sweetness for his daughter in being with him so long without his doing anything worse. The whole hour of course was to remain with her for days and weeks, ineffaceably illumined and confirmed; by the end of which she was able to read into it a hundred things that were at the moment mere miraculous pleasantness. What they then and there came to was simply that her companion was still excited, yet wished not to show it, and that just in proportion as he succeeded in this attempt he was able to encourage her to regard him as kind. He moved about the room after a little, showed her things, spoke to her as a person of taste, told her the name, which she remembered, of the famous French lady represented in one of the miniatures, and remarked, as if he had caught her wistful over a trinket or a trailing stuff, that he made no doubt the Countess, on coming in, would give her something jolly. He spied a pink satin box with a looking-glass let into the cover, which he raised, with a quick, facetious flourish, to offer her the privilege of six rows of chocolate bonbons, cutting out thereby Sir Claude, who had never gone beyond four rows. 'I can do what I like with these,' he said, 'for I don't mind telling you I gave 'em to her myself.' The Countess had evidently appreciated the gift; there were numerous gaps, a ravage now quite unchecked, in the array. Even while they waited together Maisie had her sense, which was the mark of what their separation had become, of her having grown for him, since the last time he had, as it were, noticed her, and by increase of years and of inches if by nothing else, much more of a little person to reckon with. Yes, that was a part of the positive awkwardness that he carried off by being almost foolishly tender. There was a passage during which, on a yellow silk sofa under one of the palms, he had her on his knee, stroking her hair, playfully holding her off while he showed his shining fangs and let her, with a vague, affectionate, helpless, pointless 'Dear old girl, dear little daughter', inhale the fragrance of his cherished beard. She must have been sorry for him, she afterwards knew, so well could she privately follow his difficulty in being specific to her about anything. She had such possibilities of vibration, of response, that it needed nothing more than this to make up to her in fact for omissions. The tears came into her eyes again as they had done when in the Park that day the Captain told her so excitingly that her mother was good. What was this but exciting too – this still directer goodness of her father and this unexampled shining solitude with him, out of which everything had dropped but that he was papa and that he was magnificent? It didn't spoil it that she finally felt he must have, as he became restless, some purpose he didn't quite see his way to bring out, for in the freshness of their recovered fellowship she would have lent herself gleefully to his suggesting, or even to his pretending, that their relations were easy and graceful. There was something in him that seemed, and quite touchingly, to ask her to help him to pretend – pretend he knew enough about her life and her education, her means of subsistence and her view of himself, to give the questions he couldn't put her a natural domestic tone. She would have pretended with ecstasy if he could only have given her the cue.

She waited for it while, between his big teeth, he breathed the sighs she didn't know to be stupid. And as if he had drawn – rather red with the confusion of it – the pledge of her preparation from her tears, he floundered about, wondering what the devil he could lay hold of.

XIX

When he had lighted a cigarette and begun to smoke in her face it was as if he had struck with the match the note of some queer, clumsy ferment of old professions, old scandals, old duties, a dim perception of what he possessed in her and what, if everything had only – damn it! – been totally different, she might still be able to give him. What she was able to give him, however, as his blinking eyes seemed to make out through the smoke, would be simply what he should be able to get from her. To give something, to give here on the spot, was all her own desire. Among the old things that came back was her little instinct of keeping the peace; it made her wonder more sharply what particular thing she could do or not do, what particular word she could speak or not speak, what particular line she could take or not take, that might for every one, even for the Countess, give a better turn to the crisis. She was ready, in this interest, for an immense surrender, a surrender of everything but Sir Claude, of everything but Mrs. Beale. The immensity didn't include *them*; but if he had an idea at the back of his head she had also one in a recess as deep, and for a time, while they sat together, there was an extraordinary mute passage between her vision of this vision of his, his vision of her vision, and her vision of his vision of her vision. What there was no effective record of indeed was the small strange pathos on the child's part of an innocence so saturated with knowledge and so directed to diplomacy. What, further, Beale finally laid hold of while he masked again with his fine presence half the flounces of the fireplace was: 'Do you know, my dear, I shall soon be off to America?' It struck his daughter both as a short cut and as the way he wouldn't have said it to his wife. But his wife figured with a bright superficial assurance in her response.

'Do you mean with Mrs. Beale?'

Her father looked at her hard. 'Don't be a little ass!'

Her silence appeared to represent a concentrated effort not to be. 'Then with the Countess?'

'With her or without her, my dear; that concerns only your poor daddy. She has big interests over there, and she wants me to take a look at them.'

Maisie threw herself into them. 'Will that take very long?'

'Yes; they're in such a muddle – it may take months. Now what I want to hear, you know, is whether you would like to come along?'

Planted once more before him in the middle of the room she felt herself turning white. 'I?' she gasped, yet feeling as soon as she had spoken that such a note of dismay was not altogether pretty. She felt it still more while her father replied, with a shake of his legs, a toss of his cigarette-ash and a fidgety look – he was for ever taking one – all the length of his waistcoat and trousers, that she needn't be quite so disgusted. It helped her in a few seconds to appear more as he would like her that she saw, in the lovely light of the Countess's splendour, exactly, however she appeared, the right answer to make. 'Dear papa, I'll go with you anywhere.'

He turned his back to her and stood with his nose at the glass of the chimneypiece while he brushed specks of ash out of his beard. Then he abruptly said: 'Do you know anything about your brute of a mother?'

It was just of her brute of a mother that the manner of the question in a remarkable degree reminded her: it had the free flight of one of Ida's fine bridgings of space. With the sense of this was kindled for Maisie at the same time an inspiration. 'Oh yes, I know everything!' and she became so radiant that her father, seeing it in the mirror, turned back to her and presently, on the sofa, had her on his knee again and was again particularly stirring. Maisie's inspiration was to the effect that the more she should be able to say about mamma the less she would be called upon to speak of her step-parents. She kept

hoping the Countess would come in before her power to protect them was exhausted; and it was now, in closer quarters
with her companion, that the idea at the back of her head
shifted its place to her lips. She told him she had met her mother
in the Park with a gentleman who, while Sir Claude had strolled
with her ladyship, had been kind and had sat and talked to her;
narrating the scene with a remembrance of her pledge of secrecy
to the Captain quite brushed away by the joy of seeing Beale
listen without profane interposition. It was almost an amazement, but it was indeed all a joy, thus to be able to guess that
papa was at last quite tired of his anger – of his anger at any
rate about mamma. He was only bored with her now. That
made it, however, the more imperative that his spent displeasure shouldn't be blown out again. It charmed the child to see
how much she could interest him; and the charm remained
even when, after asking her a dozen questions, he observed
musingly and a little obscurely: 'Yes, damned if she won't!' For
in this too there was a detachment, a wise weariness that made
her feel safe. She had had to mention Sir Claude, though she
mentioned him as little as possible and Beale only appeared to
look quite over his head. It pieced itself together for her that
this was the mildness of general indifference, a source of profit
so great for herself personally that if the Countess was the
author of it she was prepared literally to hug the Countess. She
betrayed that eagerness by a restless question about her, to
which her father replied:

'Oh, she has a head on her shoulders. I'll back her to get out
of anything!' He looked at Maisie quite as if he would trace the
connection between her inquiry and the impatience of her gratitude. 'Do you mean to say,' he presently went on, 'that you'd
really come with me?'

She felt as if he were now looking at her very hard indeed,
and also as if she had grown ever so much older. 'I'll do anything in the world you ask me, papa.'

He gave again, with a laugh and with his legs apart, his proprietary glance at his waistcoat and trousers. 'That's a way, my
dear, of saying "No, thank you!" You know you don't want to
go the least little mite. You can't humbug *me*!' Beale Farange

laid down. 'I don't want to bully you – I never bullied you in
my life; but I make you the offer, and it's to take or to leave.
Your mother will never again have any more to do with you
than if you were a kitchenmaid she had turned out for going
wrong. Therefore of course I'm your natural protector, and
you've a right to get everything out of me you can. Now's your
chance, you know – you'll be a great fool if you don't. You
can't say I don't put it before you – you can't say I ain't kind to
you or that I don't play fair. Mind you never say that, you
know – it *would* bring me down on you. I know what's proper.
I'll take you again, just as I *have* taken you again and again.
And I'm much obliged to you for making up such a face.'

She was conscious enough that her face indeed couldn't please
him if it showed any sign – just as she hoped it didn't – of her
sharp impression of what he now really wanted to do. Wasn't he
trying to turn the tables on her, embarrass her somehow into
admitting that what would really suit her little book would be,
after doing so much for good manners, to leave her wholly at
liberty to arrange for herself? She began to be nervous again; it
rolled over her that this was their parting, their parting for ever,
and that he had brought her there for so many caresses only
because it was important such an occasion should look better for
him than any other. For her to spoil it by the note of discord
would certainly give him ground for complaint; and the child was
momentarily bewildered between her alternatives of agreeing
with him about her wanting to get rid of him and displeasing him
by pretending to stick to him. So she found for the moment no
solution but to murmur very helplessly: 'Oh papa – oh papa!'

'I know what you're up to – don't tell *me*!' After which he
came straight over and, in the most inconsequent way in the
world, clasped her in his arms a moment and rubbed his beard
against her cheek. Then she understood as well as if he had
spoken it that what he wanted, hang it, was that she should let
him off with all the honours – with all the appearance of virtue
and sacrifice on his side. It was exactly as if he had broken out
to her: 'I say, you little donkey, help me to be irreproachable, to
be noble, and yet to have none of the beastly bore of it. There's
only impropriety enough for one of us; so *you* must take it all.

Repudiate your dear old daddy – in the face, mind you, of his tender supplications. He can't be rough with you – it isn't in his nature: therefore you will have successfully chucked him because he was too generous to be as firm with you, poor man, as was, after all, his duty.' This was what he communicated in a series of tremendous pats on the back; that portion of her person had never been so thumped since Moddle thumped her when she choked. After a moment he gave her the further impression of having become sure enough of her to be able very gracefully to say out: 'You know your mother loathes you, loathes you simply. And I've been thinking over your precious man – the fellow you told me about.'

'Well,' Maisie replied with competence, 'I'm sure of *him*.'

Her father was vague in an instant. 'Do you mean sure of his liking you?'

'Oh no; of his liking *her*!'

Beale had a return of gaiety. 'There's no accounting for tastes! It's what they all say, you know.'

'I don't care – I'm sure of him!' Maisie repeated.

'Sure, you mean, that she'll bolt?'

Maisie knew all about bolting, but, decidedly, she *was* older, and there was something in her that could wince at the way her father made the word boom out. It prompted her to amend his allusion, which she did by returning: 'I don't know what she'll do. But she'll be happy.'

'Let us hope so,' said Beale with bright, unusual mildness. 'The more happy she is at any rate the less she'll want you about. That's why I press you,' he agreeably pursued, 'to consider this handsome offer – I mean seriously, you know – of your sole surviving parent.' Their eyes, at this, met again in a long and extraordinary communion which terminated in his ejaculating: 'Ah, you little scoundrel!' She took it from him in the manner that it seemed to her he would prefer and with a success that encouraged him to go on: 'You *are* a deep little devil!' Her silence, ticking like a watch, acknowledged even this, in confirmation of which he finally brought out: 'You've settled it with the other pair!'

'Well, what if I have?' She sounded to herself most bold.

Her father, quite as in the old days, broke into a peal.

'Why, don't you know they're awful?'

She grew bolder still. 'I don't care – not a bit!'

'But they're probably the worst people in the world and the very greatest criminals,' Beale pleasantly urged. 'I'm not the man, my dear, not to let you know it.'

'Well, it doesn't prevent them from loving me. They love me tremendously.' Maisie turned crimson to hear herself.

Her companion fumbled; almost any one – let alone a daughter – would have seen how conscientious he wanted to be. 'I daresay. But do you know why?' She braved his eyes and he added: 'You're a jolly good pretext.'

'For what?' Maisie asked.

'Why, for their game. I needn't tell you what that is.'

The child reflected. 'Well, then, that's all the more reason.'

'Reason for what, pray?'

'For their being kind to me.'

'And for your keeping in with them?' Beale roared again; it was as if his spirits rose and rose. 'Do you realize, pray, that in saying that you're a monster?'

Maisie turned it over. 'A monster?'

'They've made one of you. Upon my honour it's quite awful. It shows the kind of people they are. Don't you understand,' Beale pursued, 'that when they've made you as horrid as they can – as horrid as themselves – they'll just simply chuck you?'

Maisie, at this, had a flicker of passion. 'They *won't* chuck me!'

'Excuse me,' her father courteously insisted; 'it's my duty to put it before you. I shouldn't forgive myself if I didn't point out to you that they'll cease to require you.' He spoke as if with an appeal to her intelligence that she must be ashamed not adequately to meet, and this gave a real distinction to his superior delicacy.

It had after an instant the illumining effect he intended. 'Cease to require me because they won't care?' She paused with that sketch of her idea.

'Of course Sir Claude won't care if his wife bolts. That's his game. It will suit him down to the ground.'

This was a proposition Maisie could perfectly embrace, but it still left a loophole for triumph. She considered a little. 'You mean if mamma doesn't come back ever at all?' The composure with which her face was presented to that prospect would have shown a spectator the long road she had travelled. 'Well, but that won't put Mrs. Beale——'

'In the same comfortable position——?' Beale took her up with relish; he had sprung to his feet again, shaking his legs and looking at his shoes. 'Right you are, darling! Something more will be wanted for Mrs. Beale.' He hesitated, then he added: 'But she may not have long to wait for it.'

Maisie also for a minute looked at his shoes, though they were not the pair she most admired, the laced yellow 'uppers' and patent-leather complement. At last, with a question, she raised her eyes. 'Are you not coming back?'

Once more he hung fire; after which he gave a small laugh that in the oddest way in the world reminded her of the unique sounds she had heard emitted by Mrs. Wix. 'It may strike you as extraordinary that I should make you such an admission; and in point of fact you're not to understand that I do. But we'll put it that way to help your decision. The point is that that's the way my wife will presently be sure to put it. You'll hear her shrieking that she's deserted, so that she may just pile up her wrongs. She'll be as free as she likes then – as free, you see, as your mother's ass of a husband. They won't have anything more to consider and they'll just put you into the street. Do I understand,' Beale inquired, 'that, in the face of what I press upon you, you still prefer to take the risk of that?' It was the most wonderful appeal any gentleman had ever addressed to his daughter, and it had placed Maisie in the middle of the room again while her father moved slowly about her with his hands in his pockets and something in his step that seemed, more than anything else he had done, to show the habit of the place. She turned her fevered little eyes over his friend's brightnesses, as if, on her own side, to press for some help in a quandary unexampled. As if also the pressure reached him he after an instant stopped short, completing the prodigy of his attitude and the pride of his loyalty by a supreme formulation of the general inducement. 'You have an eye, love! Yes, there's money. No end of money.'

This affected her for a moment like some great flashing dazzle in one of the pantomimes to which Sir Claude had taken her: she saw nothing in it but what it directly conveyed. 'And shall I never, never see you again——?'

'If I do go to America?' Beale brought it out like a man. 'Never, never, never!'

Hereupon, with the utmost absurdity, she broke down; everything gave way, everything but the horror of hearing herself definitely utter such an ugliness as the acceptance of that. So she only stiffened herself and said: 'Then I can't give you up.'

She held him some seconds looking at her, showing her a strained grimace, a perfect parade of all his teeth, in which it seemed to her she could read the disgust he didn't quite like to express at this departure from the pliability she had practically promised. But before she could attenuate in any way the crudity of her collapse he gave an impatient jerk which took him to the window. She heard a vehicle stop; Beale looked out; then he freshly faced her. He still said nothing, but she knew the Countess had come back. There was a silence again between them, but with a different shade of embarrassment from that of their united arrival; and it was still without speaking that, abruptly repeating one of the embraces of which he had already been so prodigal, he whisked her back to the lemon sofa just before the door of the room was thrown open. It was thus in renewed and intimate union with him that she was presented to a person whom she instantly recognized as the brown lady.

The brown lady looked almost as astonished, though not quite as alarmed, as when, at the Exhibition, she had gasped in the face of Mrs. Beale. Maisie in truth almost gasped in her own; this was with the fuller perception that she was brown indeed. She literally struck the child more as an animal than as a 'real' lady; she might have been a clever, frizzled poodle in a frill or a dreadful human monkey in a spangled petticoat. She had a nose that was far too big and eyes that were far too small and a moustache that was, well, not so happy a feature as Sir Claude's. Beale jumped up to her; while, to the child's astonishment, though as if in a quick intensity of thought, the Countess advanced as gaily as if, for many a day, nothing awkward had happened for any one. Maisie, in spite of a large acquaintance with the phenomenon, had never seen it so promptly established that nothing awkward was to be mentioned. The next minute the Countess had kissed her and exclaimed to Beale with bright, tender reproach: 'Why, you never told me *half*! My dear child,' she cried, 'it was awfully nice of you to come!'

'But she hasn't come – she won't come!' Beale answered. 'I've put it to her how much you'd like it, but she declines to have anything to do with us.'

The Countess stood smiling, and after an instant that was mainly taken up with the shock of her weird aspect Maisie felt herself reminded of another smile, which was not ugly, though also interested – the kind light thrown, that day in the Park, from the clean, fair face of the Captain. Papa's Captain – yes – was the Countess; but she wasn't nearly so nice as the other: it all came back, doubtless, to Maisie's minor appreciation of ladies. 'Shouldn't you like me,' said this one endearingly, 'to take you to Spa?'

'To Spa?' The child repeated the name to gain time, not to show how the Countess brought back to her a dim remembrance of a strange woman with a horrid face who once, years before, in an omnibus, bending to her from an opposite seat, had suddenly produced an orange and murmured 'Little dearie, won't you have it?' She had felt then, for some reason, a small, silly terror, though afterwards conscious that her interlocutress, unfortunately hideous, had particularly meant to be kind. This was also what the Countess meant; yet the few words she had uttered and the smile with which she had uttered them immediately cleared everything up. Oh no, she wanted to go nowhere with *her*, for her presence had already, in a few seconds, dissipated the happy impression of the room and put an end to the pride momentarily suggested by Beale's association with so much taste. There was no taste in his association with the short, fat, wheedling, whiskered person who had approached her and in whom she had to recognize the only figure wholly without attraction that had become a party to an intimate connection formed in her immediate circle. She was abashed meanwhile, however, at having appeared to weigh the place to which she

had been invited; and she added as quickly as possible: 'It isn't
to America then?' The Countess, at this, looked sharply at
Beale, and Beale, airily enough, asked what the deuce it mattered when she had already given him to understand that she
wanted to have nothing to do with them. There followed between her companions a passage of which the sense was drowned
for her in the deepening inward hum of her mere desire to get
off; though she was able to guess later on that her father must
have put it to his friend that it was no use talking, that she was
an obstinate little pig and that, besides, she was really old
enough to choose for herself. It glimmered back to her indeed
that she must have failed quite dreadfully to seem responsive
and polite, inasmuch as before she knew it she had visibly given
the impression that if they didn't allow her to go home she
should cry. Oh! if there had ever been a thing to cry about it
was being found in that punishable little attitude toward the
handsomest offers one had ever received. The great pain of the
thing was that she could see the Countess liked her enough to
wish to be liked in return, and it was from the idea of a return
she sought to flee. It was the idea of a return that after a confusion of loud words had arisen between the others brought to
her lips with the tremor preceding disaster: 'Can't I, please, be
sent home in a cab?' Yes, the Countess wanted her and the
Countess was wounded and chilled, and she couldn't help it,
and it was all the more dreadful because it only made the
Countess more seductive and more impossible. The only thing
that sustained either of them perhaps till the cab came – Maisie
presently saw it would come – was its being in the air somehow
that Beale had done what he wanted. He went out to look for
a conveyance; the servants, he said, had gone to bed, but she
shouldn't be kept beyond her time. The Countess left the room
with him, and, alone in the possession of it, Maisie hoped she
wouldn't come back. It was all the effect of her face – the child
simply couldn't look at it and meet its expression half-way. All
in a moment too that queer expression had leaped into the
lovely things – all in a moment she had had to accept her father
as liking some one whom she was sure neither her mother, nor
Mrs. Beale, nor Mrs. Wix, nor Sir Claude, nor the Captain, nor

even Mr. Perriam and Lord Eric could possibly have liked. Three minutes later, downstairs, with the cab at the door, it was perhaps as a final confession of not having much to boast of that, on taking leave of her, he managed to press her to his bosom without her seeing his face. For herself she was so eager to go that their parting reminded her of nothing, not even of a single one of all the 'nevers' that above, as the penalty of not cleaving to him, he had attached to the question of their meeting again. There was something in the Countess that falsified everything, even the great interests in America and yet more the first flush of that superiority to Mrs. Beale and to mamma which had been expressed in silver boxes. These were still there, but perhaps there were no great interests in America. Mamma had known an American who was not a bit like this one. She was not, however, of noble rank; her name was only Mrs. Tucker. Maisie's detachment would all the same have been more complete if she had not suddenly had to exclaim: 'Oh dear, I haven't any money!'

Her father's teeth, at this, were such a picture of appetite without action as to be a match for any plea of poverty. 'Make your stepmother pay.'

'Stepmothers *don't* pay!' cried the Countess. 'No stepmother ever paid in her life!' The next moment they were in the street together, and the next the child was in the cab, with the Countess, on the pavement, but close to her, quickly taking money from a purse whisked out of a pocket. Her father had vanished and there was even yet nothing in that to reawaken the pang of loss. 'Here's money,' said the brown lady: 'go!' The sound was commanding: the cab rattled off. Maisie sat there with her hand full of coin. All that for a cab? As they passed a street lamp she bent to see how much. What she saw was a cluster of sovereigns. There *must* then have been great interests in America. It was still at any rate the Arabian Nights.

XX

The money was far too much even for a fee in a fairy-tale, and in the absence of Mrs. Beale, who, though the hour was now late, had not yet returned to the Regent's Park, Susan Ash, in the hall, as loud as Maisie was low and as bold as she was bland, produced, on the exhibition offered under the dim vigil of the lamp that made the place a contrast to the child's recent scene of light, the half-crown that an unsophisticated cabman could pronounce to be the least he would take. It was apparently long before Mrs. Beale would arrive, and in the interval Maisie had been induced by the prompt Susan not only to go to bed like a darling dear, but, in still richer expression of that character, to devote to the repayment of obligations general as well as particular one of the sovereigns in the fanciful figure that, on the dressing-table upstairs, was naturally not less dazzling to a lone orphan of a housemaid than to the subject of the manœuvres of a quartette. This subject went to sleep with her property under her pillow; but the explanations that on the morrow were inevitably more complete with Mrs. Beale than they had been with her humble friend found a climax in a surrender also more becomingly free. There were explanations indeed that Mrs. Beale had to give as well as to ask, and the most striking of these was to the effect that it was dreadful for a little girl to take money from a woman who was simply the vilest of their sex. The sovereigns were examined with some attention, the result of which, however, was to make Mrs. Beale desire to know what, if one really went into the matter, they could be called but the wages of sin. Her companion went into it merely to the point of inquiring what then they were to do with them; on which Mrs. Beale, who had by this time put them into her pocket, replied with dignity and with her hand on the place: 'We're to send them back on the spot!' Susan, the child soon afterwards learnt, had been invited to contribute to this act of restitution her one appropriated coin; but a closer clutch of the treasure showed in her private assurance to Maisie that there was a limit to the way she could be 'done'. Maisie had been open with Mrs. Beale about the whole of last night's transaction; but she now found herself on the part of their indignant inferior a recipient of remarks that she must feel to be scaring secrets. One of these bore upon the extraordinary hour – it was three in the morning if she really wanted to know – at which Mrs. Beale had re-entered the house; another, in accents as to which Maisie's criticism was still intensely tacit, characterized that lady's appeal as such a 'gime', such a 'shime' as one had never had to put up with; a third treated with some vigour the question of the enormous sums due below stairs, in every department, for gratuitous labour and wasted zeal. Our young lady's consciousness was indeed mainly filled for several days with the apprehension created by the too slow subsidence of her attendant's sense of wrong. These days would be exciting indeed if an outbreak in the kitchen should crown them; and to promote that prospect she had more than one glimpse through Susan's eyes of forces making for an earthquake. To listen to Susan was to gather that the spark applied to the inflammables and already causing them to crackle was the circumstance of one's being called a horrid low thief for refusing to part with one's own.

The redeeming point of this tension was, on the fifth day, that it actually appeared to have had to do with a breathless perception in our heroine's breast that scarcely more as the centre of Sir Claude's than as that of Susan's energies she had soon after breakfast been conveyed from London to Folkestone and established at a lovely hotel. These agents, before her wondering eyes, had combined to carry through the adventure and to give it the air of having owed its success to the fact that Mrs. Beale had, as Susan said, but just stepped out. When Sir Claude, watch in hand, had met this fact with the exclamation

'Then pack Miss Farange and come off with us!' there had ensued on the stairs a series of gymnastics of a nature to bring Miss Farange's heart into her mouth. She sat with Sir Claude in a four-wheeler while he still held his watch; held it longer than any doctor who had ever felt her pulse; long enough to give her a vision of something like the ecstasy of neglecting such an opportunity to show impatience. The ecstasy had begun in the schoolroom and over the Berceuse, quite in the manner of the same foretaste on the day, a little while back, when Susan had panted up and she herself, after the hint about the duchess, had sailed down; for what harm then had there been in drops and disappointments if she could still have, even only a moment, the sensation of such a name 'brought up'? It had remained with her that her father had told her that she would some day be in the street, but it clearly wouldn't be this day, and she felt justified of her preference as soon as her visitor had set Susan in motion and laid his hand, while she waited with him, kindly on her own. That was what the Captain, in Kensington Gardens, had done; her present situation reminded her a little of that one and renewed the dim wonder of the way in which, from the first, such pats and pulls had struck her as the steps and signs of other people's business and even a little as the wriggle or the overflow of their difficulties. What had failed her and what had frightened her on the night of the Exhibition lost themselves at present alike in the impression that what would come from Sir Claude was too big to come all at once. Any awe that might have sprung from his air of leaving out her stepmother was corrected by the force of a general rule, the odd truth that if Mrs. Beale now never came nor went without making her think of him, it was not, to balance that, the main character of his own contact to appear to be a reference to Mrs. Beale. To be with Sir Claude was to think of Sir Claude, and that law governed Maisie's mind until, through a sudden lurch of the cab, which had at last taken in Susan and ever so many bundles and almost reached Charing Cross, it popped again somehow into her dizzy head the long-lost image of Mrs. Wix.

It was singular, but from this time she understood and she followed, followed with the sense of an ample filling-out of any

void created by symptoms of avoidance and of flight. Her
ecstasy was a thing that had yet more of a face than of a back
to turn, a pair of eyes still directed to Mrs. Wix even after the
slight surprise of their not finding her, as the journey expanded,
either at the London station or at the Folkestone hotel. It took
few hours to make the child feel that if she was in neither of
these places she was at least everywhere else. Maisie had known
all along a great deal, but never so much as she was to know
from this moment on and as she learned in particular during
the couple of days that she was to hang in the air, as it were,
over the sea which represented in breezy blueness and with a
summer charm a crossing of more spaces than the Channel.
It was granted her at this time to arrive at divinations so ample
that I shall have no room for the goal if I attempt to trace the
stages; as to which therefore I must be content to say that the fullest
expression we may give to Sir Claude's conduct is a poor and pale
copy of the picture it presented to his young friend. Abruptly,
that morning, he had yielded to the action of the idea pumped
into him for weeks by Mrs. Wix on lines of approach that she
had been capable of the extraordinary art of preserving from
entanglement with the fine network of his relations with Mrs.
Beale. The breath of her sincerity, blowing without a break,
had puffed him up to the flight by which, in the degree I have
indicated, Maisie too was carried off her feet. This consisted in
neither more nor less than the brave stroke of his getting off
from Mrs. Beale as well as from his wife – of making with the
child straight for some such foreign land as would give a support to Mrs. Wix's dream that she might still see his errors
renounced and his delinquencies redeemed. It would all be a
sacrifice – under eyes that would miss no faintest shade – to what
even the strange frequenters of her ladyship's earlier period used
to call the real good of the little unfortunate. Maisie's head
held a suspicion of much that, during the last long interval, had
confusedly, but quite candidly, come and gone in his own; a
glimpse, almost awe-stricken in its gratitude, of the miracle her
old governess had wrought. That functionary could not in this
connection have been more impressive, even at second-hand, if
she had been a prophetess with an open scroll or some ardent

abbess speaking with the lips of the Church. She had clung day by day to their plastic associate, plying him with her deep, narrow passion, doing her simple utmost to convert him, and so inspiring him that he had at last really embraced his fine chance. That the chance was not delusive was sufficiently guaranteed by the completeness with which he could finally figure it out that, in case of his taking action, neither Ida nor Beale, whose book, on each side, it would only too well suit, would make any sort of row.

It sounds, no doubt, too penetrating, but it was by no means all through Sir Claude's betrayals that Maisie was able to piece together the beauty of the special influence through which, for such stretches of time, he had refined upon propriety by keeping, so far as possible, his sentimental interests distinct. She had ever of course in her mind fewer names than conceptions, but it was only with this drawback that she now made out her companion's absences to have had for their ground that he was the lover of her stepmother and that the lover of her stepmother could scarce logically pretend to a superior right to look after her. Maisie had by this time embraced the implication of a kind of natural divergence between lovers and little girls. It was just this indeed that could throw light on the probable contents of the pencilled note deposited on the hall-table in the Regent's Park and which would greet Mrs. Beale on her return. Maisie freely figured it as provisionally jocular in tone, even though to herself on this occasion Sir Claude turned a graver face than he had shown in any crisis but that of putting her into the cab when she had been horrid to him after her parting with the Captain. He might really be embarrassed, but he would be sure, to her view, to have muffled in some bravado of pleasantry the disturbance produced at her father's by the removal of a valued servant. Not that there wasn't a great deal too that wouldn't be in the note – a great deal for which a more comfortable place was Maisie's light little brain, where it hummed away hour after hour and caused the first outlook at Folkestone to swim in a softness of colour and sound. It became clear in this medium that her stepfather had really now only to take into account his entanglement with Mrs. Beale. Wasn't he at last disentangled from every one and everything else? The obstacle to the rupture pressed upon him by Mrs. Wix in the interest of his virtue would be simply that he was in love, or rather, to put it more precisely, that Mrs. Beale had left him no doubt of the degree in which *she* was. She was so much so as to have succeeded in making him accept for a time her infatuated grasp of him and even to some extent the idea of what they yet might do together with a little diplomacy and a good deal of patience. I may not even answer for it that Maisie was not aware of how, in this, Mrs. Beale failed to share his all but insurmountable distaste for their allowing their little charge to breathe the air of their gross irregularity – his contention, in a word, that they should either cease to be irregular or cease to be parental. Their little charge, for herself, had long ago adopted the view that even Mrs. Wix had at one time not thought prohibitively coarse – the view that she was after all, *as* a little charge, morally at home in atmospheres it would be appalling to analyse. If Mrs. Wix, however, ultimately appalled, had now set her heart on strong measures, Maisie, as I have intimated, could also work round both to the reasons for them and to the quite other reasons for that lady's not, as yet at least, appearing in them at first hand.

Oh, decidedly, I shall never get you to believe the number of things she saw and the number of secrets she discovered! Why in the world, for instance, couldn't Sir Claude have kept it from her – except on the hypothesis of his not caring to – that, when you came to look at it and so far as it was a question of vested interests, he had quite as much right in her as her stepmother and a right that Mrs. Beale was in no position to dispute? He failed at all events of any such successful ambiguity as could keep her, when once they began to look across at France, from regarding even what was least explained as most in the spirit of their old happy times, their rambles and expeditions in the easier, better days of their first acquaintance. Never before had she had so the sense of giving him a lead for the sort of treatment of what was between them that would best carry it off, or of his being grateful to her for meeting him so much in the right place. She met him literally at the very point where Mrs. Beale was most to be reckoned with, the point of the jealousy that

was sharp in that lady and of the need of their keeping it as
long as possible obscure to her that poor Mrs. Wix had still a
hand. Yes, she met him too in the truth of the matter that, as
her stepmother had had no one else to be jealous of, she had
made up for so gross a privation by directing the sentiment to
a moral influence. Sir Claude appeared absolutely to convey in
a wink that a moral influence that could pull a string was after
all a moral influence that could have its eyes scratched out; and
that, this being the case, there was somebody they couldn't
afford to expose before they should see a little better what Mrs.
Beale was likely to do. Maisie, true enough, had not to put it
into words to rejoin, in the coffee-room, at luncheon: 'What
can she do but come to you if papa does take a step that will
amount to legal desertion?' Neither had he then, in answer,
to articulate anything but the jollity of their having found a
table at a window from which, as they partook of cold beef and
apollinaris – for he hinted they would have to save lots of
money, they could let their eyes hover tenderly on the far-off
white cliffs that so often had signalled to the embarrassed English
a promise of safety. Maisie stared at them as if she might really
make out after a little a queer, dear figure perched on them – a
figure as to which she had already the subtle sense that, wherever perched, it would be the very oddest yet seen in France.
But it was at least as exciting to feel where Mrs. Wix wasn't as
it would have been to know where she was, and if she wasn't
yet at Boulogne this only thickened the plot.

If she was not to be seen that day, however, the evening was
marked by an apparition before which, none the less, the savour
of suspense folded on the spot its wings. Adjusting her respira-
tions and attaching, under dropped lashes, all her thoughts to a
smartness of frock and frill for which she could reflect that she
had not appealed in vain to a loyalty in Susan Ash triumphant
over the nice things their feverish flight had left behind, Maisie
spent on a bench in the garden of the hotel the half-hour before
dinner, that mysterious ceremony of the *table d'hôte* for which
she had prepared with a punctuality of flutter. Sir Claude,
beside her, was occupied with a cigarette and the afternoon
papers; and though the hotel was full the garden showed the

particular void that ensues upon the sound of the dressing-bell.
She had almost had time to weary of the human scene; her own
humanity at any rate, in the shape of a smutch on her scanty
skirt, had held her so long that as soon as she raised her eyes
they rested on a high, fair drapery by which smutches were put
to shame and which had glided towards her over the grass
without her noting its rustle. She followed up its stiff sheen –
up and up from the ground, where it had stopped – till at the
end of a considerable journey her impression felt the shock of
the fixed face which, surmounting it, seemed to offer the climax
of the dressed condition. 'Why, mamma!' she cried the next
instant – cried in a tone that, as she sprang to her feet, brought
Sir Claude to his own beside her and gave her ladyship, a few
yards off, the advantage of their momentary confusion. Poor
Maisie's was immense; her mother's drop had the effect of one
of the iron shutters that, in evening walks with Susan Ash, she
had seen suddenly, at the touch of a spring, rattle down over
shining shop-fronts. The light of foreign travel was darkened at
a stroke; she had a horrible sense that they were caught; and
for the first time in her life in Ida's presence she so far translated
an impulse into an invidious act as to clutch straight at the
hand of her responsible confederate. It didn't help her that he
appeared at first equally hushed with horror; a minute during
which, in the empty garden, with its long shadows on the lawn,
its blue sea over the hedge and its startled peace in the air, both
her elders remained as stiff as tall tumblers filled to the brim
and held straight for fear of a spill. At last, in a tone that in its
unexpected softness enriched the whole surprise, her mother
said to Sir Claude: 'Do you mind at all my speaking to her?'

'Oh no; *do* you?' His reply was so long in coming that
Maisie was the first to find the right note.

He laughed as he seemed to take it from her, and she felt a
sufficient concession in his manner of addressing their visitor.
'How in the world did you know we were here?'

His wife, at this, came the rest of the way and sat down on
the bench with a hand laid on her daughter, whom she gracefully drew to her and in whom, at her touch, the fear just kindled
gave a second jump, but now in quite another direction. Sir Claude,

on the further side, resumed his seat and his newspapers, and the three grouped themselves like a family party; his connection, in the oddest way in the world, almost cynically and in a flash acknowledged, and the mother patting the child into conformities unspeakable. Maisie could already feel that it was not Sir Claude and she who were caught. She had the positive sense of catching their relative, catching her in the act of getting rid of her burden with a finality that showed her as unprecedentedly relaxed. Oh yes, the fear had dropped, and she had never been so irrevocably parted with as in the pressure of possession now supremely exerted by Ida's long-gloved and much-bangled arm. 'I went to the Regent's Park' – this was presently her ladyship's answer to Sir Claude.

'Do you mean to-day?'

'This morning; just after your own call there. That's how I found you out; that's what has brought me.'

Sir Claude considered and Maisie waited. 'Whom then did you see?'

Ida gave a sound of indulgent mockery. 'I like your scare. I know your game. I didn't see the person I risked seeing, but I had been ready to take my chance of her.' She addressed herself to Maisie; she had encircled her more closely. 'I asked for *you*, my dear, but I saw no one but a dirty parlourmaid. She was red in the face with the great things that, as she told me, had just happened in the absence of her mistress; and she luckily had the sense to have made out the place to which Sir Claude had come to take you. If he hadn't given a false scent I should find you here: that was the supposition on which I've proceeded.' Ida had never been so explicit about proceeding or supposing, and Maisie, drinking this in, was aware that Sir Claude shared her fine impression of it. 'I wanted to see you,' his wife continued, 'and now you can judge of the trouble I've taken. I had everything to do in town to-day, but I managed to get off.'

Maisie and her companion, for a moment, did justice to this achievement; but Maisie was the first to express it. 'I'm glad you wanted to see me, mamma.' Then, after a concentration more deep and with a plunge more brave: 'A little more and you'd have been too late.' It stuck in her throat, but she brought it out: 'We're going to France.'

Ida was magnificent: Ida kissed her on the forehead. 'That's just what I thought likely; it made me decide to run down. I fancied that in spite of your scramble you'd wait to cross, and it added to the reason I have for seeing you.'

Maisie wondered intensely what the reason could be, but she knew ever so much better than to ask. She was slightly surprised indeed to perceive that Sir Claude didn't, and to hear him immediately inquire: 'What in the name of goodness can you have to say to her?'

His tone was not exactly rude, but it was impatient enough to make his wife's response a fresh specimen of the new softness. 'That, my dear man, is all my own business.'

'Do you mean,' Sir Claude asked, 'that you wish me to leave you with her?'

'Yes, if you'll be so good; that's the extraordinary request I take the liberty of making.' Her ladyship had dropped to a mildness of irony by which, for a moment, poor Maisie was mystified and charmed, puzzled with a glimpse of something that in all the years had at intervals peeped out. Ida smiled at Sir Claude with the strange air she had on such occasions of defying an interlocutor to keep it up as long; her huge eyes, her red lips, the intense marks in her face formed an illumination as distinct and public as a lamp set in a window. The child seemed quite to see in it the very lamp that had lighted her path; she suddenly found herself reflecting that it was no wonder the gentlemen were guided. This must have been the way mamma had first looked at Sir Claude; it brought back the lustre of the time they had outlived. It must have been the way she looked also at Mr. Perriam and Lord Eric; above all, it contributed in Maisie's mind to a completer view of the Captain. Our young lady grasped this idea with a quick lifting of the heart; there was a stillness during which her mother flooded her with a wealth of support to the Captain's striking tribute. This stillness remained long enough unbroken to represent that Sir Claude too might literally be struggling again with the element that had originally upset him; so that Maisie quite hoped he

would at least say something to show a recognition that she
could be charming.

What he presently said was: 'Are you putting up for the
night?'

His wife hesitated. 'Not here – I've come from Dover.'

Over Maisie's head, at this, they still faced each other. 'You
spend the night there?'

'Yes, I brought some things. I went to the hotel and hastily
arranged; then I caught the train that whisked me on here. You
see what a day I've had of it.'

The statement may surprise, but these were really as obliging if not as lucid words as, into her daughter's ears at least,
Ida's lips had ever dropped; and there was a quick desire in the
daughter that for the hour at any rate they should duly be welcomed as a ground of intercourse. Certainly mamma had a
charm which, when turned on, became a large explanation;
and the only danger now in an impulse to applaud it would be
that of appearing to signalize its rarity. Maisie, however, risked
the peril in the geniality of an admission that Ida had indeed
had a rush; and she invited Sir Claude to expose himself by
agreeing with her that the rush had been even worse than theirs.
He appeared to meet this appeal by saying with detachment
enough: 'You go back there to-night?'

'Oh yes – there are plenty of trains.'

Again Sir Claude hesitated; it would have been hard to say
if the child, between them, more connected or divided them.
Then he brought out quietly: 'It will be late for you to knock
about. I'll see you over.'

'You needn't trouble, thank you. I think you won't deny that
I can help myself and that it isn't the first time in my dreadful
life that I've somehow managed it.' Save for this allusion to her
dreadful life they talked there, Maisie noted, as if they were
only rather superficial friends; a special effect that she had
often wondered at before in the midst of what she supposed to
be intimacies. This effect was augmented by the almost casual
manner in which her ladyship went on: 'I daresay I shall go
abroad.'

'From Dover do you mean, straight?'

'How straight I can't say. I'm excessively ill.' This for a minute struck Maisie as but a part of the conversation; at the end of which time she became aware that it ought to strike her – as it apparently didn't strike Sir Claude – as a part of something graver. It helped her to twist nearer. 'Ill, mamma – really ill?'

She regretted her 'really' as soon as she had spoken it; but there couldn't be a better proof of her mother's present polish than that Ida showed no gleam of a temper to take it up. She had taken up at other times much tinier things. She only pressed Maisie's head against her bosom and said: 'Shockingly, my dear. I must go to that new place.'

'What new place?' Sir Claude inquired.

Ida thought, but couldn't recall it. 'Oh, "Chose", don't you know? – where every one goes. I want some proper treatment. It's all I've ever asked for on earth. But that's not what I came to say.'

Sir Claude, in silence, folded one by one his newspapers; then he rose and stood whacking the palm of his hand with the bundle. 'You'll stop and dine with us?'

'Dear no – I can't dine at this sort of hour. I ordered dinner at Dover.'

Her ladyship's tone in this one instance showed a certain superiority to those conditions in which her daughter had artlessly found Folkestone a paradise. It was yet not so crushing as to nip in the bud the eagerness with which the latter broke out: 'But won't you at least have a cup of tea?'

Ida kissed her again on the brow. 'Thanks, love. I had tea before coming.' She raised her eyes to Sir Claude. 'She *is* sweet!' He made no more answer than if he didn't agree; but Maisie was at ease about that and was still taken up with the joy of this happier pitch of their talk, which put more and more of a meaning into the Captain's version of her ladyship and literally kindled a conjecture that this admirer might, over there at the other place, be waiting for her to dine. Was the same conjecture in Sir Claude's mind? He partly puzzled her, if it had risen there, by the slight perversity with which he returned to a question that his wife evidently thought she had disposed of.

He whacked his hand again with his papers. 'I had really much better take you.'

'And leave Maisie here alone?'

Mamma so clearly didn't want it that Maisie leaped at the vision of a Captain who had seen her on from Dover and who, while he waited to take her back, would be hovering just at the same distance at which, in Kensington Gardens, the companion of his walk had herself hovered. Of course, however, instead of breathing any such guess she let Sir Claude reply; all the more that his reply could contribute so much to her own present grandeur. 'She won't be alone when she has a maid in attendance.'

Maisie had never before had so much of a retinue, and she waited also to enjoy the effect of it on her ladyship. 'You mean the woman you brought from town?' Ida considered. 'The person at the house spoke of her in a way that scarcely made her out company for my child.' Her tone was that her child had never wanted, in her hands, for prodigious company. But she as distinctly continued to decline Sir Claude's. 'Don't be an old goose,' she said charmingly. 'Let us alone.'

In front of them on the grass he looked graver than Maisie at all now thought the occasion warranted. 'I don't see why you can't say it before me.'

His wife smoothed one of her daughter's curls. 'Say what, dear?'

'Why, what you came to say.'

At this Maisie at last interposed: she appealed to Sir Claude. 'Do let her say it to me.'

He looked hard for a moment at his little friend. 'How do you know what she may say?'

'She must risk it,' Ida remarked.

'I only want to protect you,' he continued to the child.

'You want to protect yourself – that's what you mean,' his wife replied. 'Don't be afraid. I won't touch you.'

'She won't touch you – she *won't*!' Maisie declared. She felt by this time that she could really answer for it, and something of the emotion with which she had listened to the Captain came back to her. It made her so happy and so secure that she could positively patronize mamma. She did so in the Captain's very language. 'She's good, she's good!' she proclaimed.

'Oh Lord!' – Sir Claude, at this, let himself go. He appeared to have emitted some sound of derision that was smothered, to Maisie's ears, by her being again embraced by his wife. Ida released her and held her off a little, looking at her with a very queer face. Then the child became aware that their companion had left them and that from the face in question a confirmatory remark had proceeded.

'I *am* good, love,' said her ladyship.

XXI

A good deal of the rest of Ida's visit was devoted to explaining, as it were, so extraordinary a statement. This explanation was more copious than any she had yet indulged in, and as the summer twilight gathered and she kept her child in the garden she was conciliatory to a degree that let her need to arrange things a little perceptibly peep out. It was not merely that she explained; she almost conversed; all that was wanting to that was that she should have positively chattered a little less. It was really the occasion of Maisie's life on which her mother was to have most to say to her. That alone was an implication of generosity and virtue, and no great stretch was required to make our young lady feel that she should best meet her and soonest have it over by simply seeming struck with the propriety of her contention. They sat together while the parent's gloved hand sometimes rested sociably on the child's and sometimes gave a corrective pull to a ribbon too meagre or a tress too thick; and Maisie was conscious of the effort to keep out of her eyes the wonder with which they were occasionally moved to blink. Oh, there would have been things to blink at if one had let one's self go; and it was lucky they were alone together, without Sir Claude or Mrs. Wix or even Mrs. Beale to catch an imprudent glance. Though profuse and prolonged her ladyship was not exhaustively lucid, and her account of her situation, so far as it could be called descriptive, was a muddle of inconsequent things, bruised fruit of an occasion she had rather too lightly affronted. None of them were really thought out and some were even not wholly insincere. It was as if she had asked outright what better proof could have been wanted of her

goodness and her greatness than just this marvellous consent to
give up what she had so cherished. It was as if she had said in
so many words: 'There have been things between us – between
Sir Claude and me – which I needn't go into, you little nuisance,
because you wouldn't understand them.' It suited her to convey
that Maisie had been kept, so far as *she* was concerned or could
imagine, in a holy ignorance and that she must take for granted
a supreme simplicity. She turned this way and that in the predicament she had sought and from which she could neither
retreat with grace nor emerge with credit: she draped herself in
the tatters of her impudence, postured to her utmost before the
last little triangle of cracked glass to which so many fractures
had reduced the polished plate of filial superstition. If neither
Sir Claude nor Mrs. Wix was there this was perhaps all the
more a pity: the scene had a style of its own that would have
qualified it for presentation, especially at such a moment as
that of her letting it betray that she quite did think her wretched
offspring better placed with Sir Claude than in her own soiled
hands. There was at any rate nothing scant either in her admis-
sions or her perversions, the mixture of her fear of what Maisie
might undiscoverably think and of the support she at the same
time gathered from a necessity of selfishness and a habit of
brutality. This habit flushed through the merit she now made,
in terms explicit, of not having come to Folkestone to kick up
a vulgar row. She had not come to box any ears or to bang any
doors or even to use any language: she had come at the worst
to lose the thread of her argument in an occasional dumb, disgusted twitch of the toggery in which Mrs. Beale's low domestic had had the impudence to serve up Miss Farange. She
checked all criticism, not committing herself even as much
as about those missing comforts of the schoolroom on which
Mrs. Wix had presumed.

'I *am* good – I'm crazily, I'm criminally good. But it won't
do for *you* any more, and if I've ceased to contend with him,
and with you too, who have made most of the trouble
between us, it's for reasons that you'll understand one of
these days but too well – one of these days when I hope you'll
know what it is to have lost a mother. I'm awfully ill, but you

mustn't ask me anything about it. If I don't get off somewhere my doctor won't answer for the consequences. He's
stupefied at what I've borne – he says it has been put on me
because I was formed to suffer. I'm thinking of South Africa,
but that's none of your business. You must take your choice –
you can't ask me questions if you're so ready to give me up.
No, I won't tell you; you can find out for yourself. South
Africa is wonderful, they say, and if I do go it must be to give
it a fair trial. It must be either one thing or the other; if he
takes you, you know, he takes you. I've struck my last blow
for you; I can follow you no longer from pillar to post. I must
live for myself at last, while there's still a handful left of me.
I'm very, very ill; I'm very, very tired; I'm very, very determined.
There you have it. Make the most of it. Your frock is too
filthy; but I came to sacrifice myself.' Maisie looked at the
peccant places; there were moments when it was a relief to
her to drop her eyes even on anything so sordid. All her inter-
views, all her ordeals with her mother had, as she had grown
older, seemed to have, before any other, the hard quality of
duration; but longer than any, strangely, were these minutes
offered to her as so pacific and so agreeably winding up the
connection. It was her anxiety that made them long, her fear
of some hitch, some check of the current, one of her ladyship's
famous quick jumps. She held her breath; she only wanted, by
playing into her visitor's hands, to see the thing through. But
her impatience itself made at instants the whole situation
swim; there were things Ida said which she perhaps didn't hear,
and there were things she heard that Ida perhaps didn't say.
'You're all I have, and yet I'm capable of this. Your father wishes
you were dead – that, my dear, is what your father wishes. You'll
have to get used to it as I've done – I mean to his wishing that
I'm dead. At all events you see for yourself how wonderful I am
to Sir Claude. He wishes me dead quite as much; and I'm sure
that if making me scenes about *you* could have killed me——!'
It was the mark of Ida's eloquence that she started more hares
than she followed, and she gave but a glance in the direction
of this one; going on to say that the very proof of her treating
her husband like an angel was that he had just stolen off not

to be fairly shamed. She spoke as if he had retired on tiptoe, as he might have withdrawn from a place of worship in which he was not fit to be present. 'You'll never know what I've been through about you – never, never, never. I spare you everything, as I always have; though I daresay you know things that, if I did (I mean if you knew them) would make me – well, no matter! You're old enough at any rate to know there are a lot of things I don't say that I easily might; though it would do me good, I assure you, to have spoken my mind for once in my life. I don't speak of your father's infamous wife: that may give you a notion of the way I'm letting you off. When I say "you" I mean your precious friends and backers. If you don't do justice to my forbearing, out of delicacy, to mention, just as a last word, about your stepfather, a little fact or two of a kind that really I should only *have* to mention to shine myself in comparison and after every calumny like pure gold: if you don't do me *that* justice you'll never do me justice at all!'

Maisie's desire to show what justice she did her had by this time become so intense as to have brought with it an inspiration. The great effect of their encounter had been to confirm her sense of being launched with Sir Claude, to make it rich and full beyond anything she had dreamed, and everything now conspired to suggest that a single soft touch of her small hand would complete the good work and set her ladyship so promptly and majestically afloat as to leave the great seaway clear for the morrow. This was the more the case as her hand had for some moments been rendered free by a marked man-œuvre of both of her mother's. One of these capricious members had fumbled with visible impatience in some backward depth of drapery and had presently reappeared with a small article in its grasp. The act had a significance for a little person trained, in that relation, from an early age, to keep an eye on manual motions, and its possible bearing was not darkened by the memory of the handful of gold that Susan Ash would never, never believe Mrs. Beale had sent back – 'not she; she's too false and too greedy!' – to the munificent Countess. To have guessed, none the less, that her ladyship's purse might be the

real figure of the object extracted from the rustling covert of
her rear – this suspicion gave on the spot to the child's eyes a
direction carefully distant. It added moreover to the optimism
that for an hour could ruffle the surface of her deep diplomacy,
ruffle it to the point of making her forget that she had never
been safe unless she had also been stupid. She in short forgot
her habitual caution in her impulse to adopt her ladyship's
practical interests and show her ladyship how perfectly she
understood them. She saw without looking that her mother
pressed a little clasp; heard, without wanting to, the sharp click
that marked the closing portemonnaie from which something
had been taken. What this was she just didn't see; it was not
too substantial to be locked with ease in the fold of her ladyship's fingers. Nothing was less new to Maisie than the art of
not thinking singly, so that at this instant she could both bring
out what was on her tongue's end and weigh, as to the object
in her mother's palm, the question of its being a sovereign
against the question of its being a shilling. No sooner had she
begun to speak than she saw that within a few seconds this
question would have been settled: she had foolishly checked
the rising words of the little speech of presentation to which,
under the circumstances, even such a high pride as Ida's had
had to give some thought. She had checked it completely – that
was the next thing she felt: the note she sounded brought into
her companion's eyes a look that quickly enough seemed at
variance with presentations.

'That was what the Captain said to me that day, mamma.
I think it would have given you pleasure to hear the way he
spoke of you.'

The pleasure, Maisie could now in consternation reflect,
would have been a long time coming if it had come no faster
than the response evoked by her allusion to it. Her mother gave
her one of the looks that slammed the door in her face; never in
a career of unsuccessful experiments had Maisie had to take
such a stare. It reminded her of the way that once, at one of the
lectures in Glower Street, something in a big jar that, amid an
array of strange glasses and bad smells, had been promised as
a beautiful yellow was produced as a beautiful black. She had

been sorry on that occasion for the lecturer, but she was at this moment sorrier for herself. Oh, nothing had ever made for twinges like mamma's manner of saying: 'The Captain? What Captain?'

'Why, when we met you in the Gardens – the one who took me to sit with him. That was exactly what *he* said.'

Ida met her so far as to appear for an instant to pick up a lost thread. 'What on earth did he say?'

Maisie faltered supremely, but supremely she brought it out. 'What you say, mamma – that you're so good.'

'What "I" say?' Ida slowly rose, keeping her eyes on her child, and the hand that had busied itself in her purse conformed at her side and amid the folds of her dress to a certain stiffening of the arm. 'I say you're a precious idiot, and I won't have you put words into my mouth!' This was much more peremptory than a mere contradiction. Maisie could only feel on the spot that everything had broken short off and that their communication had abruptly ceased. That came out as Ida went on. 'What business have you to speak to me of him?'

Her daughter turned scarlet. 'I thought you liked him.'

'Him! – the biggest cad in London!' Her ladyship towered again, and in the gathering dusk the whites of her eyes were huge.

Maisie's own, however, could by this time pretty well match them; and she had at least now, with the first flare of anger that had ever yet lighted her face for a foe, the sense of looking up quite as hard as any one could look down. 'Well, he was kind about you then; he *was*, and it made me like him. He said things – they were beautiful, they were, they were!' She was almost capable of the violence of forcing this home, for even in the midst of her surge of passion – of which in fact it was a part – there rose in her a fear, a pain, a vision ominous, precocious, of what it might mean for her mother's fate to have forfeited such a loyalty as that. There was literally an instant in which Maisie fully saw – saw madness and desolation, saw ruin and darkness and death. 'I've thought of him often since, and I hoped it was with him – with him——' Here, in her emotion, it failed her, the breath of her filial hope.

But Ida got it out of her. 'You hoped, you little horror——?'

'That it was he who's at Dover, that it was he who's to take you. I mean to South Africa,' Maisie said with another drop.

Ida's stupefaction, on this, kept her silent unnaturally long, so long that her daughter could not only wonder what was coming, but perfectly measure the decline of every symptom of her liberality. She loomed there in her grandeur, merely dark and dumb; her wrath was clearly still, as it had always been, a thing of resource and variety. What Maisie least expected of it was by this law what now occurred. It melted, in the summer twilight, gradually into pity, and the pity after a little found a cadence, to which the renewed click of her purse gave an accent. She had put back what she had taken out. 'You're a dreadful, dismal, deplorable little thing,' she murmured. And with this she turned back and rustled away over the lawn.

After she had disappeared Maisie dropped upon the bench again and for some time, in the empty garden and the deeper dusk, sat and stared at the image her flight had still left standing. It had ceased to be her mother only, in the strangest way, that it might become her father, the father of whose wish that she were dead the announcement still lingered in the air. It was a presence with vague edges – it continued to front her, to cover her. But what reality that she need reckon with did it represent if Mr. Farange were, on his side, also going off – going off to America with the Countess, or even only to Spa? That question had from the house a sudden gay answer in the great roar of a gong, and at the same moment she saw Sir Claude look out for her from the wide, lighted doorway. At this she went to him, and he came forward and met her on the lawn. For a minute she was with him there in silence, as, just before, at the last, she had been with her mother.

'She's gone?'

'She's gone.'

Nothing more, for the instant, passed between them but to move together to the house, where, in the hall, he indulged in one of those sudden pleasantries with which, to the delight of his stepdaughter, his native animation abounded. 'Will Miss Farange do me the honour to accept my arm?'

There was nothing in all her days that Miss Farange had accepted with such bliss, a bright, rich element that floated them together to their feast; before they reached which, however, she uttered, in the spirit of a glad young lady taken in to her first dinner, a sociable word that made him stop short. 'She goes to South Africa.'

'To South Africa?' His face, for a moment, seemed to swing for a jump; the next it took its spring into the extreme of hilarity. 'Is that what she said?'

'Oh yes, quite distinctly. For the climate.'

Sir Claude was now looking at a young woman with black hair, a red frock and a tiny terrier tucked under her elbow. She swept past them on her way to the dining-room, leaving an impression of a strong scent which mingled, amid the clatter of the place, with the hot aroma of food. He had become a little graver; he still stopped to talk. 'I see – I see.' Other people brushed by; he was not too grave to notice them. 'Did she say anything else?'

'Oh yes, a lot more.'

On this he met her eyes again with some intensity, but only repeated: 'I see – I see.'

Maisie had still her own vision, which she brought out. 'I thought she was going to give me something.'

'What kind of a thing?'

'Some money that she took out of her purse and then put back.'

Sir Claude's amusement reappeared. 'She thought better of it. Dear thrifty soul! How much did she make by that manœuvre?'

Maisie considered. 'I didn't see. It was very small.'

Sir Claude threw back his head. 'Do you mean very little? Sixpence?'

Maisie resented this almost as if, at dinner, she were already bandying jokes with an agreeable neighbour. 'It may have been a sovereign.'

'Or even,' Sir Claude suggested, 'a ten-pound note.' She flushed at this sudden picture of what she perhaps had lost, and he made it more vivid by adding: 'Rolled up in a tight little ball, you know – her way of treating bank-notes as if they were curl-papers!' Maisie's flush deepened both with the immense plausibility of this and with a fresh wave of the consciousness that was always there to remind her of his cleverness – the consciousness of how immeasurably more after all he knew about mamma than she. She had lived with her so many times without discovering the material of her curl-papers or assisting at any other of her dealings with bank-notes. The tight little ball had at any rate rolled away from her for ever – quite like one of the other balls that Ida's cue used to send flying. Sir Claude gave her his arm again and by the time she was seated at table she had perfectly made up her mind as to the amount of the sum she had forfeited. Everything about her, however – the crowded room, the bedizened banquet, the savour of dishes, the drama of figures – ministered to the joy of life. After dinner she smoked with her friend – for that was exactly what she felt she did – on a porch, a kind of terrace, where the red tips of cigars and the light dresses of ladies made, under the happy stars, a poetry that was almost intoxicating. They talked but little, and she was slightly surprised at his asking for no more news of what her mother had said; but she had no need of talk, for it seemed to her that without it her sense of everything overflowed. They smoked and smoked, and there was a sweetness in her stepfather's silence. At last he said: 'Let us take another turn – but you must go to bed soon. Oh, you know, we're going to have a system!' Their turn was back into the garden, along the dusky paths from which they could see the black masts and the red lights of boats and hear the calls and cries that evidently had to do with happy foreign travel; and their system was once more to get on beautifully in this further lounge without a definite exchange. Yet he finally spoke – he broke out as he tossed away the match from which he had taken a fresh light: 'I must go for a stroll. I'm in a fidget – I must walk it off.' She fell in with this as she fell in with everything; on which he went on: 'You go up to Miss Ash' – it was the name they had started; 'you must see she's not in mischief. Can you find your way alone?'

'Oh yes; I've been up and down seven times.' She positively enjoyed the prospect of an eighth.

Still they didn't separate; they stood smoking together under the stars. Then at last Sir Claude produced it. 'I'm free – I'm free.'

She looked up at him; it was the very spot on which a couple of hours before she had looked up at her mother. 'You're free – you're free.'

'To-morrow we go to France.' He spoke as if he had not heard her; but it didn't prevent her again concurring.

'To-morrow we go to France.'

Again he appeared not to have heard her; and after a moment – it was an effect evidently of the depth of his reflections and the agitation of his soul – he also spoke as if he had not spoken before. 'I'm free – I'm free!'

She repeated her form of assent. 'You're free – you're free.'

This time he did hear her; he fixed her through the darkness with a grave face. But he said nothing more; he simply stooped a little and drew her to him – simply held her a little and kissed her good-night; after which, having given her a silent push upstairs to Miss Ash, he turned round again to the black masts and the red lights. Maisie mounted as if France were at the top.

XXII

The next day it seemed to her at the bottom – down too far, in shuddering plunges, even to leave her a sense, on the Channel boat, of the height at which Sir Claude remained and which had never in every way been so great as when, much in the wet, though in the angle of a screen of canvas, he sociably sat with his stepdaughter's head in his lap and that of Mrs. Beale's housemaid fairly pillowed on his breast. Maisie was surprised to learn as they drew into port that they had had a lovely passage; but this emotion, at Boulogne, was speedily quenched in others, above all in the great ecstasy of a larger impression of life. She was 'abroad' and she gave herself up to it, responded to it, in the bright air, before the pink houses, among the bare-legged fishwives and the red-legged soldiers, with the instant certitude of a vocation. Her vocation was to see the world and to thrill with enjoyment of the picture; she had grown older in five minutes and had by the time they reached the hotel recognized in the institutions and manners of France a multitude of affinities and messages. Literally in the course of an hour she found her initiation; a consciousness much quickened by the superior part that, as soon as they had gobbled down a French breakfast – which was indeed a high note in the concert – she observed herself to play to Susan Ash. Sir Claude, who had already bumped against people he knew and who, as he said, had business and letters, sent them out together for a walk, a walk in which the child was avenged, so far as poetic justice required, not only for the loud giggles that in their London trudges used to break from her attendant, but for all the years of her tendency to produce socially that impression of an excess of the queer something which had seemed to waver so widely between innocence and guilt. On the spot, at Boulogne, though there might have been excess there was at least no wavering; she recognized, she understood, she adored and took possession; feeling herself attuned to everything and laying her hand, right and left, on what had simply been waiting for her. She explained to Susan, she laughed at Susan, she towered over Susan; and it was somehow Susan's stupidity, of which she had never yet been so sure, and Susan's bewilderment and ignorance and antagonism, that gave the liveliest rebound to her immediate perceptions and adoptions. The place and the people were all a picture together, a picture that, when they went down to the wide sands, shimmered, in a thousand tints, with the pretty organization of the *plage*, with the gaiety of spectators and bathers, with that of the language and the weather and above all with that of our young lady's unprecedented situation. For it appeared to her that no one since the beginning of time could have had such an adventure or, in an hour, so much experience; as a sequel to which she only needed, in order to feel with conscious wonder how the past was changed, to hear Susan, inscrutably aggravated, express a preference for the Edgware Road. The past was so changed and the circle it had formed already so overstepped that on that very afternoon, in the course of another walk, she found herself inquiring of Sir Claude – and without a single scruple – if he were prepared as yet to name the moment at which they should start for Paris. His answer, it must be said, gave her the least little chill.

'Oh Paris, my dear child – I don't quite know about Paris!'

This required to be met, but it was much less to challenge him than for the rich joy of her first discussion of the details of a tour that, after looking at him a minute, she replied: 'Well, isn't that the *real* thing, the thing that when one does come abroad——?'

He had turned grave again, and she merely threw that out; it was a way of doing justice to the seriousness of their life. She couldn't moreover be so much older since yesterday without reflecting that if by this time she probed a little he would recognize that she had done enough for mere patience.

There was in fact something in his eyes that suddenly, to her own, made her discretion shabby. Before she could remedy this he had answered her last question, answered it in a way that, of all ways, she had least expected. 'The thing it doesn't do not to do? Certainly, Paris is charming. But, my dear fellow, Paris eats your head off; I mean it's so beastly expensive.'

That note gave her a pang – it suddenly let in a harder light. Were they poor then, that is was *he* poor, really poor beyond the pleasantry of apollinaris and cold beef? They had walked to the end of the long jetty that enclosed the harbour and were looking out at the dangers they had escaped, the grey horizon that was England, the tumbled surface of the sea and the brown smacks that bobbed upon it. Why had he chosen an embarrassed time to make this foreign dash? unless indeed it was just the dash economic, of which she had often heard and on which, after another look at the grey horizon and the bobbing boats, she was ready to turn round with elation. She replied to him quite in his own manner: 'I see, I see.' She smiled up at him. 'Our affairs are involved.'

'That's it.' He returned her smile. 'Mine are not quite so bad as yours; for yours are really, my dear man, in a state I can't see through at all. But mine will do – for a mess.'

She thought this over. 'But isn't France cheaper than England?'

England, over there in the thickening gloom, looked just then remarkably dear.

'I daresay; some parts.'

'Then can't we live in those parts?'

There was something that for an instant, in satisfaction of this, he had the air of being about to say and yet not saying. What he presently said was: 'This very place is one of them.'

'Then we shall live here?'

He didn't treat it quite as definitely as she liked. 'Since we've come to save money!'

This made her press him more. 'How long shall we stay?'

'Oh, three or four days.'

It took her breath away. 'You can save money in that time?'

He burst out laughing, starting to walk again and taking her under his arm. He confessed to her on the way that she too had put a finger on the weakest of all his weaknesses, the fact, of which he was perfectly aware, that he probably might have lived within his means if he had never done anything for thrift. 'It's the happy thoughts that do it,' he said; 'there's nothing so ruinous as putting in a cheap week.' Maisie heard afresh among the pleasant sounds of the closing day that steel click of Ida's change of mind. She thought of the ten-pound note it would have been delightful at this juncture to produce for her companion's encouragement. But the idea was dissipated by his saying irrelevantly, in the presence of the next thing they stopped to admire: 'We shall stay till she arrives.'

She turned upon him. 'Mrs. Beale?'

'Mrs. Wix. I've had a wire,' he went on. 'She has seen your mother.'

'Seen mamma?' Maisie stared. 'Where in the world?'

'Apparently in London. They've been together.'

For an instant this looked ominous – a fear came into her eyes. 'Then she hasn't gone?'

'Your mother? – to South Africa? I give it up, dear boy,' Sir Claude said; and she seemed literally to see him give it up as he stood there and with a kind of absent gaze – absent, that is, from *her* affairs – followed the fine stride and shining limbs of a young fishwife who had just waded out of the sea with her basketful of shrimps. His thought came back to her sooner than his eyes. 'But I daresay it's all right. She wouldn't come if it wasn't, poor old thing: she knows rather well what she's about.'

This was so reassuring that Maisie, after turning it over, could make it fit into her dream. 'Well, what *is* she about?'

He stopped looking at last at the fishwife – he met his companion's inquiry. 'Oh, you know!' There was something in the way he said it that made, between them, more of an equality than she had yet imagined; but it had also more the effect of raising her up than of letting him down, and what it did with her was shown by the sound of her assent.

'Yes – I know!' What she knew, what she *could* know is by this time no secret to us: it grew and grew at any rate, the rest of that day, in the air of what he took for granted. It was better he should do that than attempt to test her knowledge; but there at the worst was the gist of the matter: it was open between them at last that their great change, as, speaking as if it had already lasted weeks, Maisie called it, was somehow built up round Mrs. Wix. Before she went to bed that night she knew further that Sir Claude, since, as *he* called it, they had been on the rush, had received more telegrams than one. But they separated again without speaking of Mrs. Beale.

Oh what a crossing for the straighteners and the old brown dress – which latter appurtenance the child saw thriftily revived for the possible disasters of travel! The wind got up in the night and from her little room at the inn Maisie could hear the noise of the sea. The next day it was raining and everything different: this was the case even with Susan Ash, who positively crowed over the bad weather, partly, it seemed, for relish of the time their visitor would have in the boat, and partly to point the moral of the folly of coming to such holes. In the wet, with Sir Claude, Maisie went to the Folkestone packet, on the arrival of which, with many signs of the fray, he made her wait under an umbrella on the quay; whence, almost ere the vessel touched, he was to be descried, in quest of their friend, wriggling – that had been his word – through the invalids massed upon the deck. It was long till he reappeared – it was not indeed till every one had landed; when he presented the object of his benevolence in a light that Maisie scarce knew whether to deem the depth of prostration or the climax of success. The lady on his arm, still bent beneath her late ordeal, was muffled in such draperies as had never before offered so much support to so much woe. At the hotel, an hour later, this ambiguity dropped: assisting Mrs. Wix in private to refresh and reinvest herself, Maisie heard from her in detail how little she could have achieved if Sir Claude hadn't put it in her power. It was a phrase that in her room she repeated in connections indescribable: he had put it in her power to have 'changes', as she said, of the most intimate order, adapted to climates and occasions so various as to

foreshadow in themselves the stages of a vast itinerary. Cheap
weeks would of course be in their place after so much money
spent on a governess; sums not grudged, however, by this lady's
pupil even on her feeling her own appearance give rise, through
the straighteners, to an attention perceptibly mystified. Sir
Claude in truth had had less time to devote to it than to
Mrs. Wix's; and moreover she would rather be in her own
shoes than in her friend's creaking new ones in the event of an
encounter with Mrs. Beale. Maisie was too lost in the idea of
Mrs. Beale's judgment of so much newness to pass any judgment herself. Besides, after much luncheon and many endearments, the question took quite another turn, to say nothing of
the pleasure of the child's quick view that there were other eyes
than Susan Ash's to open to what she could show. She couldn't
show much, alas, till it stopped raining, which it declined to do
that day; but this had only the effect of leaving more time for
Mrs. Wix's own demonstration. It came as they sat in the little
white and gold *salon* which Maisie thought the loveliest place
she had ever seen except perhaps the apartment of the Countess;
it came while the hard summer storm lashed the windows and
blew in such a chill that Sir Claude, with his hands in his pockets and cigarettes in his teeth, fidgeting, frowning, looking out
and turning back, ended by causing a smoky little fire to be
made in the dressy little chimney. It came in spite of something
that could only be named his air of wishing to put it off; an air
that had served him – oh, as all his airs served him! – to the
extent of his having for a couple of hours confined the conversation to gratuitous jokes and generalities, kept it on the level
of the little empty coffee-cups and *petits verres* (Mrs. Wix had
two of each!) that struck Maisie, through the fumes of the
French fire and the English tobacco, as a token more than ever
that they were launched. She felt now, in close quarters and as
clearly as if Mrs. Wix had told her, that what this lady had
come over for was not merely to be chaffed and to hear her
pupil chaffed; not even to hear Sir Claude, who knew French in
perfection, imitate the strange sounds emitted by the English
folk at the hotel. It was perhaps half an effect of her present
renovations, as if her clothes had been somebody's else: she had

at any rate never produced such an impression of high colour, of a redness really so vivid as to be feverish. Her heart was not at all in the gossip about Boulogne; and if her complexion was partly the result of the *déjeuner* and the *petits verres* it was also the brave signal of what she was there to say. Maisie knew when this did come how anxiously it had been awaited by the youngest member of the party. 'Her ladyship packed me off – she almost put me into the cab!' That was what Mrs. Wix at last brought out.

XXIII

Sir Claude was stationed at the window; he didn't so much as turn round, and it was left to Maisie to take up the remark. 'Do you mean you went to see her yesterday?'

'She came to see *me*. She knocked at my shabby door. She mounted my squalid stair. She told me she had seen you at Folkestone.'

Maisie wondered. 'She went back that evening?'

'No; yesterday morning. She drove to me straight from the station. It was most remarkable. If I had a job to get off she did nothing to make it worse – she did a great deal to make it better.' Mrs. Wix hung fire, though the flame in her face burned brighter; then she became capable of saying: 'Her ladyship is kind! She did what I didn't expect.'

Maisie, on this, looked straight at her stepfather's back; it might well have been for her at that hour a monument of her ladyship's kindness. It remained, as such at all events, monumentally still, and for a time that permitted the child to ask of their companion: 'Did she really help you?'

'Most practically.' Again Mrs. Wix paused; again she quite resounded. 'She gave me a ten-pound note.'

At that, still looking out, Sir Claude, at the window, laughed loud. 'So you see, Maisie, we've not quite lost it.'

'Oh no,' Maisie responded. 'Isn't that too charming?' She smiled at Mrs. Wix. 'We know all about it.' Then on her friend's showing such blankness as was compatible with such a flush she pursued: 'She does want me to have you?'

Mrs. Wix showed a final hesitation, which, however, while Sir Claude drummed on the window-pane, she presently surmounted.

It came to Maisie that in spite of his drumming and of his not turning round he was really so much interested as to leave himself in a manner in her hands; which somehow suddenly seemed to her a greater proof than he could have given by interfering. 'She wants me to have *you*!' Mrs. Wix declared.

Maisie answered this bang at Sir Claude. 'Then that's nice for all of us.'

Of course it was, his continued silence sufficiently admitted, while Mrs. Wix rose from her chair and, as if to take more of a stand, placed herself, not without majesty, before the fire. The incongruity of her smartness, the circumference of her stiff frock presented her as really more ready for Paris than any of them. She also gazed hard at Sir Claude's back. 'Your wife was different from anything she had ever shown me. She recognizes certain proprieties.'

'Which? Do you happen to remember?' Sir Claude asked.

Mrs. Wix's reply was prompt. 'The importance for Maisie of a gentlewoman, of some one who is not – well, so bad! She objects to a mere maid, and I don't in the least mind telling you what she wants me to do.' One thing was clear – Mrs. Wix was now bold enough for anything. 'She wants me to persuade you to get rid of the person from Mrs. Beale's.'

Maisie waited for Sir Claude to pronounce on this; then she could only understand that he on his side waited, and she felt particularly full of common sense as she met her responsibility. 'Oh, I don't want Susan with *you*!' she said to Mrs. Wix.

Sir Claude, always from the window, approved. 'That's quite simple. I'll take her back.'

Mrs. Wix gave a positive jump; Maisie caught her look of alarm. '"Take" her? You don't mean to go over on purpose?'

Sir Claude said nothing for a moment; after which, 'Why shouldn't I leave you here?' he inquired.

Maisie, at this, sprang up. 'Oh do, oh do, oh do!' The next moment she was interlaced with Mrs. Wix, and the two, on the hearth-rug, their eyes in each other's eyes, considered the plan with intensity. Then Maisie perceived the difference of what they saw in it.

'She can surely go back alone: why should you put yourself out?' Mrs. Wix demanded.

'Oh, she's an idiot – she's incapable. If anything should happen to her it would be awkward: it was I who brought her – without her asking. If I turn her away I ought with my own hand to place her exactly where I found her.'

Mrs. Wix's face appealed to Maisie on such folly, and her manner, as directed to their companion, had, to her pupil's surprise, an unprecedented sharpness. 'Dear Sir Claude, I think you're perverse. Pay her fare and give her a sovereign. She has had an experience that she never dreamed of and that will be an advantage to her through life. If she goes wrong on the way it will be simply because she wants to, and, with her expenses and her remuneration – make it even what you like! – you will have treated her as handsomely as you always treat every one.'

This was a new tone – as new as Mrs. Wix's cap; and it could strike a perceptive person as the upshot of a relation that had taken on a new character. It brought out for Maisie how much more even than she guessed her friends were fighting side by side. At the same time it needed so definite a justification that as Sir Claude now at last did face them she at first supposed it in resentment of excessive familiarity. She was therefore yet more puzzled to see him show the whole of his serene beauty as well as an equal interest in a matter quite distinct from any freedom but her ladyship's. 'Did my wife come alone?' He could ask even that good-humouredly.

'When she called on me?' Mrs. Wix *was* red now: his good-humour wouldn't keep down her colour, which for a minute glowed there like her ugly honesty. 'No – there was some one in the cab.' The only attenuation she could think of was after a minute to add: 'But they didn't come up.'

Sir Claude broke into a laugh – Maisie herself could guess what it was at: while he now walked about, still laughing, and at the fire-place gave a gay kick to a displaced log, she felt more vague about almost everything than about the drollery of such a 'they'. She in fact could scarce have told you if it was to deepen or to cover the joke that she bethought herself to observe: 'Perhaps it was her maid.'

Mrs. Wix gave her a look that at any rate deprecated the wrong tone. 'It was not her maid.'

'Do you mean there are this time two?' Sir Claude asked as if he had not heard.

'Two maids?' Maisie went on as if she might assume he had.

The reproach of the straighteners darkened; but Sir Claude cut across it with a sudden: 'See here; what do you mean? And what do you suppose *she* meant?'

Mrs. Wix let him for a moment, in silence, understand that the answer to his question, if he didn't take care, might give him more than he wanted. It was as if, with this scruple, she measured and adjusted all that she gave him in at last saying: 'What she meant was to make me know that you're definitely free. To have that straight from her was a joy I, of course, hadn't hoped for: it made the assurance, and my delight at it, a thing I could really proceed upon. You already know I would have started even if she hadn't pressed me; you already know what, so long, we have been looking for and what, as soon as she told me of her step taken at Folkestone, I recognized with rapture that we *have*. It's your freedom that makes me right' – she fairly bristled with her logic. 'But I don't mind telling you that it's her action that makes me happy!'

'Her action?' Sir Claude echoed. 'Why, my dear woman, her action is just a hideous crime. It happens to satisfy our sympathies in a way that's quite delicious; but that doesn't in the least alter the fact that it's the most abominable thing ever done. She has chucked our friend here overboard not a bit less than if she had shoved her, shrieking and pleading, out of that window and down two floors to the paving-stones.'

Maisie surveyed serenely the parties to the discussion. 'Oh, your friend here, dear Sir Claude, doesn't plead and shriek!'

He looked at her a moment. 'Never. Never. That's one, only one, but charming so far as it goes, of about a hundred things we love her for.' Then he pursued to Mrs. Wix: 'What I can't for the life of me make out is what Ida is *really* up to, what game she was playing in turning to you with that cursed cheek after the beastly way she has used you. Where – to explain her at all – does she fancy she can presently, when we least expect it, take it out of us?'

'She doesn't fancy anything, nor want anything out of any one. Her cursed cheek, as you call it, is the best thing I've ever seen in her. I don't care a fig for the beastly way she used me – I forgive it all a thousand times over!' Mrs. Wix raised her voice as she had never raised it; she quite triumphed in her lucidity. 'I understand her, I almost admire her!' she proclaimed. She spoke as if this might practically suffice; yet in charity to fainter lights she threw out an explanation. 'As I've said, she was different; upon my word I wouldn't have known her. She had a glimmering, she had an instinct; they brought her. It was a kind of happy thought, and if you couldn't have supposed she would ever have had such a thing, why, of course, I quite agree with you. But she did have it! There!'

Maisie could see that, from what it with liveliness lacked, this demonstration gathered a certain something that might almost have exasperated. But as she had often watched Sir Claude in apprehension of displeasures that didn't come, so now, instead of his saying 'Oh hell!' as her father used, she observed him only to take refuge in a question that at the worst was abrupt.

'Who *is* it this time, do you know?'

Mrs. Wix tried blind dignity. 'Who is what, Sir Claude?'

'The man who stands the cabs. Who was in the one that waited at your door?'

At this challenge she faltered so long that it occurred to Maisie's conscience to give her a hand. 'It wasn't the Captain.'

Her good intention, however, only changed her old friend's scruple to a more ambiguous stare; besides of course making Sir Claude go off. Mrs. Wix fairly appealed to him. 'Must I really tell you?'

His amusement continued. 'Did she make you promise not to?'

Mrs. Wix looked at him still harder. 'I mean before Maisie.'

Sir Claude laughed again. 'Why, *she* can't hurt him!'

Maisie felt herself, as it passed, brushed by the light humour of this. 'Yes, I can't hurt him.'

The straighteners again roofed her over; after which they seemed to crack with the explosion of their wearer's honesty. Amid the flying splinters Mrs. Wix produced a name. 'Mr. Tischbein.'

There was for an instant a silence that, under Sir Claude's influence and while he and Maisie looked at each other, suddenly pretended to be that of gravity. 'We don't know Mr. Tischbein, do we, dear?'

Maisie gave the point all needful thought. 'No, not Mr. Tischbein.'

It was a passage that worked visibly on their friend. 'You must excuse me, Sir Claude,' she said, with an austerity of which the note was real, 'if I thank God to your face that he has in his mercy – I mean his mercy to our charge – allowed me to achieve this act.' She gave out a long puff of pain. 'It was time!' Then as if still more to point the moral: 'I said just now I understood your wife. I said just now I admired her. I stand to it: I did both of those things when I saw how even *she*, poor thing, saw. If you want the dots on the i's you shall have them. What she came to me for, in spite of everything was that I'm just' – she quavered it out – 'well, just clean! What she saw for her daughter was that there must at last be a *decent* person!'

Maisie was quick enough to jump a little at the sound of this implication that such a person was what Sir Claude was not; the next instant, however, she more profoundly guessed against whom the discrimination was made. She was therefore left the more surprised at the complete candour with which he embraced the worst. 'If she's bent on decent persons, why has she given her to *me*? You don't call me a decent person, and I'll do Ida the justice that *she* never did. I think I'm as indecent as any one and that there's nothing in my behaviour that makes my wife's surrender a bit less ignoble!'

'Don't speak of your behaviour!' Mrs. Wix cried. 'Don't say such horrible things; they're false, and they're wicked, and I forbid you! It's to *keep* you decent that I'm here and that I've done everything I have done. It's to save you – I won't say from yourself, because in yourself you're beautiful and good! It's to save you from the worst person of all. I haven't, after all, come over to be afraid to speak of her! That's the person in whose place her ladyship wants such a person as even me; and if she thought herself, as she as good as told me, not fit for Maisie's company, it's not, as you may well suppose, that she may make room for Mrs. Beale!'

Maisie watched his face as it took this outbreak, and the most she saw in it was that it turned a little white. That indeed made him look, as Susan Ash would have said, queer; and it was, perhaps, a part of the queerness that he intensely smiled. 'You're too hard on Mrs. Beale. She has great merits of her own.'

Mrs. Wix, at this, instead of immediately replying, did what Sir Claude had been doing before: she moved across to the window and stared awhile into the storm. There was for a minute, to Maisie's sense, a hush that resounded with wind and rain. Sir Claude, in spite of these things, glanced about for his hat; on which Maisie spied it first and, making a dash for it, held it out to him. He took it with a gleam of a 'thank-you' in his face, but as he did so something moved her still to hold the other side of the brim, so that, united by their grasp of this object, they stood some seconds looking many things at each other. By this time Mrs. Wix had turned round. 'Do you mean to tell me,' she demanded, 'that you *are* going back?'

'To Mrs. Beale?' Maisie surrendered his hat, and there was something that touched her in the embarrassed, almost humiliated way their companion's challenge made him turn it round and round. She had seen people do that who, she was sure, did nothing else that Sir Claude did. 'I can't just say, my dear thing. We'll see about it – we'll talk of it to-morrow. Meantime I must get some air.'

Mrs. Wix, with her back to the window, threw up her head to a height that, still for a moment, had the effect of detaining him. 'All the air in France, Sir Claude, won't, I think, give you the courage to deny that you're simply afraid of her!'

Oh, this time he did look queer; Maisie had no need of Susan's vocabulary to note it! It would have come to her of itself as, with his hand on the door, he turned his eyes from his stepdaughter to her governess and then back again. Resting on Maisie's, though for ever so short a time, there was something they gave up to her and tried to explain. His lips, however, explained nothing; they only surrendered to Mrs. Wix. 'Yes. I'm simply afraid of her!' He opened the door and passed out.

It brought back to Maisie his confession of fear of her mother; it made her stepmother then the second lady about whom he failed of the particular virtue that was supposed most to mark a gentleman. In fact there were three of them, if she counted in Mrs. Wix, before whom he had undeniably quailed. Well, his want of valour was but a deeper appeal to her tenderness. To thrill with response to it she had only to remember all the ladies she herself had, as they called it, funked.

XXIV

It continued to rain so hard that our young lady's private dream
of explaining the Continent to their visitor had to contain a
provision for some adequate treatment of the weather. At the
table d'hôte that evening she threw out a variety of lights: this
was the second ceremony of the sort she had sat through, and
she would have neglected her privilege and dishonoured her
vocabulary – which indeed consisted mainly of the names of
dishes – if she had not been proportionately ready to dazzle
with interpretations. Preoccupied and overawed, Mrs. Wix was
apparently dim: she accepted her pupil's version of the mysteries of the *menu* in a manner that might have struck the child as
the depression of a credulity conscious not so much of its needs
as of its dimensions. Maisie was soon enough – though it scarce
happened before bedtime – confronted again with the different
sort of programme for which she reserved her criticism. They
remounted together to their sitting-room while Sir Claude, who
said he would join them later, remained below to smoke and to
converse with the old acquaintances that he met wherever he
turned. He had proposed his companions, for coffee, the enjoyment of the *salon de lecture*, but Mrs. Wix had replied promptly
and with something of an air that it struck her their own apartments offered them every convenience. They offered the good
lady herself, Maisie could immediately observe, not only that
of this rather grand reference, which, already emulous, so far as
it went, of her pupil, she made as if she had spent her life in
salons; but that of a stiff French sofa where she could sit and
stare at the faint French lamp, in default of the French clock
that had stopped, as if for some account of the time Sir Claude

would so markedly interpose. Her demeanour accused him so
directly of hovering beyond her reach that Maisie sought to
divert her by a report of Susan's quaint attitude toward what
they had talked of after lunch. Maisie had mentioned to the
young woman for sympathy's sake the plan for her relief, but
her disapproval of alien ways appeared, strange to say, only to
prompt her to hug her gloom; so that between Mrs. Wix's effect
of displacing her and the visible stiffening of her back the child
had the sense of a double office, an enlarged play for pacific
powers.

These powers played to no great purpose, it was true, in
keeping before Mrs. Wix the vision of Sir Claude's perversity,
which hung there in the pauses of talk and which he himself,
after unmistakable delays, finally made quite lurid by bursting
in – it was near ten o'clock – with an object held up in his hand.
She knew, before he spoke, what it was; she knew at least from
the underlying sense of all that, since the hour spent after the
Exhibition with her father, had not sprung up to reinstate
Mr. Farange – she knew it meant a triumph for Mrs. Beale. The
mere present sight of Sir Claude's face caused her on the spot to
drop straight through her last impression of Mr. Farange a
plummet that reached still deeper down than the security of
these days of flight. She had wrapped that impression in silence –
a silence that had parted with half its veil to cover also, from
the hour of Sir Claude's advent, the image of Mr. Farange's
wife. But as the object in Sir Claude's hand revealed itself as a
letter which he held up very high, so there was something in his
mere motion that laid Mrs. Beale again bare. 'Here we are!' he
cried almost from the door, shaking his trophy at them and
looking from one to the other. Then he came straight to Mrs.
Wix; he had pulled two papers out of the envelope and glanced
at them again to see which was which. He thrust one out open
to Mrs. Wix. 'Read that.' She looked at him hard, as if in fear:
it was impossible not to see that he was excited. Then she took
the letter, but it was not her face that Maisie watched while she
read. Neither, for that matter, was it this countenance that Sir
Claude scanned: he stood before the fire and, more calmly, now
that he had acted, communed in silence with his stepdaughter.

This silence was in truth quickly broken; Mrs. Wix rose to her feet with the violence of the sound she emitted. The letter had dropped from her and lay upon the floor; it had made her turn ghastly white and she was speechless with the effect of it. 'It's too abominable – it's too unspeakable!' she then cried.

'Isn't it a charming thing?' Sir Claude asked. 'It has just arrived, enclosed in a word of her own. She sends it on to me with the remark that comment is superfluous. I really think it is. That's all you can say.'

'She oughtn't to pass such a horror about,' said Mrs. Wix. 'She ought to put it straight in the fire.'

'My dear woman, she's not such a fool! It's much too precious.' He had picked the letter up and he gave it again a glance of complacency which produced a light in his face. 'Such a document' – he considered, then concluded with a slight drop – 'such a document is, in fine, a basis!'

'A basis for what?'

'Well——for proceedings.'

'Hers?' Mrs. Wix's voice had become outright the voice of derision. 'How can *she* proceed?'

Sir Claude turned it over. 'How can she get rid of him? Well – she *is* rid of him.'

'Not legally.' Mrs. Wix had never looked to her pupil so much as if she knew what she was talking about.

'I daresay,' Sir Claude laughed; 'but she's not a bit less deprived than I am!'

'Of the power to get a divorce? It's just your want of the power that makes the scandal of your connection with her. Therefore it's just her want of it that makes that of hers with you. That's all I contend!' Mrs. Wix concluded with an unparalleled neigh of battle. Oh, she did know what she was talking about!

Maisie had meanwhile appealed mutely to Sir Claude, who judged it easier to meet what she didn't say than to meet what Mrs. Wix did.

'It's a letter to Mrs. Beale from your father, my dear, written from Spa and making the rupture between them perfectly irrevocable. It lets her know, and not in pretty language, that, as we technically say, he deserts her. It puts an end for ever to their relations.' He ran his eyes over it again, then appeared to make up his mind. 'In fact it concerns you, Maisie, so nearly and refers to you so particularly that I really think you ought to see the terms in which this new situation is created for you.' And he held out the letter.

Mrs. Wix, at this, pounced upon it; she had grabbed it too soon even for Maisie to become aware of being rather afraid of it. Thrusting it instantly behind her she positively glared at Sir Claude. 'See it, wretched man? – the innocent child *see* such a thing? I think you must be mad, and she shall not have a glimpse of it while I'm here to prevent!'

The breadth of her action had made Sir Claude turn red – he even looked a little foolish. 'You think it's too bad, eh? But it's precisely because it's bad that it seemed to me it would have a lesson and a virtue for her.'

Maisie could do a quick enough justice to his motive to be able clearly to interpose. She fairly smiled at him. 'I assure you I can quite believe how bad it is!' She hesitated an instant; then she added: 'I know what's in it!'

He of course burst out laughing, and while Mrs. Wix groaned an 'Oh heavens!' he replied: 'You wouldn't say that, old boy, if you did! The point I make is,' he continued to Mrs. Wix with a blandness now re-established – 'the point I make is simply that it sets Mrs. Beale free.'

She hung fire but an instant. 'Free to live with *you*?'

'Free not to live, not to pretend to live, with her husband.'

'Ah, they're mighty different things!' – a truth as to which her earnestness could now with a fine, inconsequent look invite the participation of the child.

Before Maisie could commit herself, however, the ground was occupied by Sir Claude, who, as he stood before their visitor with an expression half rueful, half persuasive, rubbed his hand sharply up and down the back of his head. 'Then why the deuce do you grant so – do you, I may even say, rejoice so – that by the desertion of my own precious partner I'm free?'

Mrs. Wix met this challenge first with silence, then with a demonstration the most extraordinary, the most unexpected.

Maisie could scarcely believe her eyes as she saw the good lady, with whom she had never associated the faintest form of coquetry, actually, after an upward grimace, give Sir Claude a great giggling, insinuating, naughty slap. 'You wretch – you *know* why!' And she turned away. The face that with this movement she left him to present to Maisie was to abide with his stepdaughter as the very image of stupefaction; but the pair lacked time to communicate either amusement or alarm before their interlocutress was upon them again. She had begun in fact to show infinite variety and she flashed about with a still quicker change of tone. 'Have you brought me that thing as a pretext for going over?'

Sir Claude braced himself. 'I can't, after such news, in common decency not. I mean, don't you know, in common courtesy and humanity. My dear lady, you can't chuck a woman that way, especially taking the moment when she has been most insulted and wronged. A fellow must behave like a gentleman, damn it, dear good Mrs. Wix. We didn't come away, we two, to hang right on, you know: it was only to try our paces and just put in a few days that might prove to every one concerned that we're in earnest. It's exactly because we're in earnest that, hang it, we needn't be so awfully particular. I mean, don't you know, we needn't be so awfully afraid.' He showed a vivacity, an intensity of argument, and if Maisie counted his words she was all the more ready to swallow after a single swift gasp those that, the next thing, she became conscious he paused for a reply to. 'We didn't come, old girl, did we,' he pleaded straight, 'to stop right away for ever and put it all in *now*?'

Maisie had never doubted she could be heroic for him. 'Oh no!' It was as if she had been shocked at the bare thought. 'We're just taking it as we find it.' She had a sudden inspiration, which she backed up with a smile. 'We're just seeing what we can afford.' She had never yet in her life made any claim for herself, but she hoped that this time, frankly, what she was doing would somehow be counted to her. Indeed she felt Sir Claude *was* counting it, though she was afraid to look at him – afraid she should show him tears. She looked at Mrs. Wix; she reached her maximum. 'I don't think I should be bad to Mrs. Beale.'

She heard, on this, a deep sound, something inarticulate and sweet, from Sir Claude; but tears were what Mrs. Wix didn't scruple to show. 'Do you think you should be bad to *me*?' The question was the more disconcerting that Mrs. Wix's emotion didn't deprive her of the advantage of her effect. 'If you see that woman again you're lost!' she declared to their companion.

Sir Claude looked at the moony globe of the lamp; he seemed to see for an instant what seeing Mrs. Beale would consist of. It was also apparently from this vision that he drew strength to return: 'Her situation, by what has happened, is completely changed; and it's no use your trying to prove to me that I needn't take any account of that.'

'If you see that woman you're lost!' Mrs. Wix with greater force repeated.

'Do you think she'll not let me come back to you? My dear lady, I leave you here, you and Maisie, as a hostage to fortune, and I promise you by all that's sacred that I shall be with you again at the very latest on Saturday. I provide you with funds; I install you in these lovely rooms; I arrange with the people here that you be treated with every attention and supplied with every luxury. The weather, after this, will mend; it will be sure to be exquisite. You'll both be as free as air and you can roam all over the place and have tremendous larks. You shall have a carriage to drive you; the whole house shall be at your call. You'll have in a word a magnificent position.' He paused, he looked from one of his companions to the other as if to see the impression he had made. Whether or no he judged it adequate he subjoined after a moment: 'And you'll oblige me above all by not making a fuss.'

Maisie could only answer for the impression on herself, though indeed from the heart even of Mrs. Wix's rigour there floated to her sense a faint fragrance of depraved concession. Maisie had her dumb word for the show such a speech could make, for the exquisite charm it could take from his exquisite sincerity; and before she could do anything but blink at excess of light she heard this very word sound on Mrs. Wix's lips, just as if the poor lady had guessed it and wished, snatching it from her, to blight it like a crumpled flower. 'You're dreadful, you're terrible, for you know but too well that it's not a small thing to me that you should address me in a fashion that's princely!' Princely was what he stood there and looked and sounded; that was what Maisie for the occasion found herself reduced to simple worship of him for being. Yet strange to say too, as Mrs. Wix went on, an echo rang within her that matched the echo she had herself just produced. 'How much you must *want* to see her to say such things as that and to be ready to do so much for the poor little likes of Maisie and me! She has a hold of you, and you know it, and you want to feel it again and – God knows, or at least *I* do, what's your motive and desire – enjoy it once more and give yourself up to it! It doesn't matter if it's one day or three: enough is as good as a feast and the lovely time you'll have with her is something you're willing to pay for! I daresay you'd like me to believe that your pay is to get her to give you up; but that's a matter on which I adjure you not to put down your money in advance. Give *her* up first. Then pay her what you please!'

Sir Claude took this to the end, though there were things in it that made him colour, called into his face more of the apprehension than Maisie had ever perceived there of a particular sort of shock. She had an odd sense that it was the first time she had seen any one but Mrs. Wix really and truly scandalized, and this fed her inference, which grew and grew from moment to moment, that Mrs. Wix was proving more of a force to reckon with than either of them had allowed so much room for. It was true that, long before, she had obtained a 'hold' of him, as she called it, different in kind from that obtained by Mrs. Beale and originally by her ladyship. But Maisie could quite feel with him now that he had really not expected this advantage to be driven so home. Oh, they hadn't at all got to where Mrs. Wix would stop, for the next minute she was driving harder than ever. It was the result of his saying with a certain dryness, though so kindly that what most affected Maisie in it was his patience: 'My dear friend, it's simply a matter in which I must judge for myself. You've judged *for* me, I know, a good deal, of late, in a way that I appreciate, I assure you, down to the ground. But you can't do it always; no one can do that for

another, don't you see, in every case. There are exceptions, particular cases that turn up and that are awfully delicate. It would
be too easy if I could shift it all off on you: it would be allowing
you to incur an amount of responsibility that I should simply
become quite ashamed of. You'll find, I'm sure, that you'll have
quite as much as you'll enjoy if you'll be so good as to accept
the situation as circumstances happen to make it for you and to
stay here with our friend, till I rejoin you, on the footing of as
much pleasantness and as much comfort – and I think I have
a right to add, to both of you, of as much faith in *me* – as
possible.'

Oh, he was princely indeed: that came out more and more
with every word he said and with the particular way he said it,
and Maisie could feel his monitress stiffen almost with anguish
against the increase of his spell and then hurl herself as a desperate defence from it into the quite confessed poorness of violence,
of iteration. 'You're afraid of her – afraid, afraid, afraid! Oh
dear, oh dear, oh dear!' Mrs. Wix wailed it with a high quaver,
then broke down into a long shudder of helplessness and woe.
The next minute she had flung herself again on the lean sofa and
had burst into a passion of tears.

Sir Claude stood and looked at her a moment; he shook his
head slowly, altogether tenderly. 'I've already admitted it – I'm
in mortal terror; so we'll let that settle the question. I think you
had best go to bed,' he added; 'you've had a tremendous day
and you must both be tired to death. I shall not expect you to
concern yourselves in the morning with my movements. There's
an early boat on; I shall have cleared out before you're up; and
I shall moreover have dealt directly and most effectively,
I assure you, with the haughty, but not quite hopeless Miss
Ash.' He turned to his stepdaughter as if at once to take leave
of her and give her a sign of how, through all tension and fric-
tion, they were still united in such a way that she at least needn't
worry. 'Maisie, boy!' – he opened his arms to her. With her
culpable lightness she flew into them and, while he kissed her,
chose the soft method of silence to promise him the silence that
after battles of talk was the best balm she could offer his
wounds. They held each other long enough to reaffirm intensely

their vows; after which they were almost forced apart by Mrs.
Wix's jumping to her feet.

Her jump, either with a quick return or with a final lapse of
courage, was also to supplication almost abject. 'I beseech you
not to take a step so miserable and so fatal. I know her but too
well, even if you jeer at me for saying it; little as I've seen her I
know her, I know her. I know what she'll do – I see it as I stand
here. Since you are afraid of her it's the mercy of heaven. Don't,
for God's sake, be afraid to show it, to profit by it and to arrive
at the very safety that it gives you. *I'm* not afraid of her, I assure
you; you must already have seen for yourself that there's nothing I'm afraid of now. Let me go to her – *I'll* settle her and I'll
take that woman back without a hair of her touched. Let me
put in the two or three days – let me wind up the connection.
You stay here with Maisie, with the carriage and the larks and
the luxury; then I'll return to you and we'll go off together –
we'll live together without a cloud. Take me, take me,' she went
on and on – the tide of her eloquence was high. 'Here I am; I
know what I am and what I ain't; but I say boldly to the face of
you both that I'll do better for you, far, than ever she will even
try to. I say it to yours, Sir Claude, even though I owe you the
very dress on my back and the very shoes on my feet. I owe you
everything – that's just the reason; and to pay it back, in profu-
sion, what can that be but what I want? Here I am, here I am!' –
she spread herself into an exhibition that, combined with her
intensity and her decorations, appeared to suggest her for
strange offices and devotions, for ridiculous replacements and
substitutions. She manipulated her gown as she talked, she
insisted on the items of her debt. 'I have nothing of my own, I
know – no money, no clothes, no appearance, no anything,
nothing but my hold of this little one truth, which is all in the
world I can bribe you with: that the pair of you are more to me
than all besides, and that if you'll let me help you and save you,
make what you both want possible in the one way it *can* be,
why, I'll work myself to the bone in your service!'

Sir Claude wavered there without an answer to this magnificent appeal; he plainly cast about for one, and in no small
agitation and pain. He addressed himself in his quest, however,

only to vague quarters until he met once more, as he so frequently and actively met it, the more than filial gaze of his intelligent little charge. That gave him – poor plastic and dependent male – his issue. If she was still a child she was yet of the sex that could help him out. He signified as much by a renewed invitation to an embrace. She freshly sprang to him and again they inaudibly conversed. 'Be nice to her, be nice to her,' he at last distinctly articulated; 'be nice to her as you've not even been to *me*!' On which, without another look at Mrs. Wix, he somehow got out of the room, leaving Maisie under the slight oppression of these words as well as of the idea that he had unmistakably once more dodged.

XXV

Every single thing he had prophesied came so true that it was after all no more than fair to expect quite as much for what he had as good as promised. His pledges they could verify to the letter, down to his very guarantee that a way would be found with Miss Ash. Roused in the summer dawn and vehemently squeezed by that interesting exile, Maisie fell back upon her couch with a renewed appreciation of his policy, a memento of which, when she rose later on to dress, glittered at her from the carpet in the shape of a sixpence that had overflowed from Susan's pride of possession. Sixpences really for the forty-eight hours that followed seemed to abound in her life; she fancifully computed the number of them represented by such a period of 'larks'. The number was not kept down, she presently noticed, by any scheme of revenge for Sir Claude's flight which should take on Mrs. Wix's part the form of a refusal to avail herself of the facilities he had so bravely ordered. It was in fact impossible to escape them; it was in the good lady's own phrase ridiculous to go on foot when you had a carriage prancing at the door. Everything about them pranced: the very waiters even as they presented the dishes to which, from a similar sense of the absurdity of perversity, Mrs. Wix helped herself with a freedom that spoke to Maisie quite as much of her depletion as of her logic. Her appetite was a sign to her companion of a great many things and testified no less on the whole to her general than to her particular condition. She had arrears of dinner to make up, and it was touching that in a dinnerless state her moral passion should have burned so clear. She partook largely as a refuge from depression, and yet the opportunity to partake was just a

mark of the sinister symptoms that depressed her. The affair
was in short a combat in which the baser element triumphed
between her refusal to be bought off and her consent to be
clothed and fed. It was not at any rate to be gainsaid that there
was comfort for her in the developments of France; comfort so
great as to leave Maisie free to take with her all the security for
granted and brush all the danger aside. That was the way to
carry out in detail Sir Claude's injunction to be 'nice'; that was
the way, as well, to look, with her, in a survey of the pleasures
of life abroad, straight over the head of any doubt.

They shrank at last, all doubts, as the weather cleared up: it
had an immense effect on them and became quite as lovely as
Sir Claude had engaged. This seemed to have put him so into
the secret of things and the joy of the world so waylaid the
steps of his friends that little by little the spirit of hope filled
the air and finally took possession of the scene. To drive on the
long cliff was splendid, but it was perhaps better still to creep
in the shade – for the sun was strong – along the many-
coloured and many-odoured *port* and through the streets in
which, to English eyes, everything that was the same was a
mystery and everything that was different a joke. Best of all
was to continue the creep up the long Grand' Rue to the gate
of the *haute ville* and, passing beneath it, mount to the quaint
and crooked rampart, with its rows of trees, its quiet corners
and friendly benches where brown old women in such white
frilled caps and such long gold earrings sat and knitted or
snoozed; its little yellow-faced houses that looked like the
homes of misers or of priests and its dark château where small
soldiers lounged on the bridge that stretched across an empty
moat and military washing hung from the windows of towers.
This was a part of the place that could lead Maisie to inquire
if it didn't just meet one's idea of the middle ages; and since it
was rather a satisfaction than a shock to perceive, and not for
the first time, the limits in Mrs. Wix's mind of the historic
imagination, that only added one more to the variety of kinds
of insight that she felt it her own present mission to show.
They sat together on the old grey bastion; they looked down
on the little new town which seemed to them quite as old, and

across at the great dome and the high gilt Virgin of the church
that, as they gathered, was famous and that pleased them by
its unlikeness to any place in which they had worshipped.
They wandered in this temple afterwards and Mrs. Wix
confessed that for herself she had probably early in life made,
in not being a Catholic, a fatal mistake. Her confession in its
turn caused Maisie to wonder rather interestedly what degree
of maturity it was that shut the door against an escape from
such an error. They went back to the rampart on the second
morning; the spot on which they appeared to have come furthest
in the journey that was to separate them from everything that
in the past had been objectionable: it gave them afresh the
impression that had most to do with their having worked
round to a confidence that on Maisie's part was determined
and that she could see to be on her companion's desperate. She
had had for many hours the sense of showing Mrs. Wix so
much that she was comparatively slow to become conscious
of being at the same time the subject of a similar process. The
process went the faster, however, from the moment she got her
glimpse of it; it then fell into its place in her general, her
habitual view of the particular phenomenon that, had she felt
the need of words for it, she might have called her personal
relation to her knowledge. This relation had never been so
lively as during the time she waited with her old governess for
Sir Claude; and what made it so was exactly that Mrs. Wix
struck her as having a new suspicion of it. Mrs. Wix had never
yet had a suspicion – that was certain – so calculated to throw
her pupil, in spite of the closer union of such adventurous
hours, upon the deep defensive. Her pupil made out indeed as
many marvels as she had made out on the rush to Folkestone;
and if in Sir Claude's company on that occasion Mrs. Wix was
the constant implication, so in Mrs. Wix's in the actual crisis
Sir Claude was – and most of all through long pauses – the
perpetual, the insurmountable theme. It all took them back to
the first flush of his marriage and to the place he held in the
schoolroom in those months of love and pain: only he had
himself blown to a much bigger balloon the large consciousness
he then filled out.

They went through it all again, and indeed while the interval lingered with the very weight of its charm they went, in spite of defences and suspicions, through everything. Their intensified clutch of the future throbbed like a clock ticking seconds; but this was a timepiece that inevitably, as well, at the best, rang occasionally a portentous hour. Oh, there were several of these, and two or three of the worst on the old city-wall where everything else so made for peace. There was nothing in the world Maisie more wanted than to be to Mrs. Wix as nice as Sir Claude had desired; but it was exactly because this fell in with her inveterate instinct of keeping the peace that the instinct itself was quickened. From the moment it was quickened, however, it found other work, and that was how, to begin with, she produced the very complication she most sought to avert. What she had essentially done, these days, had been to read the unspoken into the spoken; so that thus, with accumulations, it had become more definite to her that the unspoken was, unspeakably, the completeness of the sacrifice of Mrs. Beale. There were times when every minute that Sir Claude stayed away was like a nail in Mrs. Beale's coffin. That brought back to Maisie – it was a roundabout way – the beauty and antiquity of her connection with the flower of the Overmores as well as that lady's own grace and charm, her peculiar prettiness and cleverness and even her peculiar tribulations. A hundred things hummed at the back of her head, but two of these were simple enough. Mrs. Beale was by the way, after all, just her step-mother and her relative. She was just – and partly for that very reason – Sir Claude's greatest intimate ('lady-intimate' was Maisie's term), so that what together they were on Mrs. Wix's programme to give up and break short off with was for one of them his particular favourite and for the other her father's wife. Strangely, indescribably her perception of reasons kept pace with her sense of trouble; but there was something in her that, without a supreme effort not to be shabby, could not take the reasons for granted. What it comes to perhaps for ourselves is that, disinherited and denuded as we have seen her, there still lingered in her life an echo of parental influence – she was still reminiscent of one of the sacred lessons of home. It was the only one she retained, but luckily she retained it with force. She enjoyed in a word an ineffaceable view of the fact that there were things papa called mamma and mamma called papa a low sneak for doing or for not doing. Now this rich memory gave her a name that she dreaded to invite to the lips of Mrs. Beale: she would personally wince so just to hear it. The very sweetness of the foreign life she was steeped in added with each hour of Sir Claude's absence to the possibility of such pangs. She watched beside Mrs. Wix the great golden Madonna, and one of the ear-ringed old women who had been sitting at the end of their bench got up and pottered away.

'Adieu, mesdames!' said the old woman in a little cracked, civil voice – a demonstration by which our friends were so affected that they bobbed up and almost curtsied to her. They subsided again, and it was shortly after, in a summer hum of French insects and a phase of almost somnolent reverie, that Maisie most had the vision of what it was to shut out from such a perspective so appealing a participant. It had not yet appeared so vast as at that moment, this prospect of statues shining in the blue and of courtesy in romantic forms.

'Why, after all, should we have to choose between you? Why shouldn't we be four?' she finally demanded.

Mrs. Wix gave the jerk of a sleeper awakened or the start even of one who hears a bullet whiz at the flag of truce. Her stupefaction at such a breach of the peace delayed for a moment her answer. 'Four improprieties, do you mean? Because two of us happen to be decent people! Do I gather you to wish that I should stay on with you even if that woman *is* capable——?'

Maisie took her up before she could further phrase Mrs. Beale's capability. 'Stay on as *my* companion – yes. Stay on as just what you were at mamma's. Mrs. Beale *would* let you!' the child proclaimed.

Mrs. Wix had by this time fairly sprung to her arms. 'And who, I'd like to know, would let Mrs. Beale? Do you mean, little unfortunate, that *you* would?'

'Why not, if now she's free?'

'Free? Are you imitating *him*? Well, if Sir Claude's old enough to know better, upon my word I think it's right to treat you as

if you also were. You'll have to, at any rate, to know better, if
that's the line you're proposing to take.' Mrs. Wix had never
been so harsh; but on the other hand Maisie could guess that
she herself had never appeared so wanton. What was underlying, however, rather overawed than angered her; she felt she
could still insist, not for contradiction, but for ultimate calm.
Her wantonness meanwhile continued to work upon her friend,
who caught again, on the rebound, the sound of deepest provo-
cation. 'Free, free, free? If she's as free as *you* are, my dear, she's
free enough, to be sure!'

'As I am?' Maisie, after reflection and in the face of what, of
portentous, this seemed to convey, risked a critical echo.

'Well,' said Mrs. Wix, 'nobody, you know, is free to commit
a crime.'

'A crime!' The word had come out in a way that made the
child echo it again.

'You'd commit as great a one as their own – and so should
I – if we were to condone their immorality by our presence.'

Maisie waited a little; this seemed so fiercely conclusive.

'Why is it immorality?' she nevertheless presently inquired.

Her companion now turned upon her with a reproach softer
because it was somehow deeper. 'You're too unspeakable! Do
you know what we're talking about?'

In the interest of ultimate calm Maisie felt that she must be
above all clear. 'Certainly; about their taking advantage of their
freedom.'

'Well, to do what?'

'Why, to live with us.'

Mrs. Wix's laugh, at this, was literally wild. '"Us"? Thank
you!'

'Then to live with *me*.'

The words made her friend jump. 'You give me up? You
break with me for ever? You turn me into the street?'

Maisie was dazzled by the enumeration, but she bore bravely
up. 'Those, it seems to me, are the things you do to *me*.'

Mrs. Wix made little of her valour. 'I can promise you that,
whatever I do, I shall never let you out of my sight! You ask me
why it's immorality when you've seen with your own eyes that

Sir Claude has felt it to be so to that dire extent that, rather than make you face the shame of it, he has for months kept away from you altogether? Is it any more difficult to see that the first time he tries to do his duty he washes his hands of *her* – takes you straight away from her?'

Maisie turned this over, but more for apparent consideration than from any impulse to yield too easily. 'Yes, I see what you mean. But at that time they weren't free.' She felt Mrs. Wix rear up again at the offensive word, but she succeeded in touching her with a remonstrant hand. 'I don't think you know how free they've become.'

'I know, I believe, at least as much as you do!'

Maisie hesitated. 'About the Countess?'

'Your father's – temptress?' Mrs. Wix gave her a sidelong squint. 'Perfectly. She pays him!'

'Oh, *does* she?' At this the child's countenance fell: it seemed to give a reason for papa's behaviour and place it in a more favourable light. She wished to be just. 'I don't say she's not generous. She was so to me.'

'How, to you?'

'She gave me a lot of money.'

Mrs. Wix stared. 'And, pray, what did you do with a lot of money?'

'I gave it to Mrs. Beale.'

'And what did Mrs. Beale do with it?'

'She sent it back.'

'To the Countess? Gammon!' said Mrs. Wix. She disposed of that plea as effectually as Susan Ash.

'Well, I don't care!' Maisie replied. 'What I mean is that you don't know about the rest.'

'The rest? What rest?'

Maisie wondered how she could best put it. 'Papa kept me there an hour.'

'I do know – Sir Claude told me. Mrs. Beale had told him.'

Maisie looked incredulity. 'How could she – when I didn't speak of it?'

Mrs. Wix was mystified. 'Speak of what?'

'Why, of her being so frightful.'

'The Countess? Of course she's frightful,' Mrs. Wix declared. After a moment she added: 'That's why she pays him.'

Maisie pondered. 'It's the best thing about her then – if she gives him as much as she gave *me*.'

'Well, it's not the best thing about *him*! Or rather perhaps it is too!' Mrs. Wix subjoined.

'But she's awful – really and truly,' Maisie went on.

Mrs. Wix arrested her. 'You needn't go into details!' It was visibly at variance with this injunction that she yet inquired: 'How does that make it any better?'

'Their living with me? Why, for the Countess – and for her whiskers! – he has put me off on them. I understood him,' Maisie profoundly said.

'I hope then he understood you. It's more than I do!' Mrs. Wix admitted.

That was a real challenge to be plainer, and our young lady immediately became so. 'I mean it isn't a crime.'

'Why then did Sir Claude steal you away?'

'He didn't steal – he only borrowed me. I knew it wasn't for long,' Maisie audaciously professed.

'You must allow me to reply to that,' cried Mrs. Wix, 'that you knew nothing of the sort, and that you rather basely failed to back me up last night when you pretended so plump that you did! You hoped, in fact, exactly as much as I did and as in my senseless passion I even hope now, that this may be the beginning of better things.'

Oh yes, Mrs. Wix was indeed, for the first time, sharp; so that there at last stirred in our heroine the sense not so much of being proved disingenuous as of being precisely accused of the meanness that had brought everything down on her through her very desire to shake herself clear of it. She suddenly felt herself swell with a passion of protest. 'I never, *never* hoped I wasn't going again to see Mrs. Beale! I didn't, I didn't, I didn't!' she repeated. Mrs. Wix bounced about with a force of rejoinder of which she also felt that she must anticipate the concussion and which, though the good lady was evidently charged to the brim, hung fire long enough to give time for an aggravation. 'She's beautiful and I love her! I love her and she's beautiful!'

'And I'm hideous and you hate *me*?' Mrs. Wix fixed her a moment, then caught herself up. 'I won't embitter you by absolutely accusing you of that; though, as for my being hideous, it's hardly the first time I've been told so! I know it so well that even if I haven't whiskers – have I? – I daresay there are other ways in which the Countess is a Venus to me! My pretensions must therefore seem to you monstrous – which comes to the same thing as your not liking me. But do you mean to go so far as to tell me that you *want* to live with them in their sin?'

'You know what I want, you know what I want!' – Maisie spoke with the shudder of rising tears.

'Yes, I do; you want me to be as bad as yourself! Well, I won't. There! Mrs. Beale's as bad as your father!' Mrs. Wix went on.

'She's not! – she's not!' her pupil almost shrieked in retort.

'You mean because Sir Claude at least has beauty and wit and grace? But he pays just as the Countess pays!' Mrs. Wix, who now rose as she spoke, fairly revealed a latent cynicism.

It raised Maisie also to her feet; her companion had walked off a few steps and paused. The two looked at each other as they had never looked, and Mrs. Wix seemed to flaunt there in her finery. 'Then doesn't he pay *you* too?' her unhappy charge demanded.

At this she bounded in her place. 'Oh, you incredible little waif!' She brought it out with a wail of violence; after which, with another convulsion, she marched straight away.

Maisie dropped back on the bench and burst into sobs.

XXVI

Nothing so dreadful of course could be final or even for many minutes prolonged: they rushed together again too soon for either to feel that either had kept it up, and though they went home in silence it was with a vivid perception for Maisie that her companion's hand had closed upon her. That hand had shown altogether, these twenty-four hours, a new capacity for closing, and one of the truths the child could least resist was that a certain greatness had now come to Mrs. Wix. The case was indeed that the quality of her motive surpassed the sharpness of her angles; both the combination and the singularity of which things, when in the afternoon they used the carriage, Maisie could borrow from the contemplative hush of their grandeur the freedom to feel to the utmost. She still bore the mark of the tone in which her friend had thrown out that threat of never losing sight of her. This friend had been converted in short from feebleness to force; and it was the light of her present power that showed from how far she had come. The threat in question, sharply exultant, might have produced defiance; but before anything so ugly could happen another process had insidiously forestalled it. The moment at which this process had begun to mature was that of Mrs. Wix's breaking out with a dignity attuned to their own apartments and with an advantage now measurably gained. They had ordered coffee after luncheon, in the spirit of Sir Claude's provision, and it was served to them while they awaited their equipage in the white and gold saloon. It was flanked moreover with a couple of liqueurs, and Maisie felt that Sir Claude could scarce have been taken more at his word had it been followed by anecdotes and cigarettes. The influence of these luxuries was at any rate in the air. It seemed to her while she tiptoed at the chimney-glass, pulling on her gloves and with a motion of her head shaking a feather into place, to have had something to do with Mrs. Wix's suddenly saying: 'Haven't you really and truly *any* moral sense?'

Maisie was aware that her answer, though it brought her down to her heels, was vague even to imbecility and that this was the first time she had appeared to practise with Mrs. Wix an intellectual inaptitude to meet her – the infirmity to which she had owed so much success with papa and mamma. The appearance did her injustice, for it was not less through her candour than through her playfellow's pressure that after this the idea of a moral sense mainly coloured their intercourse. She began, the poor child, with scarcely knowing what it was; but it proved something that, with scarce an outward sign save her surrender to the swing of the carriage, she could, before they came back from their drive, strike up a sort of acquaintance with. The beauty of the day only deepened, and the splendour of the afternoon sea, and the haze of the far headlands, and the taste of the sweet air. It was the coachman indeed who, smiling and cracking his whip, turning in his place, pointing to invisible objects and uttering unintelligible sounds – all, our tourists recognized, strict features of a social order principally devoted to language: it was this polite person, I say, who made their excursion fall so much short that their return left them still a stretch of the long daylight and an hour that, at his obliging suggestion, they spent on foot on the shining sands. Maisie had seen the *plage* the day before with Sir Claude, but that was a reason the more for showing on the spot to Mrs. Wix that it was, as she said, another of the places on her list and of the things of which she knew the French name. The bathers, so late, were absent and the tide was low; the sea-pools twinkled in the sunset and there were dry places as well, where they could sit again and admire and expatiate: a circumstance that, while they listened to the lap of the waves, gave Mrs. Wix a fresh fulcrum for her challenge. 'Have you absolutely none at all?'

She had no need now, as to the question itself at least, to be specific; that on the other hand was the eventual result of their quiet conjoined apprehension of the thing that – well, yes, since they must face it – Maisie absolutely and appallingly had so little of. This marked more particularly the moment of the child's perceiving that her friend had risen to a level which might – till superseded at all events – pass almost for sublime. Nothing more remarkable had taken place in the first heat of her own departure, no phenomenon of perception more inscrutable by our rough method, than her vision, the rest of that Boulogne day, of the manner in which she figured. I so despair of tracing her steps that I must crudely give you my word for its being from this time on a picture literally present to her. Mrs. Wix saw her as a little person knowing so extraordinarily much that, for the account to be taken of it, what she still didn't know would be ridiculous if it hadn't been embarrassing. Mrs. Wix was in truth more than ever qualified to meet embarrassment; I am not sure that Maisie had not even a dim discernment of the queer law of her own life that made her educate to that sort of proficiency those elders with whom she was concerned. She promoted, as it were, their development; nothing could have been more marked for instance than her success in promoting Mrs. Beale's. She judged that if her whole history, for Mrs. Wix, had been the successive stages of her knowledge, so the very climax of the concatenation would, in the same view, be the stage at which the knowledge should overflow. As she was condemned to know more and more, how could it logically stop before she should know Most? It came to her in fact as they sat there on the sands that she was distinctly on the road to know Everything. She had not had governesses for nothing: what in the world had she ever done but learn and learn and learn? She looked at the pink sky with a placid foreboding that she soon should have learnt All. They lingered in the flushed air till at last it turned to grey and she seemed fairly to receive new information from every brush of the breeze. By the time they moved homeward it was as if for Mrs. Wix this inevitability had become a long, tense cord, twitched by a nervous hand, on which the counted pearls of intelligence were to be neatly strung.

In the evening upstairs they had another strange sensation, as to which Maisie could not afterwards have told you whether it was bang in the middle or quite at the beginning that her companion sounded with fresh emphasis the note of the moral sense. What mattered was merely that she did exclaim, and again, as at first appeared, most disconnectedly: 'God help me, it does seem to peep out!' Oh, the queer confusions that had wooed it at last to such peeping! None so queer, however, as the words of woe, and it might verily be said of rage, in which the poor lady bewailed the tragic end of her own rich ignorance. There was a point at which she seized the child and hugged her as close as in the old days of partings and returns; at which she was visibly at a loss how to make up to such a victim for such contaminations; appealing, as to what she had done and was doing, in bewilderment, in explanation, in supplication, for reassurance, for pardon and even out-right for pity.

'I don't know what I've said to you, my own: I don't know what I'm saying or what the turn you've given my life has rendered me, heaven forgive me, capable of saying. Have I lost all delicacy, all decency, all measure of how far and how bad? It seems to me mostly that I have, though I'm the last of whom you would ever have thought it. I've just done it for *you*, precious – not to lose you, which would have been worst of all: so that I've had to pay with my own innocence, if you do laugh! for clinging to you and keeping you. Don't let me pay for nothing; don't let me have been thrust for nothing into such horrors and such shames. I never knew anything about them and I never wanted to know! Now I know too much, too much!' the poor woman lamented and groaned. 'I know so much that with hearing such talk I ask myself where I am; and with uttering it too, which is worse, say to myself that I'm far, too far, from where I started! I ask myself what I should have thought with my lost one if I had heard myself cross the line. There are lines I've crossed with *you* that I should have fancied I had come to a pretty pass!' She gasped at the mere supposi-tion. 'I've gone from one thing to another, and all for the real love of you; and now what would any one say – I mean any one but *them* – if they were to hear the way I go on? I've had to keep up with you, haven't I? – and therefore what could I do less than look to you to keep up with *me*? But it's not *them* that are the worst – by which I mean to say it's not *him*: it's your dreadfully base papa and the one person in the world whom he could have found, I do believe – and she's not the Countess, duck – wickeder than himself. While they were about it at any rate, since they *were* ruining you, they might have done it so as to spare an honest woman. Then I shouldn't have had to do whatever it is that's the worst: throw up at you the badness you haven't taken in, or find my advantage in the vileness you *have*! What I did lose patience at this morning was at how it was without your seeming to condemn – for you didn't, you remember! – you yet did seem to *know*. Thank God in his mercy, at last, *if* you do!'

The night, this time, was warm and one of the windows stood open to the small balcony over the rail of which, on coming up from dinner, Maisie had hung a long time in the enjoyment of the chatter, the lights, the life of the quay made brilliant by the season and the hour. Mrs. Wix's requirements had drawn her in from this posture and Mrs. Wix's embrace had detained her even though midway in the outpouring her confusion and sympathy had permitted, or rather had positively helped, her to disengage herself. But the casement was still wide, the spectacle, the pleasure were still there, and from her place in the room, which, with its polished floor and its panels of elegance, was lighted from without more than from within, the child could still take account of them. She appeared to watch and listen; after which she answered Mrs. Wix with a question: 'If I do know?'

'If you do condemn.' The correction was made with some austerity.

It had the effect of causing Maisie to heave a vague sigh of oppression and then after an instant and as if under cover of this ambiguity pass out again upon the balcony. She hung again over the rail; she felt the summer night; she dropped down into the manners of France. There was a *café* below the hotel, before which, with little chairs and tables, people sat on a space

enclosed by plants in tubs; and the impression was enriched by
the flash of the white aprons of waiters and the music of a man
and a woman who, from beyond the precinct, sent up the strum
of a guitar and the drawl of a song about 'amour'. Maisie
knew what 'amour' meant too, and wondered if Mrs. Wix did:
Mrs. Wix remained within, as still as a mouse and perhaps not
reached by the performance. After a while, but not till the musi-
cians had ceased and begun to circulate with a little plate, her
pupil came back to her. '*Is* it a crime?' Maisie then asked.

Mrs. Wix was as prompt as if she had been crouching in a
lair. 'Branded by the Bible.'

'Well, he won't commit a crime.'

Mrs. Wix looked at her gloomily. 'He's committing one
now.'

'Now?'

'In being with her.'

Maisie had it on her tongue's end to return once more: 'But
now he's free.' She remembered, however, in time that one of
the things she had known for the last entire hour was that this
made no difference. After that and as if to turn the right way
she was on the point of a blind dash, a weak reversion to the
reminder that it might make a difference, might diminish the
crime for Mrs. Beale; till such a reflection was in its order also
quashed by the visibility in Mrs. Wix's face of the collapse produced by her inference from her pupil's manner that after all
her pains her pupil didn't even yet adequately understand.
Never so much as when confronted had Maisie wanted to
understand, and all her thought for a minute centred in the
effort to come out with something which should be a disproof
of her simplicity. 'Just trust me, dear; that's all!' – she came out
finally with that; and it was perhaps a good sign of her action
that with a long, impartial moan Mrs. Wix floated her to bed.

There was no letter the next morning from Sir Claude –
which Mrs. Wix let out that she deemed the worst of omens;
yet it was just for the quieter communion they so got with him
that, when after the coffee and rolls which made them more
foreign than ever, it came to going forth for fresh drafts upon
his credit they wandered again up the hill to the rampart instead

of plunging into distraction with the crowd on the sands or into the sea with the semi-nude bathers. They gazed once more at their gilded Virgin; they sank once more upon their battered bench; they felt once more their distance from the Regent's Park. At last Mrs. Wix became definite about their friend's silence. 'He *is* afraid of her! She has forbidden him to write.' The fact of his fear Maisie already knew; but her companion's mention of it had at this moment two unexpected results. The first was her wondering in dumb remonstrance how Mrs. Wix, with a devotion not after all inferior to her own, could put into such an allusion such a grimness of derision; the second was that she found herself suddenly drop into a deeper view of it. She too had been afraid, as we have seen, of the people of whom Sir Claude was afraid, and by that law she had had her due measure of latest apprehension of Mrs. Beale. What occurred at present, however, was that, whereas this sympathy appeared vain as for him, the ground of it loomed dimly as a reason for selfish alarm. That uneasiness had not carried her far before Mrs. Wix spoke again and with an abruptness so great as almost to seem irrelevant. 'Has it never occurred to you to be jealous of her?'

It never had in the least; yet the words were scarce in the air before Maisie had jumped at them. She held them well, she looked at them hard; at last she brought out with an assurance which there was no one, alas, but herself to admire: 'Well, yes – since you ask me.' She hesitated, then continued: 'Lots of times!'

Mrs. Wix glared askance an instant; such approval as her look expressed was not wholly unqualified. It expressed at any rate something that presumably had to do with her saying once more: 'Yes. He's afraid of her.'

Maisie heard, and it had afresh its effect on her even through the blur of the attention now required by the possibility of that idea of jealousy – a possibility created only by her feeling that she had thus found the way to show she was not simple. It stuck out of Mrs. Wix that this lady still believed her moral sense to be interested and feigned; so what could be such a gage of her sincerity as a peep of the most restless of the passions? Such a revelation would baffle discouragement, and discouragement was in fact so baffled that, helped in some degree by the mere intensity of their need to hope, which also, according to its nature, sprang from the dark portent of the absent letter, the real pitch of their morning was reached by the note, not of mutual scrutiny, but of unprecedented frankness. There were broodings indeed and silences, and Maisie sank deeper into the vision that for her friend she was, at the most, superficial, and that also, positively, she was the more so the more she tried to appear complete. Was the sum of all knowledge only to know how little in this presence one would ever reach it? The answer to that question luckily lost itself in the brightness suffusing the scene as soon as Maisie had thrown out in regard to Mrs. Beale such a remark as she had never dreamed she should live to make. 'If I thought she was unkind to him – I don't know *what* I should do!'

Mrs. Wix dropped one of her squints; she even confirmed it by a wild grunt. 'I know what *I* should!'

Maisie at this felt that she lagged. 'Well, I can think of *one* thing.'

Mrs. Wix more directly challenged her. 'What is it then?'

Maisie met her expression as if it were a game with forfeits for winking. 'I'd *kill* her!' That at least, she hoped as she looked away, would guarantee her moral sense. She looked away, but her companion said nothing for so long that she at last turned her head again. Then she saw the straighteners all blurred with tears which after a little seemed to have sprung from her own eyes. There were tears in fact on both sides of the spectacles, and they were even so thick that it was presently all Maisie could do to make out through them that slowly, finally Mrs. Wix put forth a hand. It was the material pressure that settled that and even at the end of some minutes more things besides. It settled in its own way one thing in particular, which, though often, between them, heaven knew, hovered round and hung over, was yet to be established without the shadow of an attenuating smile. Oh, there was no gleam of levity, as little of humour as of deprecation in the long time they now sat together or in the way in which at some unmeasured point of it Mrs. Wix became distinct enough for her own dignity and yet not loud enough for the snoozing old women.

'I adore him. I adore him.'

Maisie took it well in; so well that in a moment more she would have answered profoundly: 'So do I.' But before that moment passed something took place that brought other words to her lips; nothing more, very possibly, than the closer consciousness in her hand of the significance of Mrs. Wix's. Their hands remained linked in unutterable sign of their union, and what Maisie at last said was simply and serenely: 'Oh, I know!'

Their hands were so linked and their union was so confirmed that it took the far, deep note of a bell, borne to them on the summer air, to call them back to a sense of hours and proprieties. They had touched bottom and melted together, but they gave a start at last: the bell was the voice of the inn and the inn was the image of luncheon. They should be late for it; they got up, and their quickened step on the return had something of the swing of confidence. When they reached the hotel the *table d'hôte* had begun; this was clear from the threshold, clear from the absence in the hall and on the stairs of the 'personnel', as Mrs. Wix said – she had picked *that* up – all collected in the dining-room. They mounted to their apartments for a brush before the glass, and it was Maisie who, in passing and from a vain impulse, threw open the white and gold door. She was thus first to utter the sound that brought Mrs. Wix almost on top of her, as by the other accident it would have brought her on top of Mrs. Wix. It had at any rate the effect of leaving them bunched together in a strained stare at their new situation. This situation had put on in a flash the bright form of Mrs. Beale: she stood there in her hat and her jacket, amid bags and shawls, smiling and holding out her arms. If she had just arrived it was a different figure from either of the two that for *their* benefit, wan and tottering and none too soon to save life, the Channel had recently disgorged. She was as lovely as the day that had brought her over, as fresh as the luck and the health that attended her: it came to Maisie on the spot that she was more beautiful than she had ever been. All this was too quick to count, but there was still time in it to give the child the sense of what had kindled the light. That leaped out of the open arms, the open eyes, the open mouth; it leaped out with Mrs. Beale's loud cry at her: 'I'm free, I'm free!'

XXVII

The greatest wonder of all was the way Mrs. Beale addressed her announcement, so far as could be judged, equally to Mrs. Wix, who, as if from sudden failure of strength, sank into a chair while Maisie surrendered to the visitor's embrace. As soon as the child was liberated she met with profundity Mrs. Wix's stupefaction and actually was able to see that while in a manner sustaining the encounter her face yet seemed with intensity to say: 'Now, for God's sake, don't crow "I told you so!"' Maisie was somehow on the spot aware of an absence of disposition to crow; it had taken her but an extra minute to arrive at such a quick survey of the objects surrounding Mrs. Beale as showed that among them was no appurtenance of Sir Claude's. She knew his dressing-bag now – oh, with the fondest knowledge! – and there was an instant during which its not being there was a stroke of the worst news. She was yet to learn what it could be to recognize in some perception of a gap the sign of extinction, and therefore remained unaware that this momentary pang was a foretaste of the experience of death. It passed in a flash of course with Mrs. Beale's brightness and with her own instant appeal. 'You've come alone?'

'Without Sir Claude?' Strangely, Mrs. Beale looked even brighter. 'Yes; in the eagerness to get *at* you. You abominable little villain!' – and her stepmother, laughing clear, administered to her cheek a pat that was partly a pinch. 'What were you up to and what did you take me for? But I'm glad to be abroad, and after all it's you who have shown me the way. I mightn't without you have been able to come; that is so soon. Well, here I am at any rate and in a moment more I should have begun to

worry about you. This will do very well' – she was good-natured
about the place and even presently added that it was charming.
Then with a rosier glow she made again her great point: 'I'm free,
I'm free!' Maisie made on her side her own: she carried back her
gaze to Mrs. Wix, whom amazement continued to hold; she drew
afresh her old friend's attention to the superior way she didn't
take that up. What she did take up, the next minute, was the question of Sir Claude. 'Where is he? Won't he come?'

Mrs. Beale's consideration of this oscillated with a smile
between the two expectancies with which she was flanked: it
was conspicuous, it was extraordinary, her unblinking acceptance of Mrs. Wix, a miracle of which Maisie had even now
begun to read a reflection in that lady's long visage. 'He'll come,
but we must *make* him!' she gaily brought forth.

'Make him?' Maisie echoed.

'We must give him time. We must play our cards.'

'But he promised us awfully,' Maisie replied.

'My dear child, he has promised *me* awfully; I mean lots of
things, and not in every case kept his promise to the letter.'
Mrs. Beale's good-humour insisted on taking for granted Mrs.
Wix's, to whom her attention had suddenly grown prodigious.
'I daresay he has done the same with you and not always
come to time. But he makes it up in his own way; and it isn't
as if we didn't know exactly what he is. There's one thing he
is,' she went on, 'which makes everything else only a question,
for us, of tact.' They scarce had time to wonder what this was
before it was, as they might have said, right there. 'He's as free
as I am!'

'Yes, I know,' said Maisie; as if, however, independently
weighing the value of that. She really weighed also the oddity
of her stepmother's treating it as news to *her*, who had been the
first person literally to whom Sir Claude had mentioned it. For
a few seconds, as if with the sound of it in her ears, she stood
with him again, in memory and in the twilight, in the hotel
garden at Folkestone.

Anything Mrs. Beale overlooked was, she indeed divined, but
the effect of an exaltation of high spirits, a tendency to soar that
showed even when she dropped – still quite impartially – almost

to the confidential. 'Well, then – we've only to wait. He can't do without us long. I'm sure, Mrs. Wix, he can't do without *you*! He's devoted to you; he has told me so much about you. The extent I count on you, you know, count on you to help me!' – was an extent that even all her radiance couldn't express. What it couldn't express quite as much as what it could made at any rate every instant her presence and even her famous freedom loom larger; and it was this mighty mass that once more led her companions, bewildered and scattered, to exchange with each other as through a thickening veil confused and ineffectual signs. They clung together at least on the common ground of unpreparedness, and Maisie watched without relief the havoc of wonder in Mrs. Wix. It had reduced her to perfect impotence, and, but that gloom was black upon her, she sat as if fascinated by Mrs. Beale's high style. It had plunged her into a long deep hush; for what had happened was the thing she had least allowed for and before which the particular rigour she had worked up could only grow limp and sick. Sir Claude was to have reappeared with his accomplice or without her; never, never his accomplice without *him*. Mrs. Beale had gained apparently by this time an advantage she could pursue: she looked at the droll, dumb figure with jesting reproach. 'You really won't shake hands with me? Never mind; you'll come round!' She put the matter to no test, going on immediately and, instead of offering her hand, raising it, with a pretty gesture that her bent head met, to a long black pin that played a part in her back hair. 'Are hats worn at luncheon? If you're as hungry as I am we must go right down'.

Mrs. Wix stuck fast, but she met the question in a voice her pupil scarce recognized. 'I wear mine.'

Mrs. Beale, swallowing at one glance her brand-new bravery, which she appeared at once to refer to its origin and to follow in its flights, accepted this as conclusive. 'Oh, but I've not such a beauty!' Then she turned rejoicingly to Maisie. 'I've got a beauty for *you*, my dear.'

'A beauty?'

'A love of a hat – in my luggage. I remembered *that*' – she nodded at the object on her stepdaughter's head – 'and I've

brought you one with a peacock's breast. It's the most gorgeous blue!'

It was too strange, this talking with her there already not
about Sir Claude, but about peacocks – too strange for the
child to have the presence of mind to thank her. But the felicity
in which she had arrived was so proof against everything that
Maisie felt more and more the depth of the purpose that must
underlie it. She had a vague sense of its being abysmal, the spirit
with which Mrs. Beale carried off the awkwardness, in the white
and gold *salon*, of such a want of breath and of welcome.
Mrs. Wix was more breathless than ever; the embarrassment of
Mrs. Beale's isolation was as nothing to the embarrassment of
her grace. The perception of this dilemma was the germ on the
child's part of a new question altogether. What if *with* this
indulgence——? But the idea lost itself in something too frightened for hope and too conjectured for fear; and while everything went by leaps and bounds one of the waiters stood at the
door to remind them that the *table d'hôte* was half over.

'Had you come up to wash hands?' Mrs. Beale hereupon
asked them. 'Go and do it quickly and I'll be with you: they've
put my boxes in that nice room – it was Sir Claude's. Trust
him,' she laughed, 'to have a nice one!' The door of a neigh-
bouring room stood open, and now from the threshold, addressing herself again to Mrs. Wix, she launched a note that gave the
very key of what, as she would have said, she was up to. 'Dear
lady, please attend to my daughter.'

She was up to a change of deportment so complete that it
represented – oh, for offices still honourably subordinate if not
too explicitly menial – an absolute coercion, an interested
clutch of the old woman's respectability. There was response, to
Maisie's view, I may say at once, in the jump of that respectability to its feet: it was itself capable of one of the leaps, one of the
bounds just mentioned, and it carried its charge, with this
momentum and while Mrs. Beale popped into Sir Claude's
chamber, straight away to where, at the end of the passage,
pupil and governess were quartered. The greatest stride of all,
for that matter, was that within a few seconds the pupil had, in
another relation, been converted into a daughter. Maisie's eyes

were still following it when, after the rush, with the door almost slammed and no thought of soap and towels, the pair stood face to face. Mrs. Wix, in this position, was the first to gasp a sound. 'Can it ever be that *she* has one?'

Maisie felt still more bewildered. 'One what?'

'Why, moral sense.'

They spoke as if you might have two, but Mrs. Wix looked as if it were not altogether a happy thought, and Maisie didn't see how even an affirmative from her own lips would clear up what had become most of a mystery. It was to this she sprang pretty straight. '*Is* she my mother now?'

It was a point as to which an horrific glimpse of the responsibility of an opinion appeared to affect Mrs. Wix like a blow in the stomach. She had evidently never thought of it; but she could think and rebound. 'If she is, he's equally your father.'

Maisie, however, thought further. 'Then my father and my mother——!'

But she had already faltered and Mrs. Wix had already glared back: 'Ought to live together? Don't begin it again!' She turned away with a groan, to reach the washing-stand, and Maisie could by this time recognize with a certain ease that that way verily madness did lie. Mrs. Wix gave a great untidy splash, but the next instant had faced round. 'She has taken a new line.'

'She was nice to you,' Maisie concurred.

'What *she* thinks so – "go and dress the young lady!" But it's something!' she panted. Then she thought out the rest. 'If he won't have her, why she'll have *you*. She'll be the one.'

'The one to keep me abroad?'

'The one to give you a home.' Mrs. Wix saw further; she mastered all the portents. 'Oh, she's cruelly clever! It's not a moral sense.' She reached her climax: 'It's a game!'

'A game?'

'Not to lose him. She has sacrificed him – to her duty.'

'Then won't he come?' Maisie pleaded.

Mrs. Wix made no answer; her vision absorbed her. 'He has fought. But she has won.'

'Then won't he come?' the child repeated.

Mrs. Wix hesitated. 'Yes, hang him!' She had never been so profane.

For all Maisie minded! 'Soon – to-morrow?'

'Too soon – whenever. Indecently soon.'

'But then we *shall* be together!' the child went on. It made Mrs. Wix look at her as if in exasperation; but nothing had time to come before she precipitated: 'Together with *you*!' The air of criticism continued, but took voice only in her companion's bidding her wash herself and come down. The silence of quick ablutions fell upon them, presently broken, however, by one of Maisie's sudden reversions. 'Mercy, isn't she handsome?'

Mrs. Wix had finished; she waited. 'She'll attract attention.' They were rapid, and it would have been noticed that the shock the beauty had given them acted, incongruously, as a positive spur to their preparations for rejoining her. She had none the less when they returned to the sitting-room already descended; the open door of her room showed it empty and the chambermaid explained. Here again they were delayed by another sharp thought of Mrs. Wix's. 'But what will she live on meanwhile?'

Maisie stopped short. 'Till Sir Claude comes?'

It was nothing to the violence with which her friend had been arrested. 'Who'll pay the bills?'

Maisie thought. 'Can't *she*?'

'She? She hasn't a penny.'

The child wondered. 'But didn't papa——?'

'Leave her a fortune?' Mrs. Wix would have appeared to speak of papa as dead had she not immediately added: 'Why, he lives on other women!'

Oh yes, Maisie remembered. 'Then can't he send——?' She faltered again; even to herself it sounded queer.

'Some of their money to his wife?' Mrs. Wix gave a laugh still stranger than the weird suggestion. 'I daresay she'd take it!'

They hurried on again; yet again, on the stairs, Maisie pulled up. 'Well, if she had stopped in England——!' she threw out.

Mrs. Wix considered. 'And he had come over instead?'

'Yes, as we expected.' Maisie launched her speculation. 'What then would she have lived on?'

Mrs. Wix hung fire but an instant. 'On other men!' And she marched downstairs.

XXVIII

Mrs. Beale, at table between the pair, plainly attracted the attention Mrs. Wix had foretold. No other lady present was nearly so handsome, nor did the beauty of any other accommodate itself with such art to the homage it produced. She talked mainly to her other neighbour, and that left Maisie leisure both to note the manner in which eyes were riveted and nudges interchanged, and to lose herself in the meanings that, dimly as yet and disconnectedly, but with a vividness that fed apprehension, she could begin to read into her stepmother's independent move. Mrs. Wix had helped her by talking of a game; it was a connection in which the move could put on a strategic air. Her notions of diplomacy were thin, but it was a kind of cold diplomatic shoulder and an elbow of more than usual point that, temporarily at least, were presented to her by the averted inclination of Mrs. Beale's head. There was a phrase familiar to Maisie, so often was it used by this lady to express the idea of one's getting what one wanted: one got it – Mrs. Beale always said *she* at all events always got it or proposed to get it – by 'making love'. She was at present making love, singular as it appeared, to Mrs. Wix, and her young friend's mind had never moved in such freedom as on thus finding itself face to face with the question of what she wanted to get. This period of the *omelette aux rognons* and the *poulet sauté*, while her sole surviving parent, her fourth, fairly chattered to her governess, left Maisie rather wondering if her governess would hold out. It was strange, but she became on the spot quite as interested in Mrs. Wix's moral sense as Mrs. Wix could possibly be in hers: it had risen before her so pressingly that this was something new for Mrs. Wix to resist. Resisting Mrs. Beale herself promised at such a rate to become a very different business from resisting Sir Claude's view of her. More might come of what had happened – whatever it was – than Maisie felt she could have expected. She put it together with a suspicion that, had she ever in her life had a sovereign changed, would have resembled an impression, baffled by the want of arithmetic, that her change was wrong: she groped about in it that she had perhaps become the victim of a violent substitution. A victim was what she should surely be if the issue between her step-parents had been settled by Mrs. Beale's saying: 'Well, if she can live with but one of us alone, with which in the world should it be but me?' That answer was far from what, for days, she had nursed herself in, and the desolation of it was deepened by the absence of anything from Sir Claude to show he had not had to take it as triumphant. Had not Mrs. Beale, upstairs, as good as given out that she had quitted him with the snap of a tension, left him, dropped him in London, after some struggle as a sequel to which her own advent represented that she had practically sacrificed him? Maisie assisted in fancy at the probable episode in the Regent's Park, finding elements almost of terror in the suggestion that Sir Claude had not had fair play. They drew something, as she sat there, even from the pride of an association with such beauty as Mrs. Beale's; and the child quite forgot that, though the sacrifice of Mrs. Beale herself was a solution she had not invented, she would probably have seen Sir Claude embark upon it without a direct remonstrance.

What her stepmother had clearly now promised herself to wring from Mrs. Wix was an assent to the great modification, the change, as smart as a juggler's trick, in the interest of which nothing so much mattered as the new convenience of Mrs. Beale. Maisie could positively seize the moral that her elbow seemed to point in ribs thinly defended – the moral of its not mattering a straw which of the step-parents was the guardian. The essence of the question was that a girl wasn't a boy: if Maisie had been a mere trousered thing Sir Claude would have been welcome. As the case stood he had simply tumbled out, and Mrs. Wix would henceforth find herself in the

employ of the right person. These arguments had really fallen,
for our young lady, into their place at the very touch of that
tone in which she had heard her new title declared. She was
still, as a result of so many parents, a daughter to somebody
even after papa and mamma were to all intents dead. If her
father's wife and her mother's husband, by the operation of a
natural or, for all she knew, a legal rule, were in the shoes of
their defunct partners, then Mrs. Beale's was exactly as defunct
as Sir Claude's and her shoes the very pair to which, in 'Farange
v. Farange and Others', the divorce court had given priority.
The subject of that celebrated settlement saw the rest of her day
really filled out with the pomp of all that Mrs. Beale assumed.
The assumption rounded itself there between this lady's
entertainers, flourished in a way that left them, in their
bottomless element, scarce a free pair of eyes to exchange
signals. It struck Maisie even a little that there was a rope or
two Mrs. Wix might have thrown out if she would, or a rocket
or two she might have sent up. They had at any rate never been
so long together without communion or telegraphy, and their
companion kept them apart by simply keeping them with her.
From this situation they saw the grandeur of their intenser
relation to her pass and pass like an endless procession. It was
a day of lively movement and of talk on Mrs. Beale's part so
brilliant and overflowing as to represent music and banners.
She took them out with her promptly to walk and to drive, and
even – towards night – sketched a plan for carrying them to the
Établissement, where, for only a franc apiece, they should listen
to a concert of celebrities. It reminded Maisie, the plan, of the
side-shows at Earl's Court, and the franc sounded brighter than
the shillings which had at that time failed; yet this too, like the
other, was a frustrated hope: the francs failed like the shillings
and the side-shows had set an example to the concert. The
Établissement in short melted away, and it was little wonder
that a lady who from the moment of her arrival had been so
gallantly in the breach should confess herself at last done up.
Maisie could appreciate her fatigue; the day had not passed
without such an observer's discovering that she was excited
and even mentally comparing her state to that of the breakers

after a gale. It had blown hard in London, and she would take time to subside. It was of the condition known to the child by report as that of talking against time that her decision, her spirit, her humour, which had never dropped, now gave the impression.

She too was delighted with foreign manners; but her daughter's opportunities of explaining them to her were unexpectedly forestalled by her tone of large acquaintance with them. One of the things that nipped in the bud all response to her volubility was Maisie's surprised retreat before the fact that Continental life was what she had been almost brought up on. It was Mrs. Beale, disconcertingly, who began to explain it to her friends; it was she who, wherever they turned, was the interpreter, the historian and the guide. She was full of reference to her early travels – at the age of eighteen: she had at that period made, with a distinguished Dutch family, a stay on the Lake of Geneva. Maisie had in the old days been regaled with anecdotes of these adventures, but they had with time become phantasmal, and the heroine's quite showy exemption from bewilderment at Boulogne, her acuteness on some of the very subjects on which Maisie had been acute to Mrs. Wix, were a high note of the majesty, of the variety of advantage, with which she had alighted. It was all a part of the wind in her sails and of the weight with which her daughter was now to feel her hand. The effect of it on Maisie was to add already the burden of time to her separation from Sir Claude. This might, to her sense, have lasted for days; it was as if, with their main agitation transferred thus to France and with neither mamma now nor Mrs. Beale nor Mrs. Wix nor herself at his side, he must be fearfully alone in England. Hour after hour she felt as if she were waiting; yet she couldn't have said exactly for what. There were moments when Mrs. Beale's flow of talk was a mere rattle to smother a knock. At no part of the crisis had the rattle so public a purpose as when, instead of letting Maisie go with Mrs. Wix to prepare for dinner, she pushed her – with a push at last incontestably maternal – straight into the room inherited from Sir Claude. She titivated her little charge with her own brisk hands; then she brought out; 'I'm going to divorce your father.'

This was so different from anything Maisie had expected that it took some time to reach her mind. She was aware meanwhile that she probably looked rather wan. 'To marry Sir Claude?'

Mrs. Beale rewarded her with a kiss. 'It's sweet to hear you put it so.'

This was a tribute, but it left Maisie balancing for an objection. 'How *can* you when he's married?'

'He isn't – practically. He's free, you know.'

'Free to marry?'

'Free, first, to divorce his own fiend.'

The benefit that these last days she had felt she owed a certain person left Maisie a moment so ill-prepared for recognizing this lurid label that she hesitated long enough to risk: 'Mamma?'

'She isn't your mamma any longer,' Mrs. Beale replied. 'Sir Claude has paid her money to cease to be.' Then as if remembering how little, to the child, a pecuniary transaction must represent: 'She lets him off supporting her if he'll let her off supporting you.'

Mrs. Beale appeared, however, to have done injustice to her daughter's financial grasp. 'And support me himself?' Maisie asked.

'Take the whole bother and burden of you and never let her hear of you again. It's a regular signed contract.'

'Why, that's lovely of her!' Maisie cried.

'It's not so lovely, my dear, but that he'll get his divorce.'

Maisie was briefly silent; after which, 'No – he won't get it,' she said. Then she added still more boldly: 'And you won't get yours.'

Mrs. Beale, who was at the dressing-glass, turned round with amusement and surprise. 'How do you know that?'

'Oh, I know!' cried Maisie.

'From Mrs. Wix?'

Maisie debated, then, after an instant, was determined by Mrs. Beale's absence of anger, which struck her the more as she had felt she must take her courage in her hands. 'From Mrs. Wix,' she admitted.

Mrs. Beale, at the glass again, made play with a powder-puff. 'My own sweet, she's mistaken!' was all she said.

There was a certain force in the very amenity of this, but our young lady reflected long enough to remember that it was not the answer Sir Claude himself had made. The recollection nevertheless failed to prevent her saying: 'Do you mean then that he won't come till he has got it?'

Mrs. Beale gave a last touch; she was ready; she stood there in all her elegance. 'I mean, my dear, that it's because he hasn't got it that I left him.'

This opened out a view that stretched further than Maisie could reach. She turned away from it, but she spoke before they went out again. 'Do you like Mrs. Wix now?'

'Why, my chick, I was just going to ask you if you think she has come at all to like poor bad me!'

Maisie thought, at this hint; but unsuccessfully. 'I haven't the least idea. But I'll find out.'

'Do!' said Mrs. Beale, rustling out with her in a scented air and as if it would be a very particular favour.

The child tried promptly at bed-time, relieved now of the fear that their visitor would wish to separate her for the night from her attendant. 'Have you held out?' she began as soon as the two doors at the end of the passage were again closed on them.

Mrs. Wix looked hard at the flame of the candle. 'Held out——?'

'Why, she has been making love to you. Has she won you over?'

Mrs. Wix transferred her intensity to her pupil's face. 'Over to what?'

'To *her* keeping me instead.'

'Instead of Sir Claude?' Mrs. Wix was distinctly gaining time. 'Yes; who else? since it's not instead of you.'

Mrs. Wix coloured at this lucidity. 'Yes, that *is* what she means.'

'Well, do you like it?' Maisie asked.

She actually had to wait, for, oh, her friend was embarrassed! 'My opposition to the connection – theirs – would then natu-rally to some extent fall. She has treated me to-day with peculiar consideration; not that I don't know very well where she got the pattern of it! But of course,' Mrs. Wix hastened to add, 'I shouldn't like her as *the* one nearly so well as him.'

"Nearly so well!" Maisie echoed: 'I should hope indeed not.' She spoke with a firmness under which she was herself the first to quiver. 'I thought you "adored" him.'

'I do,' Mrs. Wix sturdily allowed.

'Then have you suddenly begun to adore her too?'

Mrs. Wix, instead of directly answering, only blinked in support of her sturdiness. 'My dear, in what a tone you ask that! You're coming out.'

'Why shouldn't I? You've come out. Mrs. Beale has come out. We each have our turn!' And Maisie threw off the most extraordinary little laugh that had ever passed her young lips.

There passed Mrs. Wix's indeed the next moment a sound that more than matched it. 'You're most remarkable!' she neighed.

Her pupil faltered a few seconds. 'I think you've done a great deal to make me so.'

'Very true, I have.' She dropped to humility, as if she recalled her so recent self-arraignment.

'Would you accept her then? That's what I ask,' said Maisie.

'As a substitute?' Mrs. Wix turned it over; she met again the child's eyes. 'She has literally almost fawned upon me.'

'She hasn't fawned upon *him*. She hasn't even been kind to him.'

Mrs. Wix looked as if she had now an advantage. 'Then do you propose to "kill" her?'

'You don't answer my question,' Maisie persisted. 'I want to know if you accept her.'

Mrs. Wix continued to dodge. 'I want to know if *you* do!'

Everything in the child's person, at this, announced that it was easy to know. 'Not for a moment.'

'Not the two now?' Mrs. Wix had caught on; she flushed with it. 'Only him alone?'

'Him alone or nobody.'

'Not even *me*?' cried Mrs. Wix.

Maisie looked at her a moment, then began to undress. 'Oh, you're nobody!'

XXIX

Her sleep was drawn out; she instantly recognized lateness in the way her eyes opened to Mrs. Wix, erect, completely dressed, more dressed than ever, and gazing at her from the centre of the room. The next thing she was sitting straight up, wide awake with the fear of the hours of 'abroad' that she might have lost. Mrs. Wix looked as if the day had already made itself felt, and the process of catching up with it began for Maisie with hearing her distinctly say: 'My poor dear, he has come!'

'Sir Claude?' Maisie, clearing the little bed-rug with the width of her spring, felt the polished floor under her bare feet.

'He crossed in the night; he got in early.' Mrs. Wix's head jerked stiffly backward. 'He's there.'

'And you've seen him?'

'No. He's there – he's there,' Mrs. Wix repeated. Her voice came out with a queer extinction that was not a voluntary drop, and she trembled so that it added to their common emotion. Visibly pale, they gazed at each other.

'Isn't it too *beautiful*?' Maisie panted back at her; an appeal to which, however, she was not ready with a response. The term Maisie had used was a flash of diplomacy – to prevent at any rate Mrs. Wix's using another. To that degree it was successful; there was only an appeal, strange and mute, in the white old face, which produced the effect of a want of decision greater than could by any stretch of optimism have been associated with her attitude toward what had happened. For Maisie herself indeed what had happened was oddly, as she could feel, less of a simple rapture than any arrival or return of the same supreme friend had ever been before. What had become overnight, what had become while she slept, of the comfortable faculty of gladness? She tried to wake it up a little wider by talking, by rejoicing, by plunging into water and into clothes, and she made out that it was ten o'clock, but also that Mrs. Wix had not yet breakfasted. The day before, at nine, they had had together a *café complet* in their sitting-room. Mrs. Wix on her side had evidently also a refuge to seek. She sought it in checking the precipitation of some of her pupil's present steps, in recalling to her with an approach to sternness that of such preliminaries ablutions should be the most thorough, and in throwing even a certain reprobation on the idea of hurrying into clothes for the sake of a mere stepfather. She took her in fact with a sort of silent insistence in hand; she reduced the process to sequences more definite than any it had known since the days of Moddle. Whatever it might be that was now, with a difference, attached to Sir Claude's presence was still after all compatible, for our young lady, with the instinct of dressing to see him with almost untidy haste. Mrs. Wix meanwhile luckily was not wholly directed to repression. 'He's there – he's there!' she had said over several times. It was her answer to every invitation to mention how long she had been up and her motive for respecting so rigidly the slumber of her companion. It formed for some minutes her only account of the whereabouts of the others and her reason for not having yet seen them, as well as of the possibility of their presently being found in the *salon*.

'He's there – he's there!' she declared once more as she made, on the child, with an almost invidious tug, a strained undergarment 'meet'.

'Do you mean he's in the *salon*?' Maisie asked again.

'He's *with* her,' Mrs. Wix desolately said. 'He's with her,' she reiterated.

'Do you mean in her own room?' Maisie continued.

She waited an instant. 'God knows!'

Maisie wondered a little why, or how, God should know; this, however, delayed but an instant her bringing out: 'Well, won't she go back?'

'Go back? Never!'

'She'll stay all the same?'

'All the more.'

'Then won't Sir Claude go?' Maisie asked.

'Go back – if *she* doesn't?' Mrs. Wix appeared to give this question the benefit of a minute's thought. 'Why should he have come – only to go back?'

Maisie produced an ingenious solution. 'To *make* her go. To take her.'

Mrs. Wix met it without a concession. 'If he can make her go so easily, why should he have let her come?'

Maisie considered. 'Oh, just to see *me*. She has a right.'

'Yes – she has a right.'

'She's my mother!' Maisie tentatively tittered.

'Yes – she's your mother.'

'Besides,' Maisie went on, 'he didn't let her come. He doesn't like her coming, and if he doesn't like it——'

Mrs. Wix took her up. 'He must lump it – that's what he must do! Your mother was right about him – I mean your real one. He has no strength. No – none at all.' She seemed more profoundly to muse. 'He might have had some even with *her* – I mean with her ladyship. He's just a poor, sunk slave,' she asserted with sudden energy.

Maisie wondered again. 'A slave?'

'To his passions.'

She continued to wonder and even to be impressed; after which she went on: 'But how do you know he'll stay?'

'Because he likes us!' – and Mrs. Wix, with her emphasis of the word, whirled her charge round again to deal with posterior hooks. She had positively never shaken her so.

It was as if she quite shook something out of her. 'But how will that help him if we – in spite of his liking! – don't stay?'

'Do you mean if we go off and leave him with her?' – Mrs. Wix put the question to the back of her pupil's head. 'It *won't* help him. It will be his ruin. He'll have got nothing. He'll have lost everything. It will be his utter destruction, for he's certain after a while to loathe her.'

'Then when he loathes her' – it was astonishing how she caught the idea – 'he'll just come right after us!' Maisie announced.

'Never.'

'Never?'

'She'll keep him. She'll hold him for ever.'

Maisie doubted. 'When he "loathes" her?'

'That won't matter. She won't loathe *him*. People don't!' Mrs. Wix brought up.

'Some do. Mamma does,' Maisie contended.

'Mamma does *not*!' It was startling – her friend contradicted her flat. 'She loves him – she adores him. A woman knows.' Mrs. Wix spoke not only as if Maisie were not a woman, but as if she would never be one. '*I* know!' she cried.

'Then why on earth has she left him?'

Mrs. Wix hesitated. 'He hates *her*. Don't stoop so – lift up your hair. You know how I'm affected toward him,' she added with dignity; 'but you must also know that I see clear.'

Maisie all this time was trying hard to do likewise. 'Then, if she has left him for that, why shouldn't Mrs. Beale leave him?'

'Because she's not such a fool!'

'Not such a fool as mamma?'

'Precisely – if you *will* have it. Does it look like her leaving him?' Mrs. Wix inquired. She hung fire again; then she went on with more intensity: 'Do you want to know really and truly why? So that she may be his wretchedness and his punishment.'

'His punishment?' – this was more than as yet Maisie could quite accept. 'For what?'

'For everything. That's what will happen: he'll be tied to her for ever. She won't mind in the least his hating her, and she won't hate him back. She'll only hate *us*.'

'Us?' the child faintly echoed.

'She'll hate *you*.'

'Me? Why, I brought them together!' Maisie resentfully cried.

'You brought them together.' There was a completeness in Mrs. Wix's assent. 'Yes; it was a pretty job. Sit down.' She began to brush her pupil's hair and, as she took up the mass of it with some force of hand, went on with a sharp recall: 'Your mother adored him at first – it might have lasted. But he began too soon with Mrs. Beale. As you say,' she pursued with a brisk application of the brush, 'you brought them together.'

'I brought them together' – Maisie was ready to reaffirm it. She felt none the less for a moment at the bottom of a hole; then she seemed to see a way out. 'But I didn't bring mamma together——' She just faltered.

'With all those gentlemen?' – Mrs. Wix pulled her up. 'No; it isn't quite so bad as that.'

'I only said to the Captain' – Maisie had the quick memory of it – 'that I hoped he at least (he was awfully nice!) would love her and keep her.'

'And even that wasn't much harm,' threw in Mrs. Wix.

'It wasn't much good,' Maisie was obliged to recognize. 'She can't bear him – not even a mite. She told me at Folkestone.'

Mrs. Wix suppressed a gasp; then after a bridling instant during which she might have appeared to deflect with difficulty from her odd consideration of Ida's wrongs: 'He was a nice sort of person for her to talk to you about!'

'Oh, I *like* him!' Maisie promptly rejoined; and at this, with an inarticulate sound and an inconsequence still more marked, her companion bent over and dealt her on the cheek a rapid peck which had the apparent intention of a kiss.

'Well, if her ladyship doesn't agree with you, what does it only prove?' Mrs. Wix demanded in conclusion. 'It proves that she's fond of Sir Claude!'

Maisie, in the light of some of the evidence, reflected on that till her hair was finished, but when she at last started up she gave a sign of no very close embrace of it. She grasped at this moment Mrs. Wix's arm. 'He must have got his divorce!'

'Since day before yesterday? Don't talk trash.'

This was spoken with an impatience which left the child nothing to reply; whereupon she sought her defence in a completely different relation to the fact. 'Well, I knew he would come!'

'So did I; but not in twenty-four hours. I gave him a few days!' Mrs. Wix wailed.

Maisie, whom she had now released, looked at her with interest. 'How many did *she* give him?'

Mrs. Wix faced her a moment; then as if with a bewildered sniff: 'You had better ask her!' But she had no sooner uttered the words than she caught herself up. 'Lord of mercy, how we talk!'

Maisie felt that however they talked she must see him, but she said nothing more for a time, a time during which she conscientiously finished dressing and Mrs. Wix also kept silence. It was as if they each had almost too much to think of and even as if the child had the sense that her friend was watching her and seeing if she herself were watched. At last Mrs. Wix turned to the window and stood – sightlessly, as Maisie could guess – looking away. Then our young lady, before the glass, gave the supreme shake. 'Well, I'm ready. And now to *see* him!'

Mrs. Wix turned round, but as if without having heard her. 'It's tremendously grave.' There were slow, still tears behind the straighteners.

'It is – it is.' Maisie spoke as if she were now dressed quite up to the occasion; as if indeed with the last touch she had put on the judgment-cap. 'I must see him immediately.'

'How can you see him if he doesn't send for you?'

'Why can't I go and find him?'

'Because you don't know where he is.'

'Can't I just look in the *salon*?' That still seemed simple to Maisie.

Mrs. Wix, however, instantly cut it off. 'I wouldn't have you look in the *salon* for all the world!' Then she explained a little: 'The *salon* isn't ours now.'

'Ours?'

'Yours and mine. It's theirs.'

'Theirs?' Maisie, with her stare, continued to echo. 'You mean they want to keep us out?'

Mrs. Wix faltered; she sank into a chair and, as Maisie had often enough seen her do before, covered her face with her hands. 'They ought to, at least. The situation's too monstrous!'

Maisie stood there a moment – she looked about the room. 'I'll go to him – I'll find him.'

'*I* won't! I won't go *near* them!' cried Mrs. Wix.

'Then I'll see him alone.' The child spied what she had been looking for – she possessed herself of her hat. 'Perhaps I'll take him out!' And with decision she quitted the room.

When she entered the *salon* it was empty, but at the sound of the opened door some one stirred on the balcony, and Sir Claude, stepping straight in, stood before her. He was in light, fresh clothes and wore a straw hat with a bright ribbon; these things, besides striking her in themselves as the very promise of the grandest of grand tours, gave him a certain radiance and, as it were, a tropical ease; but such an effect only marked rather more his having stopped short and, for a longer minute than had ever at such a juncture elapsed, not opened his arms to her. His pause made her pause and enabled her to reflect that he must have been up some time, for there were no traces of breakfast; and that though it was so late he had rather markedly not caused her to be called to him. Had Mrs. Wix been right about their forfeiture of the *salon*? Was it all his now, all his and Mrs. Beale's? Such an idea, at the rate her small thoughts throbbed, could only remind her of the way in which what had been hers hitherto was what was exactly most Mrs. Beale's and his. It was strange to be standing there and greeting him across a gulf, for he had by this time spoken, smiled and said: 'My dear child, my dear child!' but without coming any nearer. In a flash she saw that he was different – more so than he knew or designed. The next minute indeed it was as if he caught an impression from her face: this made him hold out his hand. Then they met, he kissed her, he laughed, she thought he even blushed: something of his affection rang out as usual. 'Here I am, you see, again – as I promised you.'

It was not as he had promised them – he had not promised them Mrs. Beale; but Maisie said nothing about that. What she said was simply: 'I knew you had come. Mrs. Wix told me.'

'Oh yes. And where is she?'

'In her room. She got me up – she dressed me.'

Sir Claude looked at her up and down; a sweetness of mockery that she particularly loved came out in his face whenever he did that, and it was not wanting now. He raised his eyebrows and his arms to play at admiration; he was evidently after all disposed to be gay. 'Got you up? – I should think so! She has dressed you most beautifully. Isn't she coming?'

Maisie wondered if she had better tell. 'She said not.'

'Doesn't she want to see a poor devil?'

She looked about under the vibration of the way he described himself, and her eyes rested on the door of the room he had previously occupied. 'Is Mrs. Beale in there?'

Sir Claude looked blankly at the same object. 'I haven't the least idea!'

'You haven't seen her?'

'Not the tip of her nose.'

Maisie thought: there settled on her, in the light of his beautiful smiling eyes, the faintest, purest, coldest conviction that he was not telling the truth. 'She hasn't welcomed you?'

'Not by a single sign.'

'Then where is she?'

Sir Claude laughed; he seemed both amused and surprised at the point she made of it. 'I give it up!'

'Doesn't she know you've come?'

He laughed again. 'Perhaps she doesn't care!'

Maisie, with an inspiration, pounced on his arm. 'Has she *gone*?'

He met her eyes and then she could see that his own were really much graver than his manner. 'Gone?' She had flown to the door, but before she could raise her hand to knock he was beside her and had caught it. 'Let her be. I don't care about her. I want to see *you*.'

Maisie fell back with him. 'Then she *hasn't* gone?'

He still looked as if it were a joke, but the more she saw of him the more she could make out that he was troubled. 'It wouldn't be like her!'

She stood wondering at him. 'Did you want her to come?'

'How can you suppose——?' He put it to her candidly. 'We had an immense row over it.'

'Do you mean you've quarrelled?'

Sir Claude was at a loss. 'What has she told you?'

'That I'm hers as much as yours. That she represents papa.'

His gaze struck away through the open window and up to the sky; she could hear him rattle in his trousers-pocket his money or his keys. 'Yes – that's what she keeps saying.' It gave him for a moment an air that was almost helpless.

'You say you don't care about her,' Maisie went on. '*Do* you mean you've quarrelled?'

'We do nothing in life but quarrel.'

He rose before her, as he said this, so soft and fair, so rich, in spite of what might worry him, in restored familiarities, that it gave a bright blur to the meaning – to what would otherwise perhaps have been the tangible promise – of the words. 'Oh, *your* quarrels!' she exclaimed with discouragement.

'I assure you hers are quite fearful!'

'I don't speak of hers. I speak of yours.'

'Ah, don't do it till I've had my coffee! You're growing up clever,' he added. Then he said: 'I suppose you've breakfasted?'

'Oh no – I've had nothing.'

'Nothing in your room?' – he was all compunction. 'My dear old man! – we'll breakfast then together.' He had one of his happy thoughts. 'I say – we'll go out.'

'That was just what I hoped. I've brought my hat.'

'You *are* clever! We'll go to a *café*.' Maisie was already at the door; he glanced round the room. 'A moment – my stick.' But there appeared to be no stick. 'No matter; I left it – oh!' He remembered with an odd drop and came out.

'You left it in London?' she asked as they went downstairs.

'Yes – in London: fancy!'

'You were in such a hurry to come,' Maisie explained.

He had his arm round her. 'That must have been the reason.' Half way down he stopped short again, slapping his leg. 'And poor Mrs. Wix?'

Maisie's face just showed a shadow. 'Do you want her to come?'

'Dear, no – I want to see you alone.'

'That's the way I want to see *you*!' she replied. 'Like before.'

'Like before!' he gaily echoed. 'But I mean has she had her coffee?'

'No, nothing.'

'Then I'll send it up to her. Madame!' He had already, at the foot of the stair, called out to the stout *patronne*, a lady who turned to him from the bustling, breezy hall a countenance covered with fresh matutinal powder and a bosom as capacious as the velvet shelf of a chimneypiece, over which her round white face, framed in its golden frizzle, might have figured as a showy clock. He ordered, with particular recommendations, Mrs. Wix's repast, and it was a charm to hear his easy, brilliant French: even his companion's ignorance could measure the perfection of it. The *patronne*, rubbing her hands and breaking in with high, swift notes as into a florid duet, went with him to the street, and while they talked a moment longer Maisie remembered what Mrs. Wix had said about every one's liking him. It came out enough through the morning powder, it came out enough in the heaving bosom how the landlady liked him. He had evidently ordered something lovely for Mrs. Wix. '*Et bien soigné, n'est-ce-pas?*'

'*Soyez tranquille*' – the *patronne* beamed upon him. '*Et pour Madame?*'

'*Madame?*' he echoed – it just pulled him up a little.

'*Rien encore?*'

'*Rien encore*. Come, Maisie.' She hurried along with him, but on the way to the *café* he said nothing.

XXX

After they were seated there it was different: the place was not below the hotel, but further along the quay; with wide, clear windows and a floor sprinkled with bran in a manner that gave it for Maisie something of the added charm of a circus. They had pretty much to themselves the painted spaces and the red plush benches; these were shared by a few scattered gentlemen who picked teeth, with facial contortions, behind little bare tables, and by an old personage in particular, a very old personage with a red ribbon in his buttonhole, whose manner of soaking buttered rolls in coffee and then disposing of them in the little that was left of the interval between his nose and chin might at a less anxious hour have cast upon Maisie an almost envious spell. They too had their *café au lait* and their buttered rolls, determined by Sir Claude's asking her if she could with that light aid wait till the hour of *déjeuner*. His allusion to this meal gave her, in the shaded, sprinkled coolness, the scene, as she vaguely felt, of a sort of ordered, mirrored licence, the haunt of those – the irregular, like herself – who went to bed or who rose too late, something to think over while she watched the white-aproned waiter perform as nimbly with plates and saucers as a certain conjurer her friend had in London taken her to a music-hall to see. Sir Claude had presently begun to talk again, to tell her how London had looked and how long he had felt himself, on either side, to have been absent; all about Susan Ash too and the amusement as well as the difficulty he had had with her; then all about his return journey and the Channel in the night and the crowd of people coming over and the way there were always too many one knew. He spoke of other

matters beside, especially of what she must tell him of the occu-
pations, while he was away, of Mrs. Wix and her pupil. Hadn't
they had the good time he had promised? – had he exaggerated
a bit the arrangements made for their pleasure? Maisie had
something – not all there was – to say of his success and of their
gratitude: she had a complication of thought that grew every
minute, grew with the consciousness that she had never seen
him in this particular state in which he had been given back.

Mrs. Wix had once said – it was once or fifty times; once was
enough for Maisie, but more was not too much – that he was
wonderfully various. Well, he was certainly so, to the child's
mind, on the present occasion: he was much more various than
he was anything else. The fact that they were together in a shop,
at a nice little intimate table as they had so often been in London,
only, besides, made greater the difference of what they were
together about. This difference was in his face, in his voice, in
every look he gave her and every movement he made. They
were not the looks and the movements he really wanted to
show, and she could feel as well that they were not those
she herself wanted. She had seen him nervous, she had seen
every one she had come in contact with nervous, but she had
never seen him so nervous as this. Little by little it gave her a
settled terror, a terror that partook of the coldness she had felt
just before, at the hotel, to find herself, on his answer about
Mrs. Beale, disbelieve him. She seemed to see at present, to
touch across the table, as if by laying her hand on it, what he
had meant when he confessed on those several occasions to
fear. Why was such a man so often afraid? It must have begun
to come to her now that there was one thing just such a man
above all could be afraid of. He could be afraid of himself. His
fear at all events was there; his fear was sweet to her, beautiful
and tender to her, was having coffee and buttered rolls and
talk and laughter that were no talk and laughter at all with
her; his fear was in his jesting, postponing, perverting voice; it
was in just this make-believe way he had brought her out to
imitate the old London playtimes, to imitate indeed a relation
that had wholly changed, a relation that she had with her very
eyes seen in the act of change when, the day before in the

salon, Mrs. Beale rose suddenly before her. She rose before her, for that matter, now, and even while their refreshment delayed Maisie arrived at the straight question for which, on their entrance, his first word had given opportunity. 'Are we going to have *déjeuner* with Mrs. Beale?'

His reply was anything but straight. 'You and I?'

Maisie sat back in her chair. 'Mrs. Wix and me.'

Sir Claude also shifted. 'That's an inquiry, my dear child, that Mrs. Beale herself must answer.' Yes, he had shifted; but abruptly, after a moment during which something seemed to hang there between them and, as it heavily swayed, just fan them with the air of its motion, she felt that the whole thing was upon them. 'Do you mind,' he broke out, 'my asking you what Mrs. Wix has said to you?'

'Said to me?'

'This day or two – while I was away.'

'Do you mean about you and Mrs. Beale?'

Sir Claude, resting on his elbows, fixed his eyes a moment on the white marble beneath them. 'No; I think we had a good deal of that – didn't we? – before I left you. It seems to me we had it pretty well all out. I mean about yourself, about your – don't you know? – associating with us, as I might say, and staying on with us. While you were alone with our friend what did she say?'

Maisie felt the weight of the question; it kept her silent for a space during which she looked at Sir Claude, whose eyes remained bent. 'Nothing,' she rejoined at last.

He showed incredulity. 'Nothing?'

'Nothing,' Maisie repeated; on which an interruption descended in the form of a tray bearing the preparations for their breakfast.

These preparations were as amusing as everything else; the waiter poured their coffee from a vessel like a watering-pot and then made it froth with the curved stream of hot milk that dropped from the height of his raised arm; but the two looked across at each other through the whole play of French pleasantness with a gravity that had now ceased to dissemble. Sir Claude sent the waiter off again for something and then took up her answer. 'Hasn't she tried to affect you?'

Face to face with him thus it seemed to Maisie that she had tried so little as to be scarce worth mentioning; again therefore an instant she shut herself up. Presently she found her middle course. 'Mrs. Beale likes her now; and there's one thing I've found out – a great thing. Mrs. Wix enjoys her being so kind. She was tremendously kind all day yesterday.'

'I see. And what did she do?' Sir Claude asked.

Maisie was now busy with her breakfast, and her companion attacked his own; so that it was all, in form at least, even more than their old sociability. 'Everything she could think of. She was as nice to her as you are,' the child said. 'She talked to her all day.'

'And what did she say to her?'

'Oh, I don't know.' Maisie was a little bewildered with his pressing her so for knowledge; it didn't fit into the degree of intimacy with Mrs. Beale that Mrs. Wix had so denounced and that, according to that lady, had now brought him back in bondage. Wasn't he more aware than his stepdaughter of what would be done by the person to whom he was bound? In a moment, however, she added: 'She made love to her.'

Sir Claude looked at her harder, and it was clearly something in her tone that made him quickly say: 'You don't mind my asking you, do you?'

'Not at all; only I should think you'd know better than I.'

'What Mrs. Beale did yesterday?'

She thought he coloured a trifle; but almost simultaneously with that impression she found herself answering: 'Yes – if you *have* seen her.'

He broke into the loudest of laughs. 'Why, my dear boy, I told you just now I've absolutely not. I say, don't you believe me?'

There was something she was already so afraid of that it covered up other fears. 'Didn't you come back to see her?' she inquired in a moment. 'Didn't you come back because you always want to so much?'

He received her inquiry as he had received her doubt – with an extraordinary absence of resentment. 'I can imagine of course why you think that. But it doesn't explain my doing what I have. It was, as I said to you just now at the inn, really and truly you I wanted to see.'

She felt an instant as she used to feel when, in the back-garden at her mother's, she took from him the highest push of a swing – high, high, high – that he had had put there for her pleasure and that had finally broken down under the weight and the extravagant patronage of the cook. 'Well, that's beautiful. But to see me, you mean, and go away again?'

'My going away again is just the point. I can't tell yet – it all depends.'

'On Mrs. Beale?' Maisie asked. '*She* won't go away.' He finished emptying his coffee-cup and then, when he had put it down, leaned back in his chair, where she could see that he smiled at her. This only added to her idea that he was in trouble, that he was turning somehow in his pain and trying different things. He continued to smile and she went on: 'Don't you know that?'

'Yes, I may as well confess to you that as much as that I do know. *She* won't go away. She'll stay.'

'She'll stay. She'll stay,' Maisie repeated.

'Just so. Won't you have some more coffee?'

'Yes, please.'

'And another buttered roll?'

'Yes, please.'

He signed to the hovering waiter, who arrived with the shining spout of plenty in either hand and with the friendliest interest in mademoiselle. '*Les tartines sont là.*' Their cups were replenished and, while he watched almost musingly the bubbles in the fragrant mixture, 'Just so – just so,' Sir Claude said again and again. 'It's awfully awkward!' he exclaimed when the waiter had gone.

'That she won't go?'

'Well – everything! Well, well, well!' But he pulled himself together; he began again to eat. 'I came back to ask you something. That's what I came back for.'

'I know what you want to ask me,' Maisie said.

'Are you very sure?'

'I'm *almost* very.'

'Well then, risk it. You mustn't make *me* risk everything.'

She was struck with the force of this. 'You want to know if I should be happy with *them*.'

'With those two ladies only? No, no, old man: *vous n'y êtes pas*. So now – there!' Sir Claude laughed.

'Well then, what is it?'

The next minute, instead of telling her what it was, he laid his hand across the table on her own and held her as if under the prompting of a thought. 'Mrs. Wix would stay with *her*?'

'Without you? Oh yes – now.'

'On account, as you just intimated, of Mrs. Beale's changed manner?'

Maisie, with her sense of responsibility, focused both Mrs. Beale's changed manner and Mrs. Wix's human weakness. 'I think she talked her over.'

Sir Claude thought a moment. 'Ah, poor dear!'

'Do you mean Mrs. Beale?'

'Oh no – Mrs. Wix.'

'She likes being talked over – treated like any one else. Oh, she likes great politeness,' Maisie expatiated. 'It affects her very much.'

Sir Claude, to her surprise, demurred a little to this. 'Very much – up to a certain point.'

'Oh, up to any point!' Maisie returned with emphasis.

'Well, haven't I been polite to her?'

'Lovely – and she perfectly worships you.'

'Then, my dear child, why can't she let me alone?' – this time Sir Claude unmistakably blushed. Before Maisie, however, could answer his question, which would indeed have taken her long, he went on in another tone: 'Mrs. Beale thinks she has probably quite broken her down. But she hasn't.'

Though he spoke as if he were sure, Maisie was strong in the impression she had just uttered and that she now again produced. 'She has talked her over.'

'Ah yes; over to herself, but not over to me.'

Oh, she couldn't bear to hear him say that! 'To you? Don't you really believe how she loves you?'

Sir Claude examined his belief. 'Of course I know she's wonderful.'

'She's just every bit as fond of you as *I* am,' said Maisie. 'She told me so yesterday.'

'Ah then,' he promptly exclaimed, 'she *has* tried to affect you! I don't love *her*, don't you see? I do her perfect justice,' he pursued, 'but I mean I don't love her as I do you, and I'm sure you wouldn't seriously expect it. She's not my daughter – come, old chap! She's not even my mother, though I daresay it would have been better for me if she had been. I'll do for her what I'd do for my mother, but I won't do more.' His real excitement broke out in a need to explain and justify himself, though he kept trying to correct and conceal it with laughs and mouthfuls and other vain familiarities. Suddenly he broke off, wiping his moustache with sharp pulls and coming back to Mrs. Beale. 'Did she try to talk *you* over?'

'No – to me she said very little. Very little indeed,' Maisie continued.

Sir Claude seemed struck with this. 'She was only sweet to Mrs. Wix?'

'As sweet as sugar!' cried Maisie.

He looked amused at her comparison, but he didn't contest it; he uttered on the contrary, in an assenting way, a little inarticulate sound. 'I know what she *can* be. But much good may it have done her! Mrs. Wix won't come round. That's what makes it so fearfully awkward.'

Maisie knew it was fearfully awkward; she had known this now, she felt, for some time, and there was something else it more pressingly concerned her to learn. 'What is it that you meant you came over to ask me?'

'Well,' said Sir Claude, 'I was just going to say. Let me tell you it will surprise you.' She had finished breakfast now and she sat back in her chair again: she waited in silence to hear. He had pushed the things before him a little way and had his elbows on the table. This time, she was convinced, she knew what was coming, and once more, for the crash, as with Mrs. Wix lately in her room, she held her breath and drew together her eyes. He was going to say that she must give him up. He looked hard at her again; then he made his effort. 'Should you see your way to let her go?'

She was bewildered. 'To let who——?'

'Mrs. Wix, simply. I put it at the worst. Should you see your way to sacrifice her? Of course I know what I'm asking.'

Maisie's eyes opened wide again; this was so different from what she had expected. 'And stay with you alone?'

He gave another push to his coffee-cup. 'With me and Mrs. Beale. Of course it would be rather rum; but everything in our whole story is rather rum, you know. What is more unusual than for any one to be given up, like you, by her parents?'

'Oh, nothing is more unusual than *that*!' Maisie concurred, relieved at the contact of a proposition as to which concurrence could have lucidity.

'Of course it would be quite unconventional,' Sir Claude went on – 'I mean the little household we three should make together; but things have got beyond that, don't you see? They got beyond that long ago. We shall stay abroad at any rate – it's ever so much easier and it's our affair and nobody else's: it's no one's business but ours on all the blessed earth. I don't say that for Mrs. Wix, poor dear – I do her absolute justice. I respect her; I see what she means; she has done me a lot of good. But there are the facts. There they are, simply. And here am I, and here are you. And she won't come round. She's right from her point of view. I'm talking to you in the most extraordinary way – I'm always talking to you in the most extraordinary way, ain't I? One would think you were about sixty and that I – I don't know what any one would think *I* am. Unless a beastly cad!' he suggested. 'I've been awfully worried, and this is what it has come to. You've done us the most tremendous good, and you'll do it still and always, don't you see? We can't let you go – you're everything. There are the facts as I say. She *is* your mother now, Mrs. Beale, by what has happened, and I, in the same way, I'm your father. No one can contradict that, and we can't get out of it. My idea would be a nice little place – somewhere in the south – where she and you would be together and as good as any one else. And I should be as good too, don't you see? for I shouldn't live with you, but I should be close to you – just round the corner, and it would be just the same. My idea would be that it should all be perfectly open and frank.

Honi soit qui mal y pense, don't you know? You're the best
thing – you and what we can do for you – that either of us has
ever known:' he came back to that. 'When I say to her "Give her
up, come," she lets me have it bang in the face: "Give her up
yourself!" It's the same old vicious circle – and when I say
vicious I don't mean a pun or a what-d'ye-call-'em. Mrs. Wix is
the obstacle; I mean, you know, if she has affected you. She has
affected *me*, and yet here I am. I never was in such a tight place:
please believe it's only that that makes me put it to you as I do.
My dear child, isn't that – to put it so – just the way out of it?
That came to me yesterday, in London, after Mrs. Beale had
gone: I had the most infernal, atrocious day. "Go straight over
and put it to her: let her choose, freely, her own self." So I do,
old girl – I put it to you. *Can* you choose freely?'

This long address, slowly and brokenly uttered, with fidgets
and falterings, with lapses and recoveries, with a mottled face
and embarrassed but supplicating eyes, reached the child from
a quarter so close that after the shock of the first sharpness she
could see intensely its direction and follow it from point to
point; all the more that it came back to the point at which it
had started. There was a word that had hummed all through it.
'Do you call it a "sacrifice"?'

'Of Mrs. Wix? I'll call it whatever *you* call it. I won't funk it –
I haven't, have I? I'll face it in all its baseness. Does it strike you
it *is* base for me to get you well away from her, to smuggle you
off here into a corner and bribe you with sophistries and buttered rolls to betray her?'

'To betray her?'

'Well – to part with her.'

Maisie let the question wait; the concrete image it presented was the most vivid side of it. 'If I part with her where
will she go?'

'Back to London.'

'But I mean what will she do?'

'Oh, as for that I won't pretend I know. I don't. We all have
our difficulties.'

That, to Maisie, was at this moment more striking than it
had ever been. 'Then who will teach me?'

Sir Claude laughed out. 'What Mrs. Wix teaches?'

Maisie smiled dimly; she saw what he meant. 'It isn't so very, very much.'

'It's so very, very little,' he rejoined, 'that that's a thing we've positively to consider. We probably shouldn't give you another governess. To begin with, we shouldn't be able to get one – not of the only kind that would do. It wouldn't do – the kind that *would* do,' he queerly enough explained. 'I mean they wouldn't stay – heigh-ho! We'd do you ourselves. Particularly me. You see I *can* now; I haven't got to mind – what I used to. I won't fight shy as I did – she can show out *with* me. Our relation, all round, is more regular.'

It seemed wonderfully regular, the way he put it; yet none the less, while she looked at it as judiciously as she could, the picture it made persisted somehow in being a combination quite distinct – an old woman and a little girl seated in deep silence on a battered old bench by the rampart of the *haute ville*. It was just at that hour yesterday; they were hand in hand; they had melted together. 'I don't think you yet understand how she clings to you,' Maisie said at last.

'I do – I do. But for all that——!' And he gave, turning in his conscious exposure, an oppressed, impatient sigh; the sigh, even his companion could recognize, of the man naturally accustomed to that argument, the man who wanted thoroughly to be reasonable, but who, if really he had to mind so many things, would be always impossibly hampered. What it came to indeed was that he understood quite perfectly. If Mrs. Wix clung it was all the more reason for shaking Mrs. Wix off.

This vision of what she had brought him to occupied our young lady while, to ask what he owed, he called the waiter and put down a gold piece that the man carried off for change. Sir Claude looked after him, then went on: 'How could a woman have less to reproach a fellow with? I mean as regards herself.'

Maisie entertained the question. 'Yes. How *could* she have less? So why are you so sure she'll go?'

'Surely you heard why – you heard her come out three nights ago? How can she do anything but go – after what she then said? I've done what she warned me of – she was absolutely right. So here we are. Her liking Mrs. Beale, as you call it now, is a motive sufficient with other things to make her, for your sake, stay on without me; it's not a motive sufficient to make her, even for yours, stay on *with* me – swallow, in short, what she can't swallow. And when you say she's as fond of me as you are I think I can, if that's the case, challenge you a little on it. Would *you*, only with those two, stay on without me?' The waiter came back with the change, and that gave her, under this appeal, a moment's respite. But when he had retreated again with the 'tip' gathered in with graceful thanks on a subtle hint from Sir Claude's forefinger, the latter, while he pocketed the money, followed the appeal up. 'Would you let her make you live with Mrs. Beale?'

'Without you? Never,' Maisie then answered. 'Never,' she said again.

It made him quite triumph, and she was indeed herself shaken by the mere sound of it. 'So you see you're not, like her,' he exclaimed, 'so ready to give me away!' Then he came back to his original question. '*Can* you choose? I mean can you settle it, by a word, yourself? Will you stay on with us without her?'

Now in truth she felt the coldness of her terror, and it seemed to her that suddenly she knew, as she knew it about Sir Claude, what she was afraid of. She was afraid of herself. She looked at him in such a way that it brought, she could see, wonder into his face, a wonder held in check, however, by his frank pretension to play fair with her, not to use advantages, not to hurry nor hustle her – only to put her chance clearly and kindly before her. 'May I think?' she finally asked.

'Certainly, certainly. But how long?'

'Oh, only a little while,' she said meekly.

He had for a moment the air of wishing to look at it as if it were the most cheerful prospect in the world. 'But what shall we do while you're thinking?' He spoke as if thought were compatible with almost any distraction.

There was but one thing Maisie wished to do, and after an instant she expressed it. 'Have we got to go back to the hotel?'

'Do you want to?'

'Oh no.'

'There's not the least necessity for it.' He bent his eyes on his watch; his face was now very grave. 'We can do anything else in the world.' He looked at her again almost as if he were on the point of saying that they might for instance start off for Paris. But even while she wondered if that were not coming he had a sudden drop. 'We can take a walk.'

She was all ready, but he sat there as if he had still something more to say. This too, however, didn't come; so she herself spoke. 'I think I should like to see Mrs. Wix first.'

'Before you decide? All right – all right.' He had put on his hat, but he had still to light a cigarette. He smoked a minute, with his head thrown back, looking at the ceiling; then he said: 'There's one thing to remember – I've a right to impress it on you: we stand absolutely in the place of your parents. It's their defection, their extraordinary baseness, that has made our responsibility. Never was a young person more directly committed and confided.' He appeared to say this over, at the ceiling, through his smoke, a little for his own illumination. It carried him after a pause somewhat further. 'Though, I admit, it was to each of us separately.'

He gave her so, at that moment and in that attitude, the sense of wanting, as it were, to be on her side – on the side of what would be in every way most right and wise and charming for her – that she felt a sudden desire to show herself as not less delicate and magnanimous, not less solicitous for his own interests. What were these but that of the 'regularity' he had just before spoken of? 'It *was* to each of you separately,' she accordingly with much earnestness remarked. 'But don't you remember? I brought you together.'

He jumped up with a delighted laugh. 'Remember? Rather! You brought us together, you brought us together. Come!'

XXXI

She remained out with him for a time of which she could take no measure save that it was too short for what she wished to make of it – an interval, a barrier indefinite, insurmountable. They walked about, they dawdled, they looked in shop-windows; they did all the old things exactly as if to try toget back all the old safety, to get something out of them that they had always got before. This had come before, whatever it was, without their trying, and nothing came now but the intenser consciousness of their quest and their subterfuge. The strangest thing of all was what had really happened to the old safety. What had really happened was that Sir Claude was 'free' and that Mrs. Beale was 'free', and yet that the new medium was somehow still more oppressive than the old. She could feel that Sir Claude concurred with her in the sense that the oppression would be worst at the inn, where, till something should be settled, they would feel the want of something – of what could they call it but a footing? The question of the settlement loomed larger to her now: it depended, she had learned, so completely on herself. Her choice, as her friend had called it, was there before her like an impossible sum on a slate, a sum that in spite of her plea for consideration she simply got off from doing while she walked about with him. She must see Mrs. Wix before she could do her sum; therefore the longer before she saw her the more distant would be the ordeal. She met at present no demand whatever of her obligation; she simply plunged, to avoid it, deeper into the company of Sir Claude. She saw nothing that she had seen hitherto – no touch in the foreign picture that had at first been always before her. The only touch was

that of Sir Claude's hand, and to feel her own in it was her mute
resistance to time. She went about as sightlessly as if he had
been leading her blindfold. If they were afraid of themselves it
was themselves they would find at the inn. She was certain
now that what awaited them there would be to lunch with
Mrs. Beale. All her instinct was to avoid that, to draw out their
walk, to find pretexts, to take him down upon the beach, to
take him to the end of the pier. He said not another word to her
about what they had talked of at breakfast, and she had a dim
vision of how his way of not letting her see that he was waiting
for anything from her would make any one who should know
of it, would make Mrs. Wix for instance, think him more than
ever a gentleman. It was true that once or twice, on the jetty, on
the sands, he looked at her for a minute with eyes that seemed
to propose to her to come straight off with him to Paris. That,
however, was not to give her a nudge about her responsibility.
He evidently wanted to procrastinate quite as much as she did;
he was not a bit more in a hurry to get back to the others.
Maisie herself at this moment could be secretly merciless to
Mrs. Wix – to the extent at any rate of not caring if her continued disappearance did make that lady begin to worry about
what had become of her, even begin to wonder perhaps if
the truants hadn't found their remedy. Her want of mercy to
Mrs. Beale indeed was at least as great; for Mrs. Beale's worry
and wonder would be as much greater as the object at which
they were directed. When at last Sir Claude, at the far end of the
plage, which they had already, in the many-coloured crowd,
once traversed, suddenly, with a look at his watch, remarked
that it was time, not to get back to the *table d'hôte*, but to get
over to the station and meet the Paris papers – when he did this
she found herself thinking quite with intensity what Mrs. Beale
and Mrs. Wix *would* say. On the way over to the station she
had even a mental picture of the stepfather and the pupil established in a little place in the south while the governess and the
stepmother, in a little place in the north, remained linked by a
community of blankness and by the endless theme of intercourse it would afford. The Paris papers had come in and her
companion with a strange extravagance bought no less of them

than nine: it took up time while they hovered at the bookstall on the restless platform, where the little volumes in a row were all yellow and pink and one of her favourite old women in one of her favourite old caps absolutely wheedled him into the purchase of three. They had thus so much to carry home that it would have seemed simpler, with such a provision for a nice straight journey through France, just to 'nip', as she phrased it to herself, into the *coupé* of the train that, a little further along, stood waiting to start. She asked Sir Claude where it was going.

'To Paris. Fancy!'

She could fancy well enough. They stood there and smiled, he with all the newspapers under his arm and she with the three books, one yellow and two pink. He had told her the pink were for herself and the yellow one for Mrs. Beale, implying in an interesting way that these were the vivid divisions in France of literature for the young and for the old. She knew that they looked exactly as if they were going to get into the train, and she presently brought out to her companion: 'I wish we could go. Won't you take me?'

He continued to smile. 'Would you really come?'

'Oh yes, oh yes. Try.'

'Do you want me to take our tickets?'

'Yes, take them.'

'Without any luggage?'

She showed their two armfuls, smiling at him as he smiled at her, but so conscious of being more frightened than she had ever been in her life that she seemed to see her whiteness as in a glass. Then she knew that what she saw was Sir Claude's whiteness: he was as frightened as herself. 'Haven't we got plenty of luggage?' she asked. 'Take the tickets – haven't you time? When does the train go?'

Sir Claude turned to a porter. 'When does the train go?'

The man looked up at the station clock. 'In two minutes. *Monsieur est placé?*'

'*Pas encore.*'

'*Et vos billets? – vous n'avez que le temps.*' Then, after a look at Maisie, '*Monsieur veut-il que je les prenne?*' the man inquired.

Sir Claude turned back to her. '*Veux-tu bien qu'il en prenne?*'

It was the most extraordinary thing in the world: in the intensity of her excitement she not only by illumination understood all their French, but fell into it with an active perfection. She addressed herself straight to the porter. '*Prenny, prenny. Oh prenny!*'

'*Ah, si mademoiselle le veut——*' He waited there for the money.

But Sir Claude only stared – stared at her with his white face. 'You *have* chosen then? You'll let her go?'

Maisie carried her eyes wistfully to the train, where, amid cries of '*En voiture, en voiture!*' heads were at windows and doors banging loud. The porter was pressing. '*Ah, vous n'avez plus le temps!*'

'It's going – it's going!' cried Maisie.

They watched it move, they watched it start; then the man went his way with a shrug. 'It's gone!' Sir Claude said.

Maisie crept some distance up the platform; she stood there with her back to her companion, following it with her eyes, keeping down tears, nursing her pink and yellow books. She had had a real fright, but had fallen back to earth. The odd thing was that in her fall her fear too had been dashed down and broken. It was gone. She looked round at last from where she had paused at Sir Claude's, and then she saw that his was not. It sat there with him on the bench to which, against the wall of the station, he had retreated, and where, leaning back and, as she thought, rather queer, he still waited. She came down to him and he continued to offer his ineffectual intention of pleasantry. 'Yes, I've chosen,' she said to him. 'I'll let her go if you – if you——'

She faltered; he quickly took her up. 'If I, if I——?'

'If you'll give up Mrs. Beale.'

'Oh!' he exclaimed; on which she saw how much, how hopelessly he was afraid. She had supposed at the *café* that it was of his rebellion, of his gathering motive; but how could that be when his temptations – that temptation for example of the train they had just lost – were after all so slight? Mrs. Wix was right. He was afraid of his weakness – of his weakness.

She could not have told you afterwards how they got back to the inn: she could only have told you that even from this point they had not gone straight, but once more had wandered and loitered and, in the course of it, had found themselves on the edge of the quay where – still apparently with half an hour to spare – the boat prepared for Folkestone was drawn up. Here they hovered as they had done at the station; here they exchanged silences again, but only exchanged silences. There were punctual people on the deck, choosing places, taking the best; some of them already contented, all established and shawled, facing to England and attended by the steward, who, confined on such a day to the lighter offices, tucked up the ladies' feet or opened bottles with a pop. They looked down at these things without a word; they even picked out a good place for two that was left in the lee of a lifeboat; and if they lingered rather stupidly, neither deciding to go aboard nor deciding to come away, it was quite as much as she Sir Claude who wouldn't move. It was Sir Claude who cultivated the supreme stillness by which she knew best what he meant. He simply meant that he knew all she herself meant. But there was no pretence of pleasantry now: their faces were grave and tired. When at last they lounged off it was as if his fear, his fear of his weakness, leaned upon her heavily as they followed the harbour. In the hall of the hotel as they passed in she saw a battered old box that she recognized, an ancient receptacle with dangling labels that she knew and a big painted W, lately done over and intensely personal, that seemed to stare at her with a recognition and even with some suspicion of its own. Sir Claude caught it too, and there was agitation for both of them in the sight of this object on the move. Was Mrs. Wix going and was the responsibility of giving her up lifted, at a touch, from her pupil? Her pupil and her pupil's companion, transfixed a moment, held, in the presence of the omen, communication more intense than in the presence either of the Paris train or of the Channel steamer; then, and still without a word, they went straight upstairs. There, however, on the landing, out of sight of the people below, they collapsed so that they had to sink down together for support: they simply seated themselves on the uppermost step while Sir Claude grasped the hand of his stepdaughter with a pressure that at another moment would probably have made her squeal. Their books and papers were all scattered. 'She thinks you've given her up!'

'Then I must see her – I must see her,' Maisie said.

'To bid her good-bye?'

'I must see her – I must see her,' the child only repeated.

They sat a minute longer, Sir Claude with his tight grip of her hand and looking away from her, looking straight down the staircase to where, round the turn, electric bells rattled and the pleasant sea-draught blew. At last, loosening his grasp, he slowly got up while she did the same. They went together along the lobby, but before they reached the *salon* he stopped again. 'If I give up Mrs. Beale——?'

'I'll go straight out with you again and not come back till she has gone.'

He seemed to wonder. 'Till Mrs. Beale——?'

He had made it sound like a bad joke. 'I mean till Mrs. Wix leaves – in that boat.'

Sir Claude looked almost foolish. 'Is she going in that boat?'

'I suppose so. I won't even bid her good-bye,' Maisie continued. 'I'll stay out till the boat has gone. I'll go up to the old rampart.'

'The old rampart?'

'I'll sit on that old bench where you see the gold Virgin.'

'The gold Virgin?' he vaguely echoed. But it brought his eyes back to her as if after an instant he could see the place and the thing she named – could see her sitting there alone. 'While I break with Mrs. Beale?'

'While you break with Mrs. Beale.'

He gave a long, deep, smothered sigh. 'I must see her first.'

'You won't do as I do? Go out and wait?'

'Wait?' – once more he appeared at a loss.

'Till they both have gone,' Maisie said.

'Giving *us* up?'

'Giving *us* up.'

Oh, with what a face, for an instant, he wondered if that could be! But his wonder the next moment only made him go to the door and, with his hand on the knob, stand as if listening for voices. Maisie listened, but she heard none. All she heard presently was Sir Claude's saying with speculation quite averted, but so as not to be heard in the *salon*: 'Mrs. Beale will never go.' On this he pushed open the door and she went in with him. The *salon* was empty, but as an effect of their entrance the lady he had just mentioned appeared at the door of the bedroom. 'Is she going?' he then demanded.

Mrs. Beale came forward, closing her door behind her. 'I've had the most extraordinary scene with her. She told me yesterday she'd stay.'

'And my arrival has altered it?'

'Oh, we took that into account!' Mrs. Beale was flushed, which was never quite becoming to her, and her face visibly testified to the encounter to which she alluded. Evidently, however, she had not been worsted, and she held up her head and smiled and rubbed her hands as if in sudden emulation of the *patronne*. 'She promised she'd stay even if you should come.'

'Then why has she changed?'

'Because she's a hound. The reason she herself gives is that you've been out too long.'

Sir Claude stared. 'What has that to do with it?'

'You've been out an age,' Mrs. Beale continued; 'I myself couldn't imagine what had become of you. The whole morning,' she exclaimed, 'and luncheon long since over!'

Sir Claude appeared indifferent to that. 'Did Mrs. Wix go down with you?' he only asked.

'Not she; she never budged!' – and Mrs. Beale's flush, to Maisie's vision, deepened. 'She moped there – she didn't so much as come out to me; and when I sent to invite her she simply declined to appear. She said she wanted nothing, and I went down alone. But when I came up, fortunately a little primed' – and Mrs. Beale smiled a fine smile of battle – 'she *was* in the field!'

'And you had a big row?'

'We had a big row' – she assented with a frankness as large. 'And while you left me to that sort of thing, I should like to know where you were!' She paused for a reply, but Sir Claude merely looked at Maisie; a movement that promptly quickened her challenge. 'Where the mischief have you been?'

'You seem to take it as hard as Mrs. Wix,' Sir Claude returned.

'I take it as I choose to take it, and you don't answer my question.'

He looked again at Maisie, and as if for an aid to this effort; whereupon she smiled at her stepmother and offered: 'We've been everywhere.'

Mrs. Beale, however, made her no response, thereby adding to a surprise of which our young lady had already felt the light brush. She had received neither a greeting nor a glance, but perhaps this was not more remarkable than the omission, in respect to Sir Claude, parted with in London two days before, of any sign of a sense of their reunion. Most remarkable of all was Mrs. Beale's announcement of the pledge given by Mrs. Wix and not hitherto revealed to her pupil. Instead of heeding this witness she went on with acerbity: 'It might surely have occurred to you that something would come up.'

Sir Claude looked at his watch. 'I had no idea it was so late, nor that we had been out so long. We weren't hungry. It passed like a flash. What *has* come up?'

'Oh, that she's disgusted,' said Mrs. Beale.

'With whom then?'

'With Maisie.' Even now she never looked at the child, who stood there equally associated and disconnected. 'For having no moral sense.'

'How *should* she have?' Sir Claude tried again to shine a little at the companion of his walk. 'How at any rate is it proved by her going out with me?'

'Don't ask *me*; ask that woman. She drivels when she doesn't rage,' Mrs. Beale declared.

'And she leaves the child?'

'She leaves the child,' said Mrs. Beale with great emphasis and looking more than ever over Maisie's head.

In this position suddenly a change came into her face, caused, as the others could the next thing see, by the reappearance of Mrs. Wix in the doorway which, on coming in at Sir Claude's heels, Maisie had left gaping. 'I *don't* leave the child – I don't, I don't!' she thundered from the threshold, advancing upon the opposed three, but addressing herself directly to Maisie. She was girded – positively harnessed – for departure, arrayed as she had been arrayed on her advent and armed with a small, fat, rusty reticule which, almost in the manner of a battle-axe, she brandished in support of her words. She had clearly come straight from her room, where Maisie in an instant guessed she had directed the removal of her minor effects. 'I don't leave you till I've given you another chance: will you come *with* me?'

Maisie turned to Sir Claude, who struck her as having been removed to a distance of about a mile. To Mrs. Beale she turned no more than Mrs. Beale had turned: she felt as if already their difference had been disclosed. What had come out about that in the scene between the two women? Enough came out now, at all events, as she put it practically to her stepfather. 'Will *you* come? Won't you?' she inquired as if she had not already seen that she should have to give him up. It was the last flare of her dream. By this time she was afraid of nothing.

'I should think you'd be too proud to ask!' Mrs. Wix interposed. Mrs. Wix was herself conspicuously too proud.

But at the child's words Mrs. Beale had fairly bounded. 'Come away from *me*, Maisie?' It was a wail of dismay and reproach, in which her stepdaughter was astonished to read that she had had no hostile consciousness and that if she had been so actively grand it was not from suspicion, but from strange entanglements of modesty.

Sir Claude presented to Mrs. Beale an expression positively sick. 'Don't put it to her *that* way!' There had indeed been something in Mrs. Beale's tone, and for a moment our young lady was reminded of the old days in which so many of her friends had been 'compromised'.

This friend blushed – it was before Mrs. Wix, and though she bridled she took the hint. 'No – it isn't the way.' Then she showed she knew the way. 'Don't be a still bigger fool, dear, but go straight to your room and wait there till I can come to you.'

Maisie made no motion to obey, but Mrs. Wix raised a hand that forestalled every evasion. 'Don't move till you've heard me. *I'm* going, but I must first understand. Have you lost it again?'

Maisie surveyed for the idea of a describable loss the immensity of space. Then she replied lamely enough: 'I feel as if I had lost everything.'

Mrs. Wix looked dark. 'Do you mean to say you *have* lost what we found together with so much difficulty two days ago?' As her pupil failed of response she continued: 'Do you mean to say you've already forgotten what we found together?'

Maisie dimly remembered. 'My moral sense?'

'Your moral sense. *Haven't* I, after all, brought it out?' She spoke as she had never spoken even in the schoolroom and with the book in her hand.

It brought back to the child's recollection of how sometimes she couldn't repeat on Friday the sentence that had been glib on Wednesday, and she thought with conscious stupidity of the mystery on which she was now pulled up. Sir Claude and Mrs. Beale stood there like visitors at an 'exam'. She had indeed an instant a whiff of the faint flower that Mrs. Wix pretended to have plucked and now with such a peremptory hand passed under her nose. Then it left her, and, as if she were sinking with a slip from a foothold, her arms made a short jerk. What this jerk represented was the spasm within her of something still deeper than a moral sense. She looked at her examiner; she looked at the visitors; she felt the rising of the tears she had kept down at the station. The only thing was the old flat, shameful schoolroom plea. 'I don't know – I don't know.'

'Then you've lost it.' Mrs. Wix seemed to close the book as she fixed the straighteners on Sir Claude. 'You've nipped it in the bud. You've killed it when it had begun to live.'

She was a newer Mrs. Wix than ever, a Mrs. Wix high and great; but Sir Claude was not after all to be treated as a little boy with a missed lesson. 'I've not killed anything,' he said; 'on the contrary I think I've produced life. I don't know what to call it – I haven't even known how decently to deal with it, to approach it; but, whatever it is, it's the most beautiful thing I've ever met – it's exquisite, it's sacred.' He had his hands in his pockets and, though a trace of the sickness he had just shown still perhaps lingered there, his face bent itself with extraordinary gentleness on both the friends he was about to lose. 'Do you know what I came back for?' he asked of the elder.

'I think I do!' cried Mrs. Wix, surprisingly unmollified and with a crimson on her brow that was like a wave of colour reflected from the luridness lately enacted with Mrs. Beale. That lady, as if a little besprinkled by such turns of the tide, uttered a loud inarticulate protest and, averting herself, stood a moment at the window.

'I came back with a proposal,' said Sir Claude.

'To me?' Mrs. Wix asked.

'To Maisie. That she should give you up.'

'And does she?'

Sir Claude wavered. 'Tell her!' he then exclaimed to the child, also turning away as if to give her the chance. But Mrs. Wix and her pupil stood confronted in silence, Maisie whiter than ever – more awkward, more rigid and yet more dumb. They looked at each other hard, and as nothing came from them Sir Claude faced about again. 'You won't tell her? – you can't?' Still she said nothing: whereupon, addressing Mrs. Wix, he broke into a kind of ecstasy. 'She refused – she refused!'

Maisie, at this, found her voice. 'I didn't refuse. I didn't,' she repeated.

It brought Mrs. Beale straight back to her. 'You accepted, angel – you accepted!' She threw herself upon the child and, before Maisie could resist, had sunk with her upon the sofa, possessed of her, encircling her. 'You've given her up already, you've given her up for ever, and you're ours and ours only now, and the sooner she's off the better!'

Maisie had shut her eyes, but at a word of Sir Claude's they opened. 'Let her go!' he said to Mrs. Beale.

'Never, never, never!' cried Mrs. Beale. Maisie felt herself more compressed.

'Let her go!' Sir Claude more intensely repeated. He was looking at Mrs. Beale and there was something in his voice. Maisie knew from a loosening of arms that she had become conscious of what it was; she slowly rose from the sofa, and the child stood there again dropped and divided. 'You're free – you're free,' Sir Claude went on; at which Maisie's back became aware of a push that vented resentment and that placed her again in the centre of the room, the cynosure of every eye and not knowing which way to turn.

She turned with an effort to Mrs. Wix. 'I didn't refuse to give you up. I said I would if *he'd* give up——!'

'Give up Mrs. Beale?' burst from Mrs. Wix.

'Give up Mrs. Beale. What do you call that but exquisite?' Sir Claude demanded of all of them, the lady mentioned included; speaking with a relish as intense now as if some lovely work of art or of nature had suddenly been set down among them. He was rapidly recovering himself on this basis of fine appreciation. 'She made her condition – with such a sense of what it should be! She made the only right one.'

'The only right one?' – Mrs. Beale returned to the charge. She had taken a moment before a snub from him, but she was not to be snubbed on this. 'How can you talk such rubbish and how can you back her up in such impertinence? What in the world have you done to her to make her think of such stuff?' She stood there in righteous wrath; she flashed her eyes round the circle. Maisie took them full in her own, knowing that here at last was the moment she had had most to reckon with. But as regards her stepdaughter Mrs. Beale subdued herself to an inquiry deeply mild. '*Have* you made, my own love, any such condition as that?'

Somehow, now that it was there, the great moment was not so bad. What helped the child was that she knew what she wanted. All her learning and learning had made her at last learn that; so that if she waited an instant to reply it was only from the desire to be nice. Bewilderment had simply gone or at any rate was going fast. Finally she answered. 'Will you give *him* up? Will you?'

'Ah, leave her alone – leave her, leave her!' Sir Claude in sudden supplication murmured to Mrs. Beale.

Mrs. Wix at the same instant found another apostrophe. 'Isn't it enough for you, madam, to have brought her to discussing your relations?'

Mrs. Beale left Sir Claude unheeded, but Mrs. Wix could make her flame. 'My relations? What do you know, you hideous creature, about my relations, and what business on earth have you to speak of them? Leave the room this instant, you horrible old woman!'

'I think you had better go – you must really catch your boat,' Sir Claude said distressfully to Mrs. Wix. He was out of it now, or wanted to be; he knew the worst and had accepted it: what now concerned him was to prevent, to dissipate vulgarities. 'Won't you go – won't you just get off quickly?'

'With the child as quickly as you like. Not without her.' Mrs. Wix was adamant.

'Then why did you lie to me, you fiend?' Mrs. Beale almost yelled. 'Why did you tell me an hour ago that you had given her up?'

'Because I despaired of her – because I thought she had left me.' Mrs. Wix turned to Maisie. 'You were *with* them – in their connection. But now your eyes are open, and I take you!'

'No you don't!' and Mrs. Beale made, with a great fierce jump, a wild snatch at her stepdaughter. She caught her by the arm and, completing an instinctive movement, whirled her round in a further leap to the door, which had been closed by Sir Claude the instant their voices had risen. She fell back against it and, even while denouncing and waving off Mrs. Wix, kept it closed in an incoherence of passion. 'You don't take her, but you bundle yourself: she stays with her own people and she's rid of you! I never heard anything so monstrous!' Sir Claude had rescued Maisie and kept hold of her; he held her in front of him, resting his hands very lightly on her shoulders and facing the loud adversaries. Mrs. Beale's flush had dropped; she had turned pale with a splendid wrath. She kept protesting and dismissing Mrs. Wix; she glued her back to the door to prevent Maisie's flight; she drove out Mrs. Wix by the window or the chimney. 'You're a nice one – "discussing relations" – with your talk of our "connection" and your insults! What in the world is our connection but the love of the child who is our duty and our life and who holds us together as closely as she originally brought us?'

'I know, I know!' Maisie said with a burst of eagerness. 'I did bring you.'

The strangest of laughs escaped from Sir Claude. 'You did bring us – you did!' His hands went up and down gently on her shoulders.

Mrs. Wix so dominated the situation that she had something sharp for every one. 'There you have it, you see!' she pregnantly remarked to her pupil.

'*Will* you give him up?' Maisie persisted to Mrs. Beale.

'To *you*, you abominable little horror?' that lady indignantly inquired, 'and to this raving old demon who has filled your dreadful little mind with her wickedness? Have you been a hideous little hypocrite all these years that I've slaved to make you love me and deludedly believed that you did?'

'I love Sir Claude – I love *him*,' Maisie replied with a sense slightly rueful and embarrassed that she appeared to offer it as something that would do as well. Sir Claude had continued to pat her, and it was really an answer to his pats.

'She hates you – she hates you,' he observed with the oddest quietness to Mrs. Beale.

His quietness made her blaze. 'And you back her up in it and give me up to outrage?'

'No; I only insist that she's free – she's free.'

Mrs. Beale stared – Mrs. Beale glared. 'Free to starve with this pauper lunatic?'

'I'll do more for her than *you* ever did!' Mrs. Wix retorted. 'I'll work my fingers to the bone.'

Maisie, with Sir Claude's hands still on her shoulders, felt, just as she felt the fine surrender in them, that over her head he looked in a certain way at Mrs. Wix. 'You needn't do that,' she heard him say. 'She has means.'

'Means? – Maisie?' Mrs. Beale shrieked. 'Means that her vile father has stolen!'

'I'll get them back – I'll get them back. I'll look into it.' He smiled and nodded at Mrs. Wix.

This had a fearful effect on his other friend. 'Haven't *I* looked into it, I should like to know, and haven't I found an abyss? It's too inconceivable – your cruelty to me!' she wildly broke out. She had hot tears in her eyes.

He spoke to her very kindly, almost coaxingly. 'We'll look into it again; we'll look into it together. It *is* an abyss, but he *can* be made – or Ida can. Think of the money they're getting now!' he laughed. 'It's all right, it's all right,' he continued.

'It wouldn't do – it wouldn't do. We *can't* work her in. It's perfectly true – she's unique. We're not good enough – oh no!' and, quite exuberantly, he laughed again.

'Not good enough, and that beast *is*?' Mrs. Beale shouted.

At this for a moment there was a hush in the room, and in the midst of it Sir Claude replied to the question by moving with Maisie to Mrs. Wix. The next thing the child knew she was at that lady's side with an arm firmly grasped. Mrs. Beale still guarded the door. 'Let them pass,' said Sir Claude at last.

She remained there, however; Maisie saw the pair look at each other. Then she saw Mrs. Beale turn to her. 'I'm your mother now, Maisie. And he's your father.'

'That's just where it is!' sighed Mrs. Wix with an effect of irony positively detached and philosophic.

Mrs. Beale continued to address her young friend, and her effort to be reasonable and tender was in its way remarkable. 'We're representative, you know, of Mr. Farange and his former wife. This person represents mere illiterate presumption. We take our stand on the law.'

'Oh the law, the law!' Mrs. Wix superbly jeered. 'You had better indeed let the law have a look at you!'

'Let them pass – let them pass!' Sir Claude pressed his friend – he pleaded.

But she fastened herself still to Maisie. '*Do* you hate me, dearest?'

Maisie looked at her with new eyes, but answered as she had answered before. 'Will you give him up?'

Mrs. Beale's rejoinder hung fire, but when it came it was noble. 'You shouldn't talk to me of such things!' She was shocked, she was scandalized to tears.

For Mrs. Wix, however, it was her discrimination that was indelicate. 'You ought to be ashamed of yourself!' she roundly cried.

Sir Claude made a supreme appeal. 'Will you be so good as to allow these horrors to terminate?'

Mrs. Beale fixed her eyes on him, and again Maisie watched them. 'You should do him justice,' Mrs. Wix went on to Mrs. Beale. 'We've always been devoted to him, Maisie and

I – and he has shown how much he likes us. He would like to please her; he would like even, I think, to please me. But he hasn't given you up.'

They stood confronted, the step-parents, still under Maisie's observation. That observation had never sunk so deep as at this particular moment. 'Yes, my dear, I haven't given you up,' Sir Claude said to Mrs. Beale at last, 'and if you'd like me to treat our friends here as solemn witnesses I don't mind giving you my word for it that I never, never will. There!' he dauntlessly exclaimed.

'He can't!' Mrs. Wix tragically commented.

Mrs. Beale, erect and alive in her defeat, jerked her handsome face about. 'He can't!' she literally mocked.

'He can't, he can't, he can't!' Sir Claude's gay emphasis wonderfully carried it off.

Mrs. Beale took it all in, yet she held her ground; on which Maisie addressed Mrs. Wix. 'Shan't we lose the boat?'

'Yes, we shall lose the boat,' Mrs. Wix remarked to Sir Claude.

Mrs. Beale meanwhile faced full at Maisie. 'I don't know what to make of you!' she launched.

'Good-bye,' said Maisie to Sir Claude.

'Good-bye, Maisie,' Sir Claude answered.

Mrs. Beale came away from the door. 'Good-bye!' she hurled at Maisie; then passed straight across the room and disappeared in the adjoining one.

Sir Claude had reached the other door and opened it. Mrs. Wix was already out. On the threshold Maisie paused; she put out her hand to her stepfather. He took it and held it a moment, and their eyes met as the eyes of those who have done for each other what they can. 'Good-bye,' he repeated.

'Good-bye.' And Maisie followed Mrs. Wix.

They caught the steamer, which was just putting off, and, hustled across the gulf, found themselves on the deck so breathless and so scared that they gave up half the voyage to letting their emotion sink. It sank slowly and imperfectly; but at last, in mid-channel, surrounded by the quiet sea, Mrs. Wix had courage to revert. 'I didn't look back, did you?'

'Yes. He wasn't there,' said Maisie.

'Not on the balcony?'

Maisie waited a moment; then, 'He wasn't there,' she simply said again.

Mrs. Wix also was silent awhile. 'He went to *her*,' she finally observed.

'Oh, I know!' the child replied.

Mrs. Wix gave a sidelong look. She still had room for wonder at what Maisie knew.

FIVE REVIEWS (1897) OF
WHAT MAISIE KNEW

1. Unsigned review, *Manchester Guardian*
(28 September 1897)

The problem of the possible aspects which life might take for a small girl-child whose parents have found in divorce only a wider licence for temper and vice, though probably repellent to most people, is sufficiently complex to attract a mental analyst of the stamp of Mr. Henry James. In *What Maisie Knew* (W. Heinemann, pp. 304, 6s.) Mr. James has so far triumphed over the difficulties of the subject as to present us with a credible picture of childish innocence, preserved in the midst of glaring evil by means, not of stupid obtuseness, but of a rare sensibility, tact, and sweet power of devotion. This is indeed a victory, and one of no mean order, for, although largely due to the author's unrivalled skill in the art of allusiveness and skating over thin ice, we are yet conscious that verbal dialectics alone could not have saved from besmirchment the small figure of this helpless toy of chance and evil passions. From other points of view, such, for instance, as the enjoyment of the reader, success is more questionable. More even than in some of his other works are we haunted here by the impression that it is the thorny setting of the fruit rather than its succulence which has tempted the author to lay hands on it. It is a study, not a story or a drama. The portion of Maisie's life which it covers is only a few years of childhood, and they may be described roughly as a duel for the possession of her person. On one side the forces of respectability are represented by Mrs. Wix, an elderly and outwardly grotesque but wholly devoted governess, and by Sir Claude, the second husband of Maisie's mother, who is resolved to put the child outside an atmosphere from which he has no moral strength himself to escape; on the other are arrayed (though in succession rather than side by side) Maisie's father and mother, and the woman who has become first her step-mother and then the lover of Sir Claude. These persons, hostile in everything else, are at one in using Maisie simply as a tool to be picked up or dropped to suit their own needs. The crucial point of the complication arises from the *liaison* between two members of the opposing parties – the step-mother and step-father – of which the child herself, in her lively affection for both, has been the innocent instrument. The battle and the book close with Mrs. Wix bearing Maisie across the Channel in triumphant flight, but the horizon of the future is left veiled in cloud. From the nature of the case the book is monotonous, and, in spite of the changeful dialogue and the delicious insight into childish character with which every page is full, this monotony presses hard on the reader before the close. We feel that the author has performed his task as perhaps no other man could. Only, whatever entertainment or admiration the book may call forth, we cannot imagine anyone reading it a second time. It is undoubtedly a work of art, but hardly one which we wish to hang on our walls.

2. From an unsigned review, *Pall Mall Gazette* (11 October 1897)

This latest novel from Mr. James's pen seems, beyond doubt, to touch his highest point. It is a work very difficult to criticize, very perplexing to appraise. But beyond and above all the one fact of its astounding cleverness stands forth. It is quite impossible to ignore that, if the word have any significance, and is ever to be used at all, we are here dealing with genius. This is a work of genius, as much as Mr. Meredith's best work, though on quite other human lines, as the readers of both need not be reminded. And the next point which may occur to a reader, as he lays down the book, is that the author has generously, wilfully, almost wantonly handicapped himself. He had selected a strange medley of sordid intrigue, in which some vivid and curious characters perform the antics of that human comedy on which Mr. James loves to dwell as much as his great contemporary. It was a *partie carrée*, a group hard enough in itself to conceive, set forth, and illumine in the subtle manner to which the author has accustomed us. But conceive that this medley, these intricacies of motive, this tangle and confusion of emotion, are all transmuted, reflected, determined through the mind of a little girl of eight years! The thing, one would say, was preposterous. What on earth, indeed, *did* Maisie know of all this terrible human imbroglio? She knew nothing – that is obviously the answer which Mr. James desires us to take from his story; and that very fact that she knew nothing, was really aware of nothing, stared on life through childish and innocent eyes, surveyed the dustheap and the dungheap with her incomplete and wondering vision – that fact composes the amazing difficulty of Mr. James's task. To render the action and the motives through Maisie's mind to the reader, and yet leave upon that virginal spirit the stain or shadow of no comprehension – such has been the author's work. His success is commensurate with the difficulty. Of all the figures that tread the mazes of the story – Farange, her father, Mrs. Beale, Sir Claude, even Ida herself – none is fixed so indelibly and marked with such personality as the child. Mr. James's plots do not bear the bald analysis of a review; they must be taken in the context. To any one who will drop his Hall Caines and Marie Corellis for a time and take the trouble to read through this book, every single act and feeling of the child will be pathetically convincing. The grime and squalor of the life of these characters make an impression upon the reader. But they never touch Maisie. She is no heroine, of course; she is what her unnatural life made her – weak, yielding, a little deceitful, feebly affectionate, but above all ignorant, peace-loving, and possessed of that weary craving for rest and home and some one to cling to. To the last she is defeated, and even when Mrs. Wix carries her off in triumph, we are not quite certain if she has gained what was the desire of her heart.

What did Maisie know? There was little that she had not heard. Every vain, selfish, or cowardly character in the book pours confidences into her ears. She herself boasted to her father that she knew everything; she liked to know. The pathetic part of it, and yet the best part of it also, was that, as we have said, she knew nothing. We have remarked upon the surprising difficulties which Mr. James has thrown in his own way; and yet we should not be astounded to learn that Mr. James had conceived the book entirely for the sake of that central figure with its distressing problem. He is used to set himself hard tasks, and executes them whether any one cares or not. This time we venture to think that he has achieved something which must strike even that mysterious and loose-headed person, the general reader. And yet, perhaps not; and, if not, at least he has enriched the heritage of our descendants.

3. From an unsigned review, *The Academy* (16 October 1897)

I have read this book with amazement and delight: with amazement at its supreme delicacy; with delight that its author, in spite of such discouragement as may come from lack of popular acclaim, retains an unswerving allegiance, to a literary conscience that forbids him to leave a slipshod phrase, or a single word out of its appointed place. As admirers of Mr. James foresee – and Mr. James has a devoted band of admirers, who follow every line that he writes – the bare outline of the story is of the simplest . . . But to state the plot of one of Mr. James's books is to state next to nothing. He deals not in events, but in events as they mirror themselves in the thoughts, the fleeting impulses, of his characters. By a rare psychological intuition, he lays bare the under side of his story. And in this book the whole sordid drama of petty jealousy, rancour, wantonness, and vacillation plays itself out for the amusement of Maisie. You follow the story through the mind of Maisie; you see and hear only what Maisie saw and heard; and yet, such is the combined humour and pathos of the presentment, you know so much more than Maisie could possibly know, though Maisie had her childish moral arithmetic, whereby she could put two and two together . . .

Certainly there is no living writer who has achieved the feat which Mr. James has here achieved, in analysing and purifying the baser passions of our nature by passing them through the pure mind of a little child.

4. Unsigned review, *The Spectator* (30 October 1897)

In *What Maisie Knew* Mr. Henry James presents the unedifying spectacle of a man of great talent and subtlety, whose sympathies are obviously on the side of the angels, toiling with unflagging persistence and desperate attention to detail over the portraiture of half a dozen as unlovely and squalid souls – spite of their fashionable surroundings and showy exteriors – as it has been our misfortune to encounter in the range of modern fiction. It reminds us of nothing so much as a beautifully dressed child making an elaborate mud-pie in the gutter. The mud-pie is a regular work of art, and the child continues to keep its own hands and dress unsoiled. But when all is said and done, the result is only a mud-pie and nothing more. Maisie is the only child of thoroughly disreputable parents, who have just been divorced at the opening of the tale. According to the arrangement, Maisie spends her time alternately with her father and mother. Governesses are provided, and her father marries the younger, handsomer, and incomparably more worthless of the two. The mother also marries again, her second husband being a feeble, invertebrate creature called Sir Claude. Then Maisie, who all the time is tossed about like a shuttlecock between this disreputable quartet, is the innocent means of bringing her new stepmother and stepfather together, with results that can be easily imagined from their antecedents. Mr. James, it is true, refrains from the crowning feat of making the father and mother marry each other again. That would have exposed him to the charge of attempting to enter into rivalry with the hideous finale of *Jude the Obscure*. But it could not have rendered the book more disagreeable than it is. The elaborate ingenuity with which this wretched little child is hemmed round with undesirable relatives in our opinion entirely robs the figure of its intended pathos. Maisie escapes in the end, thanks chiefly to the dogged determination of the ugly governess, and to the gradual emergence in the child of a moral sense. There are a great many passages in the book which are evidently meant to be humorous. This, for example, from the description of the divorce proceedings – 'The father, who, though bespattered from head to foot, had made good his case, was, in pursuance of this triumph, appointed to keep her: it was not so much that the mother's character had been more absolutely damaged as that the brilliancy of a lady's complexion (and this lady's, in court, was immensely remarked) might be more regarded as showing the spots.' For the life of us we fail to see where the fun comes in, though no doubt this strenuous facetiousness has its admirers. We note, in conclusion, that some of the names – Wix and Moddle, for example – remind one of Dickens. But we hasten to add, in justice to Mr. Henry James, that there is absolutely nothing else in the book which the most fanatical plagiary-hunter could indicate as recalling in the faintest way the manner or matter of the immortal 'Boz'.

5. Unsigned review, *Literary World* (Boston, 11 December 1897)

Mr. Henry James, it is reported, remarked lately to a friend that he had reached that point in his literary career when he could write exactly what he liked. The first uses to which he has put this newly attained freedom seem to us regrettable; being, firstly, his paper on Du Maurier ['George Du Maurier', *Harper's New Monthly Magazine* (September 1897)], an orphic utterance, unintelligible except to the initiated, and secondly, the novel whose name heads this paper.

What Maisie Knew is of a quality incredible in a writer whose work has heretofore been, morally, beyond reproach. In what it says, still more in what it suggests, it ranks, except for a terrible underlying dullness, with the worst schools of French fiction. Maisie is a little child, not more than five or six years old, when her parents obtain a mutual divorce with an agreement that she shall divide her year equally between them. In the six months spent with her worthless father she hears her mother's name daily mentioned with oaths and foulest reproach. Going thence to an equally worthless mother, she learns, in language only less profane and foul, that her father is a profligate wretch. Neither spares one detail of coarse objurgation for pity at her helpless babyhood. Presently the pretty governess, hired by the mother, follows Maisie to the home of the father and becomes that father's mistress. A little later the mother makes a second marriage. Husband No.2, a good-natured man, as weak and dissipated as, but less violent than, his predecessor, takes a fancy to the little girl, and she learns to adore him. She also adores the ex-governess, her father's mistress and later his wife. When, therefore, father No.1 deserts wife No.2, and goes to live with (and on) a third lady, and mother No.1, having tried a variety of lovers (all with Maisie's knowledge and connivance), elopes with the latest, and father No.2 and mother No.2 form a connection, Maisie, by this time nine years old or so, sees no harm in the arrangement. She talks the situation over with her governess, and is prepared to accept it happily.

Such a plot seems inconceivable. Its author exhibits not one ray of pity or dismay at this spectacle of a child with the pure current of its life thus poisoned at its source. To him she is merely the *raison d'être* of a curiously complicated situation, which he can twist and untwist for purposes of fiction. One feels in the reading that every manly feeling, every possibility of generous sympathy, every comprehension of the higher standards, has become atrophied in Mr. James's nature from long disuse, and that all relation between him and his kind has perished except to serve him coldly by way of 'material'.

It goes without saying that the style of the book is jerkily incoherent. The characters, Maisie included, converse in vague innuendoes, and, as no answer is promised 'in the next number', the readers of the story – may they be few – will probably never understand exactly what any one concerned said or did or meant. This is just as well, for what little one is able to understand is alike repellent to taste and feeling, to law and gospel.

HENRY JAMES ON
WHAT MAISIE KNEW

THE NOTEBOOKS (1892–96)

34 De Vere Gardens, W., November 12th, 1892.

—Two days ago, at dinner at James Bryce's Mrs. Ashton, Mrs. Bryce's sister, mentioned to me a situation that she had known of, of which it immediately struck me that something might be made in a tale. A child (boy or girl would do, but I see a girl, which would make it different from *The Pupil*) was *divided* by its parents in consequence of their being divorced. The court, for some reason, didn't, as it might have done, give the child exclusively to either parent, but decreed that it was to spend its time equally with each—that is alternately. Each parent married again, and the child went to them a month, or three months, about—finding with the one a new mother and with the other a new father. Might not something be done with the idea of an odd and particular relation springing up 1st between the child and each of these new parents, 2d between one of the new parents and the other—through the child—over and on account of and by means of the child? Suppose the real parents die, etc.—then the new parents marry each other in order to take care of it, etc. The basis of almost any story, any development would be, that the child should prefer the new husband and the new wife to the old; that is that these latter should (from the moment they have ceased to *quarrel* about it), become indifferent to it, whereas the others have become interested and attached, finally passionately so. Best of all perhaps would be to make the child a fresh bone of contention, a fresh source of dramatic situations, *du vivant* of the original parents. *Their* indifference throws the new parents, through a common sympathy, together. Thence a 'flirtation', a love affair between them which produces suspicion, jealousy, a fresh separation, etc.—with the innocent child in the midst.

August 26th, 1893 (34 De Vere Gdns.).
I am putting my hand to the idea of the little story on the subject of the *partagé* child of the divorced parents—as to which I have already made a note here. The little *donnée* will yield most, I think—most *ironic* effect, and this is the sort of thing mainly to try for in it—if I make the old parents, the original parents, *live*, not die, and transmit the little girl to the persons they each have married *en secondes noces*. This at least is what I ask myself. May I not combine the ironic and the *other* interest (the 'touch of tenderness'—or sweetness—or sympathy or poetry—or whatever the needed thing is), by a conception of this sort; viz.: that Hurter [subsequently Farange] and his former wife each marry again and cease to care for the child—as I have originally posited as soon as they have her no longer to quarrel about? The new husband and the new wife then take the interest in her, and meet on this common ground. The Hurters quarrel with *them* over this, and they separate: I mean each of the Hurters separate afresh. Make *Hurter* die? His 1st wife survives and becomes extremely jealous of his 2d. I must remember that if Hurter dies, the situation breaks, for his wife then gets the whole care of Maisie; which won't do. No, they both live.

December 22d. [1895] Promising H. Harland a 10,000 (a *real* 10,000) for the April *Yellow Book*, I have put my pen to the little subject of the child, the little girl, whose parents are divorced, and then each marry again, then die, leaving her divided between the 2d husband of the one and the 2d wife of the other. But the thing, before I go further, requires some more ciphering out, more extraction of the subject, of the drama—if such there really *be* in it. *Voyons un peu*—what little drama *does* reside in it?—I catch it, I catch it: I seize the tail of the little latent action *qu'il recèle*. I made a mistake, above, in thinking—in speaking—of the divorced parents as 'dying': they live—the very essence of the subject is in that. Make my point of view, my *line*, the consciousness, the dim, sweet, sacred, wondering, clinging perception of the child, and one gets something like *this*. The parents become indifferent to her as soon as they cease to have her to quarrel about; then each marry again. The father *first*— it's *his* new spouse who first takes an interest in the child. But let me state it, rather [in] 8 or 10 little chapters.

I. 12½ pages about the parents.

II. 10 pages: the child's perceptions of the situation at first—its wonderings, bewilderments, then gradual clever little perception of what it must do. Boyd [Beale] first takes her— his pretended arrangement of his life for it, his playing at being occupied with her and devoted to her. His talk to her about her mother—her dread and awe of going to her. Then her going—the mother's wild caresses, and her getting from the child all the father has said of her. The results of this—her behaviour on going back to her father, etc. The results don't show the *1st* time: she repeats to her father what her mother has said, as she has repeated to her mother what her father has said. Then, on her 2d visit to her mother, she takes the line of *not* telling—she gets a glimpse, in her little prematurely troubled and sharpened mind, of what she can do in the way of *peace*. This disappoints and angers her mother on the second visit—so that, with her vicious activity dropping, her mother neglects her, neglects her badly, and she is eager to return to her father. On her return she finds a governess. Or does her MOTHER get her the governess? I seem to see reasons for that. The mother hires the governess for the last three months of the visit—but under penalty of her displeasure if she goes to the other place with the child. She's to wait and take her six months later—that had been the arrangement under which she is hired. But she takes such a fancy to Maisie that she breaks the vow and goes, knowing what displeasure she incurs, and offers herself to Boyd. He is horrified, learning that she comes from his wife—from Maisie under that roof. But he relents on finding what promise she has broken, and binds her by another not to go back there. *She* gives it—her line is now, secretly, to keep the child at the father's. She falls in love with Boyd. The scene between Boyd and the governess takes place before Maisie. This is all in II.

III. Relation between Maisie and the governess. Then Maisie goes back once again to her mother, and stays there without the governess—with another, who also gets embroiled about her. Her mother *drops* her, after this third period, and she stays on—on and on. A young man comes to her father's in the latter's absence, to see about her. He proves to be her mother's new husband. He has been put up to it—egged on by the embroiled governess—who adores the child and wants to get her back or get back *to* her. Essence of the little drama this— the strange, fatal, complicating action of the child's lovability. It occurs to me, however, that instead of making the young man come himself, outright (a little unnatural and *invraisemblable*), I had better make the 'embroiled governess'—the second, elder, plain one—come herself, hungrily, desperately, to see if the child *isn't* coming back to her mother. She has come to see Boyd Farange, but he is away. She sees *his* governess, the pretty one, my second 'heroine'; and the scene between the 2 women takes place before Maisie. The plain governess, the honest frump, *tells* of Mrs. Farange's marriage—this is the 1st they know of it. She has married Captain So-and-So [Sir Claude]—she tells who: she is abroad—it has taken place at Florence. She has written to the frump, characteristically— enclosing the portrait of her *sposo*—younger than herself, very handsome. (The 'Pretty' governess must not be very handsome—too much beauty—only a marked type.) *The* SPOSI *are coming home*—hence the poor woman's officious, pathetic errand. Her passion for the child—it breaks out. She catches her up, hugs her. She must be a widow—MRS. Something: she has lost her only little girl. Movement between the women precipitating the younger one's announcement of the kind of place she holds—the authority with which she speaks: she is engaged to be married to Boyd Farange.

IV. I must handle freely and handsomely the years—treat my *intervals* with art and courage; master the little secrets in regard to the expression of duration—be superior I mean, on the question of time. Maisie does go back to her mother—she sees her new stepfather—she stays a year. Her new stepfather—the Captain—attaches himself to her tenderly. Simple, good, mild chap, bullied, hustled by his wife, and not destined, as he is already sure, or at any rate definitely apprehensive, to have a child of his own: the thing he has almost predominantly married for—and not *been* married, grabbed and appropriated, by Mrs. Farange. (I must get a name, a Xtian name, for Mrs. F. early—so as not to speak of her by a *changed* surname.) It occurs to me that it will be well to make Ida have a confinement—a *very*, VERY prompt one—which is what, in its results, dashes the Captain's hope of paternity. She is awfully ill—the child dies— her convalescence is long—her attitude about another episode of the same kind unmistakable. It is during this—for him— worried and lonely time that the Captain fraternizes and fore- gathers with Maisie, who is as 'lonely' as himself—*délaissée* in a way that touches him. The year that she is now by way of staying with her mother is to make up for the time that Ida DIDN'T insist, antecedently to that event. It is the Captain, really, who, from his fancy for the child, carries out the rule of the time to be made up, stickles for it, puts it through. Trace as vividly as may be, *mark strongly*, the *drop*, the cynical surren- der, on each side of the *real parents'* responsibility—of their sense of it and pretension *to* it, and tolerance of the trouble of it. Mark the point of the *full change*—the change that leaves only the step-parents to keep the matter up. It is, e.g., the Cap- tain who now keeps Maisie—the Captain only. All this in section IV. Section IV must terminate with the second wife's visit to the Captain, to *get back* the child. This is their MEETING— their 1st being brought face to face over Maisie. It takes place before Maisie—EVERYTHING TAKES PLACE BEFORE MAISIE. That is a part of the essence of the thing—that, with the tenderness she inspires, the rest of the essence, the second of the golden threads of my *form*. Maisie is really more—much more—than a year with the Captain and her mother. It is as married to Boyd Farange—married now *depuis bientôt 2 ans*—that the pretty governess presents herself. She has realized, too, that she will have no children. She may have been confined (yes, that is right) and lost her little girl. Yes, yes, she *tells* that to the Captain. This

1st meeting marks practically the middle of my tale. I am not
SURE, now, that it will be well for her—at the end of III—to
have ANNOUNCED to the frumpy governess her engagement
to Boyd. And yet why not? When I can prepare so little, and
must take such jumps, so much preparation as that may be
valuable to me. *Nous verrons bien*. This relation established
between the 2 step-parents evidently, at any rate, flows over
into section V.

SECTION V consists, therefore, of the sharp, vivid establishment of the contact in question and of:—

(b) The second wife's second visit to the Captain to *continue*
the effort to get Maisie. Ida is away—Boyd is away: this marks
what has become of *their* duty. The Captain is at the seaside
somewhere—in lodgings—with the child: say at Brighton. The
second wife, this second time, comes down to Brighton. The
frumpy governess is back again with the little girl—now 10
years old. She has come to her [in spite of everything? [James's
brackets]]—she clings to her: she is her only REAL guardian.
Sound that note in her feeling—in her sense, her deep foreboding. She sees what is to happen between the younger
pair—SHOW that she sees it.

(c) Maisie's return to her father and her stepmother.

(d) The Captain's going to see her there. *Boyd consents* to
this—is jolly over it, seeing how unhappy he too is with Ida.
This *rapprochement* between the 2 men takes place in the
child's presence. The frumpy governess is meanwhile forbidden the house by the second wife—who is jealous and suspicious of her, has *her* vague foretaste and foreknowledge of
what may happen, and an intuition of the old woman's perception of it which makes her keep her at a distance. The old
woman gets in once—to express this to Maisie. That is, she
formulates to the child exactly what *I* have just formulated.
Everything is formulated and formulatable to the child. May
not V terminate with this formula?—leaving VI to consist
virtually of the *growth* of the extraordinary relation between
the step-parents as witnessed by Maisie? Yes, that is it. The
formula from the frump at the end of V *facilitates* my making
the child witness the phenomenon in question—prepares the

mirror, the plate, on which it is represented as reflected. Therefore we have:—

VI. (*sixth*) The freedom, the facility, of the step-parents together over the child. *Cela se passe chez* Boyd—since the Captain can come there. *Description of it in form of picture of the child's dim sense.* It terminates in irruption of Ida—an outbreak of jealousy. The Captain is out somewhere with Maisie in Kensington Gardens—out with her, *as brought from Boyd's house*—where they suddenly encounter Ida, who is there with a strange gentleman—strange to Maisie, but known, very well, to the Captain. Scene of jealousy from Ida to anticipate, to FORESTALL her 2d husband's (the Captain's) suspicion of her relations with the strange gentleman. The strange gentleman takes Maisie off—at Ida's request—to walk a little. That moment is, in 3 lines, described (*the gentleman* PERFECTLY SILENT—Maisie also), and the situation the child finds on their rejoining the others. VI ends up with Maisie going back to her mother, who has to have her to back up the grievance she has hurled at the Captain, but she really doesn't care for it a bit, *ou* that her being there only keeps the Captain more on the premises—or *may* do so: a state of affairs that doesn't suit her book, as she has her lover to receive and be with. However, the chapter terminates with the little girl's redomicilement under her mother's roof.

VII embodies:—(a) What I have surrounded with a red line just above. [Who has to . . . be with] (b) The Captain's veto on the tattling frump. (c) The incident of Maisie being out with her stepmother—out from her mother's house—and meeting (as a counterpart of the incident of VI) her father with a strange lady, a lady strange to Maisie but known, well known, to her stepfather. The same things happen as before. There is the same scene between the 2 *sposi*. Maisie is taken off to walk a little by the strange lady—only the strange lady is extraordinarily loquacious, almost violently chatters. The *bout de scène* that, before the child, Boyd makes his wife, is a scene of *insincere jealousy*—like the scene Ida has made the Captain. But before introducing the incident I must have made it clear that the Captain has forbidden the frumpy governess his house—kept her off. Maisie knows the reason from him—knows that, to be well with Ida and get *at* the child (since Mrs. Farange no. 2 has turned her out—has banged *her* door in her face), she (the frump) has communicated to Ida her idea about the 2 step-parents. This to make Ida bring the child home, where she (the frump) may see her. She has reckoned without the Captain's divination (or knowledge *through* Ida) and resentment, which does not keep her out. He says *he* will teach Maisie.

In VIII, Ida 'bolts' with the strange little gentleman. The Captain formulates this to Maisie. He takes her to her stepmother and there she learns—through the latter's formulation—that Boyd Farange has bolted with the strange little lady.

In IX, Maisie sees her step-parents very definitively come together—unite in devotion to her. *They* will take care of her, take care of her together—they will both be to her everything she has lost. She is wonderstruck and charmed with this—she sees them *really exalted and magnificent over it*; and she accepts the prospect, tells them it's them she prefers, etc., and prepares to give herself altogether to them. Then, with—

X, The old frumpy governess arrives, intervenes, has her great scene with them, *leur dit leur fait*, grandly, vividly (puts everything into her mouth), and carries off the child, to rescue her, to save her. *She* will bring her up.

The Vicarage, Rye, September 22d, 1896.
I've brought my little history of 'Maisie' to the point at which I ought to be able to go on very straight with it, the point at which the child comes back to her father and the domesticated Miss Overmore *after* her 1st period with Mrs. Wix at her mother's. The relations between Miss Overmore and Beale exist—she is his mistress. This is my V, I find, and it must include the *prolongation* of Maisie's stay and the visit of Mrs. Wix as noted *supra*.

34 De Vere Gardens, October 26th.
I have brought this little matter of Maisie to a point at which a really detailed scenario of the rest is indispensable for a straight and sure advance to the end. Let me not, just Heaven—not,

God knows, that I *incline* to!—slacken in my deep observance of this strong and beneficent method—this intensely structural, intensely hinged and jointed preliminary frame. In proportion as this frame is vague do I directly pay for the vagueness; in proportion as it is full and finished do I gain, do I rejoice in the strength. Sir Claude—in my VIII—has come for the child to Mrs. Beale and taken her to her mother's. What then is the function and office of my IX? To develop the relation between Maisie and Sir Claude and, through her, between him and Mrs. Beale. It must picture a little Ida's *intérieur*—poor Sir Claude's relation to *her*—her own relation to Maisie, etc. She's very much in love with Sir Claude. She mustn't be too monstrous about Maisie—she must welcome her at 1st. Mrs. Wix is there—Mrs. Wix must explain things to the child. She adores—they BOTH adore—Sir Claude. He must be very nice, very charming to Maisie, but he must get a little tired of her. As the whole thing is an action, so the little chapter is its little *piece* of the action; and to what point must the latter be brought by it? *Voyons, voyons.* Don't I best see the whole thing reflected in the talk, the confidences, the intercourse of Mrs. Wix? Something very pretty may be made of this—her going a little further and further, in the way of communication, of 'crudity', with the child than her own old dingy decencies, her old-fashioned conscience quite warrants—her helpless pathetic sighs at what she *has*, perforce, to tell her, at what Maisie *already* has seen and learnt—so that *she* doesn't make her any more initiated—any 'worse': etc., etc., and thus serves as a sort of a dim, crooked little reflector of the conditions that I desire to present on the part of the others. The rest of my story—*voyons*—consists of the sharp notation, at a series of moments, of these conditions. Each little chapter *is*, thereby, a moment, a stage. What is this IX, then, the moment, the stage, *of*? Well, of a more *presented*, a more visible *cynisme* on the part of everybody. But what *step* does the action take in it? *That of Sir C.'s detachment from Ida—Mrs. Beale's from Beale—*OVER the little opportunity and pretext of Maisie. Furthermore the distinct indifferent parental surrender of Maisie. Beale has 'surrendered' her practically in VIII—her mother, getting her back through Sir Claude, and putting up with her, to please him, at 1st (exhibit this through Mrs. Wix, to the child), her mother breaks down and resents her presence—or rather resents Beale's shirking—at the last. Yes, I *see* thus, I think, my little *act* of my little drama here. Ah, this *divine* conception of one's little masses and periods in the scenic light—as rounded ACTS, this patient, pious, nobly 'vindictive' [corrected by James to 'vindicating' in a note on the manuscript page] application of the scenic philosophy and method—I feel as if it still (above *all*, YET) had a great deal to give me, and might carry me as far as I dream! God knows how far—into the flushed, dying day—*that* is! *De part et d'autre* Maisie has become a bore to her parents—with Mrs. Wix to help to prove it. They must still hate each other, and Ida must be furiously jealous—of Mrs. Beale. Beale is more indifferent, but he won't (if he can help it) have back Maisie. What my IX brings me to is the coming together of Sir Claude and Mrs. B. on the basis of '*What* the devil are they to do with the child?' Sir Claude says that Ida at last demands that Beale shall do, again, his turn; Mrs. Beale says that her husband is tremendously recalcitrant. Then they are *together*—with the child on their hands. *They* have a moment together, to this effect—a moment which seems to me to be the right climax of my IX. I must *enjamber* my period—my time for the child with her mother—from the 1st: hold out my cup—of this year—and then pour my little chapter—express my little act—into it. It must 'transpire' that Claude's visit to Mrs. Beale, his snatch at Maisie, has been 'unbeknown' to Ida. This has been his little way of doing it—quite sincere and generous and really tender to the child—in his pretty, pleasant, weak, bullied, finally disgusted nature—disgusted, of course, with Ida. Ida refuses to see Maisie at first—and Mrs. W. puts her *au courant*. Then Ida's relenting and what Maisie does see—the painted Idol, the sharp, showy, fiercely questioning mamma. She 'gets it out' of Maisie—the scene at Mrs. Beale's. It's the way it has been done—his going there to that woman—that she resents. But to the child she is at first pretentiously endearing. She must, however, take Sir Claude AWAY a great deal at 1st—through her absorption in him—her passion for him. He resents her neglect of her child and makes up for it to the little girl: comes up to the nursery or schoolroom, rather, to see her, charms Mrs. Wix more and more (she's in love with him), braves ridicule by going out with them when he can, taking them to the theatre, etc. Then comes the transition, the change. Ida becomes unfaithful. Beale becomes unfaithful. Sir Claude and Mrs. Beale come together on it and on 'What's to be done with Maisie?' I seem to see that I must keep Mrs. Beale AWAY for a year. I show it through Mrs. W.'s presentation of it to the child. Mrs. Wix shows Maisie that it's impossible she should come. Maisie knows fully how jealous her mother is of her (Mrs. B.). So there's an interval after the beginning, that I have shown in VIII, of the relations between Mrs. Beale and Sir Claude. The climax of the act, then, the *resumption* of them, the confrontation of the pair (at Brighton?), the 'Will *you* take her?' the 'Can't *you* keep her?' etc. They must have been, before this, in correspondence—toward the end of the year—ABOUT her. Mrs. Wix *clutches* her. But Sir Claude, in spite of Mrs. Wix, and not wishing in the least to pain her, but *having* to act, to do something, and wishing to see again—for Maisie's sake—Mrs. Beale, in whose tenderness for her he *believes*—Claude *does act*, takes her off alone, takes her down to Brighton.

X.

What then does my X give me? It gives me primarily 2 things: one of them that Maisie *goes* back to her father's; the other that I get, till the end, rid of Mrs. Wix. I *must* get rid of Mrs. W., to give effect to her return *at* the end, when everything else has failed. And I must replace Maisie at her father's as the only possible basis for the carrying on of the intrigue between her step-parents. Claude can go there—Mrs. Beale could never go to Ida's. Claude is now Mrs. Beale's lover, and it is in this X that I must make the scene in Kensington Gardens occur—the outbreak of 'jealousy' on Ida's part when she—being there with a lover of her own—meets her husband and her daughter. I have sketched this scene *supra*—and here refer myself to it. It must *begin* my X—for the little picture of Sir Claude's *fréquentation* of Beale's house must come *after* it—resting *upon* it.

Beale is constantly away—after *his* woman; and this X must contain a passage between him and Maisie. But what's to be its climax? That of the chapter—this passage of the child with her father? Or must that come AFTER the pendant-scene to the foregoing—the scene of Maisie's being out with Mrs. Beale and meeting Beale with a strange lady as, out with Sir Claude, she has *met* Ida with a strange gentleman? I think it *must* come after XI (brief), must consist of this second episode and the passage between the child and her father. The latter, it seems to me, can really be *fine* in its picture of the brutality of Beale's cynicism and baseness. It prepares for the 'bolt' and it is the climax of the little chapter. I must now *leave* Maisie under his roof—I can't take her back again to her mother's. But do we *see* Ida again?—after the scene of the meeting? I *think* so—I think I can get an effect from it. Yes, Maisie has her passage with her father—she has her passage with her mother. Then if the former, following the *second* meeting, forms the climax of XI, the latter must be the *beginning* of XII. I imagine Ida coming—oh yes, oh yes, frankly, brazenly, to see the child *at* Beale's to tell her that—well, she's weary of the struggle—she surrenders her to her father. She is strange—she cries, she lies, she hugs her as she used to do of old—and she disappears. This is my 1st half of XII. The next thing Maisie 'knows' is that her mother has 'bolted'. Sir Claude arrives at her father's, where she is, with this news for Mrs. Beale. He is a 'free man', but they greet the news as a supreme trick she has played Beale—about the child; unfitting herself—by her act—for further bother about it. Sir Claude, on this, asks Maisie if she will come now and live—stay with him: he will do her mother's turn for her. She must have had, over her mother's flight, a burst of grief and shame—her *one* EXPRESSION of perceptive violence: she cries, she breaks down. Her *one* break down. This *moves* Sir Claude; makes him want more to have her. He *urges* her—but on this Mrs. Beale protests. No—*she'll* keep her: he'll come and see her there. It reaches almost a dispute between them. I must have it that Mrs. Beale *really* clings to her—partly from her old affection, the charm of the child (formulate *to* the child—*for* the reader, *through* Mrs. Wix or Sir Claude, this

charm so complicating and entangling for others); and partly
because her presence is a way of *attracting* Sir Claude and
making a tie *with* him. But he is the person, who, after
Mrs. Wix, loves her most and he does get her away from
Mrs. Beale—for a week; succeeds in taking her to the empty
house, where, abandoned of Ida, they moon about, vaguely
and tenderly, together. That is, I *think* he takes her to the empty
house: this is to settle, to *creuser. Voyons, voyons—arrangeons
un peu cela.* What I seem to want is that a little interval should
occur before the revelation that Beale, too, has bolted with a
'paramour'. If I can only keep this—that is, *make* it, really dramatic, it may perhaps be something of a little triumph. Mrs.
Beale must come down, somewhere, *to* Sir Claude and Maisie
with her great news for the former and her 'Now we're free!'
My climax is that what this freedom conveys for them is the
freedom to live together—to do now what they like—with the
rather perplexed and slightly ashamed consciousness that now,
charged with the child, if they keep her they keep her mixed up
with their *malpropreté,* their illegitimate tie. The embarrassment, the awkwardness, the irony, the *cynisme,* the melancholy
comedy, or whatever one may call it, of this. *Then* poor Mrs.
Wix's descent—her indignant rise in her might, her putting
before them the horror (for *her,* at least), of what they're doing;
the way, in a word, in which *elle leur dit leur fait,* winding up
with her *taking* Maisie to her own poor, bare shabbiness of
home and life—her rescuing her, declaring that *she* will do for
her. That is my clear climax and denouement; BUT what I've
been asking myself is whether I may not with effect, whether I,
indeed, *must* not, represent a little prior descent of Mrs. Wix's
after Ida's flight and *before* Beale's—in the interval that I'm
obliged to make. (Put it in the episode of the empty house?) It
is not only that this interval—the wait for the effect of Mrs.
Beale's advent with *her* news, the tidings of what has happened
to *her* home—it is not only that this little interval requires to
be filled; but, further, that there are 2 other reasons. One of
these is that, given the attitude already imputed to Mrs. W.
toward Sir Claude, it seems to me she mustn't reprobate him,
break with him *tout d'un coup.* The other is that I do well to

give her a chance to *appeal* to him—do it well from the point of view of dramatic prettiness and pathos. Isn't there a grotesque *pathos*, in especial, in her turning up on learning (I must settle *how* she learns—with her relation to Ida *that* is manageable very naturally) of her ladyship's flight and hurrying down to him to put his present chance for beauty and virtue (of behaviour) before him. She sees how the event must throw him into Mrs. Beale's arms, and *elle se démène* as *against* that. She pictures to him his chance—his chance to come off now with Maisie and *her*. They will be together—they will make a *trio*. The small touching oddity (with her secret passion for him) of her offering *herself* as a rescue from the temptation, the impropriety of Mrs. Beale. ADMIRABLE, this. He resists—he doesn't see it yet; and she *has* to go off, with her return, her next entrance, prepared for, as it were, and led up to. I seem to see this out of town—at Brighton, at a watering-place *quelconque*. I see Mrs. W. 'come down';—I see Mrs. Beale 'come down';—I see Mrs. W. 'come down' again. She leaves, in snatching up Maisie. Mrs. Beale and Sir Claude to go *abroad*. Yes, she goes back with the child to London. They stay there—behind—together: to embark together for the continent. Don't I get an effect from *Folkestone*? It's to Folkestone Sir Claude has taken Maisie, and after Mrs. Beale, on Beale's 'bolt', has rushed down, it is *there*, a very good place, I think, that they find themselves with the problem of having her between them in their adulterous relation. I thought of making Mrs. Wix arrive the same day as Mrs. Beale—in the afternoon—but I think I strengthen my effect by making her not come till *3 or 4* days after. A part of the ugly little comedy is their—the 'guilty couple's'—at once exalted and rueful *consideration* of what they are face to face with—and I must give that a little time—a few days—to go on. They go about with her—looking over to France and 'abroad'—meanwhile; and it is this *accomplished* situation that Mrs. Wix breaks into. Susan Ash is also with the child—Susan Ash has accompanied her and Sir Claude down to Folkestone when he goes and possesses himself of *Maisie* after Ida's flight. And Susan Ash *too* is a hussy, whom Mrs. Wix also *dit son fait* to—or about.

December 21st, 34 De Vere Gdns., W.

I realize—none too soon—that the *scenic* method is my absolute, my imperative, my *only* salvation. The *march of an action* is the thing for me to, more and more, *attach* myself to: it is the only thing that really, for *me*, at least, will *produire* L'ŒUVRE, and L'ŒUVRE is, before God, what I'm going in for. Well, the scenic scheme is the only one that *I* can trust, with my tendencies, to stick to the march of an action. How reading Ibsen's splendid *John Gabriel* a day or two ago (in proof) brought that, FINALLY AND FOREVER, home to me! I must now, I fully recognize, have a splendid recourse to it to see me out of the wood, at all, of this interminable little *Maisie*; *10,000 more words* of which I have still to do. They can be magnificent in movement if I resolutely and triumphantly take this course with them, and *only if I do so.*

PREFACE TO THE NEW YORK
EDITION, VOLUME IX, 1908

[What Maisie Knew, "In the Cage", "The Pupil"]
I recognize again, for the first of these three Tales, another instance of the growth of the 'great oak' from the little acorn; since 'What Maisie Knew' is at least a tree that spreads beyond any provision its small germ might on a first handling have appeared likely to make for it. The accidental mention had been made to me of the manner in which the situation of some luckless child of a divorced couple was affected, under my informant's eyes, by the re-marriage of one of its parents – I forget which; so that, thanks to the limited desire for its company expressed by the step-parent, the law of its little life, its being entertained in rotation by its father and its mother, wouldn't easily prevail. Whereas each of these persons had at first vindictively desired to keep it from the other, so at present the re-married relative sought now rather to be rid of it – that is to leave it as much as possible, and beyond the appointed times and seasons, on the hands of the adversary; which malpractice, resented by the latter as bad faith, would of

course be repaid and avenged by an equal treachery. The wretched infant was thus to find itself practically disowned, rebounding from racquet to racquet like a tennis-ball or a shuttlecock. This figure could but touch the fancy to the quick and strike one as the beginning of a story – a story commanding a great choice of developments. I recollect, however, promptly thinking that for a proper symmetry the second parent should marry too – which in the case named to me indeed would probably soon occur, and was in any case what the ideal of the situation required. The second step-parent would have but to be correspondingly incommoded by obligations to the offspring of a hated predecessor for the misfortune of the little victim to become altogether exemplary. The business would accordingly be sad enough, yet I am not sure its possibility of interest would so much have appealed to me had I not soon felt that the ugly facts, so stated or conceived, by no means constituted the whole appeal.

The light of an imagination touched by them couldn't help therefore projecting a further ray, thanks to which it became rather quaintly clear that, not less than the chance of misery and of a degraded state, the chance of happiness and of an improved state might be here involved for the child, round about whom the complexity of life would thus turn to fineness, to richness – and indeed would have but so to turn for the small creature to be steeped in security and ease. Sketchily clustered even, these elements gave out that vague pictorial glow which forms the first appeal of a living 'subject' to the painter's consciousness; but the glimmer became intense as I proceeded to a further analysis. The further analysis is for that matter almost always the torch of rapture and victory, as the artist's firm hand grasps and plays it – I mean, naturally, of the smothered rapture and the obscure victory, enjoyed and celebrated not in the street but before some innermost shrine; the odds being a hundred to one, in almost any connexion, that it doesn't arrive by any easy first process at the *best* residuum of truth. That was the charm, sensibly, of the picture thus at first confusedly showing; the elements so couldn't but flush, to their very surface, with some deeper depth of irony than the mere obvious. It lurked in the crude postulate like a buried scent; the more the attention hovered the more aware it became of the fragrance. To which I may add that the more I scratched the surface and penetrated, the more potent, to the intellectual nostril, became this virtue. At last, accordingly, the residuum, as I have called it, reached, I was in presence of the red dramatic spark that glowed at the core of my vision and that, as I gently blew upon it, burned higher and clearer. This precious particle was the *full* ironic truth – the most interesting item to be read into the child's situation. For satisfaction of the mind, in other words, the small expanding consciousness would have to be saved, have to become presentable as a register of impressions; and saved by the experience of certain advantages, by some enjoyed profit and some achieved confidence, rather than coarsened, blurred, sterilized, by ignorance and pain. This better state, in the young life, would reside in the exercise of a function other than that of disconcerting the selfishness of its parents – which was all that had on the face of the matter seemed reserved to it in the way of criticism applied to their rupture. The early relation would be exchanged for a later; instead of simply submitting to the inherited tie and the imposed complication, of suffering from them, our little wonder-working agent would create, without design, quite fresh elements of this order – contribute, that is, to the formation of a fresh tie, from which it would then (and for all the world as if through a small demonic foresight) proceed to derive great profit.

This is but to say that the light in which the vision so readily grew to a wholeness was that of a second marriage on both sides; the father having, in the freedom of divorce, but to take another wife, as well as the mother, under a like licence, another husband, for the case to begin, at least, to stand beautifully on its feet. There would be thus a perfect logic for what might come – come even with the mere attribution of a certain sensibility (if but a mere relative fineness) to either of the new parties. Say the prime cause making for the ultimate attempt to shirk on one side or the other, and better still if on both, a due share of the decreed burden should have been, after all, in each progenitor, a constitutional inaptitude for *any* burden, and a base intolerance of it: we should thus get a motive not requiring, but happily dispensing with, too particular a perversity in the step-parents. The child seen as creating by the fact of its forlornness a relation between its step-parents, the more intimate the better, dramatically speaking; the child, by the mere appeal of neglectedness and the mere consciousness of relief, weaving about, with the best faith in the world, the close web of sophistication; the child becoming a centre and pretext for a fresh system of misbehaviour, a system moreover of a nature to spread and ramify: *there* would be the 'full' irony, there the promising theme into which the hint I had originally picked up would logically flower. No themes are so human as those that reflect for us, out of the confusion of life, the close connexion of bliss and bale, of the things that help with the things that hurt, so dangling before us for ever that bright hard medal, of so strange an alloy, one face of which is somebody's right and ease and the other somebody's pain and wrong. To live with all intensity and perplexity and felicity in its terribly mixed little world would thus be the part of my interesting small mortal; bringing people together who would be at least more correctly separate; keeping people separate who would be at least more correctly together; flourishing, to a degree, at the cost of many conventions and proprieties, even decencies; really keeping the torch of virtue alive in an air tending infinitely to smother it; really in short making confusion worse confounded by drawing some stray fragrance of an ideal across the scent of selfishness, by sowing on barren strands, through the mere fact of presence, the seed of the moral life.

All this would be to say, I at once recognized, that my light vessel of consciousness, swaying in such a draught, couldn't be with verisimilitude a rude little boy; since, beyond the fact that little boys are never so 'present,' the sensibility of the female young is indubitably, for early youth, the greater, and my plan would call, on the part of my protagonist, for 'no end' of sensibility. I might impute that amount of it without extravagance to a slip of a girl whose faculties should have been well shaken up; but I should have so to depend on its action to keep my story clear that I must be able to show it in all assurance as naturally intense. To this end I should have of course to suppose for my heroine dispositions originally promising, but above all I should have to invest her with perceptions easily and almost infinitely quickened. So handsomely fitted out, yet not in a manner too grossly to affront probability, she might well see me through the whole course of my design; which design, more and more attractive as I turned it over, and dignified by the most delightful difficulty, would be to make and to keep her so limited consciousness the very field of my picture while at the same time guarding with care the integrity of the objects represented. With the charm of this possibility, therefore, the project for 'Maisie' rounded *itself* and loomed large – any subject looming large, for that matter, I am bound to add, from the moment one is ridden by the law of entire expression. I have already elsewhere noted, I think, that the memory of my own work preserves for me no theme that, at some moment or other of its development, and always only waiting for the right connexion or chance, hasn't signally refused to remain humble, even (or perhaps all the more resentfully) when fondly selected for its conscious and hopeless humility. Once 'out,' like a house-dog of a temper above confinement, it defies the mere whistle, it roams, it hunts, it seeks out and 'sees' life; it can be brought back but by hand and then only to take its futile thrashing. It wasn't at any rate for an idea seen in the light I here glance at not to have due warrant of its value – how could the value of a scheme so finely workable *not* be great? The one presented register of the whole complexity would be the play of the child's confused and obscure notation of it, and yet the whole, as I say, should be unmistakeably, should be honourably there, seen through the faint intelligence, or at the least attested by the imponderable presence, and still advertising its sense.

I recall that my first view of this neat possibility was as the attaching problem of the picture restricted (while yet achieving, as I say, completeness and coherency) to what the child might be conceived to have *understood* – to have been able to interpret and appreciate. Further reflexion and experiment showed me my subject strangled in that extreme of rigour. The infant mind would at the best leave great gaps and voids; so that with a systematic surface possibly beyond reproach we should

nevertheless fail of clearness of sense. I should have to stretch
the matter to what my wondering witness materially and inevitably *saw*; a great deal of which quantity she either wouldn't
understand at all or would quite misunderstand – and on those
lines, only on those, my task would be prettily cut out. To that
then I settled – to the question of giving it *all*, the whole situation surrounding her, but of giving it only through the occasions
and connexions of her proximity and her attention; only as it
might pass before her and appeal to her, as it might touch her
and affect her, for better or worse, for perceptive gain or perceptive loss: so that we fellow witnesses, we not more invited
but only more expert critics, should feel in strong possession of
it. This would be, to begin with, a plan of absolutely definite
and measurable application – that in itself always a mark of
beauty; and I have been interested to find on re-perusal of the
work that some such controlling grace successfully rules it.
Nothing could be more 'done,' I think, in the light of its happi-
est intention; and this in spite of an appearance that at moments
obscures my consistency. Small children have many more perceptions than they have terms to translate them; their vision is
at any moment much richer, their apprehension even constantly
stronger, than their prompt, their at all producible, vocabulary.
Amusing therefore as it might at the first blush have seemed to
restrict myself in this case to the terms as well as to the experience, it became at once plain that such an attempt would fail.
Maisie's terms accordingly play their part – since her simpler
conclusions quite depend on them; but our own commentary
constantly attends and amplifies. This it is that on occasion,
doubtless, seems to represent us as going so 'behind' the facts of
her spectacle as to exaggerate the activity of her relation to
them. The difference here is but of a shade: it is her relation, her
activity of spirit, that determines all our own concern – we
simply take advantage of these things better than she herself.
Only, even though it is her interest that mainly makes matters
interesting for us, we inevitably note this in figures that are not
yet at her command and that are nevertheless required whenever those aspects about her and those parts of her experience
that she understands darken off into others that she rather

tormentedly misses. All of which gave me a high firm logic to observe; supplied the force for which the straightener of almost any tangle is grateful while he labours, the sense of pulling at threads intrinsically worth it – strong enough and fine enough and entire enough.

Of course, beyond this, was another and well-nigh equal charm – equal in spite of its being almost independent of the acute constructional, the endless expressional question. This was the quite different question of the particular kind of truth of resistance I might be able to impute to my central figure – *some* intensity, some continuity of resistance being naturally of the essence of the subject. Successfully to resist (to resist, that is, the strain of observation and the assault of experience) what would that be, on the part of so young a person, but to remain fresh, and still fresh, and to have even a freshness to communicate? – the case being with Maisie to the end that she treats her friends to the rich little spectacle of objects embalmed in her wonder. She wonders, in other words, to the end, to the death – the death of her childhood, properly speaking; after which (with the inevitable shift, sooner or later, of her point of view) her situation will change and become another affair, subject to other measurements and with a new centre altogether. The particular reaction that will have led her to that point, and that it has been of an exquisite interest to study in her, will have spent itself; there will be another scale, another perspective, another horizon. Our business meanwhile therefore is to extract from her current reaction whatever it may be worth; and for that matter we recognize in it the highest exhibitional virtue. Truly, I reflect, if the theme had had no other beauty it would still have had this rare and distinguished one of its so expressing the variety of the child's values. She is not only the extraordinary 'ironic centre' I have already noted; she has the wonderful importance of shedding a light far beyond any reach of her comprehension; of lending to poorer persons and things, by the mere fact of their being involved with her and by the special scale she creates for them, a precious element of dignity. I lose myself, truly, in appreciation of my theme on noting what she does by her 'freshness' for appearances in themselves vulgar and empty

enough. They become, as she deals with them, the stuff of
poetry and tragedy and art; she has simply to wonder, as I say,
about them, and they begin to have meanings, aspects, solidities,
connexions – connexions with the 'universal!' – that they could
scarce have hoped for. Ida Farange alone, so to speak, or Beale
alone, that is either of them otherwise connected – what intensity, what 'objectivity' (the most developed degree of *being* anyhow thinkable for them) would they have? How would they
repay at all the favour of our attention?

Maisie makes them portentous all by the play of her good
faith, makes her mother above all, to my vision – unless I have
wholly failed to render it – concrete, immense and awful; so
that we get, for our profit, and get by an economy of process
interesting in itself, the thoroughly pictured creature, the striking figured symbol. At two points in particular, I seem to recognize, we enjoy at its maximum this effect of associational
magic. The passage in which her father's terms of intercourse
with the insinuating but so strange and unattractive lady whom
he has had the detestable levity to whisk her off to see late at
night, is a signal example of the all but incalculable way in
which interest may be constituted. The facts involved are that
Beale Farange is ignoble, that the friend to whom he introduces
his daughter is deplorable, and that from the commerce of the
two, *as* the two merely, we would fain avert our heads. Yet the
thing has but to become a part of the child's bewilderment for
these small sterilities to drop from it and for the *scene* to emerge
and prevail – vivid, special, wrought hard, to the hardness of
the unforgettable; the scene that is exactly what Beale and Ida
and Mrs. Cuddon, and even Sir Claude and Mrs. Beale, would
never for a moment have succeeded in making their scant unre-
deemed importances – namely *appreciable*. I find another
instance in the episode of Maisie's unprepared encounter, while
walking in the Park with Sir Claude, of her mother and that
beguiled attendant of her mother, the encouraging, the appealing 'Captain', to whom this lady contrives to commit her for
twenty minutes while she herself deals with the second husband. The human substance here would have seemed in advance
well-nigh too poor for conversion, the three 'mature' figures of

too short a radiation, too stupid (*so* stupid it was for Sir Claude to have married Ida!), too vain, too thin, for any clear application; but promptly, immediately, the child's own importance, spreading and contagiously acting, has determined the *total* value otherwise. Nothing of course, meanwhile, is an older story to the observer of manners and the painter of life than the grotesque finality with which such terms as 'painful', 'unpleasant' and 'disgusting' are often applied to his results; to that degree, in truth, that the free use of them as weightily conclusive again and again re-enforces his estimate of the critical sense of circles in which they artlessly flourish. Of course under that superstition I was punctually to have had read to me the lesson that the 'mixing-up' of a child with anything unpleasant confessed itself an aggravation of the unpleasantness, and that nothing could well be more disgusting than to attribute to Maisie so intimate an 'acquaintance' with the gross immoralities surrounding her.

The only thing to say of such lucidities is that, however one may have 'discounted' in advance, and as once for all, their general radiance, one is disappointed if the hour for them, in the particular connexion, doesn't strike – they so keep before us elements with which even the most sedate philosopher must always reckon. The painter of life has indeed work cut out for him when a considerable part of life offers itself in the guise of that sapience. The effort really to see and really to represent is no idle business in face of the *constant* force that makes for muddlement. The great thing is indeed that the muddled state too is one of the very sharpest of the realities, that it also has colour and form and character, has often in fact a broad and rich comicality, many of the signs and values of the appreciable. Thus it was to be, for example, I might gather, that the very principle of Maisie's appeal, her undestroyed freshness, in other words that vivacity of intelligence by which she indeed does vibrate in the infected air, indeed does flourish in her immoral world, may pass for a barren and senseless thing, or at best a negligible one. For nobody to whom life at large is *easily* interesting do the finer, the shyer, the more anxious small vibrations, fine and shy and anxious with the passion that precedes knowledge, succeed in being negligible: which is doubtless one of many reasons why the passage between the child and the kindly, friendly, ugly gentleman who, seated with her in Kensington Gardens under a spreading tree, positively answers to her for her mother as no one has ever answered, and so stirs her, filially and morally, as she has never been stirred, throws into highest relief, to my sense at least, the side on which the subject is strong, and becomes the type-passage – other advantages certainly aiding, as I may say – for the expression of its beauty. The active, contribute close-circling wonder, as I have called it, in which the child's identity is guarded and preserved, and which makes her case remarkable exactly by the weight of the tax on it, provides distinction for her, provides vitality and variety, through the operation of the tax – which would have done comparatively little for us hadn't it been monstrous. A pity for us surely to have been deprived of this just reflexion. "Maisie" is of 1907.

NOTES

Society

One mark of James's powers is that he exercises a prudent courtesy towards his readers, and does not ask that we be especially knowledgeable, for instance as to social history. As a good writer will, he succeeds in conveying, even to the uninitiated, the nature of the world into which he is happy to conduct us all. Take the social comedy of table manners.

> Miss Overmore never, like Moddle, had on an apron, and when she ate she held her fork with her little finger curled out. The child, who watched her at many moments, watched her particularly at that one. 'I think you're lovely,' she often said to her; even mamma, who was lovely too, had not such a pretty way with the fork. (14)

This sufficiently brings home the genteel affectation, not harshly and rather sadly, and it doesn't need a note. Or didn't need the note that some editors supply. Perhaps these few pages of mine should be headed, not 'NOTES', but 'NOTES?'.

More widely, in the opening pages there appears a particular accomplishment of Ida Farange, one for which she pays a price:

> The sole flaw in Ida's beauty was a length and reach of arm conducive perhaps to her having so often beaten her ex-husband at billiards, a game in which she showed a superiority largely accountable, as she maintained, for the resentment finding expression in his physical violence. Billiards were her great accomplishment and the distinction her name always first produced the mention of. (6)

James intimates a touch of surprise at gender (and at class?). In the 1985 Penguin Classics edition Paul Theroux notes that 'Billiards is associated with gentlemen's clubs and masculinity and privacy – the billiard room in the English country house being essentially a male preserve. But it has known women practitioners. When in 1576 Mary Queen of Scots was imprisoned at Pontefract, she "complained of being deprived of her billiard table".' Complementarily, in the notes to the Oxford World's Classics edition (1996) Adrian Poole ranges through nineteenth-century life and fiction, stressing that 'billiards was never exclusively the diversion of men', and investigating the hint later in the novel that it is perhaps for money that Ida plays the occasional 'match'. Valuable, these, and yet *What Maisie Knew* is very good at seeing to it that when we don't know something, we will *suspect as much*. James helps us to twig things. The same applies to Sir Claude's smoking. Theroux intriguingly suggests that 'Sir Claude may be the first chain-smoker in English literature'. A brief history of the cigarette from the 1850s to the 1880s does then give pleasure, but the absence of such a note would not preclude any reader from apprehending Sir Claude's fretful addiction ('he was always smoking', 73).

A parallel between James's imaginative intimations and his annotatory ones might be prompted by the observation of an appreciative reviewer of *What Maisie Knew*: 'Most of his obtuse readers will believe Mr. James to be reticent: he is not. The "i's" are dotted; but the dots are very small ones: once, for example, a lady shows "a deficiency in the air of a honeymoon", once a gentleman forgets his stick' (*Saturday Review*, 20 November 1897). Much of James's unforgetful skill lies in his not insisting that in order to read *What Maisie Knew* you must know a lot. He often functions as his own annotator, and makes clear (for instance) those class distinctions of which a vehicle is the vehicle. 'The brougham was a token of harmony, of the fine conditions papa, this time, would offer: he had usually come for her in a hansom with a four-wheeler behind for the boxes' (24). The packing order is clear enough, even without one's being quite sure that a brougham is 'a one-horse closed carriage, with two or four wheels, for two or four persons' (*OED*, noting that *broom* 'was the accepted London pronunciation as seen in society verses, etc.'); that a hansom is a 'low-hung two-wheeled cabriolet holding two persons inside, the driver being mounted on a dickey or elevated seat behind, and the reins going over the roof'; and a four-wheeler is '*esp*. a four-wheeled hackney carriage'. The 'old lady who passed in a victoria' (25) enjoys a better class of four-wheeler, 'a light, low, four-wheeled carriage having a collapsible hood, with seats (usually) for two persons and an elevated seat in front for the driver' (*OED*). The hansom was named after an architect; the brougham, after a lord; the victoria, after the Queen.

It is the word *carriage* that can move across from a class of vehicle
to the money that sets all this in motion. 'Poor Ida, who had run
through everything, had now nothing but her carriage and her paralysed uncle' (7). (With a faint pun on how impressively she carries
herself, a lady who will in due course become her ladyship.) Contem-
plating Hyde Park, James had remarked in 'The Suburbs of London',
an essay written in 1877:

> If the spectators testify to English leisure, the carriages testify more par-
> ticularly to English incomes. To keep a carriage and pair in London costs,
> I believe, about five hundred pounds a year; the number of people driving
> about at this expense defies any powers of calculation at the command of
> the contemplative stranger. (*Collected Travel Writings: Great Britain and
> America*, p. 279)

It is not just one particular character but every character in the
book who runs through everything, and finds herself or himself
always being introduced 'afresh to the question of money' (102).
When Maisie is disappointed of the coin that her mother really did
seem to have been on the brink of giving her, we hear a sound that
is heard with variations throughout this unremittingly worldly
novel, 'the sharp click that marked the closing portemonnaie' (164).
The French for 'a flat leathern purse' (*OED*) is not italicized by
James, the word having been anglicized for half a century by the
time he wrote. But then this novel is itself a portemonnaie, and
money is then what carries this novel from beginning to end. The
beginning, in that what commands the whole divorce is the legal
judgment, 'an order that he should refund to his late wife the twenty-
six hundred pounds put down by her, as it was called, some three
years before'. The end, in that the final chapter has this exchange
between Sir Claude and his mistress:

> 'She has means.'
>   'Means? – Maisie?' Mrs. Beale shrieked. 'Means that her vile father has
>   stolen!'
>   'I'll get them back – I'll get them back. I'll look into it.' (262)

From the world of late-Victorian money, a few of the coins do now
need to be identified (without undertaking here a calculation of
the monetary value today). The *shilling* consisted of twelve pence, and
there were twenty shillings to the pound. 'There wasn't "two-
and-tuppence" for anything' (103): the paltry sum, to the well-off, of

two shillings and twopence (the pronunciation *tuppence* being standard English). The *half-a-crown* was two shillings and sixpence; there were four crowns to the pound. The *sovereign* was a gold coin worth £1.

Then there is the flourishing monetary side to other aspects of the brave new Victorian world. When it comes to education, 'an immense deal could be done for very little more than your fare in the Underground' (122). The Underground railway, with carriages that were not horse-drawn, opened in 1863, and Poole has a warm note on James's transports at the Underground. All the way from Paris there comes a fine present from Sir Claude, 'a splendid apparatus for painting in water-colours' (71), almost as exotic in its way as the magic of the magic-lantern, glimpsed anew in the very first paragraph of Chapter I. What Tennyson in 'Locksley Hall' (1842) had called – with sincere respect – 'the fairy tales of science' are here romantic in both an Eastern and a Western way. Of Maisie's entranced arrival at the Countess's house, Theroux observes: 'It sounds as though the Countess has electric lighting, a sign of affluence at a time when electricity cost eightpence a unit (the same price as half a pound of best butter).' I'd have said *looks as though*, for there before our eyes is the flash of the thing itself, even while it is by courtesy of old romance that we are ushered into this sudden amazing presence, the secular immediacy of *Let there be light*:

> By the time he had helped her out of the cab, which drove away, and she heard in the door of the house the prompt little click of his key, the Arabian Nights had quite closed round her.
>
> From this minute they were in everything, particularly in such an instant 'Open Sesame' and in the departure of the cab, a rattling void filled with relinquished step-parents; they were, with the vividness, the almost blinding whiteness of the light that sprang responsive to papa's quick touch of a little brass knob on the wall, in a place that, at the top of a short, soft staircase, struck her as the most beautiful she had ever seen in her life. (130)

Instead of what we heard earlier, 'the sharp click that marked the closing portemonnaie', there is now the no-less-moneyed click that does not close but opens a door into riches beyond the dreams of avarice, 'the prompt little click of his key'. Meanwhile, the legendary tales of the *Arabian Nights* are accommodated within an English night.

Topography

The notes by Paul Theroux and Adrian Poole make adept use of the most successful guide-book of the day, of the century: Baedeker.

Poole avails himself of the tenth edition (1896), *Baedeker's London and Its Environs*, and then – when England gives place to France of *Baedeker's Northern France: Handbook for Travellers* (second edition, 1894). So that James's reference to the hour in which Sir Claude, with Maisie, cultivates an opportunity 'on the Row and by the Drive' (103) finds itself refreshed by Poole's adducing Baedeker: 'In the Drive are seen unbroken files of elegant equipages and high-bred horses in handsome trappings, moving continually to and fro, presided over by sleek coaches and powdered lacqueys, and occupied by some of the most beautiful and exquisitely dressed women in the world. In the Row are numerous lady and gentlemen riders, who parade their spirited and glossy steeds before the admiring crowd sitting or walking at the sides.'

This is itself a spirited and glossy thing to adduce. But again I'd suggest that although Baedeker may confirm the essence of the Drive and the Row, the guide's evocation is not itself essential to a reader of the novel. Even though we may not have known as much, we did guess as much, or sense as much. For James has already coloured the scene for us with his entering sentence. 'Maisie's own park, in the north, had been nearer at hand, but they rolled westward in a hansom because at the end of the sweet June days that was the direction taken by every one that any one looked at.' Again, if a reader isn't altogether sure what 'the Serpentine' is, he or she will surely get the picture when the sentence about Sir Claude and Maisie does itself direct the reader: 'directing their steps to the banks of the Serpentine'. Kensington Gardens similarly unfold themselves for any who may be unfamiliar with the scene: 'after they had passed out of the Park and begun, under the charm of the spot and the season, to stroll in Kensington Gardens' (104).

Such are the great parks of London, among them Hyde Park, and what was then called, not Regent's Park, but the Regent's Park. Such are the powerful streets, among them Oxford Street, with its handsome shops. But then the sentence that accommodates Oxford Street does find room for its shops – 'no dawdles at shop-windows' (44) – and if 'Kensal Green' is for a moment strange in register and unclear, it is for a moment only: 'Mrs. Wix was as safe as Clara Matilda, who was in heaven and yet, embarrassingly, also in Kensal Green, where they had been together to see her little huddled grave' (21). Even if you weren't altogether certain about the National Gallery, the name tells you more than enough to be getting on with, especially when the sentence is one that speaks of 'a roomful of pictures' (84), focusing then on 'patches of gold and cataracts of purple, with stiff saints and angular angels'. You don't know what the Chrysanthemum is? Oh yes, you do.' "He was at the club – the Chrysanthemum. So!" "All night long? Why the flowers shut up at night, you know!"' (102).

There is an entry in Geoffrey Madan's *Notebooks* (ed. J. A. Gere and John Sparrow, 1981) that has something of James's interest in 'The Question of Our Speech' (a lecture James delivered in 1905), including national differences in speech:

Foreigners:
1. Italian who remained silent because it was too cold to take his hands out of his pockets.
2. Two Spaniards who stopped every now and then on a walk, because the whole body was necessary for talking.

No Spaniard, James does not find it necessary to stop in order to talk to (or rather, with) the reader; he walks on, conveying what is necessary – the genuinely needed as against the happily additional – so that everything flows, graceful in the company of sentiment and observation. Even the slang of *thingumbob* can become graceful:

'We'll go to-night to the thingumbob at Earl's Court'; an announcement putting forth its full lustre when she had made known that she referred to the great Exhibition just opened in that quarter, a collection of extraordinary foreign things, in tremendous gardens, with illuminations, bands, elephants, switchbacks and side-shows, as well as crowds of people among whom they might possibly see some one they knew. (123–4)

Sometimes the place will be so well known – Piccadilly, for example – that James can count on the likelihood of a reader's catching a cadence. We learn in the prologue to the novel that Beale Farange had once had consular ambitions: 'He had been destined in his youth for diplomacy and momentarily attached, without a salary, to a legation which enabled him often to say "In *my* time, in the East": but contemporary history had somehow had no use for him, had hurried past him and left him in perpetual Piccadilly' (5). It calls up perpetual damnation, *in perpetual Piccadilly*. It is a sly turn by James that later evokes so different a mood when Sir Claude strolls enchantingly with Maisie and Mrs Wix: 'When he met them in sunny Piccadilly he made merry and turned and walked with them, heroically suppressing his consciousness of the stamp of his company' (55). As company, Sir Claude is as different from Beale Farange as *in sunny Piccadilly* is from *in perpetual Piccadilly*.

Perhaps a test case for whether a note is strictly necessary (as against a felicitous bonus) is the moment when Maisie gets something wrong, there in London. Mrs Beale, her stepmother and formerly her governess, is taking steps to further Maisie's education, 'for the dream of lectures at an institution had at last become a reality':

> The institution – there was a splendid one in a part of the town but little known to the child – became, in the glow of such a spirit, a thrilling place, and the walk to it from the station through Glower Street – a pronunciation for which Mrs. Beale once laughed at her little friend – a pathway literally strewn with 'subjects'. (122)

James banters the reader with a touch of riddle, rather as Maisie is bantered. A shrewd guess, though, would be pretty sure to come up with Gower Street.

Still, there is much pleasure to be had from contextual settings. To the aptness of Baedeker should be added the aptness of James's own topographical writings. *English Hours* (1905) has two ranging essays on the capital, 'London' (1888) and 'London at Midsummer' (1877), and there are three others that he did not collect: 'London Sights' (1875), 'The Suburbs of London' (1877) and 'London in the Dead Season' (1878). The tone of these essays is sweeter than that of *What Maisie Knew* for reasons that are more than understandable, given what goes on in the novel, but the essays help to fill in something of the London world. A young man 'has only to cross Hyde Park Corner to find his way all grassy again. I have a weakness for the convenient, familiar, treeless, or almost treeless, expanse of the Green Park, and the friendly part it plays as a kind of encouragement to Piccadilly. I am so fond of Piccadilly that I am grateful to any one or anything that does it a service . . .' (*English Hours* (1905), *Collected Travel Writings: Great Britain and America*, p. 29). Or there are these Jamesian expanses, which out-Baedeker Baedeker:

> Every one in London, as the phrase is, goes to Hyde park of a fine afternoon; and the spectacle, therefore, may be presumed to have no small impressiveness.
>
> Before you is the Drive, with its serried ranks of carriages; behind you is the Row, with its misty, red-earthed vista, and its pacing and bounding equestrians; between the two is the broad walk in which your fellow star-ers are gathered together lolling back in the tightly-packed chairs or shuffling along with wistful looks at them.

It may really be said that Kensington Gardens contain some of the finest
rural scenery in England. If they were not a huge city square, they would
be an admirable nobleman's park. To sit down for a hour at the base of
one of the great elms and see them studding the grass around you in vistas, which, as you do not perceive their limits, may be as long-drawn as
you choose to suppose them, is one of the most accessible as well as one
of the most agreeable methods of spending a June afternoon. ('The
Suburbs of London', *Collected Travel Writings: Great Britain and America*,
pp. 277–8)

James as novelist is good at exercising one of the most accessible as
well as one of the most agreeable methods of spending our hours.

What Maisie Knew often looks, sometimes wistfully, sometimes
warily, at 'the untravelled globe'. Miss Overmore, soon to be Mrs
Beale, is highly 'qualified' as a governess, for she 'could say lots of
dates straight off (letting you hold the book yourself), state the position of Malabar, play six pieces without notes, and, in a sketch, put in
beautifully the trees and houses and difficult parts' (22). Malabar is
foreign parts. The reader is permitted to be as uncertain of its exact
position as was Maisie.

There is a world elsewhere. 'I'm thinking of South Africa, but
that's none of your business,' her father tells Maisie. 'South Africa is
wonderful, they say' (162) – wonderful, that is, for business, or
rather for dubious commercial ventures. The Countess, who gives
Maisie the creeps (and yet the book has pity for the Countess, though
it does not take pity on her) – the Countess tries to make Maisie like
her. '"Shouldn't you like me," said this one endearingly, "to take you
to Spa?"' (143). Resourceful, this, in its play with the 'suspended
quotation' – an utterance interrupted by a narrator – since the
sequence permits of a moment's plea, 'Shouldn't you like me?' (see
Mark Lambert's first-rate book, *Dickens and the Suspended
Quotation*, 1981). Despite my believing that James in his art conveys
what we most need to know, I am grateful for such a note as the one
by Theroux and by Poole, that a spa (anywhere) is named after Spa
(in Belgium, near Liège).

But it is France that beckons to the competing claimants within the
novel. Boulogne (port, resort, commercial town of northern France)
boasted at the time – I learn from Poole – roughly a thousand British
residents out of its 46,000. In an 1878 travel essay 'Occasional Paris'
(*Collected Travel Writings: The Continent*, p. 276), James took pleasure in the sight of the men and women of Boulogne, there where you
'stand upon that good Boulognese quay, among the blue and red
douaniers and soldiers, the small ugly men in cerulean blouses, the

charming fishwives, with their folded kerchiefs and their crisp cap-frills, their short striped petticoats, their tightly-drawn stockings, and their little clicking sabots – ' (I say, steady on, old chap.) Sir Claude was to be contented with the sight of a fishwife, rather ignoring Maisie, 'as he stood there and with a kind of absent gaze – absent, that is, from *her* affairs – followed the fine stride and shining limbs of a young fishwife who had just waded out of the sea with her basketful of shrimps. His thought came back to her sooner than his eyes.' The first and the last *her* are belatedly Maisie, interrupted midway by the entrance of the other *her*, the one with her basketful. Five lines later, James's thought comes back to the matter of Sir Claude's thoughts: 'He stopped looking at last at the fishwife – he met his companion's inquiry. "Oh, you know!"' (173).

In French

The scattered smattered French in the novel scarcely goes beyond the rudiments of the language (most resourcefully used, though); some simple translations sequentially through the later chapters may be of use here:

Chapter XX

table d'hôte	common table for guests at a hotel or eating house

Chapter XXII

plage	beach
petits verres	glasses of liqueur (literally 'small glasses')
déjeuner	luncheon

Chapter XXIV

salon de lecture	reading-room

Chapter XXV

haute ville	upper town
'Adieu, mesdames!'	'Goodbye, ladies!'

Chapter XXVIII

omelette aux rognons	kidney omelette
poulet sauté	chicken cooked in a pan with a little butter

| Établissement ['des Bains'] | complex of tourist facilities, including baths, in Boulogne |

Chapter XXIX

café complet	continental breakfast
patronne	manageress, proprietress
'Et bien soigné, n'est-ce-pas?'	'You'll take care with it, won't you?'
'Soyez tranquille'	'Don't worry'
'Et pour Madame?'	'And for Madame?'
'Rien encore?'	'Nothing yet?'

Chapter XXX

café au lait	coffee with milk
'Les tartines sont là'	'There's the bread and butter'
'vous n'y êtes pas'	'you haven't got it'
Honi soit qui mal y pense	Evil be to him who thinks evil [of it]

Chapter XXXI

coupé	carriage
'Monsieur est placé?'	'You're seated, sir?'
'Pas encore'	'Not yet'
'Et vos billets? – vous n'avez que le temps'	'And your tickets? – you scarcely have time'
'Monsieur veut-il que je les prenne?'	'Do you wish me to take them up, sir?'
'Veux-tu bien qu'il prenne?'	'Do you wish him to take them up?'

In this crucial scene of the final chapter, with its atmosphere of all-but-elopement, the French is playing its part. 'Monsieur est placé?': this discreetly skirts any reference to more than one person, only then turning to the plural billets. The French prendre (... que je les prenne?) is translated by both Theroux and Poole as 'get them'; this is the sense, yes, but Sir Claude and Maisie have both previously used take: 'Do you want me to take our tickets?' 'Yes, take them' 'Take the tickets', so the translation I propose would maintain the continuity better. Meanwhile, the official's Vous n'avez has contrasted with Sir Claude's more intimate Veux-tu to Maisie.

It was the most extraordinary thing in the world: in the intensity of her excitement she not only by illumination understood all their French, but fell into it with an active perfection. She addressed herself straight to the porter. '*Prenny, prenny. Oh prenny!*'

'*Ah, si mademoiselle le veut!*'   'Ah, if mademoiselle so wishes'

Maisie does not have to know French; she just *knew*. By illumination, Maisie understood all their French. By illumination, James's readers understand all his English.

'*En voiture, en voiture!*'   'All aboard, all aboard'

'*Ah, vous n'avez plus le temps!*'   'Ah, you've no more time!'

No more time. The novel is about to depart. A dozen pages later, Maisie and Mrs Wix move on, move off, aboard ship.

PENGUIN CLASSICS

DAISY MILLER
HENRY JAMES

'I'm a fearful, frightful flirt! Did you ever hear of a nice girl that was not?'

Travelling in Europe with her family, Daisy Miller, an exquisitely beautiful young
American woman, presents her fellow-countryman Winterbourne with a dilemma
he cannot resolve. Is she deliberately flouting social conventions in the way she
talks and acts, or is she simply ignorant of them? When she strikes up an intimate
friendship with an urbane young Italian, her flat refusal to observe the codes
of respectable behaviour leaves her perilously exposed. In *Daisy Miller* Henry
James brilliantly dramatized the conflict between old-world manners and nouveau
riche tourists, and created his first great portrait of an enigmatic and independent
American woman.

Part of a series of new Penguin Classics editions of Henry James's works,
this edition contains a chronology, further reading, notes and a wide-ranging
introduction by David Lodge discussing the genesis of the tale, its huge success
and James's controversial revision of the text for his New York Edition.
Appendices include Henry James's Preface from the New York Edition and a note
on James's adaptation of his story as a play.

'A small masterpiece' Leon Edel

Edited with an introduction and notes by David Lodge
Series editor Philip Horne

PENGUIN CLASSICS

THE EUROPEANS
HENRY JAMES

'They are sober; they are even severe ... But we shall cheer them up'

Eugenia, an American expatriate brought up in Europe, arrives in rural New England with her charming brother Felix, hoping to find a wealthy second husband after the collapse of her marriage to a German prince. Their exotic, sophisticated airs cause quite a stir with their affluent, God-fearing American cousins, the Wentworths – and provoke the disapproval of their father, suspicious of foreign influences. To Gertrude Wentworth, struggling against her sombre puritan upbringing, the arrival of the handsome Felix is especially enchanting. One of Henry James's most optimistic novels, *The Europeans* is a subtle and gently ironic examination of manners and morals, deftly portraying the impact of experience upon innocence.

Part of a series of new Penguin Classics editions of Henry James's works, this edition contains a chronology, further reading, notes and an introduction by Andrew Taylor exploring the novel's shifting patterns of opposites and James's portrayal of personal and national identity.

'This small book, written so early in James's career, is a masterpiece of major quality' F. R. Leavis

Edited with an introduction and notes by Andrew Taylor
Series editor Philip Horne

Penguin Classics

WASHINGTON SQUARE
HENRY JAMES

'Why, you must take me or leave me ... You can't please your father and me both; you must choose between us'

When timid and plain Catherine Sloper acquires a dashing and determined suitor, her father, convinced that the young man is nothing more than a fortune-hunter, decides to put a stop to their romance. Torn between a desire to win her father's approval and passion for the first man who has ever declared his love for her, Catherine faces an agonizing choice, and eventually becomes all too aware of the restrictions that others seek to place on her freedom. James's masterly novel deftly interweaves the public and private faces of nineteenth-century New York society, and is also a moving study of innocence destroyed.

Part of a series of new Penguin Classics editions of Henry James's works, this edition contains a chronology, suggested reading, notes and an introduction discussing the novel's lasting influence and James's depiction of the quiet strength of his heroine.

'Perhaps the only novel in which a man has successfully invaded the feminine field and produced a work comparable to Jane Austen's' Graham Greene

Edited with an introduction and notes by Martha Banta
Series editor Philip Horne

THE STORY OF PENGUIN CLASSICS

Before 1946 ... 'Classics' are mainly the domain of academics and students; readable editions for everyone else are almost unheard of. This all changes when a little-known classicist, E. V. Rieu, presents Penguin founder Allen Lane with the translation of Homer's *Odyssey* that he has been working on in his spare time.

1946 Penguin Classics debuts with *The Odyssey*, which promptly sells three million copies. Suddenly, classics are no longer for the privileged few.

1950s Rieu, now series editor, turns to professional writers for the best modern, readable translations, including Dorothy L. Sayers's *Inferno* and Robert Graves's unexpurgated *Twelve Caesars*.

1960s The Classics are given the distinctive black covers that have remained a constant throughout the life of the series. Rieu retires in 1964, hailing the Penguin Classics list as 'the greatest educative force of the twentieth century.'

1970s A new generation of translators swells the Penguin Classics ranks, introducing readers of English to classics of world literature from more than twenty languages. The list grows to encompass more history, philosophy, science, religion and politics.

1980s The Penguin American Library launches with titles such as *Uncle Tom's Cabin*, and joins forces with Penguin Classics to provide the most comprehensive library of world literature available from any paperback publisher.

1990s The launch of Penguin Audiobooks brings the classics to a listening audience for the first time, and in 1999 the worldwide launch of the Penguin Classics website extends their reach to the global online community.

The 21st Century Penguin Classics are completely redesigned for the first time in nearly twenty years. This world-famous series now consists of more than 1300 titles, making the widest range of the best books ever written available to millions – and constantly redefining what makes a 'classic'.

The Odyssey continues ...

The best books ever written

PENGUIN CLASSICS

SINCE 1946

Find out more at www.penguinclassics.com